CLINEMARK'S
TALE

CLINEMARK'S TALE

by R. W. BURDA

EVEREST HOUSE

Publishers   *New York*

LIBRARY OF CONGRESS CATALOGING IN PUBLICATION DATA

Burda, Robert W
    Clinemark's tale.

    I. Title.
PZ4.B9394Cl   1979 [PS3552.U68]   813'.5'4   79-51199
    ISBN 0-89696-066-8

Published simultaneously in Canada by
Beaverbooks, Pickering, Ontario
Manufactured in the United States of America by
American Book–Stratford Press, Inc.,
Saddle Brook, New Jersey
Designed by Sam Gantt
First Edition

To Jessica without mirrors

CLINEMARK'S
TALE

I

NANCY AND RONALD WERE, God knows why, married.

But not only God knew, Vivian did too: "To change one's status, that's why people marry. That's why I married Alan."

I admired her honesty for saying so.

"Given Alan's political position and the social status that goes with it here, I suppose that's true."

"I didn't mean that. That's why he married me, too."

"For status?"

"Yes."

"Because you're a beautiful woman?"

"No, no! Just status, *status*, Aaron! Don't people say 'What's your marital status?'"

I suppose the community of husband and wife has a status that the isolation of man and woman doesn't have.

"I see."

"I don't think you do."

"Well, damnation on your arrogance."

"You know what I'm saying. One day you aren't something and the next day you are, overnight. Absolutely everything's changed."

"Overnight?"

"Yes! Good Lord, you're immediately responsible for each other's debts. You *must* know what I'm talking about!"

"Obligations?"

She looked off as if I were hopeless.

"What about my status, Vivian? What was my status in the community when I married Funa?"

She was silent, charmingly but deviously silent. She crossed her ankles as if she knew she were sidestepping my question and said, "You're not the first white man to marry an African woman, Aaron."

I smiled until she became uncomfortable. That's been my habit here, my method, my defense: at least whenever I come away from the sanity of Ndami to the madness of the expatriate life in The Port. But I didn't need any defense against Vivian. I was even willing to become what all men become around her: defenseless. A little bit, anyway. It was a kind of unspoken agreement that I had made with her a long time ago. I lowered my defenses and she raised the level of the game she couldn't help but play. So I offered a compromise by saying I had encountered one of the darker benefits of the peculiar status that marriage confers on everyone.

"Until I got married, Vivian, everyone used to ask me how I was doing, what I had been up to—or some such thing. And whoever it was took it for granted that *I* was acting, *me*, I was up to it. I was doing the doing. Then suddenly—you're right, overnight—I was asked, 'How's married life treating you?' Within a week I had become helpless, got involved in something for which I really

4

couldn't be held responsible. I was suddenly victimized, I was no longer treating life, life was treating me. Married life! And whoever greeted me with a smile, an ever-so-knowing conspiratorial smile, now took it for granted I was bewildered how it all came about. Fascinating, yes? . . . One week I'm the captain or at least the lieutenant of my fate and the next week I'm the victim of some mysterious life process, to be commiserated with over a double Scotch at the bar of the National Hotel. I admit that's a real change in status, Vivian. And how about stature?"

Now she looked at me until I became uncomfortable.

"I don't think that's very amusing," she said in an almost hurt, childlike way.

"No, I don't think so either. Ridiculous, ludicrous, absurd—but not amusing."

Vivian sighed. And then one of those silences followed that almost tease me into believing that she has a soul after all. A small, rudimentary soul, but nevertheless a soul.

"Oh. Aaron."

"Yes?"

"What are we going to do without you after next year?"

"I'm the man everyone can do without."

I smiled but she didn't. She got up from her chair and did what I hated, or intensely disliked: walked to where I was sitting and kissed me on the forehead. Vivian always makes me feel that I have something which other men haven't but that I have it because I'm lacking in something else. She should remind me, not make me forget, that I'm a Capricorn. The Goat, known for stamina and virility, capable of becoming an old goat, even though, like Vivian, I was only forty-two. At least in that decade of the fifties I was. But my feelings about Vivian or Ronald and Nancy don't interfere much with my thinking, which I've had a lot of time for in the past months. I suspect that the worst or the weakest of reasons were behind the marriage of

Ronald and Nancy. I suspect that he did again what he had done in California, what everyone is doing everywhere: moving in with someone in order to move away from oneself. I imagine that both of them, but especially Ronald, wanted to make it their last Act. To take one final, self-conscious, even responsible action, knowing that they won't have to act again, only react: to one another, to circumstance and predicament, to kindness, injustice, misunderstanding, rekindled hopes and determination . . . all on that featureless plateau where life is nothing but one chain reaction after another. And yet, these worst and weakest of reasons aside, I have to agree with Vivian. For Ronald Keane was something of a failure, even though he was only thirty-one years old. He had tried calling himself a journalist and in fact had worked for several newspapers, but not in any creative or self-respecting way. His last position before marrying was with the *Los Angeles Times*. "Near the back door," he said. "Sixty feet from the alley, where the trucks pulled up. In circulation." So he needed a fast way to achieve a new status in life, a quick realignment. A new way of living. A way out of town, out of the country, if not out of himself.

And he needed it because he felt tricked by his father and betrayed by his grandmother. She, an old woman, was dying, and he had been summoned home from California. "Home" was a town in some mid-American state. When he got there his grandmother lingered, and so did Ronald, for three months. I imagine he spent most of his nights at some favorite bar, judging by the way he drank when he came to Africa. It was, he said, "a bad scene." And the vague one he left in my mind took place in a lawyer's very seamy office —straightback chairs, faded wallpaper, and at least two fidgeting people: Ronald and his mother. Two days after his grandmother's burial he learned that he was to get five thousand dollars. He was stunned. He expected several times that amount. When he told me about it he had that same abject look about him that he must have had that morning when he questioned his father.

"What did I do wrong?"

When I see his father I see a rather woolly-looking man; burly, less than six feet. And sixtyish. Kept vigorous by running a small construction company. Ronald had a very simple, uncomplicated, straightforward relationship with his father: he hated him.

"Nothing," was his father's answer. "That's just it, nothing. I've been waiting for you to do something, so has your mother, but it's always nothing, absolutely nothing."

Ronald didn't mean that. And he didn't want to be reminded of it.

"What did I do to Grandmother?"

"A postcard every six months! That's what you did to her, every six months. A postcard! When you knew what it would have meant to her if you had only taken five minutes a week to send her one. Five minutes a week! Her only grandchild! Damn you, damn you!"

Ronald had asked and he was answered.

He was questioned in a way he didn't want to be, too: "I hope you didn't come back just to get a dollar out of her."

Ronald lifted his lowered head.

"That's all you talked about when you called me, when you wanted me to come back—her will.

"And you've been remembered in it! I wish someone had given me five thousand dollars when I was thirty-one years old! Your mother and I were trying to live through a Depression, something you don't know anything about, when I was that age. God! And there you sit, mooning. If you think"—Mr. Keane's finger was pointing at Ronald—"if you think you can manage to undertake something constructive, something that merits giving you more of it before then, let me know. Write me a letter, call me—from some bar."

Ronald turned his head toward his mother, but if she had any thoughts or feeling she didn't express them. She squeezed her hands together in her lap. Everything was immovable: the four walls, the ceiling, the desk, and the papers with a dead woman's signature on them that could never be erased or changed. And the things that could move, seated in chairs—his mother and father—were most immovable of all. Perhaps the best he could have done was to ask why things were arranged the way they were, forever.

"When have I ever been able to merit anything as far as you're concerned?"

"Oh, don't be so sarcastic, so self-pitying! You can get control of yourself, that's what you can do! Every man's—"

"—responsible for chaining his own dog," finished Ronald.

Mr. Keane stood up. His face was flushed. He had made the remark year after year until everyone, not only Ronald, knew it. And he acknowledged it: "All right, so I've said it before. It's still true. Chain your dogs—settle down, get an aim in life, an objective, get married, have a family. Do anything you want, I don't care anymore, but just stop doing nothing, absolutely nothing! No one should complain about what someone else doesn't give them for nothing. A postcard every six months and he still gets five thousand dollars!" It can be said for Mr. Keane that he was becoming as miserable as he was accusatory. "I know what you think of me, Ronnie. Maybe that's why I've done well —I know what people think of me. It might not be much, like with you, but I'm not a fool. So I know. I know what you think of your home and this town, and I know that it's only a hole in the corner. But it's my corner, Ronnie, and you've spoiled it for me. It's not true that you haven't done anything—you've done that much, you've spoiled it for me. Now walk your mother home. I'm going to

8

my office. . . ." And he added as he started out, "To do what I do well. When you're doing something well, Ronnie, no matter what it is, let me know."

Ronald and his mother walked home in silence, almost. Mrs. Keane tried to speak once but Ronald stopped her.

"Please don't say anything now, Mother."

She didn't. But she had spoken two weeks ago while the Keanes were having dinner at their country club. She was telling Ronald that it would be nice if he asked a certain woman who was a stranger to him to dance. He didn't want to, and his way out of resisting his mother's suggestion was to make fun of the woman's name.

"Who?"

"Nancy Applegate."

"Mother, no one's called Nancy Applegate anymore."

"Why not?"

"They just aren't. It isn't done."

"Well, she's called that."

"It's a mistake," he said as he squinted toward a small woman seated on the other side of the dance floor. "I don't even know her. . . . Do I?"

"That's all the more reason it would be nice to ask her. She doesn't come home very often."

"Oh? What's *she* done wrong?"

"Wrong? Why, nothing! She hasn't done anything wrong."

"Why don't I know her?"

"Because her mother is Clara Carr. Nancy was sent to a private school in Dearborn when her parents divorced."

"Oh."

"She's a doctor."

Ronald looked again. Even from a distance, with all of Nancy's defects obscured, it didn't seem possible.

"She is?"

"Yes."

He assessed something, or appeared to. Then he patted

9

Mrs. Keane on the arm and said, "All right, Mother. I'll be sociable." He got up, ready to be impressed. But he lost all readiness when he came close enough to see Nancy better. She was small: all over, in every way. If she had status as a physician she had no noticeable stature at all. And she was plainly dressed, so plainly that the gray patterned material which covered her seemed to be something she found on an iron rack at some Salvation Army thrift shop. Naturally it couldn't conceal the fact that her chest was as boney as her back. Flat to the point of discomfort for Ronald. He would have veered off in another direction if Mr. and Mrs. Carr hadn't turned their heads at his approach. When Nancy looked too, with eyes the size of dimes pressed closely together, he noticed a growth on the left side of her nose. It was as small as the rest of her, insignificant; but a growth nevertheless. There was no choice. He had to speak.

"Good evening."

The Carrs nodded pleasantly.

He looked at Nancy and smiled.

"I was wondering if I might have this dance?"

She looked frightened, almost panicked. She turned quickly to look at her mother and stepfather as if she were an adolescent searching their faces for a cue, an answer. They smiled at her pleasantly. She seemed to take this as a sign that she had been given permission to do as Ronald asked, and she stood up and started to walk to the dance floor. She herself said nothing. Ronald followed her and noticed, first with astonishment, then with relief, that she had remarkably well-shaped legs. Even after he had been given time to find something wrong with them, he couldn't. As soon as they started to dance he tried to do away with the awkwardness by laughing.

"I haven't said who I am. Shall I introduce myself to you?"

Nancy looked up and he was surprised again. She not

"Yes. She won't be home for two years."

No one had told him. He hadn't asked. He hadn't thought to ask anything about her after he had seen her closely. It was fascination that made him walk to a place on the lawn where he could take another look at her without being seen by her: the fascination for someone who seems capable of doing something real and who seems to be living somewhere, not just anywhere. But all he saw was that she was as plainly and as tastelessly dressed as she had been ten days ago, and that the look in her eyes was distant. Not because she was looking at the darkness of the golf course beyond, for she turned her head and stared at other things: the birdbath, the gaslight burning in the rock garden, a stick she picked up from the ground. She looked at everything with an unnerving intensity. Everything about her seemed strange, weird; and Ronald went back into the house and tried to find something to do other than freshen his drink. Twenty minutes later he passed by the open door of the den and saw her sitting alone in the green leather chair in the corner, reading a book. He was amazed. Not because the Keanes only had magazines and condensed books in their den, but because Nancy had come to a place where people had gathered and instead of gathering with them she seemed to think it natural to withdraw from them. Only because she had a book in her hand did he find a way to approach her.

He stepped inside the room, smiling. He thought his obvious presence or the sound of his footsteps would cause her to raise her head, which was why he was already smiling. She didn't. So he asked the question he had already asked himself with a smile in his voice.

"What are you reading?"

She looked up. But instead of answering, she handed him the book so he could see for himself. He was still smiling because he thought it was a bit of a game, but when he saw that it was a book of her own, a medical book, he

13

felt challenged. He felt his bluff called, however harmless it was; that she knew he wasn't really interested but had only asked her to make conversation. And he couldn't cry out how peculiar it was of her to bring her own book with her to a lawn party. He was forced to turn the pages of it aimlessly and search for some intelligent remark to make about it.

"It's very technical, isn't it?"

She looked directly at the book when he handed it back to her, speaking to his outstretched hand.

"I suppose so."

She seemed more strained than shy.

"I heard that you're from Africa."

She lifted her face quickly. The sternness in her small eyes had been replaced by uncertainty and fear, as if it were frightening to know that others were talking about her. She seemed unable to speak.

"Oh, I didn't hear anything bad!" said Ronald, laughing deliberately, trying to make her feel more comfortable. It only made her look down at the book in her hand.

"I work there," she explained.

"Do you like it?"

She seemed to think about it, looking off toward a framed picture of an American Eagle on the wall.

"Oh, I suppose so."

"Tell me what it's like."

Ronald was about to sit down, but she laughed. Although he was smiling down on her averted face, he wasn't at ease. He remained standing.

"Is that funny?"

"In a way. It's what everyone asks and it's impossible to answer."

The only good thing about her laughter was that it showed her white and even teeth again.

"But it must be a fascinating place to work."

He could feel himself trying to justify why he had asked what everyone else did.

"It's interesting, of course," she acknowledged, in a way that made him feel she considered his remark naive. He was accustomed to a different response from women and had expected that one as plain as Nancy would have been grateful that he had walked in. Her eyes had gone back to her book and he was left standing, feeling ridiculous.

"Well, I didn't mean to interrupt you."

He started to back out, then turned toward the door. But he felt so dismissed or put off that he stopped and deliberately challenged her by speaking again.

"Isn't living in Africa dangerous?"

She looked up.

"What?"

"Isn't life in Africa difficult?"

"I suppose it's difficult somewhere."

She stared at him as if she expected him to acknowledge the simple truth of that.

"I meant where you were."

"Oh. Perhaps some people think so."

Her flat, commonsense answers defeated him. He knew there was no point in asking her whether she was one of the persons who thought so. But at least her eyes hadn't returned to her book. They were fastened on a marble ash tray on a table to her left. Ronald looked at the plaited skirt she was wearing: it wasn't the skirt of a doctor and it was far too youthful for her age, which he guessed was thirty-four or thirty-five. And her patterned blouse didn't go with the skirt at all. How could such a person make him feel uneasy?

"You don't say much, do you?"

Her eyes darted toward his but they changed directions before they reached them. She seemed to have no intention of answering but her small body lifted in the chair slightly, moving sideways. He thought she was going to get up.

"I, I work with my hands, and—and my eyes." She was almost stuttering. That she had even spoken surprised him and the way in which she was doing it startled him. "I, you see, don't have much to . . . to say to anyone to do what I do. . . . Do you know Albert Schweitzer? I mean, what he said? The reason he became a doctor was because he didn't want to have to talk any more. He couldn't do any good for people or in the world without their cooperation, I mean, in Europe, and so he wanted to be able to do good with his hands without having to talk. He could help life, he could take a tumor out of a man when he was unconscious, without his cooperation, and that's what he wanted to do. I didn't become a doctor for that reason, but what he said is true for me, a little. I've come to trust things that are written down"—she raised the book in her lap— "things that I can see instead of those I hear. It's become a habit." She paused an instant before she confessed, "I know I'm very awkward and clumsy with others."

She stopped talking and looked at him, almost in apology. And Ronald's eyes were drawn toward hers. They didn't appear to be merely pinched together and glassed over. He noticed a gray softness in them that he hadn't seen before. He cleared his throat, getting ready to speak quietly.

"When are you going back?"

"I have six more weeks yet, but I'm leaving on Saturday. I'm going to Morocco, to Casablanca, to work with another doctor."

She looked at him expectantly.

Ronald asked, "Do you play tennis?"

It was clear she hadn't expected to be asked that and she laughed a little.

"Only when I have to."

16

Now he laughed.

"Well, you don't have to, but would you? Would you play with me sometime tomorrow?"

2

_____

I RECALL PLEADING TO VIVIAN that we didn't know people. "And they don't know us, for God's sake. We know each other's stories, that's all—it's a kind of bargain: you tell me a little bit of your story, I'll give you a personal anecdote in return. Right? . . . Isn't that what you and I have been doing for eight or nine years? And when that's all you do, share no more than a sentence of something with someone, a sentence in a whole book of stories about yourself, and they reach over and pat you on the top of the hand, saying, 'I understand' . . . That's when you really give up! Haven't you ever undergone the humiliation of being _understood_? I have. Once. . . . It's terrible, and it'll never happen again. I told a story and when I was done the person wasn't only patting me on the top of my hand, I could feel her getting her fingers on my heart, squeezing it and massaging it with tears in her eyes, whispering how she understood me now. God! You should have seen the look of satisfaction on the otherside of her tears. So let's drop the search for understanding. I'll pay you the compliment of saying that I don't begin to understand you, and I really don't, Vivian—I just know a little bit of your story—so why not forget about trying to understand why Ronald and Nancy married?"

I really don't give it up that easily. Some things aren't

that difficult to pursue: a gentle moment on a hard day, a moment of grace in a totally judged life, a sudden glimpse of something overhead when your eyes have been on what's beneath your feet for years. Even an instant when fear forgets to be afraid of itself. And Ronald did his own bit of rationalizing one night, too. It wasn't the first or only night he sat in my cottage with me, talking; but it was one of the more memorable ones. What he said helped to make it that.

"I know we didn't know each other. But that's what made it right, the risk was the same for both of us. We were equal, we . . . we stood on the same ground together. I had come from someplace where she hadn't been living, and she'd come from someplace where I hadn't been living, so we just happened to be where we were at the same time. We hadn't been planning on getting something from each other—so we couldn't take advantage of each other. There was the same amount of risk for both of us. It was deciding to do it that counted. Just doing certain things is what matters sometimes, it doesn't even matter what it is maybe, or even who you do them with. I know all kinds of married people who say they could have married someone else just as easily—a half a dozen different people they had known and been just as happy, or not happy. What was important was when they decided to do it—making the decision."

"Are you saying that it doesn't matter whom you marry, what matters is deciding to get married? The decision?"

"Yeah, that's it, that's what made it right. The risk was the same for both of us."

There were only two noticeable sounds in the room on that still Ndami night. One came from the ice cubes melting and shifting in our glasses of Scotch. The other came from the way Ronald picked at his thumbnail, an extremely long nail on his right hand, which had been split.

It had been smashed by something at one time in the middle and corrugated ridges ran the length of the nail on each side of the central depression. The end of the nail was uneven, a series of waves, and he was constantly picking at it with the nail of his doubled-under middle finger, making a small clicking sound. The idea that it didn't make any difference whom you marry, what makes the difference is the decision to marry, was so novel to me that I couldn't think of a thing to say. I picked up my drink and looked off as I pretended to savor it, listening as his middle finger picked at his thumb nail, *click, click . . . click.*

He had managed to obscure a few facts from himself. Even though it might have been the same risk for both of them, he *was* planning on getting something. He didn't tell Nancy that it might spoil his father's corner a little more if he married a doctor whose family moved in the same circle of acquaintances and dined at the same country club, where it might be rumored that Ronald was without the means to support her. Didn't he know his father wouldn't let it be said that he was spending Dr. Applegate's money in bars, living off her? And hadn't his father been waiting for him to do something? Well, he did it: he got married. He changed his status in the twinkling of an eye. I even think I remember some offhand remark about being "harassed by phone calls from California" while he waited those three months for his grandmother to die. From some other woman he had moved out on? . . . In any case, he bought and eventually paid for a ticket out of town and briefly out of himself. I believe he thought that Nancy was living in a place in the world where something was "happening." If he had journalistic fantasies of witnessing timely events, I guess he thought the rumbling which finally broke over the skies of Nigeria might break over him. It's so like a white man to think there is a road leading from where he is to where he wants to go. He can't imagine it doesn't exist, or that he can't build one if it doesn't. But what roads and paths there are in Africa a white man doesn't know how to walk: they've never been laid down in his heart and mind, so when he sees them on the ground, at his very feet, he doesn't understand what's there. He's paralyzed. . . . Nevertheless, Ronald Keane married because he could be moved only by cataclysms, by the small catastrophisms that most people rely on: flight, someone's death, marriage. The bumps that knock a stalled piece of human machinery down the road, any road—even if it's marked *Dead End*.

And Nancy?

I understand that a revolution in our comprehension of how things got done in the world took place when a lonely Scots doctor sat at his desk one day in some misbegotten century and heard the water dripping from the gutter outside his window after a recent rain. He multiplied that dripping by thousands of years, walked to his window, saw the leaves falling to the ground, multiplied the ten thousand there by ten thousand autumns, and began to fear how the world was arranged. What happened never happened suddenly, not even a volcanic explosion. It happened gradually, silently; awesomely. Everything came about as if a leaking water faucet were dripping in the night. Sooner or later something would erode and collapse forever. I don't know what it was within Nancy that did, or at what precise moment—it may have happened while she was stuttering in the Keanes' den, or that night when she couldn't sleep, if she didn't, or when she lifted her racquet during the following days . . . or perhaps when her eyes wandered across the page of a book. But my impression is that something which had dripped from the ceiling of her isolated mind for years had eroded the boards beneath her feet in the thirty-fifth year of life.

And Ronald Keane just happened to be there.

In any case, I, who can imagine anything, cannot imagine a honeymoon in Morocco between them. It isn't a tale that would hold a wedding guest spellbound.

"I tried, I really did," said Ronald.

I don't think I believed him. He was too clearly in passage, *en route*, looking out; in need of a bewildered excuse to forget who was sitting next to him. But I'm not sure that Nancy tried, either. Any efforts must have been like the evening prayers that rise above the white buildings of Casablanca: faint, indistinct, fading quickly. A honeymoon between them is unthinkable rather than unimaginable because it's unthinkable that Ronald would have known her any better after six weeks than six days, or even six years than six months. He thought that she was nothing more than shy. Temporarily withdrawn. But her habit of being silent disoriented him. She didn't appear sullen; and she was pleasant, even affectionate sounding at times, when she told him to enjoy the day at the ocean or on the hotel tennis courts while she went off to wherever she went off to—some library or laboratory. Still, he thought she would come to trust spoken words, as she had put it; but she seemed not to speak simply because she had nothing to say. When he made a casual remark like, "It's another beautiful day," he expected her to answer. At first. Then he began to hope that she would. But she remained silent unless he repeated what he said.

"I said, it's another beautiful day."

Only then would she smile and show her white teeth, saying, "I heard you," before returning to a book that was always in her lap or hands.

For the first weeks of their marriage they lived in a hotel but apparently Nancy did little things to make it seem, not like home, but as if she were prepared to assume some traditional role. She called for coffee in the morning and not only poured it but even stirred Ronald's cup, at least for their first breakfast. It made him feel uncomfortable, and he did it himself after that. But she looked after his clothes and saw to it that they were laundered and pressed regularly. If there were two chairs and one was obviously less comfortable than the other, she always chose the less comfortable one.

"I felt like a guest," he said. "I thought she would gradually relax, but she didn't."

"Nothing personal?"

That was an oblique question, I admit. One I had no right to ask but when I did I wanted to find out anything more about her, anything. Ronald knew what I meant by the question and he looked aside. I'm not sure if I saw shame or embarrassment in his face. Maybe I wanted to see one or the other.

"She surprised me once or twice."

I don't know what that meant. But I have a better idea of what a trip to Rabat meant for Ronald. One morning over coffee Nancy told him that she was going there to have dinner with a doctor. She didn't seem to expect him to go with her and he had to ask if he could.

"Can't I come with you?"

She looked at him and seemed to deliberate about it. At first Ronald thought she was going to say no. But she didn't.

"If you think you'd like it. I'll call his wife this morning so she'll be expecting both of us. We'll have to leave by five o'clock."

"All right."

When Nancy came home that afternoon she told Ronald they would be driving.

"I ordered a car. I have an allowance for one."

It was the first he knew of it, for she traveled by bus every morning. He understood, vaguely, that she was doing some sort of research but it was hard for him to realize it because she never said anything about it. And he suspected that if he asked it would be too technical for him to understand. He felt insecure enough in her presence. He didn't want that additional humiliation.

22

He was humiliated enough when he went to Rabat.

Entering the residence of Dr. and Mme. Yousri was like falling through a trapdoor. He looked about, bewildered, surrounded by mystery and elegance: the mystery of Arabic culture and the elegance of the French language. For the Yousris spoke no English and they addressed Nancy in French. As usual, Nancy was silent; but she appeared to understand them. It was she who directed Ronald this way or that as they were shown the garden and the library, and stood examining various objects of art. And when they sat on floor cushions and were handed perfumed steaming towels, she seemed to know exactly what to do, and how to help herself to the hors d'oeuvre properly. Ronald did whatever she did. When she first said something in French he stared at her. Mme. Yousri smiled at him, thinking he had understood, and she appeared to agree with whatever Dr. Applegate—she corrected herself, *Docteur Keane*—had said. When Nancy replied and then went on, speaking not only fluently but at great length in French, Ronald was not only stunned. He sat through a dinner that assaulted his tongue with all kinds of new flavors, not knowing what he was eating, dismayed; hardly having the resolution to eat.

He felt cheated, tricked. Nancy had never uttered that many words consecutively in English. His stomach grew tight, his nerves tense. The plainness of Nancy's face revolted him, the flatness of her chest was disgusting. No matter how small it was, the growth on the side of her nose made her ugly. He had to receive the unending smiles of his Moroccan hosts by nodding and smiling in return, ridiculously, getting more insecure by the moment; upset. Nancy completely ignored him, chattering away to Dr. Yousri in French. He began to drink goblets of wine and felt satisfied when Nancy started to glance at him. He finally knew that the three of them were talking about him for they began

23

smiling in his direction together. Nancy had become one of them. He knew she had told them that he hadn't understood a word since he came in the door. And he was right to feel paranoid for Mme. Yousri lifted herself up off her cushions and gestured to him with a hand so ring-laden that it must have added a pound to her weight. She wanted him to follow and so he did, into the library with its elegant bookbindings, prints and furnishings. She pointed toward a sofa where he should sit and then went to a shelf and pulled out several volumes, handing them to him with a gracious smile before she went out. They were all novels by Dickens. One of the servants brought him coffee to drink alone and he sat on the sofa staring at a collection of Berber pistols hanging on the wall.

But his humiliation wasn't his failure to be bilingual. Or that Nancy had never told him she spoke French for she never told him anything. He didn't know the source of his humiliation as he sulked in the car driving back to Casablanca, breaking the silence with a surly voice.

"And just what did you talk about all the time I was supposed to be reading *Great Expectations?*"

"About horses, mostly."

"Horses?"

"Yes."

"Is that what you do, cure horses?"

She had the nerve to laugh.

"I couldn't help it. Dr. Yousri's a racing fan. I expect to work with him for the next month. I'll be seeing him almost every day." It sounded like a warning, which she softened by adding, "He's coming to Casablanca."

"What kind of work?"

"On a fever."

"What fever?"

"*Gras* fever."

He felt ignorant. "What's that?" He wasn't asking, he was demanding to be informed.

24

"We don't know exactly. It's called *gras* because it makes the hair oily. We can't isolate the germ yet, or even find the carrier."

It was her use of *we* that struck him, he said. That there were people in the world who were not only working but were working together because there seemed to be some point to it. He couldn't say what the point was but it made him feel left out, excluded. Useless. As useless and excluded as when they were speaking a language he didn't understand.

He asked self-pityingly, "Why didn't you tell me I wouldn't understand a word of anything?"

"You said you wanted to come along."

He stared at her. He knew there was something wrong with that but he couldn't find what it was. The tone that came into Nancy's voice suggested that she also knew there was something wrong with it.

"I've been thinking that maybe we should move closer to the sea."

Because she had begun to wonder what Ronald would do all day long when Dr. Yousri came into Casablanca? Whatever the reason, they did: went to a hotel in Mohammédia and Nancy drove into Casablanca every morning, keeping the car, while Ronald spent the day on the beach or on one of the tennis courts. The sun gave his brown hair a reddish sheen, put a bit of color on his broad forehead and square chin, and made him look like a man in a cigarette ad, older than he was, not four years younger than his wife. When Nancy came home at night now she not only read late; she appeared to read the two or three books that were open in front of her at the same time. The bar of the Miramar Hotel was alive with tourists so Ronald spent the evening there, drinking Brandy Alexanders. Was it already an imperfectly perfect arrangement? Certainly drinking at the Miramar was more comfortable for Ronald than it was at the bar of the National Hotel when they flew on to The Port. There, when the Europeans at the bar, usually British, learned who Ronald was—or to whom he belonged—there was either silence or a too-obvious curiosity. Little by little he discovered that among the expatriate community that was going to constitute "home," Nancy was not very popular. He discovered that she was a doctor without a practice. She had no patients. She worked in a laboratory, if it could be called that: miserable rooms in one of the poorest sections of The Port. She was really a biologist; her speciality was tropical diseases and, by extension, bacteriology. She made cultures. She worked with serums rather than people, which fit in with everything he knew or had experienced about her. But he hadn't guessed it. She had no car and he discovered that half of her salary, a pitiful six thousand dollars a year in addition to a place to live, was paid by some missionary society. She had no status whatever among the lingering colonials. He had thought that when she got back to Africa, where she belonged, functioned and performed, some hidden qualities would appear. They didn't. No unexpected graces showed themselves. Ronald joined the midday drinkers at the National Hotel—"getting acquainted," he called it.

But he also discovered the exoticness of The Port.

It prevented him from going about totally disgruntled, sourly disillusioned, whether he had a right to be either. His discovery gave me a hint of his susceptibility, his vulnerability as he wandered through an African market for the first time: through labyrinths as narrow and jammed as an intestine, where people brushed against his ribs and breathed into his face. Where the smell of sandalwood, musk, spices, leather being cured and oil used for frying, went up his nose. Women sat in the mud, surrounded by merchandise, crying out to him and every passerby as if they were dying. One after another adults squatted: begging, shaving, weaving, emptying their bowels, baking bread in earth-ovens or teaching a chant to some child. He didn't understand how old men could sleep on bags of saffron alongside of boys beating designs into copper trays held between their legs. Once, a mule, its back burdened with wood and its sides bleeding from a whipping, came past and left its slobber all along his arm. He watched steam coming out of cauldrons filled with dye, day after day. He couldn't get enough of it. For silk and wool were being dipped into them and the black hands that pulled the materials out were as orange as the sun, as green as emeralds, as yellow as lemons. . . . I know the effect of looking upon commonplace things as if they were miracles. I know how every white man or woman who comes to Africa always has something in mind, some vague plan. But whatever it is vanishes quickly, which is probably why I can no longer remember what ideas I started to have after the Colonial Office said I could serve a three-year term. Whatever I had in mind wasn't as important as the spider bite I got on my arm the first week I was here. There is such an abundance of life around you in Africa, outside of you, *There*, that the life within you, whatever it consists of, is paltry by comparison. No matter who you are, Africa will not make an exception of you. You realize that your feet are on a planet spinning in the sun, a theater for crawling life, human and nonhuman. Billions of mouths are moving sideways or up and down, and yours just happens to be one of them. Whatever you had in mind when you arrived gets lost, which was some vague idea of returning home. But you soon prefer the African abundance of things that are already alive outside of you to whatever is struggling to be born within you. It's easy to come to Africa for three years and want to stay for thirty. The hard ideas in your white and Western head melt under the African sun. They soften into wax. Everything begins to make an impression on you.

Especially Vivian Angle if you are Ronald Keane.

3

ALL OVER AFRICA AT THAT TIME
colonialists and nationalists were throwing darts at calendars, saying that on the
day the dart landed "colonialism" was going to be out of
date. There were celebrations and ceremonies; the air was
filled with cautious hopes and restrained hates. And maybe
colonialism did go out of date but it didn't go out of fashion.
Its remnants hung around in disguised dress. Except Alan
Angle, who needed no disguise. You might almost say that
his tall, thin frame—a bit shaggy and heronlike after fifty-
five years of living—was a natural disguise. It concealed his
strength so you respected it all the more when you learned
it was there; and decided, more likely than not, that it came
from his character as much as it did from twenty-six years'
service and experience in Africa. He was still the most important white among the expatriates when Ronald arrived
and had been governor since the last year of the War. If
there was less bloodshed in our part of Africa than most
parts, he was largely responsible for our good fortune. He
had tact, common sense and the ability to see the inevitable.
His title had been abolished along with the colony but he
still exercised numerous powers that belonged to a transi-
tional government. The reins were still changing hands and
no one could have handed them over with a more genuine
smile than Alan. He was even-tempered at all times and forgetful of his importance. Vivian often had to remind him
of protocol. He was known to pick up scrap paper from
his office floor even though his office was staffed with Africans and other minor officials. He paid more attention to
cards than he did the rumors and speculations that he would

be the first British High Commissioner to a new African nation. He spent as much time as he could at the club rooms of the National Hotel playing bridge. When the half-day ended on Saturday it was his established practice to go directly to the hotel, and it was there that he first met Ronald. Which meant they had shaken hands and said hello, nothing more. It also meant that when he came home he told Vivian he had met Nancy Applegate's husband.

"Oh? What's he like?"

"The usual American."

"He can't be *usual* if he married that woman."

"I suppose not," Alan agreed. "Still, he looks the usual sort. Tall, good looking in that absurdly boyish way young Americans are, buying everyone drinks because he wants to be well liked."

"What does he do?"

Alan shrugged.

"Nothing?"

"I think he was with newspapers or something."

If Vivian referred to Nancy as *that woman,* as I've no doubt she did, she didn't do it maliciously. She was simply a woman who could afford to smile at most women. And did. Australian by birth, she was twelve or more years younger than Alan. Once you knew she had been an Olympic swimmer you could see the musculature in her arms and legs, still there, lingering, keeping her body firm. She may very well have had the only firm body of any white over forty, male or female, in a country where the heat makes everything go limp. And she was comfortably conscious about her attractiveness without being self-conscious about it. Her own self-estimate was a relief to the men she charmed because she didn't burden them with the knowledge that they were in the presence of beauty. But not infrequently they felt the burden in her absence.

"Shall we have them up?" she asked.

"It's not strictly necessary, you know. I wouldn't

want Dr. Apple—I mean, Mrs. Keane, to think we're responsible for her."

"What's going to happen to her?"

"I don't know. I suppose the local sawbones will have to take her on, if they want to. And I doubt that they do, or will. Or even the missionary society. I don't think they have the funds to do it. It doesn't help, her being American."

"Or so pleasant."

"Quite. One can't forget that."

"Why don't I add two for Friday? We really don't have to entertain anyone—we have the latest Marlon Brando film to show everyone."

"How did you manage that?"

"I didn't. It just came in the diplomatic pouch."

Vivian sent a car around for Ronald and Nancy, and the Angles' African driver raced up the hills, honking his horn and shouting at everyone on foot. To step out of the Angles' Jaguar on The Hill at dusk for the first time is an unforgettable moment. The sun has already fallen below the rim of the ocean at that time of day and the sky is a Chinese bowl of orange and indigo. The islands in the bay become ever-deepening patches of green that grope their way like cautious stepping stones toward the darker sea beyond. There, they become almost black with mystery. On clear days you can see as far as another country, even though smoke from smoldering native fires along the hills trails up into the sky. When Ronald and Nancy arrived the lights of The Port were already on, circling the harbor. And when they are they shine and sparkle like a necklace around the beautiful throat of an illusion.

Ronald couldn't help himself: he reached across the back seat of the car and grabbed Nancy's hand.

"Nancy!"

His touch made her jump with fright and she pulled her hand away.

30

"What?"

"Look! Down below."

"Oh," she said, relieved that it was only the view. "Do you like it?"

Ronald didn't answer because he was already stepping out of the car, the door being held for him, and the aroma from the hillside fires had reached his nostrils.

"They're burning something."

"It's just their dinner fires."

Nancy led the way up the stairs to the terrace, and when they reached it Ronald felt he should have been warned. Five or six doors led off the lengthy terrace into a single large room that seemed overflowing with people. The ceiling was high, the walls were white and decorated by African masks, shields, and long strips of thin bark covered with designs made by a dull red ink. Three or four huge moths had attached themselves to the ceiling and walls and never moved all evening, making it seem they had been pinned there. African servants wearing bright garments were everywhere, handing out cocktails and hors d'oeuvre. Ronald reached for a glass as quickly as he could. He wasted no time in taking a sip from it. Perhaps that's why he didn't see Alan Angle and the woman alongside of him approach. And when he did see Vivian all he saw was a burnt-orange blur. It's hard to know what a man means or what anyone means when they say about another person: "She's the most beautiful woman I've ever seen in my life." Which is something Ronald did say to me about Vivian. I would never make such a statement myself but I can see the grounds for anyone else making it, which are Vivian's face and body. But on those grounds different people build different things and I certainly wouldn't want to tear down what Ronald constructed on them. Somehow it would be beside the point, which is that Vivian's physical presence had an effect on everyone. It's what Alan himself called "star quality." You had to pay attention to her even when you got angry at yourself for letting your attention wander from whom and what you wanted it to stick. And she even had a way of making you laugh at your own anger; making you feel that you were ridiculous in not just admitting to yourself that she was so infectiously good looking that you ought to just kick off your shoes, relax, and enjoy her. You could return to your dull seriousness when she wasn't around.

"Mrs. *Keane!*" she exclaimed to Nancy smilingly, emphasizing Nancy's new name. And status, I suppose, forsaking *doctor*.

Alan offered his hand to her before he did to Ronald, saying to him "It's nice to see you again. This is my wife, Vivian."

Vivian may have nodded to Ronald before returning her attention to Nancy, saying cooly and correctly, "It's nice that you're back. Mr. Disane will take you in to dinner, the gentleman over there." She pointed to an olive-skinned man. "You may know him already, Sloke . . . he's with *The Voice of Pan-Africa*. That may interest you, Mr. Keane. I understand that you're a journalist." Her uplifted face and smile didn't mean she wanted an answer from Ronald, who was incapable of giving one. "We will be able to visit later because I'm to have the pleasure of being escorted in to dinner by you, it seems."

Alan saw the jolt that gave Ronald.

"It *seems!* Don't pay any attention to her, Mr. Keane. She made the arrangements herself. You'll catch on to her." Alan added affectionately, "We all do."

Vivian laughed.

I imagine her eyes dropped to Ronald's slightly dimpled chin even while she was talking to Nancy.

"Please make yourselves at home. We're so glad you could come."

Yes, Ronald wished he had been warned: ten times

32

over. He didn't expect Alan Angle's wife to look as she did, or be what he discovered she was. He didn't expect to be among people from the United Nations, to be introduced to the Roman Catholic bishop for the Ivory Coast and a British petroleum official; a Frenchman with *Le Figaro*, an American with the World Bank and a Belgian financier . . . not to mention an assortment of women who accompanied these men. They looked like wives, not like Vivian Angle who seemed responsible for creating an atmosphere like that of a mountaintop *skihaus* instead of a hilltop mansion filled with seemingly important people. The world beyond or down below wasn't really a serious place. These people regarded it as their playground, somehow. Ronald who lived below, not in quarters that were squalid but graceless, was awed. And when Vivian took his arm and they walked into dinner together, he had to do everything he could to conceal his nervousness. It meant nothing to Vivian, but Ronald had never been to a dinner party before where the women were led to the table by a man they hadn't arrived with. And because she was the hostess he felt singled out. He felt even more singled out when she leaned toward him as soon as they sat down and she spoke quietly.

"I won't be able to eat a proper dinner."

She had leaned so close and said it so softly that there could be no mistaking that she didn't want anyone else to hear her; she had said it for his ears alone and they burned. Burned with wanting to know why. He leaned toward her with a kind of eager helplessness, waiting.

"Young men make me watch my diet. That's why I sit them next to me—and it's a shame, too." She smiled at Ronald and waited until he looked at her, as if she wouldn't go on until she were certain of her effect. "Zili's such a wonderful cook!"

Since she expected Ronald to smile, broadly, appreciatively, he did. But his mind raced along with the blood that filled his cheeks. By calling him *young* he knew she had drawn attention to her age and he felt that maybe he was supposed to protest in a chivalrous way that he looked no younger than she did. And by calling attention to her diet, wasn't she inviting him to say something about her figure? It seemed certain yet he couldn't believe it, for his head was filled with the liberties he might take with her, verbally. It made him dizzy enough just to want to try it and he swallowed, leaning toward her as she had done, speaking in the same soft tones; conspiratorily.

"I don't think I'll be able to eat a proper dinner, either."

She mock-exclaimed like an offended hostess: "Why ever not?"

"Because no one told me I would be sitting next to a beautiful woman."

Daring to say so made Ronald feel triumphant. He glowed in anticipation of the response he was certain such a remark would have. But Vivian was silent . . . long enough for him to fumble with his napkin before she covered her mouth with her hand and leaned close. He felt the breath from her nostrils deflected off her palm onto his cheek.

"How very, very thoughtless of them!"

He was getting one petty shock after another. But however petty, however frivilous Vivian could be in delivering her shocks, there was something to say for the way she did not—after being told that she was beautiful—lower her eyes or allow herself to be overcome by false modesty or strike a pose of embarrassed acceptance. The free and hearty way in which she dealt with the reality of her physical self shocked anyone who was not used to it. And she knew how to make others accept it, gladly. She laughed for both herself and Ronald after whispering in his ear, and all heads at the table turned in her direction. Now Ronald's face reddened with deeper pleasure because he appeared to be the source of her enjoyment. And then once more she started whispering for his searing ears alone.

"I think I should tell you that I have a son at Oxford. Yes, indeed . . . Oxford. I really expect to have a red ribbon tied around my neck any day now and be quietly led into some pasture."

Everything that took place was hard for Ronald to believe. It was hard to believe that she was over forty which he knew she must be, for she looked younger than Nancy. It was hard to believe that she ordered the bishop for the Ivory Coast, with a flick of her manicured finger, to stop being bashful and take more fish. And that the bishop enjoyed being ordered to do it and obeyed. It was hard to believe that his place next to her was merely luck and that he was losing that place rapidly; inevitably, as servants took away plates, brought others and replaced them. He was feeling stricken by the time Vivian asked him, unaccountably, if he liked Marlon Brando. To hear her mention a man of consequence threatened him.

"He's all right," he shrugged.

"Oh, dear."

She was clearly disappointed in his response.

"We're going to see his latest film."

Ronald didn't know they were going to the theater. It hadn't said so on the invitation. He looked at Vivian a bit forlornly; but just when it was hard to believe that he was going to lose sight of her in a dark theater, she laid her hand on his arm and spoke in a confiding tone.

"If the film bores you, never mind. Just slip out onto the terrace. The view is always lovely at night and I'll show you where the liqueurs are kept. You can help yourself."

He wondered if others at the table were watching the

way Vivian's hand rested in his forearm. For he could feel her fingers moving as she talked and he had trouble voicing his surprise at what she said.

"You mean we're going to see the film here?"

"Of course," she said proudly.

Alan Angle pushed the button on the wall himself; it electrically lowered a screen from the ceiling in the large room that Ronald and Nancy had first entered.

Ronald lost track of Vivian during the film until the first reel was changed. Everyone's after-dinner drink was freshened and Vivian bent low as she passed the deep chair he was sitting in.

"When I see those Tahitian women I think that maybe I should let my hair grow again."

She had straightened herself and was gone before he could catch whatever look she had on her face. But he was sure he had more than luck, much more than luck—until he saw Nancy looking at him. She immediately looked away when his eyes caught hers, but he sank into the chair as he sank into his misfortune. He hadn't for one moment wondered what Vivian thought of him because he was married to Nancy. His imagination took what his own judgment told him and shook him loose from his enchantment. When the next reel began he wanted to crawl off into the dark and not be forced to stand alongside of Nancy and face Vivian with her, exchanging pleasantries as they thanked the Angles and said goodnight. His fears were realized when Vivian never even looked at him at the door. She stood with her arm locked in Alan's and gave all her attention to Nancy.

I didn't know Ronald then.

If I had, if we had already been drinking Scotch together in my cottage at night, I could have told him that Vivian was giving all her attention to Nancy because she was thinking how convenient it was that Nancy should be just exactly what Ronald regretted.

4

RONALD SULKED FOR FOUR DAYS. He did nothing but feel depressed and nurse his depression. He stayed away from the bar of the National Hotel and drank his brandy and soda at home, often in Nancy's study when she was at her laboratory because the presence of their servants unnerved him. He relived the evening at the Angles' endlessly, searching every word and gesture of Vivian's to reassure himself of something. He was humiliated by what he imagined Vivian's opinion of him was because of Nancy's plainness; her pinched, severe look; her humorlessness, her gracelessness. He became almost as silent as Nancy herself and one night he caught her looking at him instead of her book. But as soon as he did her eyes fled quickly.

On the morning of the fifth day after the Angles' dinner party, the telephone rang and a disgusted voice said:

"Ronald, do you play tennis?"

Vivian expected him to know who it was. And he did. It was just nine o'clock and Ronald already had a brandy and soda in his hand. His head whirled, stopped, and tried to find an answer. It only came up with another question.

"Tennis?"

"Alan promised—*promised!*—he would be able to get away this morning and then the news came of that terrible mining accident. Naturally, he's off! Off! . . . Just gone and left me with a French couple to entertain. We were going to play tennis at the Hamarttan and I don't know what to do. Can you please, *please* take Alan's place?"

He was too shocked to be able to answer.

"Don't tell me you don't play tennis!"

"No, no, I can play."

"Then why aren't you flying to my rescue?"

It was his unshaven condition, his unpreparedness, that kept him so earthbound. His tennis clothes weren't clean and his racquet had a tattered string.

"My racquet—"

Vivian cut him off.

"Don't bring a thing, a thing! Just go straight to the Hamarttan and when you get there, find Samson in the men's dressing room. Tell him *I* sent you—he'll know just what to do. Can you make it by ten?"

"I'll try."

"Americans! You're lovely, you always try," she said buoyantly. "I knew you would."

Of course she did. She knew a good many other things, too. I knew some myself: that Alan never played tennis at ten o'clock in the morning. No one in their right mind did. They'd fall over flat from sunstroke. The air was too heavy and the heat too intense for every expatriate in the whole of West Africa—except Vivian Angle. And I doubt that there was a French couple to be entertained. Vivian invented emergencies so men could rescue her from them. It was one of her devices, one of her usually harmless tricks. . . .

I say *usually*.

After she hung up Ronald called a taxi, hurried to the bathroom, groaned when he saw himself in the mirror, and then shaved. After he shaved he groaned again. He saw the effects of too much brandy and too little food. But it didn't prevent him from getting to the deserted courts of the Hamarttan Club at five minutes to ten. Galvanized pipes, painted green to match the lawn, arched over each court, supporting large fans that revolved so slowly that he could see the blades distinctly at all times. To escape the heat he walked over and stood beneath one of them, waiting for an air current to touch him. When none did he found some shade. He had never played tennis on grass courts before and he had a half hour to worry about it while he waited for Vivian. When she suddenly appeared, walking briskly toward the courts, she was alone.

"Do you want to warm up?" she called.

Her white shorts had a blue trim. So did her halter. He stared at the parts of her exposed body that had been covered on The Hill the other night, until his self-consciousness made him conscious that no one was with her.

"Where are the others?"

"Mr. Vaulet called to say his wife wasn't feeling well—*five* minutes before I was to leave the house and collect them! I tried to call you again but you were already gone. Up or down? . . . We don't need to warm up in this sun, do we?"

Ronald shook his head.

"Down."

It was *Up*. Vivian's first service came so fast that he merely watched it go by. One could have hardly called it an ace. Ronald was still a spectator, not a player.

"Maybe you'd like to warm up anyway."

"No, no, go ahead," he said, squinting at her through the glare of the sun. "It's the grass—I'm not used to it."

He never did get used to it. He wasn't able to return her serve until the third game and only then at game point. Vivian rewarded him with a wonderful smile at the same time that she put a passing shot to his right and cried out, "Another love game!" before the ball even hit the base line. He was stunned and sick at the same time that he was filled with admiration. He couldn't concentrate. The pipes and fans overhead disturbed him. A coal-black man in a club uniform stood with his arms folded in front of him, watching them. Vivian's feet were white puffs of speed. Her light brown hair shined in the sun. When she lifted her racquet her arm went up like a dancer's, when she ran the muscles beneath her tanned skin ran with her. Where beads of perspiration stood out on her skin they reflected the sun-light.

As they exchanged sides she touched his forearm.

"This is the last one. I must go."

Ronald looked at his watch and saw that it was just after eleven.

"Already?"

He was answered by a ball coming over the net as if it had been fired from a cannon. Three serves later she laughed and came running toward him.

"You must like love games!"

He was too stung to feel that he was being teased, too stung to even imagine that she was saying more than she was. But her pleasure in herself was enough to make him smile and warn, "Give me time!"

"How much? I don't have a minute now, I'm afraid," she said, leading him off the court by the wrist. "I have to meet the Vaulets for lunch."

"I thought Mme. Vaulet wasn't feeling well?"

"She isn't feeling good enough for tennis but she's in perfect condition to have lunch. Would you like to take a swim with me?"

Ronald felt his luck returning to him again. He looked at the pool eagerly.

"Oh, not here!" Vivian exclaimed, as if he should have known better. "Not now, I never swim here. In the ocean, down the coast. Later this afternoon. Shall I call you? I *must* run!" She started to walk off, repeating, "Shall I?" and left him standing at the edge of the courts with his head bobbing.

He waited for Vivian's call for three hours. Expectation made a wreck of him. And when she finally called she was disgusted again and didn't bother to say hello or apologize.

"Ronald, I simply can't do it!"

He was too confused to reply.

"Ronald, are you there?"

He nodded in the dimness of the room he was in before he said, "Yes."

"How about tomorrow? Can you join me in the morning?"

He nodded, holding the telephone in his hand.

"Is anything the matter? Ronald, are you there?"

"No, no, yes, yes. I'd like to join you in the morning."

He hadn't expected to be invited again. He thought an end had been put to it.

"Do you know where Hamsun's Bay is? The place the natives call Dlanga?"

He didn't. He knew nothing.

"No."

"When you take the coast road east the pavement changes about four miles out. You can't miss noticing it because it becomes rockier. Another mile on there's a dirt road to the right. Take that until you come to a huge rock, absolutely *huge!* Stop right there and wait for me. I'll be there by nine o'clock."

As Vivian gave directions Ronald's throat became thick. Nothing was right for him, nothing.

"I don't have a car."

Vivian was silent. Her silence made him feel inept, inadequate; clumsy, a fool. A nobody.

"How is it that they've never given Nancy a car?" she puzzled.

He didn't know that either and had to say so. "I don't know." But he added quickly, "I can get a taxi. I did this morning."

"No, no, that'll never do." She didn't seem to know what to do and Ronald shifted from one leg to another. She said abruptly, "I'll have to call you in the morning."

He felt his luck slipping away from him again.

"I'm sorry, Vivian. I really am."

"Never mind, never mind," she said impatiently. "Can I call you in the morning? By eight thirty?"

The inflection in her voice tripped his heart just enough to make it slam on the next beat: he knew she was asking whether he would be alone. Nancy was always gone by seven, but he said semisecretly, "I can call you, if you like."

"No, I'll ring you," she said flatly.

Too flatly. He regretted making the suggestion.

"Eight thirty is just fine."

"I have just the solution!" she cried. "We have cars, *scads* of them for special visitors at the Kiwi Garage! Not far from you, right in Livingstone Road. Just go there in the morning, I'll have already called and they'll have something ready for you. I can't say what it'll be but it'll get you to Hamsun's Bay!"

He said, "All right," dazed.

"Be at the garage by eight."

He was there at seven thirty.

5

H E WAS PERSPIRING BY THE time he walked the length of Livingstone Road and arrived at the Kiwi Garage. The car, a Morris Minor, wasn't ready and waiting until eight forty, and he was late in getting to Hamsun's Bay. He found Vivian's car parked in the shadow thrown by the huge rock she had said would be there. When he looked in the front window of her car he saw her clothes in it. She must have done as he had: worn her swim suit under her clothes. Ronald stripped to his trunks and started along the path that led to what he could hear and smell but not see: the ocean. The path narrowed until it disappeared in the tall grass that scratched his arms and legs. Then he walked across an area covered with small rocks which abruptly ended at a long slope of sanding leading to the bay. He saw a confusion of islands and rocks and at the water's edge, Vivian stood alone. She saw him and waved. Ronald began running and when he came closer to her he saw her swimming suit of navy blue. A white swirl went around it like a coil. If she had a son at Oxford he must have passed through her like water. She was still smiling when he reached her and he took a chance on saying what he wanted to say.

"You're not wearing that suit, you're poured into it."

It was a compliment Vivian was ready to accept.

"At a very early age!" she exclaimed, wagging a finger at him. "Before you were born! I swam with the Australian team in the last Olympic Games before the war."

He searched the perfect arrangement of her body for signs of that former ability. Vivian stood still, allowing him to do it, laughing with pleasure. Her right foot was tilted inward so that the instep was pushing into the sand and her small toe reached up in the air.

"You'll see!" she promised, throwing a bronzed arm toward the water.

"What? What more can I possibly see?"

"You're a flirt. Oh, how I love this place!" she cried, turning toward the water.

"But no one's here."

He hadn't expected that. He anticipated a crowded beach.

"No, no one ever comes here. Isn't it unbeliev-able? . . . and stupid? What do they do? What do people do? Whatever it is, they must do it somewhere else, so it's mine"—she threw her arm out at the bay again—"all mine! . . . Listen!"

A vow was forming inside of Ronald to make it his also, just as he heard the screeching of sea birds. But he didn't look for them because Vivian was moving toward the water and he couldn't take his eyes off the back of her.

"That's where I swim to."

She pointed to an outcropping of rocks that cut the sea off from view.

"When we get there, we'll climb out and go on top. Do you think you can swim that far?"

Ronald answered her by walking into the water and diving into the first wave. He did well to keep up with her until the swells increased in size and force. Whenever he paused, trying to rest, the heaving pulled him back, feet first; he found that to stay afloat he had to keep his arms moving constantly. It didn't take Vivian long to outswim him and he saw her turning her head to look back at him. Each time that she did he renewed his efforts. The hollows that separated the crests of the waves lengthened until they were as long as a valley between hilltops. It was much farther to the rocks than he thought and when one of Vivian's arms lifted out of the water and pointed toward shore, he was ready to be told what to do.

"You can climb up over there!"

She had to shout it twice before he waved to her that he understood. He lost sight of her as he started for the rocks. A determination to stop drinking came over him. He damned himself for being short of breath, for having no strength. Alcohol, nothing but alcohol: that's why his thirty-one-year-old body wasn't as durable as hers was at forty, or more. When he climbed onto the rocks, with difficulty, he scanned the bay for sight of her. It took him a while before he found her on the mass of heaving water.

Why wasn't she overpowered by it? She buried her face in it longer than he thought possible and her arms kept coming out in front of her as if she not only knew where she was going, but as if she knew what she was reaching for.

From where he had stood with her on the shore the bay seemed to be a small cove. It was immense: at least a mile across. He heard the steady, dull roar of water all around him. This was the Africa he had heard about, the Africa larger than the imagination. It wasn't hard to answer what the others did who weren't there, because they did what he had been doing: crawling about on the bottom of an ocean of heat, complaining about it, instead of swimming on top of a real ocean, like Vivian. When he arrived in The Port he had encountered a group of expatriates who couldn't move through the thickness of this part of the world, the density of the air. What he encountered was the pity they had for each other. Everyone was always saying, "You'll find more shade over here" . . . "We'll feel a breeze at this end of the veranda" . . . "You'll be more comfortable if I move the fan" . . . "Let me get you a lemon squash." Life was lived in an open-air sickroom. The heat threw pale invalids into an unwilled intimacy with the atmosphere, the world. It touched their bodies and fingered them in secret places. It bred a plague-ridden sense of community in club rooms and bars, on tennis courts where fans pointlessly revolved overhead. And Ronald had fallen in with it, accepted it unquestioningly, unthinkingly.

Resolutions swept through him at the sight of Vivian. To stop drinking. To stop playing bridge. To avoid the swarm of men who invaded the National Hotel every late afternoon. To start coming to Hamsun's Bay every morning. To stop thinking that the sun was too hot to live and breath beneath. . . . He had climbed up and walked forward to the place where Vivian said she swam. He could see that you had to be like her to live in Africa, as he saw her pull herself out of the water onto the rocks. He watched her arms tighten as she reached for each ledge above her. When she reached the top she shook her head like a dog coming out of water and he smiled. With her hair close about her face she looked even younger. She wasn't merely charming and attractive, not only desirable and beautiful. She was admirable. He wanted to say so but he would never have been heard.

He shouted, "Where's the noise coming from?"

She pointed off and shouted back.

"I'll show you!"

She reached for his hand and took it, for safety's sake, it seemed. But Ronald didn't see what they were approaching until she pulled her wet fingers from his.

"There!"

The sea pounded against a reef offshore, throwing itself into the air like a sea god in the shape of a horse, tossing its angry head, roaring at the rocks on which they stood and then plunging into the surf, only to roar again. Vivian put a hand on his shoulder, pulling him close so he could hear what she said.

"I thought Australia had an ocean around it until I came to Africa!"

California floated before Ronald's eyes. He saw blurred scenes of himself along its coast: it was like looking at a small boy in a sandbox compared to what was in front of him.

Vivian pulled on his shoulder again.

"I'm going to swim back."

He looked down and his eyes widened.

"But there's no way to get down there from here!"

"I'm going to dive," she said, starting for the edge.

"You can't!"

She threw her head back to laugh, pleased that he was afraid for her.

"It's only forty feet—some native boys showed me

how to do it. Just watch," she invited. "I'll meet you back on the beach."

She stood at the edge and fell forward without jumping, like a tree falling; toppling. When she started gathering speed, arms outstretched, her swimming suit made a blue-and-white blur in the air. The rock cut off Ronald's view of her and he couldn't tell whether she fell safely into the water or not. A gnawing hole expanded in his chest, made first by fear, then by his sense of inadequacy, of self-defeat. He was unable to follow her again. He could have no control over her. He became determined to meet her, not on shore as she said, but in the water. With her, not waiting for her. So he hurried along the rocks, reached the place where they had gone into the water together and waited until he saw her head appear on one of the wave-crests. Then he dove into the water.

He rediscovered that he just couldn't swim toward her; he had to battle his way. The current kept pulling him back until he decided to tread water, giving up the attempt to go forward. He struggled to keep his head above the swells that heaved him up and down. But when Vivian swam down a foaming slope into the hollow where he was waiting, she didn't stop. Hadn't she seen him? He got his arms and legs into motion and thrashed after her. When she reached shore she picked herself up out of the subsiding waves, running easily onto the sand. When he was ready to do the same, a wave caught him off balance from behind and he stumbled, falling down. Luckily, Vivian hadn't seen him because she was already running toward the top of the sandy slope and didn't turn until she stood at the edge of the tall grass. Even though Ronald's breath was gone, he felt he had to run as far as she had; but when he was halfway up the slope she started off again, away from him, into the grass. He had a sinking, persecuted feeling. What was she trying to do to him? Still he kept after her. His lungs pained him. When he reached where their cars were parked he saw her leaning against hers, head back, her chest heaving. He was glad to see her gasping for breath and leaned next to her, doing the same. Yet she seemed to be gasping from exhilaration while he gasped from exhaustion. He became miserable at what he imagined she must think of him. But she didn't show any such thoughts if she had them. Instead she took a towel from her car, handed it to him and turned her back.

"Dry me."

When he touched her through the towel, all he wanted to find out was when they would do this again.

"How often do you come here?"

"Often."

He didn't ask whether he could come with her, he just asked for time to make him different from what he had been.

"Give me two weeks."

She took the towel from him and began drying her hair.

"And then what?"

"I'll swim all the way with you."

She laughed.

"Did you bring a towel?"

Ronald nodded.

"Get it and bring your clothes." As he did, she walked around the front of her car, continuing, "There's nothing worse than pulling clothes over a wet suit. Besides, we can't go back to town like this—it'd never do. I have friends who let me change at their place."

"Friends?"

"Solly. Africans—Solly Dodide."

She smiled as she started off, and drove much faster than he would have. She not only knew Africans who came to the Angle residence on The Hill—that was understandable. She knew Africans out here, and native boys who taught her to dive among the rocks. Ronald was all admiration.

"Do you mind if I tell you you're a remarkable woman?"

She smiled.

"You may tell me whenever you feel it is appropriate."

"How about once a day?"

She laughed, pleased, and turned off the main road, starting along a track through the bush. Within a mile the country became hot and dry, littered with sticks. Any suggestion that there was an ocean nearby vanished. The wheels of the car churned up a cloud of dust that covered them when they stopped. Wherever it was, the crows were noisy. Through the windshield Ronald saw an unpainted two-story frame structure.

"That's Solly's."

"It looks like a Wild West trading post."

"In its own way, that's *just* what it is!"

Ronald followed Vivian across the road, up three steps and along a porch whose boards swayed and creaked. The door they went through was nearly unhinged. Whoever Solly was he ran a shebeen, for Ronald could smell beer, but there were no customers inside.

"I've been swimming again, Solly!" Vivian called out.

The short, very black man came from behind the counter, smiling. But he said nothing. He went to a door and held it open for Ronald and Vivian. Ronald looked at him as he passed through it, ready to smile and nod at Solly, but Solly looked straight ahead, holding the door with a look of respect on his face. They climbed a narrow staircase where Vivian opened another door at the top. Ronald followed her into a large room that contained a low dresser with a basin and pitcher on it, several worn chairs and a brass bed. The windows were open. Their thin curtains moved listlessly in an occasional hot breeze. Beyond,

49

crows squawked. And there seemed to be only one room for them to change in: Ronald looked around for another. He saw no other doors. Vivian had stopped just in front of him and seemed to be waiting—long enough for his heart to pound. When she turned around and saw the expression on his face, she lowered her eyes.

"Oh, dear."

Then she looked up, seemingly hurt.

"Kiss me, Ronald. Please don't make me think I've done the wrong thing. I hate to feel that I've done the wrong thing. I haven't, have I?"

6

WITHIN THE SPACE OF AN hour at Solly Dodide's he had undergone the miracle of having been chosen. And nothing can be done for those who believe in miracles. Nothing needs doing because it has all been done: to be chosen is everything. He had said that deciding was everything? To have a choice and choose? To act or not to act? That's what mattered? The decision was everything? He was wrong. It was nothing. He didn't know why Vivian had chosen him but she had. That was all that mattered now. Chosen people are a people I know something about, and one of the things they do is worship the gods and goddesses who choose them. And Ronald worshiped Vivian. He thought she was divine. She had a shape and even a spirit unlike any other woman he had encountered. And she had seen him out of the corner of her eye, pointed a finger at him and said, *You!* He didn't need to see Vivian's sudden and momentary choice for what it was: the flick of an energetic finger in the wild strife of life. For he was Beauty's choice.

To be chosen by Vivian was to be chosen by Beauty. He said it, everyone said it. I say it. Or I can't disagree with it. I can only wish I had some answer, some small halfway solution to the problem of beauty. I wish it because Nancy herself raised the problem of plainness or ugliness. And I wish it because I've had my own sad experience with beauty. Before I left England I saw *Uncle Vanya* at a theatre in St. Martin's Lane, and the one human spark in that play, in that futile world of bored and useless people, had but two things to say for himself. One was that he was still "vulnerable to beauty." There wasn't any question that he considered it a saving grace. I remember the line, I recall the moment because I was sitting with my niece to whom I had become a bit vulnerable myself. Every family circle, if it's wide or sprawling enough, has its victim, I guess, and Ericka was ours. And if there was anyone as beautiful as she was, I had never met or passed that person on the street. I've been living six hundred miles north of the Bight of Benin for eleven years now and haven't returned to England or Europe for more than fifteen, so there hasn't been much chance for my judgment to be challenged. But I got challenged—challenged and defeated—by Ericka herself, the summer before I came to Africa. She visited me for several weeks, and I surprised her one morning, and shocked myself, by finding her seated on the ground against a tree with a red-serpent bracelet coiled around her wrist. She had slit her wrist. I looked at her, stupefied, while my heart went wild. I felt a kind of sheer animal terror, and I felt it in part because I couldn't grasp how something as hauntingly beautiful as she was would want to destroy itself. Not even with my knowledge of her life could I comprehend why she would want to leave a world that so wanted to look at her. What I said was pathetic: "You're too beautiful for it." I said it only because I didn't know what else to say, but she went on, two years later, and took what was beautiful out of the world, as if to prove that I was right.

I've been gone from the desk where I write, for almost two hours on this August night, searching through boxes for a picture of Ericka—one that has a shadow cast across her eyes by her uplifted hand, warding off the wan sunlight into which she was looking one afternoon in St. Ives. I took the picture myself. But I couldn't find it and I came back here, thinking *If only I could have found a mirror for her.* I tried. For beauty is a matter of mirrors, just as plainness is. The mirrors don't have to be the kind that have quicksilver behind them; they can have minds behind them instead. Other people had been mirroring Ericka for years, showing her to herself like the mirrors in a carnival fun house; bent and distorted. I foolishly thought that if she would let me be her mirror, if she would see herself in or through my eyes, she would begin to hope. "Despair of your life, go ahead," I said, "despair of the way you've had to live, but don't despair of yourself because, *look*—you've a self that's beautiful." I naively thought that it was enough for a woman who looked like Ericka just to be in the world. Like everything beautiful she was complete. A finished product. Form among formlessness, a shape moving among the shapeless. Where nature and the world were concerned, a world with its millions of bodies, she was like a lucky piece of work tossed off by an artist surrounded by his failures. But when I tried to tell her this, show her this, I ended up sounding like any passing man in the street: talking about her stunningly Byzantine nose, letting my eyes return again and again to her mouth, stopping dead still during one of our walks when a recurring incomparable look came from the depth of her dark eyes and froze my heart. She literally could not see the aura that pulsed from a physical beauty that turned the head of everyone else who saw it, and which has a lasting power over my memory. But she made me see why she could not: she refused to accept that she could be something without having struggled to become it. Refused! And she was right, right. She cared nothing about the failures of nature and couldn't live for the effect she had on others. Of course she wouldn't allow me to mirror her. What? . . . She was supposed to live by the light she put in someone else's eyes? Let us beam at her like loving idiots and have her walk around like some moon, content to reflect how she made others feel? No, not Ericka. The worth she had in my eyes was worthless when transferred to her own. It couldn't even be transferred. I saw her sit day after day among the rocks at St. Ives and they didn't soften beneath her. She looked out at the sea and it didn't mirror her: it threw nothing back but its own restlessness. Her own beauty had no more effect on her than it did the sun into which she was staring that late afternoon I photographed her. When I last saw her and said goodbye, in Charing Cross Road, our eyes weren't twenty inches apart. But I looked across the fathomless gap that exists between those who can only look longingly at something beautiful and those who indifferently possess it.

But the gap can be closed, too—the way it was closed by Vivian. She let others cross a bridge of dreams to herself. She did what Ericka refused to: accepted the fact that luckily, miraculously, she could be something without ever having struggled to become it—beautiful. She let others mirror her, happily, and she saw that she was something. Somebody. And because she was some*body* she didn't have to struggle to become some*one*. There was no depth to her eyes; their surface flashed and sparkled like blue sequins. And she also lived by the effect she had on others but that effect was no mean achievement. For Ronald was transformed. The effect of her choice was visible to everyone.

Those who had watched Ronald drink at the National Hotel a month before, and had judged him, thought they had misjudged him. Not that their judgments had been harsh. They had been tempered by a consideration of his nationality and even his marriage: for everyone considered Nancy strange, doctor or not. Some thought his marriage was responsible for the way he went without shaving for days at a time. His clothes had had a slovenly look. He looked like another displaced victim of African heat. Suddenly his clothes were never ill kept and he never appeared with a stubble of beard on his cheeks; the heavy lines were gone from under his eyes. Instead of sitting in the bar he sat in the lounge drinking tea while reading the latest *Times*. He brought international trade journals with him from the U.S. Information Agency, reading whatever he could about economic opportunities in West Africa. He began talking with transients in the hotel, introducing himself, making himself friendly; most of all, available. He had an invincible faith that something other than Vivian was out there waiting to point its finger at him again, getting ready to choose him the way she had. Giving him a job, a role, a part to play.

Craddock noticed how his complexion had changed.

"Taking the sun, Keane?"

"A bit."

"How can you stand it?"

"It's just right."

"It comes from having lived in California, I suppose."

With the trace of a smile at the corners of his mouth, Ronald said, "Just from living."

"Huh! . . . You ought to get together with Angle's wife. She makes a religion out of that sort of thing."

The remark was too unexpected. Ronald flattened his newspaper out in the air, rustling it loudly, and concealed his face behind it. He told himself that he would have to get used to hearing people talk about Vivian, but telling himself didn't bring it about. Once he unexpectedly met Alan entering the hotel as he was on his way out. He couldn't speak, even when Alan held the door for him and said pleasantly, "Hello, Keane." He managed to lift his hand in a feeble greeting while his cheeks burned red, and he worried about the incident until he saw Vivian again. When he told her about it she laughed.

"Why don't you come to the Hamarttan Club this Friday and play bridge?"

Ronald looked at her.

"But Alan will be there."

She pressed a finger on his wrist.

"Of course. I'll show you how to behave."

She showed him, all right. What she showed him was the way she could pass among the tables and smile at Bennett, put her hand on Paton's arm while talking to Alan; whisper in McCartel's ear without paying any attention to him, Ronald. It was hard for him to believe that they shared a secret world. He had expected her to put her hand on his arm rather than Paton's, to make some show of familiarity. But she didn't let the faintest recognition pass between them. It caused him to misplay his hand and when Craddock saw him he cracked a worldly smile.

"Distracted, Keane?"

It took Ronald until the next day to be able to admire Vivian for the way she ignored him. But Vivian made up for it the next night at one of the expatriate parties, when they danced together: pressures came from her hand and her knee. The suddenness of the touches and their secrecy made his head pound. Still, she was cautious and had warned him what it would be like. She warned him about difficult times ahead but Ronald was incapable of perceiving that anything could be difficult. For all the wrong roads of his life had led to the right place: Africa, Hamsun's Bay, Solly's, Vivian. How could he account for it? She asked him to be considerate of her position at a moment when he would have done a thousand things more dangerous, reckless, or extravagant than give her mere consideration.

"I'm bound hand and foot," Vivian said.

No pair of hands or feet seemed more energetic or capable of movement, but in a sense she was right for she was the wife of the most prominent man in a small community of white people. Minor officials and servants were never out of sight. When Alan was gone, as he was the morning and afternoon of the mining incident, the restrictions on her movements could even be greater. Because when Alan was away everyone preferred to consult Vivian rather than Jimison, Alan's first assistant. They called her at all hours of the night, knowing messages would get to Alan sooner that way, and she had to be there.

"I *have* to. I can never get away when I want. You'll understand, won't you? You can see that I just couldn't come by and pick you up and risk being seen, or ever let you take a taxi to Solly's?"

Ronald looked as if he could see perfectly.

"If I did, the cabbies would be chattering about it all over The Port on their talkies, speaking in their own language . . . at the very moment that one of them was driving Lynn Jimison to the airport or the hairdresser's. Good Lord! It'd get back to my servants. Life would become intolerable for me."

That was the last thing Ronald wanted. He said that he understood the situation completely but what that meant was that at the time he didn't care. He was incapable of caring. What Vivian said only underscored the risks she was taking. And for what? For whom? . . . *Him.* . . . To be able to see her more often, he persuaded Nancy to go with him to the Saturday night socials at the Hamarttan Club. But it didn't last. Not because Nancy wouldn't continue going but because Ronald saw too clearly that others considered her boring and thought their enjoyment seemed to be spoiled if she happened to be near them. What she was like reflected on him and he shrank from the imagined judgment of others. The last time they went he stood at the bar and looked at her. It was beginning to dawn on him that she wasn't merely shy or withdrawn; her detachment was haughty. She acted as if she considered herself superior to others and he couldn't imagine what opinion of herself enabled her to do that. When she stared at a mark on the wall, intently, it was obvious that she wasn't at a loss as to how to behave: she was absorbed. Completely absorbed. Intent on something inside herself. When they got home that night and Ronald told her, critically, that she was self-absorbed, she said quickly: "So is everyone else. They're just noisily self-absorbed, that's all. I'm a little more quiet about it." And then she did what she always did whenever they went out in the evening—went directly to her study when they came home. It didn't matter how late it was. She had to make up for the hours she hadn't spent there directly after dinner. She would come to bed at three or four in the morning and be up again at six, unfailingly.

Did he feel guilty about his affair with Vivian?

No. Nancy was such a machine, such a self-sufficient creature, that he tricked himself into thinking she wouldn't care. She didn't seem to feel anything else, so how could she feel anything about that? He managed to take his affair so lightheartedly where his marriage was concerned that he began to take Nancy's seriousness lightheartedly. Once when he came back from Solly's he saw a wild flower growing near their house in Tinlolo Road, picked it and set it alongside Nancy's dinner plate. Then he elaborately held her chair for her before one of their servants, Mwangi, did. When he sat down he mockingly played "the wife" and said, "Now tell me about your long, hard day at the laboratory. Tell me about your eyestrain, about how you feel like a big-game hunter looking down your microscope, which is the barrel of a rifle, killing off germs." Nancy seemed to like it. When Mwangi came in with dinner and set it on the table, she turned to Ronald with a smile and said, "This is one of my favorite dishes." He later told me you could have knocked him over with a feather. He didn't know she had a favorite anything; he didn't even know she could taste what she ate. That she cared whether she tasted it or not. . . . That one revelation wasn't enough to put him on guard, make him question whether he wasn't making a mistake about her. For he kept foolishly teasing her. When they got up from the dinner table and Nancy started for her study, he said to her back: "Now she'll take eight steps, turn to her left, brush the doorway with her shoulder and disappear for two hours and thirty-five minutes—darkly, mysteriously. If she's thinking very, very deeply she may be gone for two hours and forty minutes." Nancy stopped and Ronald put a smile on his face. But she stood motionless with her back to him for so long that his smile finally disappeared. She wouldn't speak, she wouldn't move, she wouldn't turn around.

"Nancy?"

She turned, her face deadly pale. Her eyes were so severe that he wondered what could possibly be the matter. But he couldn't tell by looking at her because it was like looking at a blind person: her irises and the whites of her eyes were all surface. She stared out of the void in which she seemed to exist and could hardly speak because her voice was so choked with emotion.

"You don't understand. I'm trying to discover something. You don't have anything to discover. I don't mock you for playing. Don't criticize me for working. Ever. Ever."

Each softly spoken word seemed filled with warning. She walked into her study and closed the door behind her, leaving him shocked.

He was shocked by Solly, too.

When he began arriving at the back country shebeen

before Vivian did, alone, he noticed that Solly gradually put a knowing grin on his face. The first time it happened Ronald thought he was wrong, mistaken in what he saw. But then Solly began coming out from behind the counter eagerly, knees bent, hurrying with Ronald toward the door that led to the stairway. And when Ronald got a frank smile from Solly he didn't know how to respond. He was shaken when he heard Solly cluck his tongue because he knew there was aggressiveness in it, going from black man to white man about a socially important woman. A white "lady." Ronald couldn't ignore the man-to-manness in it, the male sharing of snickering knowledge. What made matters worse was that Solly behaved differently when Ronald arrived with Vivian. He carefully observed "distinctions." He carried himself correctly, never looked up, never showed Vivian how his white teeth could gleam in his black face. So the day when Ronald, arriving alone once more, heard Solly's laughter after Solly closed the door behind him, he became determined to say something to Vivian. A determination had been building in him anyway to change things. It was becoming harder and harder for him to see Vivian secretly. He had tried to complain about it, casually, and Vivian had only said: "Oh, but it isn't sneaky and secretive! It's glorious!" He could become confused, especially when she put a reassuring hand on him; but when the hand was gone he lost his assurance. He found that he didn't like going to Hamsun's Bay by himself, not even for the purpose of strengthening himself—to be a more adequate swimming partner for Vivian. He didn't like listening to the roar of the sea alone. He began wavering in the resolutions he had made. I believe he needed others to see not only the effect that Vivian had on him; he wanted them to know the source. The chosen man wanted others to know or at least suspect what goddess had chosen him. And so when a determination to say something to Vivian about Solly came over him, a determination which might very well put an end to their secret meetings there, he stood at the window facing the hot breeze, listening to the crows, when he heard her coming up the stairs. He knew that if he turned around and looked at her—her tanned throat encircled with a native necklace, her eyes bright, her limbs energetic—he would change his mind and seize the moment instead of trying to reach for the future. So he didn't move when she came into the room. He kept his back to her and spoke through the open window as soon as the door closed.

"I don't like it here anymore, Vivian. It's becoming a hell."

Vivian didn't move at first. Then Ronald heard her footsteps and felt her arms come around him from behind.

"We'll make it heaven."

He couldn't prevent her from doing so, swiftly. Goddesses know their way to paradise and he let himself be taken there. When Vivian got up from the bed and walked to the low table that held the pitcher and basin he not only satisfied his admiring eyes; he spoke with a trace of wonder in his voice.

"How old are you?"

She turned quickly with fear in her face, aware of her nakedness.

"Why?"

"How old? Tell me."

She tried to control a nervous tremor in her lips and confessed, helplessly: "Forty-two."

"It's all a fake."

Vivian crossed her hands to grip her shuddering shoulders and at the same time cover her breasts with her arms.

"You're going to be found out," Ronald warned. "Any day now everyone is going to know the truth."

She was on the verge of tears.

"Wh—what do you mean?"

"You don't have a son at Oxford at all! It's not possible—you only tell people that to impress them. You're not forty-two, you're only twenty-four."

Vivian hurried back to him, crying, "Oh, Ronald! You're so good for me, so good!"

"I am?"

"I knew, I *knew* you would be!"

He was ready to believe it, eager to know.

"How?"

"The very first night at the dinner table. I could see it in your hands." Vivian rubbed the top of one of them. "See? Your knuckles? They have wrinkles around them. People who have wrinkles around their knuckles are filled with kindness toward others."

They were silent for a moment and it gave Ronald a chance to search for a tone to put into his voice, which would be a mixture of reluctance and kindness sufficient to disguise his own wishes.

"I think I should tell you something."

"Mmmm? What?"

"About Solly."

"Solly?"

Ronald nodded and looked disturbed.

"What about Solly?" Vivian coaxed.

"About the way he acts when I arrive alone. I mean, first—without you."

Vivian sat up in the bed.

"How? How does he act?"

"Well," Ronald hesitated, "it may not be important" . . . but he told her anyway. And when he did, Vivian's cheeks managed to look pale despite her tan.

"Oh God, no."

She swung her legs around to the floor, got up and slipped her underclothes on hurriedly, as if Solly were to knock on the door any instant.

Ronald got up, too.

Vivian went to the window, pulling on a thin blouse and stood to one side, leaning her forehead against the wall. She pulled her head back and even tossed it, as if she were going to say something, angrily. Her lips were parted and Ronald saw her clenched teeth but no sound came from between them. Then she put her forehead against the wall again and just stood there . . . so long that Ronald finally put both hands on her shoulders, comfortingly.

"We can never come here again," she said.

"We don't have to."

He had to control his small and secret sense of triumph and speak with reassurance and hopefulness, softly.

"I've arranged for Mwangi and Pedi to be gone on Tuesday and Friday afternoons, right after lunch. I got tired of always having someone around the house. I told Nancy I couldn't stand it all the time, so I'm completely alone. And Nancy never comes home for lunch, not at all. Not once since we've been here. She's gone from seven in the morning until six in the evening."

"Never?"

"Never."

"Are you sure?"

He kissed Vivian's slightly perfumed neck.

"Absolutely."

7

V IVIAN SAT UP IN THE BED IN
Tinlolo Road, too. She did it suddenly
in the shuttered and darkened upstairs
guest room. So suddenly that it startled Ronald.

"What's the matter?"

"Someone just tried the door!" she whispered
hoarsely.

"That's not possible," said Ronald, shaking his head.
"Pedi or Mwangi would never come around."

"Then *who* was it?"

"It wasn't anybody."

"Ronald, I *heard* a sound! Someone just tried that
door!"

He started to swing his feet around to the floor but
Vivian stopped him by her hysterical tone.

"How will I get out of here?"

He looked at her.

"How, how?"

"Vivian, there's no need for you to get out."

"Get my clothes!"

"Vivian—"

"*Get* my clothes!"

He went to the chair and got them, alarmed by her,
not by the possibility that anyone was in the house. "This
is unnecessary," he whispered, but he dropped one of her
shoes as he whispered it.

"Shhh!"

He was forced to pull his own clothes on quickly, just
to keep up with her.

"You wait here," he ordered. "Right here. I'll go out and see that everything's all right."

"It's not all right! It's Nancy!"

He thought he could feel her accusing him of bringing her to a place that wasn't safe and he walked back toward the bed and leaned down, trying to get Vivian to look at him and see the reassurance in his eyes.

"Vivian, it can't possibly be. She never leaves her laboratory until six, never."

She ignored his attempts to stay calm. Totally. She treated it as an established fact that something had gone wrong, and looked up at him like a child, helplessly. Confused.

"What will you say if she's out there?"

"Calm down!" he pleaded. And then tried to satisfy her with: "I'll say I was taking a nap."

"In the guest room? How!"

"I don't know, I don't know!" he whispered, and it was exasperating because he didn't know. "I'll say I always take a nap there in the afternoon. So what? She wouldn't know that it wasn't so—she's never come home in the afternoon, ever, and she hasn't today. Now, will you let me leave? If anyone is out there, anyone, I'll get them away from the house and then you can go. If that's what you feel you need to do."

He walked out of the room into the hallway and to the head of the stairs, calmly, naturally. He saw no one, heard no one. But he called out Nancy's name anyway—for Vivian's benefit. Of course there was no answer: he knew there wouldn't be. He walked downstairs into the sitting room and called her again. The house was completely silent, completely empty. He took the stairs up two at a time and walked into the guest room.

"There's no one there."

He spoke a little impatiently; satisfied with himself. But Vivian, on the edge of the bed, jumped when he came

64

in. He saw tears in her eyes when he walked around to her. He didn't know she could fall apart this way. And since he didn't want her to have tears in her eyes, he put a hand on her shoulder.

"There's no need for that."

"Please get me out of here, please."

He led her by the hand out of the bedroom, down the hallway and stairs. And he tried not to let the trembling of her nerves communicate itself to him. But when the drapes in front of the French doors leading to the veranda moved, they both stopped. At once, together. Vivian's mouth dropped open. He thought she was going to cry out and he put his hand over her mouth. She appeared shocked that he did it, even angry, jerking her head back.

"Mwangi!" he shouted at the moving drapes.

Vivian jumped and leaned against him, shaking.

"I didn't mean to frighten you. Vivian, Vivian, don't act this way, please—not even if someone's been here, but they haven't."

To prove it he went to the drapes and pulled them back. The veranda door was open. He looked out and found no one there. The breeze blew and the drapes moved again.

"See? It's nothing. The door was open, that's all."

"Is it usually open?"

It wasn't but he didn't admit it.

"I never pay any attention."

Vivian fell into one of the chairs.

"Vivian, can't we stop this? It *wasn't* the door handle you heard turn."

"I didn't imagine it!"

"Well, if it was one of the servants, they can be handled. I'll handle it, don't worry about it—and for the last time, Nancy never comes home during the day."

Vivian sat forward, suddenly. So suddenly that her blouse tightened across her breasts and one of the buttons slipped out of its hole. The blouse fell open to the top of her brassiere and Ronald looked at it.

"Call her laboratory and ask if she's there."

His eyes jumped up to hers. The look in her eyes confirmed that he had heard what he had: Vivian addressing a servant on The Hill. Her eyes were wide and bright, demanding in their glare.

"Go ahead."

He couldn't say no; he couldn't say yes.

"But why would I be calling? I never do. What'll I say?"

"*Think* of something!"

She flapped a braceleted hand at him; it was meant to push him toward the phone. And it did because he didn't want to appear reluctant to prove himself right. Or more inept and clumsy than he was already appearing to be.

"All right. I can say I'm going to play tennis late and won't be back until seven."

He dialed the laboratory and cleared his throat in preparation but no one answered by the fourth ring, not even Emille, one of Nancy's assistants. A small hole opened up in Ronald's stomach. It seemed to disturb his physical balance. He could feel Vivian behind him, seated, waiting for him to speak. But no one answered at Nancy's laboratory. He couldn't believe that any of this was happening. For an instant he thought he would say something into the dead phone and pretend to give a message to Nancy, but he couldn't. His throat seemed too dry. He didn't believe he could pull it off. When he finally put the receiver down, he didn't want to turn and face Vivian—not after she had addressed him the way she had—but he did, even casually; striding back, looking off.

"She's not in."

"Oh, how stupid! How—how *stupid!*"

Stupid of him? For having bungled something? Or

just the situation, the circumstances? . . . Ronald feared the answer and sat down, swallowing.

"All right, all right. It was stupid," he confessed. "Maybe, I don't know. How can we know anything? Let's"—he didn't even want to suggest what he was inviting her to consider, and he hesitated—"let's figure out what to do if it was Nancy."

Vivian leaned back and stared at the ceiling for so long that he didn't think she was going to answer. It was a relief just to sit there, breathing heavily.

"Would she care?"

Vivian said it musingly, still contemplating the ceiling. Her coolness surprised him more than the idea for she suddenly seemed poised. Ronald shifted in his chair and tried to pull himself together.

"Care?" he echoed, trying to find his way.

"Well, since she can hardly bear to be spoken to she's not going to be able to bear anything unpleasant, is she? She must know that any future position around here will probably depend on Alan, and she's not going to throw that away. She's got enough sense to realize that nothing can be gained by uncivilized behavior, hasn't she?"

Vivian was talking like the wife of the future ambassador. It unraveled Ronald at the seams. He gave up any attempt to pull himself together. To appear firm. There was something habitual about the way he lowered his head and looked at the floor. And he didn't conceal his despondency.

"I don't think I care anymore."

No attitude could have produced more concern in Vivian. She stood up and came over to him, running her fingers through his hair.

"Of course not. It's been worth everything, hasn't it?"

Ronald looked up and saw her smiling down at him. To have heard her say it! . . . He stood up.

67

"I'm sorry. You're right, I know it's my fault."

"No, it isn't. I'm not frightened any longer. And I'm glad I parked just outside—it shows we have nothing to conceal. After all, I call on all sorts of people all the time. . . . I'm going now. No, don't bother seeing me to the door." She reassured him that that didn't mean anything: "That's what I tell everyone."

She squeezed his arm and walked out.

"When will I see you?"

She didn't answer but continued quickly through the door. Ronald stood in the shadows on the porch and watched her drive away. As her car disappeared the hole in his stomach, which had never completely closed, opened up again: he knew Vivian'd never come there again. He paced around the porch. He wanted to hit, to throw a fist, at whatever it was that had frightened her. But nothing was there—and he still believed that nothing, no one, had been there. Mwangi had just forgotten to close the French doors. And the mere thought of Nancy! . . . creeping around like a spirit, not saying twenty words in a single day, while he never knew what she was thinking, whether she was dead or alive, whether she was something to be reckoned with or not. . . . In his frustration he decided to do just what he had been ready to do had she answered the phone: be gone until seven o'clock. It would throw her off balance not to find him home. So he left a note saying he would be late and they would go out for dinner at seven o'clock.

But when he returned at seven *he* was thrown off balance.

The house was empty even though the lights were on.

"Nancy?"

He looked in the obvious places for a message, but didn't find one. He went to the stairs and listened for a noise upstairs until he realized that was futile. If she was up there she wouldn't make a noise.

"Nancy!"

There was no answer. He went up and looked in the bathroom first. The bowl and tub were wet. His stomach somersaulted: she had been there and bathed. That she had done that made him feel panicky. Even though he knew she wasn't there he started to go through all the rooms— but stopped dead in front of the guest room door: he hadn't made the bed. That was something he and Vivian always did together but he had forgotten to return to do it after she had left. When he opened the door and turned on the light he saw that the bed had been made. He had to believe his eyes but he didn't want to. He went and touched the bedspread to be sure, absolutely sure. He tried to believe that one of the servants had returned and done it, but he couldn't trick himself that much. The picture of Nancy soundlessly smoothing the sheets sent him slumping against the wall.

He went out of the house, walking aimlessly.

Then he saw a taxi in Rhodes Street, hired it and started for the bar of the National Hotel. Before he was halfway there he told the driver to take him to Nancy's laboratory. When they turned the corner at Nbumi Street he saw that the lights were on. It was just one more thing he couldn't believe. What did he think he was going to do? . . . He had no clear answer but his dread began mixing itself with the relief that would come from confronting her. With everything, if necessary. So he rang the bell, ready to act—at first—as if nothing had happened, ready to pretend that she was behaving very peculiarly just because he had gone out, left a note and not come back until seven o'clock. But no one answered the door. He rapped on the windows and still she didn't come. He stood there, looking about helplessly, powerlessly. The cab driver was watching him and he got back in the taxi, went to the hotel and after a second brandy and soda lost control of himself. He imagined that Nancy was lying dead on the laboratory floor after giving herself a lethal injection. He walked from the bar to the front desk and called her office again. And again there was no answer. Finally it became too much of a strain to care anymore. His last thought before he left the bar was that it would have been just like her to have made the bed before she killed herself. Typical.

It was eleven o'clock when he reached home. Nancy still wasn't there. He laid down on the sofa to wait. Too much brandy had ruined his head. But it hadn't ruined it to the point of preventing him from reaching for a magazine when he heard her footsteps on the porch stairs. He pretended to be reading and as soon as she opened the door he took the offensive.

"Didn't you see my note?"

"I thought that since you weren't here, I'd go back to the laboratory."

He looked at her and he was sorry that he did, for her narrow-set eyes were fixed on him, like an animal's eyes that have had a light flashed on them in the dark.

"You went back to the laboratory?"

"I think I've stumbled onto something."

He waited for her to explain the possible double meaning in that but she didn't.

"You weren't at the laboratory," he accused. "I rang the bell, I knocked on the window, I called you from the hotel!"

"I must have been in the supply room. I've got to write up my reports yet, so why"—she turned her back on him mid-sentence, starting for her study—"why don't I sleep in the guest room tonight? That way I won't disturb you when I come up."

Ronald jumped up as if he were going to grab her before she got through the study door.

"You're probably not aware that I take my naps in the guest room!" he blurted. "I took one this afternoon, so—"

"But I am aware that you take your naps there," Nancy cut in. "Pedi explained why there were extra linens to wash every week."

She went into the study and closed the door behind her.

Ronald stood there sweating, for he knew she knew.

8

I CAN'T BE ABSOLUTELY CERTAIN of the clock but I believe that the following day—when Nancy went up on The Hill, when Vivian came down from it and called on Ronald, and when Nancy and Ronald confronted each other—was the day I imagined I saw the sun go red from shame. For Mc-Gowan, my closest friend, had died, and I thought that the universe ought to be ashamed of itself. Anyone would have said that he died a "natural" death—if it's natural for something as minute as a microbe to crawl into a human body and cause it to fall over and never get up. I think that's an outrage myself. To me it makes more sense for a human body to fall over by a blow from its own hand than it does for it to fall over by a blow from a microbe or a spider or a mosquito. It's more dignified, too. Maybe dignity is what I have on my mind for I don't know if anyone in The Port had a sense of shame about anything that day. All I know is that I stood in the Ndami cemetery over McGowan's grave and watched the sun blush its way over the hills. And now

71

I know that what was happening in both places brought Ronald and Nancy to *my* corner of the world. I don't really think they spoiled it. Not even Ronald. . . . When I think of the differences between life in Ndami and life in The Port, I think I feel a trace of pity for those who are condemned to learn their life-lessons in a trivial place. Saying "no" in the kitchen is a lot different than saying "no" in the highest court in the land, saying "yes" to whatever's around you at the Hamarttan Club is a lot different than being six hundred miles into the desert north of Ndami and saying "yes" to what's around you there. Everyone's life-lessons seem hard to them and Ronald's must have seemed hard to him. Still, they were trivial because they were learned in a trivial place.

That's a terrible judgment.

And I don't mean to judge him. But why is it that so many human struggles don't seem to be much more than the struggle of a fly that wanders too far into a dish of orange marmalade? It can't be because of Vivian—in Ronald's case. Venus may be the goddess of lies, as Freud said, but even if she is that still leaves you guessing at the truth. I wish that he had deliberately looked at Vivian and said, "I'm going to let that woman take over my dreams." Because then you can just sit back and let the nightmare gradually come on. It isn't true to say of Ronald that life was a preparation for something that never happened, which is what someone said it is for all of us. It was a total lack of preparation for suddenly waking up, or being awakened, and finding himself lost at the end of a trail. He did what anyone would do: panic. He panicked for days, even weeks. And like all of us he stood looking wildly about, hoping that he'd stumble on some shortcut back to dignity.

9

H E   D I D N ' T   P A N I C   W H E N   H E
woke up and found Nancy already
gone. Not quite, anyway. But he didn't
like facing the fact that he didn't have any control over her
—or anything, or anyone. And he realized that when the
telephone rang he didn't jump up only to answer it. He also
jumped because the ring was shrill: it ran right along his
nerves.

He was told what was happening even before he said
hello.

"Ronald, I'm on my way to the Palm Wine Terrace
for a morning tea. I'm going to stop by."

What rattled him was the loud *click!* which followed.
Vivian hadn't banged the receiver, as far as he could tell,
but she had obviously dropped it in a hurry. With no precautions! She didn't even ask if Nancy was there. Panic set
in over *his* appearance, not her immediate one, however.
He ran upstairs and just managed to shave by the time
Vivian's car pulled up. She was wearing a red-and-white
sun dress and high-heel shoes that gripped her toes by only
two or three straps. The usually frank and open attractiveness of her face had been softened because she looked a bit
sullen as she came through the door. Ronald was totally
unsure of himself, nervous; but to his relief Vivian suddenly smiled, took a brisk step toward him, embraced him
quickly and then drew back.

"Now tell me why Nancy's up on The Hill."

Ronald stared and gaped a lot that day. He started
right then.

Vivian had to force his tongue to move: "She's in talking with Alan right now. I want to be prepared when I go back. Tell me what's happening."

His mouth had dropped open, ready for speech. He stammered, "I—I—don't know," shaking his head until a lock of hair fell onto his forehead and he had to push it away. "Nancy was already gone when I got up."

"You *do* look a little tired under the eyes," she observed, and then turned, going to the window. She pushed one of the small curtains aside with her hand to look out. "But she must have said something last night at dinner, or acted in some way that, that—well, tell me. I can't very well guess."

Her voice was impatient and her back was still to him. Because he didn't have to look into her eyes he decided it was the moment to tell her the truth.

"She knows, Vivian."

Vivian turned and looked at him sharply, so sharply she might have been eying a servant she suspected of theft.

"What did she say?"

"Well, that's just it—not a thing."

"That makes no sense to me. She never says a thing, so how can you say that she knows?"

"Because we didn't have dinner together. She didn't stay home after she read my note."

"What note?"

"I left her a note saying I would be back at seven o'clock, and—"

"Why?"

"Why?"

"Yes. What was the point of that?"

"I just did. I needed to get out—and when I came back she wasn't here. She locked herself in her laboratory—"

"*Locked?*"

"Well, she wouldn't answer the door, wouldn't answer the telephone—"

74

"That doesn't mean anything. In fact, it makes good sense. We're having a serious epidemic in Ndami and medicine is badly needed. She's probably making serums. It would be just like her to lock herself in and not let anyone disturb her. She's always been a fanatic—of some sort."

"For the first time she slept alone—and in the guest room. She didn't come home until after eleven and when she did she said she wanted to sleep in the guest room."

Suddenly Vivian lost her sharp composure. One hand lifted toward the front of her dress, and the white bracelet around her wrist slid along her forearm.

"Naturally you had made up the bed."

"Yes."

She had said what he should have done so emphatically, so matter of factly, that he couldn't do anything else but lie. But his face got so red from nervousness and fear of not having lied well enough that he found a reason to look worried.

"But I didn't change the sheets. I thought one of the servants would do that in the morning."

Vivian's voice softened. Her eyes even lowered a bit as she asked, "Were they all right?"

He didn't know but he said, "Yes."

A long breath came from her very narrow nostrils.

"Well, maybe it's about time. Separate rooms aren't a bad idea. Alan and I have had separate bedrooms for years."

Ronald didn't know what to say to that.

"And she said nothing at all about seeing Alan? About anything?"

"No."

"It must have to do with the epidemic. She probably wants more funds for medicines—we'll just have to wait and see. Even if she knows"—Vivian stopped herself and went back to the window, pushing one of the curtains aside again to look out. She started over again: "If that was she at the door she was shocked, of course. But she can't have been surprised. That's the risk of having a handsome man for a husband. Still, it's always humiliating—but I think she'll be interested in her self-respect more than anything. She'll pretend that she doesn't know a thing, especially with Alan. A person who makes trouble is a person who loses position in a closely knit community, and she won't risk that. If she were really a doctor, and a respected one, it might be different. But she cares about things that no one else cares about—little things. You can hardly find out what they are." Vivian turned around. "Someone like that can't be very secure." She smiled, not at the certainty of what she was saying, but to encourage Ronald; to make him feel secure. He could feel her squeeze encouragement into his arm with her hand as she came up to him, smiled, kissed his cheek perfunctorily and said, "We'll see this through. Whoever finds out first what's going on will call the other, all right? But if you should call and I'm not in, don't leave a message. Call back. I don't want Alan to see your name written down anywhere. And now I must run."

She did, after flashing a smile.

And Ronald walked. He didn't know what else to do. If he thought anything, if he felt anything, did anything, it was either beyond recalling or not worth recalling. He was too cowardly to seek Nancy out at her laboratory, or too unorganized. Too unorganized, probably, for he didn't have a self that could be organized: he wasn't anything but a tension. Whenever he got jostled in the roads or one of the markets his head reverberated with a sound. He seemed to have a pain behind his right eye. He didn't know he was lost on the trail yet, but he wasn't doing anything but wandering. When he got home Nancy was already there, which she never was. The French doors leading to the porch were open and she was sitting in one of the wicker chairs, looking out. He stared at her, which was easy to do because she didn't look at him when he came through the door. He was unprepared to face her and had to think of what to say.

"You're home early."

"I think it's the usual time."

That was so blatant an untruth that all he could do for a moment was look at his watch.

"It's four thirty."

He waited for her to correct herself because he didn't know why she would lie about something so trivial. But she didn't. She only said, "I want to talk to you," tonelessly, without moving, without looking at him.

The only way Ronald could fight off the panic that started to take hold of him was to cross in front of her to a chair and not let the matter of her being home early pass.

"I'm surprised you got away from the laboratory this early."

She didn't respond. She behaved like Nancy: she continued to stare out the open doors until it unnerved him.

"Well?"

She looked at him for the first time.

"Have you ever heard of Ndami?"

If Vivian hadn't mentioned it that morning he wouldn't have.

"Yes."

"There's an epidemic there."

"I know."

"You know?"

He said smugly, "I keep in touch."

"Then you know it's one of the worst this country's had in years. Over three hundred people have died already."

"From what?"

"Cholera."

"Are you busy making serums?"

Since he was still taking his cues from Vivian he was adopting her attitude. The question came out dryly, its sarcasm not totally disguised, and Nancy looked at him intently.

"I am. Very busy," she said with a strong sense of purpose. The tone of her voice raised a bit as she began to give Ronald a series of facts in a recitative manner, certain that he was ignorant of them. "Ndami's in Muslim territory so everything is Allah's will. Nothing's done about anything until it's too late—preventive medicine, or preventive anything, doesn't occur to them. There's a small monastery which is being used as a kind of clinic or infirmary. It was a convent before the nuns were replaced by priests—from France, I believe. They're doing something about the epidemic but the only doctor, another Christian, just died. He didn't have any staff other than natives. The only other European has something to do with the mines, one of the colonials. An Englishman, Aaron Clinemark."

"Well, it sounds desolate enough."

Nancy answered Ronald's casualness with a consciously superior tone.

"I've offered to go there and take charge of the epidemic."

Ronald said he felt as if he weighed fifty pounds more, instantly; anchored in his chair. His emotions wanted him to stand but he knew from the way Nancy was looking at him that she was watching for his reaction; testing him in some way. Even as he said, "Oh?" his first thought was that she was leaving because of his affair with Vivian, and his second thought—running darkly after it—was that now he'd be free of her. "Why are you going to do that?"

"That must be obvious," Nancy said, as if he were witless. "They need a doctor!"

His cheeks flushed. He tried to intimidate her by saying, "But you don't practice medicine, you're not a doctor! You're a scientist."

It worked. Nancy looked as she had that night in the Keanes' den when Ronald said she didn't say very much.

78

Her eyes went this way and that, searching for some object to land on. She looked down at the floor and began stammering.

"I—I—interned at a very good hospital, I—know everything a doctor does. I haven't forgotten it, and"—she was able to look up, and continued more aggressively— "and I'm more qualified than the average doctor, not less. Specializing in bacteriology has *made* me more qualified. I, I suppose if I were a brain surgeon you'd be more impressed, but I'd be useless in Ndami. The city's an open-air laboratory and I've been saving animals in my laboratory for months now. Human beings are dying up there without me, without my interference, so I'll do them very little harm, and I may very well be able to do them some good— even—even though you don't think I am qualified. I know how to put a needle into flesh."

Ronald was listening without hearing. In his chair, he was sinking to a very low point: he was imagining that she was deliberately exposing herself to disease. That her response to finding him and Vivian together was to do away with herself. And he didn't jump up guiltily from his chair to tell her not to expose herself.

"Won't it be dangerous?"

Nancy displayed her pretty white teeth in a smile; but the smile was a sneer.

"Very."

She was proud of it.

Ronald shrugged.

"Well, if that's what you want to do."

"Someone has to do it, don't you agree? And there isn't any time to waste. Ndami's six hundred miles north of here and only five hundred miles can be traveled by train— to the end of the railway. After that we'll have to take a steamer upriver."

He caught her use of *we* and was glad she had some native help going with her.

"Are you taking Emille?"

"Emille?"

"Yes."

"You and I are going."

Ronald stood up and a smile appeared on Nancy's face again. Her mouth played with it, contemptuously. He stared at her, bewildered, even though he had expected that this was the way she would play her game. Indirectly, deviously.

"Me? You don't expect *me* to go with you?"

"Why, of course I do."

"What for?"

"I was sure you would want to."

She wasn't sure at all, he knew that. Knowing it left him wildly guessing and he guessed his wildest: she didn't want to expose herself to danger, she wanted to expose *him* to it? To an epidemic? To death?

"The idea's ridiculous," he breathed, fearing it.

"That a husband should accompany his wife?"

She asked it not only swiftly but artificially, not believing in the words *husband* and *wife* and the roles they implied, but using them anyway. For effect. And for further effect she didn't ask Ronald the question. She asked whatever was beyond the doors for she was staring out of them, severely. It was hard to detect whether she was being sarcastic when she continued.

"Since it's dangerous and there are only a few Europeans, I thought you'd want to accompany me. So I naturally said you would."

"Would?"

"Yes."

"To whom?"

"Alan Angle. To whom else could I have said it?"

Ronald couldn't even conceal his panic by turning away from her. He tried going to the window as Vivian had done, pushing aside one of the curtains and looking

80

out. And then he tried to pretend that she had left him behind.

"I don't understand what you're talking about."

"You should. It only takes average intelligence."

He was almost ready to thank God that he had his back turned. He was stung by the way she had said that. He knew she felt superior to others, but he never knew how far she looked down on him when she did. He wanted to be outraged but he was only frightened because he could feel her starting to blackmail him.

"Well . . . *well!* I'm not going."

Nancy got up and walked behind him to his left, directly to the French doors. She closed them and shoved the bolt in as if the sound of it sliding across the lock settled something.

"All right. I won't go either."

Ronald turned and looked at her. She nodded at him as if she were satisfied about something, went back to her chair, and sat down. She looked at him with such perfect self-control that he tried to get some himself.

He shrugged.

"Suits me."

"I'll call Alan in the morning and tell him he'll have to find someone else because you won't go with me. He'll certainly understand why a wife wouldn't want to go without her husband."

She was using those words again: *wife, husband.* Ronald was starting to feel lost in his head but his ears burned. He was getting feverish. Something in his body told him that he should know exactly where he was.

"Wh—what is this? What's all this *husband-wife* talk?"

In a quiet voice so threatening that Ronald would have never imagined Nancy capable of it if he hadn't heard it, she said: "Do you think I'm a fool?"

He didn't do anything except try to withstand it by standing still.

"I've all the proof I need, Ronald."

He had to challenge her. Or try.

"Wh—what proof? What are you talking about?"

"Stop it," she said, as if he were a child. "Sit down."

He went down like a robot and as soon as he did he realized that he had. He was stung by his obedience, his abjectness. It made him blurt, "I want a divorce."

In a high-pitched, amused tone, she echoed: "A divorce?" It appeared to be so amusing to her and he was so astonished that she said it again. "A divorce?"

"Yes."

She laughed. Nothing seemed to bother her, nothing seemed to touch her.

He tried to say angrily, "It can't make a difference to you."

"How do you know what makes a difference to me?"

He didn't. And his look admitted that he didn't.

What was more, Nancy didn't expect him to know. With no pretense at disguising that she didn't believe a word she was saying, she said airily: "Why, I feel responsible for bringing you over here. I didn't know it was going to be that much over your head—I just can't let you sink. What would your father say?"

He stiffened.

"What do you mean by that?"

Apparently it didn't mean any more than that she knew it would unnerve him if she said it.

"Don't you know you'll have to get it into more than the local headlines that you're another of Vivian Angle's gigolos? Even national headlines won't help you—you'll have to make an international political incident out of your stupidity before Alan Angle will do anything about it! And *if* you did that, dear Vivian wouldn't have anything to do with you—don't you have enough sense to know that?"

She was contemptuous of his naivete.

Because he had no shield against the kind of attack she had just mounted, he didn't have anything to throw back at her. All he could do to save himself was to lower his eyes and find within himself some picture of Vivian in love with him, of Vivian in a moment of emotion, acting. He found it and he wanted to pile the details of it on top of Nancy until she was buried. But there were no words capable of describing the scene, and he had to tighten his mouth and find something to push out through his clenched teeth. It was feeble, he knew.

"You don't know what you're talking about."

"You don't think so?"

He looked up.

"No. Vivian and I are prepared to see this thing through together."

"Is that so?"

"Yes."

"You're a child."

That seemed to be her consistent attitude. And he was incapable of changing it, so he settled for exchanging accusations with her.

"You're not such a prize specimen yourself, you know! What do you think people think of me when they find out I'm married to you? Don't worry, I've seen the way they look at me when—"

"Stop it, don't!"

The only reason he did was because she stood up. And her hand was out, toward him, the palm of it pressing against the air in his direction. Her other hand came toward the front of her dress, so pathetically unlike the way Vivian brought hers there: there was no native necklace to grasp, no loose-necked or partially unbuttoned blouse to grasp, no breasts for the underside of her forearm to lean against or press into.

"I—I—I know—"

What she knew couldn't be said. The hand whose palm had been held up to him now made little hammer-strokes in the air, like those her words were making. It went up and down, chopping away as her stammering speech began again.

"I—I know how—I look. Don't tell me, you—you don't know how to, to tell me. I can, I've known how I looked since I was a small girl, since—since my father wouldn't hold me in his lap. My mother told me I was wrong, but I know he didn't. He, he grew flowers. He loved them, he thought they were beautiful, and"—Nancy stopped both her words and her movements. She stood still and when she said, "I suppose they were," she didn't say it as if she just realized it. "I suppose they were," she repeated, looking at Ronald. "Do you know that a plant which lived for no more than three days seemed to be more valuable to him than I was, and all because it had something that he loved that I didn't have? And my mother"—she turned away—"my mother loved sounds. Beautiful music meant everything to her, everything. A look came over her face at certain sounds. It never came over her face when she looked at me, even though the sound only lasted a few seconds—and I, I tried to go on living everyday. It was wrong, stupid, vicious, unjust! I still think it's unjust—but I don't cry about it anymore. No. . . ."

She went to the doors she had closed and hung onto one of the curtains with her hand, looking out the window.

"Do you know that I might have gone through life, my whole life, believing there wasn't anything as important as being beautiful, or having beauty? Nothing as important as the pleasure it gives people, no matter what it is—human and sensible and worthwhile, or just stupid, stupidly beautiful. I was lucky because my father died when I was fourteen. Oh, I wasn't glad that he did, I was just lucky that he did, because when he got sick and died I learned that everyone hated disease even more than they loved whatever was beautiful. They were afraid of it. They feared physical suffering even more than they loved beauty. My mother's music didn't do her any good while my father was dying. Illness, real illness—cancer, malaria, meningitis, cholera—was evil, horrible. Do you know that I was glad that it was? That I went into my bedroom and cried because I had found out that there was something more horrible in the world than the way I looked?"

She seemed to stop.

She turned around and looked at Ronald as if she was waiting for an answer. But she may have turned just to make certain that he was there for he had become rapt, listening to her. She was no longer searching for words or struggling emotionally. What she was describing was a battle she had once fought and it hardly seemed to matter whether she had lost or won. She had just survived the battle and she seemed to be looking back across the field where it had taken place.

As if to emphasize the change that had taken place in her right there, she said: "It changed me. It changed my whole life—it just didn't change anything or anyone around me, that's all. You can't imagine what it's like to sit in a university classroom studying esthetics, and hearing others debate about what's beautiful, and how you can know that it is when you see it—and how you can get others to agree that it is. You can't imagine! It doesn't do you any good to know how insane it all is, insane. They were mad, I knew they were mad. That's why I stay away from people, and that's why I decided to try to keep others from physical suffering, disease—even the mad ones—because I didn't have any physical beauty that could give anyone pleasure. But look"—she thrust out one of her legs and glanced down at it—"look. I have attractive legs, even though they're different than Vivian's. They're not as long but they're every bit as attractive, aren't they?"

Ronald looked up at her after looking at them, bewildered; embarrassed. He wasn't mistaken: she was asking him to compare them.

"Aren't they?"

He never felt more foolish when he nodded his head. It seemed to weigh hundreds of pounds.

Then Nancy said sharply, "I hate them for being that way!" So sharply that she seemed to have pounced on Ronald for nodding his head in agreement with her. "I wish they were twisted, twisted! Because they're just legs—and so they only have one purpose, to get me from here to there. That's their job, that's what's important, to take us places—even though a Vivian can use hers to run around a tennis court and kick water, and be more wanted and valued by, by men—than women who use their legs to walk around a laboratory and stand over a microscope, trying to find cures for tropical diseases. Well, I think that's wrong, monstrously, stupidly wrong! And nothing, nothing in life will ever teach me or convince me that it isn't. I want to go to Ndami because I think it matters where your legs take you, even though I know Vivian Angle and her kind can stand on their legs anywhere and be wanted, and valued, and admired, simply because of what's on them—their bodies. It doesn't matter where Vivian's legs take her—she can wander from one bar stool to the next, one dance after another, and, and she's useless, absolutely useless as a human being. But somehow that doesn't make a difference, does it? I know I'm defective, Ronald—I know that not being beautiful or attractive was a defect in your eyes, but you don't have many skills, and—and I think it's fair to say that you don't have my intelligence. I knew that, too. So I forgave you your defects because I've always known my own, from a very early age. I think if I had any hope it was that you knew you were defective, too, or at least would discover that you were, and then you would forgive me for what I know I lack."

She was done.

Ronald's face burned. He didn't know whether it burned because she had said Vivian was a useless human being or because she seemed to be asking for his forgiveness and an acknowledgment of his personal deficiencies. He didn't do anything but look into her unblinking eyes for as long as he could, or until Nancy turned around again, taking hold of the curtain at the door as she looked out. He didn't remember which.

"Do you still want a divorce?"

The question pulled him to his feet. He discovered that his legs were shaking as he looked at her. He could only see the side of her face and he couldn't find any sign to tell him whether she was still playing with him. He answered waveringly, but seriously.

"Yes. I do."

"All right. Since I know what people think about you for marrying me, I'll divorce you. Just have Vivian come and see me tomorrow afternoon and tell me that she'll divorce Alan. That's all I'll ask. It won't do any good if you're the only one who's free."

10

I KNOW THE EFFECT IT CAN HAVE to look into Nancy's "unblinking eyes." I've done it at least once. They're like polished windows whose surface glitters, making you think they might, just might, be entrances into her impenetrable being. Lamps were lighted and burning in them. But they lighted only the world inside the wall of her body, a world known only to her. One could look at her with the fascination and awe that one feels for those who live in dungeons.

I say, *could*.

Because Vivian certainly wouldn't have regarded her in that way. I would have liked to have seen or overheard those two together. That wouldn't have been an encounter between two people, two women: it would have been an encounter between two self-estimates. The ground on which they stood was solider than earth. The ground on which Vivian stood—wherever her own two legs happened to be, as Nancy said—was as firm as the disease-ridden reality that Nancy had sunk her foundations into. One was absolutely sure of what she could do, the other was absolutely sure of what she was. And it was Ronald who stood nowhere by comparison, not even in between; unable to know that neither woman feared the other, or that he feared them both. But he had enough sense to know, the minute Vivian shut the library doors behind them, that he shouldn't have gone up on The Hill to see her.

"I said, *Call, call!*" she scolded. "I didn't say knock on the door! You know you shouldn't have come here."

He knew he shouldn't have come in the past but the pressures of the present and what he was certain would be the future made him do it. Still he knew it was a mistake . . . even before Vivian had said anything. For she was *at home*, powerfully at home in the richly furnished library that was jammed with the relics of a thoughtless and proud colonial history. Past colonial governors stared down at Ronald from oil paintings that went around the walls, scrutinizing his claim to be there: his purposes, his motives, demanding that they be as lofty and selfless as they imagined theirs to have been. He wished instantly that he had called Vivian and had her meet him at Hamsun's Bay, clad in swimming suits. Or back at Solly's with Vivian unclad, not wearing a lime-green blouse with puffed sleeves. Or even back in the guest room where she had been frightened and vulnerable. Instead he found himself, already a shaking collection of unorganized needs—uninvited, intimidated, put on the defensive, unable to mount any kind of offensive against what seemed to be his massive ill luck.

"Well, never mind," said Vivian, smiling quickly . . . concealing her irritation? Taking his arm . . . concealing that she too thought he was a child, one that needed guiding? "As long as you're here—which can be but a minute, one *minute*—sit down. You must want to tell me that Nancy's volunteered to go to Ndami. Alan's already told me. I think it's wonderful."

Ronald looked at her blankly, blankly.

"Nancy is ready to divorce me."

She let go of his arm.

"What do you mean?"

"She was waiting for me when I came home in the afternoon. Waiting," he repeated, though Vivian couldn't grasp the ominous significance of that for she couldn't appreciate how implacable Nancy's habits were. "She said she has all the proof she needs."

Vivian took hold of one of her lime-green sleeves.

"Proof? What proof?"

Ronald shrugged.

"She just said she has all the proof she needs."

"You didn't admit anything, did you?"

She was emphatically asking for only one answer, so Ronald gave it to her: "No." And, strictly speaking, that was true.

"Well! As long as you haven't admitted anything, we're going to deny everything. That'll be our response. If she wants to do something, we'll fight it." She must have seen the look on Ronald's face for she reached for his hand from her chair and added, "Together."

"But, Vivian, why do we have to deny anything?"

Did he know that his question was asked beggingly?

"Oh, Ronald, everything is so simple and uncomplicated to you! Look, look around you." She invited him to do so with a sweep of her lime green arm. "Whatever happens, whatever—it mustn't touch Alan. I can't think of just myself, or just you. I can't! . . . not with how important Alan is at the moment to everyone, to everything. It's certain that he'll be the ambassador and I just can't throw aside responsibilities for my own happiness—for our happiness, however much I might want to be free. Who doesn't want to be free, darling? But I told you my days weren't my own and we can't, *can't*, be selfish. I'd never forgive myself. It's rotten luck, that's all, rotten luck that this has happened! The thing we've got to do is think together how to get out of it. . . . What *are* her proofs? Can she really prove that we were in that room together? Has she got witnesses? And Solly doesn't talk—I know my natives. He may smile and lick his lips but he won't talk. What a mess we've gotten ourselves into!"

Ronald didn't know what to say to this. He was prepared for a dark and even fanatical alliance between them, for the bond that crime and guilt creates. He wasn't prepared for irritation or demands to be realistic. For he didn't think it was possible to act, only react. He felt himself in the grip of forces. He couldn't dream of being forceful himself. So he tried to make Vivian feel how forceful Nancy could be, would be, if he and Vivian didn't yield to her. For it was a yielding he wanted.

"If you don't meet with Nancy tomorrow—"

"Meet with her?"

Vivian's face was bright and alert. There wasn't a sign of panic in it, which was what he expected he would see there. Instead there was a flicker of amusement.

"—meet with her and tell her that you're going to get a divorce from Alan, she expects me to go to Ndami with her. Otherwise she won't go at all."

"Won't go at all?"

"No."

Vivian got up.

"So that's it! I see it now. You've been a naughty, naughty boy and she wants you out of my wicked way." She laughed genuinely. "I think that's marvelous! I really do. . . . Well," she went on tersely, "she has to go to Ndami, she must—that's all there is to it, because Alan is counting on it. He's already wired Aaron that someone's coming. If I went to see her, that's what I'd tell her—in no uncertain terms. That epidemic's got to be stopped, and if Nancy won't go unless you accompany her, you'll have to go—that's all. For my sake, for Alan's sake, for everyone's sake. For our sake, darling."

There were no witnesses to the expression on his face.

"Do you want me to go?"

"Of course I don't want you to go. How can you think that? But there really isn't any choice, is there?"

There was: she could divorce Alan.

"Not unless you tell her you'll divorce Alan."

His eyes were down when he reminded her of the choice.

"Why, what would persuade Alan to let me divorce him?"

"Let you?"

"Yes. After all, what grounds do *I* have for divorcing him?"

"Grounds?"

"Why yes, *grounds*. Do you know anything about British divorce laws? You and Nancy may very well have some simple American arrangement, but believe me, Alan and I haven't."

He couldn't do anything but make a personal appeal.

"Vivian, we love one another. We've made l—"

"Shhh! Of course we have, darling, and we shall again. Often. How can you doubt that? That's why we've got to be sensible, we don't want it to stop. Do you think we can live in Hamsun's Bay for the rest of our lives? Or at Solly's? Dear, dear Ronald,, what do you *do*? Your wife is a doctor, my husband is going to be an ambassador. They love doing what they do, they think it's wonderful of themselves to be so clever! They have their egos, their activities, their self-importance . . . we just can't go and interrupt their fun! If we do they'll turn around and interrupt ours, don't you see? And we don't want that."

She reached down for his arm and he lifted himself up and let himself be guided toward the door, with her hand on his elbow.

"For heaven's sake—and it *is* heaven when we're together—just go. Go! It's so simple and it can be over so quickly. Quickly, Ronald! . . . a matter of weeks, two, three at the most, and then the epidemic will be over. Don't make it seem so important—it just means it'll be all the more wonderful to see each other after a short absence, and I'll be thinking of you every day, worrying about you. So just rush out of here now or I'll have to do too much explaining. Rush to Ndami and rush right back! . . . When we step out of the door, I'm going to the right because Alan's expecting me when they serve tea to a delegation from Dahomey. You go to the left and straight on out of here. I'll tell Alan that you came up to tell us that you're accompanying Nancy and wanted to know if there was any way you could be personally helpful. He'll appreciate that. In fact, I'll announce it in front of the whole delegation—it'll show them what kind of cooperation we get around here, especially since you and Nancy are Americans. I don't know what I'll say if Alan asks me what I told you, but I'll think of something." She opened the door with one hand, squeezed Ronald's elbow with the other and whispered, "Bye, darling! Remember, *rush!*"

When Ronald turned left he knew he was going down a wide hallway which led across a receiving room. He could see the door to the main entrance immediately. So he knew exactly where he was going. And yet he was totally lost, so lost that he walked down from The Hill. A white man walking? . . . If any of the expatriates had seen him they would have murmured, "I say, I saw Keane" . . . Vivian would have been furious; scandalized. But Ronald, his head swimming in the heat, thrashed among the phrases that tossed there. *Of course we have and we shall again . . . We don't want it to stop, we don't want them to interrupt our fun . . . It'll be all the more wonderful to see each other!* What *did* he do? He tried to answer, couldn't, and his head kept swimming in the heat, reaching out for more phrases to hang on to. Vivian had been right to make him wonder where they could go, what they could do. A surge of gratitude that she was so level headed and realistic could propel him along the road for twenty paces at a fast speed. *Don't make it so important, it's only a matter of a few weeks, two, three at most . . . rush!* And he was. That seemed to be the solution: to get at it. Get it over with. A quick, simple action would cut through all the confusion and make his head stop swimming. *Rush to Ndami, rush back!* . . . He decided to walk directly to Nancy's laboratory. They had arranged that she should come home for lunch, be told what time Vivian would meet with her and stay at the house until then. Going directly to her laboratory now would throw her off balance, give him the advantage . . . he thought. What he found was near-bedlam. Not only Emille and Tully were there. Two other men, very black, were swinging hammers, crating boxes. Supplies were everywhere. Nancy was packing, readying herself. She looked around at Ronald when he walked in, startled. And in her startled eyes he saw what he had so readily obscured: that Vivian, talking about her sense of responsibility, about selfishness, about her lack of grounds for divorcing Alan, was saying that she had no intention of giving up her way of life for him. And Nancy had known it, was absolutely sure of it. He was barely able to keep a casual attitude when he spoke.

"I'm going to Ndami with you."

He worried that he hadn't tossed the phrase off. It clung to him heavily. He was stung by the fact that Nancy knew Vivian wouldn't sacrifice anything for him when he would sacrifice everything for her. He couldn't stand it.

"I talked with Alan himself."

He saw Nancy's small eyes widen to twice their size and then he couldn't look at them anymore as he continued bluffing.

"It's absolutely essential that you go to Ndami—he's counting on it—and if you won't go without me, then I'm going along. Vivian'll talk with you when we get back."

He looked at Nancy and was sure that her look was a look of defeat. The commotion around them drew his eyes toward the crates and the men working. He didn't want to make doubly sure.

"When do I have to be ready?"

"This afternoon. As long as you're here, I'll inoculate you." She turned around and went toward a table, talking as she did: "Will you remove your shirt? I'll have to give you two, one in each arm. It's a bit unusual but we don't have the usual time."

That was true: in five hours they were on the train north. He had no words for the swiftness of it. There were no words for it. The train was just one more force that was hurrying him along while he sat doing nothing. Nancy had her nose and its bump in a book the whole way, all night. She didn't do anything but read. Nothing seemed to bother her—the heat, the dirt, the flies, the smell of urine. Nothing. He didn't know when she slept. He didn't think she did. There had never been anything like her, ever. Both of his arms burned: she had thrown the needles into him like

94

darts. The only time she spoke was when he began drinking from a half pint of brandy.

"Alcohol produces low gastric acidity," she said evenly. "That's one of the predisposing factors to susceptibility. All drinking will do is make the chances of infection more likely."

"Good, good! For all I know you might have shot poison into me. What do I care?"

II

I WAS RETURNING FROM THE GOLD mines at five o'clock on the last day of Ramadan when I saw the trail of workers that I had arranged to have meet the steamer that our new doctor would be on. They were carrying crates up the hill from the river and it was a sight, believe me, a sight: I knew the crates were filled with medicines. It's odd, but for weeks I hadn't thought about deliverance. Father Jovet, the priests and I had become resigned to waiting the epidemic out, if that was possible, no longer wondering who was next or if we were included. Merely watching the death toll climb, almost without protest. To whom or against what could one protest? When Alan Angle wired that a doctor was coming to replace McGowan, a kind of savior was arriving as far as we were concerned. That it came in the shape of a small, strange-looking, incommunicative woman was typical of all messianic expectations, I suppose. When I saw the line of men coming up the hill I turned my car immediately toward their house—McGowan's old place, the mission house. When I pulled up and got out I saw only her, Nancy, standing in the courtyard giving directions where things should be placed. She didn't hear my car or see me step inside the gate but she did hear my voice.

"May I come in?"

For she seemed to give a little jump at the sound, as if it had frightened her.

"I didn't mean to surprise you. I'm sorry."

How was I to know that I hadn't surprised her? That nothing I could guess, suppose, surmise or expect in the normal course of events would apply here? Would apply to her or to Ronald? I thought I was experience itself: the knowledgable exile, ready to extend his hand to the untutored, the inexperienced. I couldn't have been more naive. If I were asked what Nancy Keane looked like and tried to answer, I don't think I'd try to place her in a scale of human unattractiveness. After all, ninety percent of the human race has to be rated on a scale of unattractiveness; myself included. I would say she looked like someone who had been confined indoors for years and was afraid to go out, at least very far. She obviously wasn't afraid to go out—for she was in Ndami—but that's the way she looked: like someone who had been kept in a room for the better part of her life. The look about her glazed eyes was apprehensive. She seemed ready for evil to appear from nowhere at any moment. And when that look, which I think was her most characteristic one, was replaced by another, it was too vacant for me to describe. You could attribute anything to her abstracted, far-off, almost hypnotized stare. What I attributed to her when I first saw her was infirmity, illness. I thought she was sick. Suffering from a disease other than cholera. I didn't think she would last twenty-four hours. Any my heart sank that it was *this* that had been sent to us. But I smiled anyway as I walked toward her.

"You must be Dr. Keane."

Putting it that way was supposed to say to her that I belonged there. I wasn't an intruder. I knew who she was and she was supposed to be glad to see me.

"Yes, I am."

Did she acknowledge it fearfully? With uncertainty? As if she were going to be judged by me because that's who in fact she was? . . . I don't know. But her acknowledgment seemed filled with guilt.

"I'm Aaron Clinemark."

"Oh, yes. Alan told me about you."

"Whatever it was, don't believe him."

She didn't smile with me so I became very matter of fact. I pointed across a depression in the land to a hill beyond.

"That small white house over there is mine, and I'll always be available to you. I hope I can be helpful. I thought you and your husband would be too worn out from your trip to come over and have dinner with me tonight, so I've already arranged to have dinner prepared for you here."

"Thank you."

"And since I was sure we would want to talk, I've invited myself."

My smile didn't help. There must have been nothing ingratiating about it. The way she looked at me made me feel like a fool. *I* had wanted to talk anyway. When there are only a half dozen Europeans living in a community of one hundred thousand people, and when five of them are priests who speak another language than yours, you look forward to company. Since McGowan had been my closest acquaintance I was probably feeling the loss of him, and I was at least curious, if not more than that, about who was taking his place. About whether they could fill his place. But I also naturally expected Dr. Keane and her husband to be eager to talk with me. Needless to say, I was wrong. When I realized that she wasn't going to invite me in,

97

dinner or no, and seemed content to let us both stand in the middle of the courtyard, I pointed to the door of the house.

"I think you should get yourself out of this sun. It doesn't lose its strength here until six o'clock."

She obeyed me without saying a word.

I followed her to the house and stayed on the subject of dinner and my apparently thoughtless self-invitation: "I think you'll find your cook's quite good. I don't need to tell you that food's a problem in an epidemic like this, so I kept him on for you. In fact, I kept all of McGowan's servants on. I didn't think you'd want to be bothered about hiring your own." She didn't agree so I had to say, "If you don't like your dinner tonight, or anything else for that matter, you can let them go."

She didn't tell me that I had been thoughtful. Or efficient.

"McGowan is the doctor who just died, is that right?"

"Yes."

We stepped into the darkness of the house.

"Did Alan tell you there's no electricity?"

She came alive and turned quickly.

"No."

"They have it in the central places. I meant just here. When the missionary society built this place fifty years ago, there wasn't any. McGowan could have relocated but he just didn't want to."

I saw a man standing in the semidarkness of the entrance, suddenly. He entered from another room and seemed surprised, almost startled, to see me. He was tall and leathery looking; he had brown hair and, when I saw them later, brown eyes. The most noticeable thing about him was his chin. It was broad and square, one of those forceful-looking ones that are considered masculine. But he was of medium build. I didn't understand why Dr. Keane wasn't going to introduce us. I knew it had to be her husband. I finally felt awkward. And confused. There was nothing to do but step forward and hold out my hand toward him.

"I'm Clinemark."

I found myself smiling pleasantly but smiling alone again. I started to get nervous. Were they both sick?

"You must be exhausted by your journey . . . and here I just told Dr. Keane that I had invited myself to dinner. I hope you don't mind." I paused and gave him a chance to say *no* but he didn't, so I found myself explaining: "I thought there might be some things you'd both like to ask me about Ndami and the conditions here." And when he didn't agree to that I even admitted: "Since McGowan died I haven't talked to anyone except Father Jovet and the priests, and I can't do myself justice in French."

He looked quickly at his wife.

"French?"

There seemed to be something wrong with that. I looked at her, then back at him.

"Yes. Weren't you told?"

I don't know why they should have been, yet I asked as if that had been a serious oversight and I was ready to make amends for it.

"No," he clipped.

"Well, I don't think you have to worry. There are a limited number of topics you can talk to a French priest about, anyway." There I was, smiling alone again. "And Father Jovet speaks tolerable English, if he wants. He usually doesn't want to," I admitted, but turned to Nancy to assure her that in her case he would. "But he'll be only too glad to with you."

"Oh, he won't have to talk English to her," said Ronald in a surly tone, or a tone that made me take notice of it anyway. "She speaks French. I'm the one who doesn't."

Whatever was behind that made Nancy walk off without even excusing herself. Naturally I was made to feel I had made a serious mistake. All I could do was utter a lame, "Oh," and then suggest the most obvious thing that came to my mind. "Would you like to come across to my place for a drink before dinner?"

"Alcohol lowers your gastric acidity. That's one of the predisposing factors to susceptibility. If you drink, your chances of infection go up."

I backed off quickly and I did it by laughing.

"Well, Mboye will probably put supper on at six, out of habit—McGowan always ate early. That'll just give me time to go down to the river and see that everything you brought with you has been handled properly. That's a better idea than whiskey."

I smiled and backed out the door without waiting for him to say anything. I didn't think he would anyway. Naturally, I didn't have to go to the river and I walked only halfway there. That was far enough to stand and look around, to gaze at what was so familiar to me. And to get support from the familiar. And not a small part of that was the sense of myself, standing there. . . . How often had I falsely expected something in Africa? Not something that might happen—arrive, change, alter, even *deliver* me from anything, including cholera. Just expected something, anything—because a long exile makes you suspect that you're ignoring half the world in a cowardly way. That your decision to leave what you called "home," a decision that seemed to demand the best from you, was a desertion of the living room for a dark corner into which you crept. After eight or nine years in Africa I began to feel that at any moment something or someone might arrive from somewhere and force me to acknowledge the uncertainty if not the guilt that I felt for living a life that blinded its eyes and deafened its ears to its own culture. Or at least the major part of it. I don't know what I had anticipated when Alan had wired and in effect told me that I would be seeing two new faces, both white, and hearing two new voices that both spoke my native language. But I had anticipated something and when my expectations weren't met and I was left standing in the road, watching the strong current in the Dalaga River below, I felt somewhat childish. The dust, the ever-present sun, the moving black bodies, the sense of my own flesh hanging a bit heavily on my bones: that's all there was. That's all there had ever been. Why was I always expecting something? There was nothing to expect, ever. And with that realization I think I breathed a sigh of relief. Dr. Keane and her husband weren't going to alter or challenge the ageless arrangement of things as I had come to know them. They were just two more lost people, doubly lost because they were white and, God knows why, in Africa. My job was going to be what it had always been: to see to it that they didn't make too many mistakes and smooth it over whenever and wherever they did. I knew Americans had no curiosity about foreign things in general, were never disturbed by the alien. Oh, they might fake a momentary conversational interest in a custom, express a social delight in it. But that's all. They were incapable of seeing the world except in their own terms. The thing that made me pause about the Keanes was that they didn't even see the world in those terms. They didn't look at it at all. They had no momentary interest, no curiosity about anything. At least not in that first encounter with them. They were self-contained. By what, I didn't know. It was obvious that they weren't contained together, that Nancy was in some way hermetically sealed. Fatigue and exhaustion didn't seem to account for their peculiarities. Or being obviously ill matched, at least physically. The picture I already had of them left me disturbed, the way you might be disturbed if you were standing in front of a painting and the shadows in it suddenly made you think: the shading in the pictures of a right-handed artist go from the bottom left-hand corner to the top right-hand corner. But the shading in the picture in front of you runs from the bottom right-hand corner to the top left-hand corner. And that meant the artist who did it was left-handed. . . . As I walked back into the courtyard of the mission house I was on the lookout for a moving left hand, watchful, ready to look for and discover something.

That was hard to do because of the silence.

Ronald, whom I still thought of as Mr. Keane, brought a whisky and soda to the table with him. So that business about gastric acidity and susceptibility was part of the game he was obviously playing, and playing bitterly. I could see that his attitude was temporary, brought on by something, and that it would change. But when I looked at his wife, Nancy, Dr. Keane, I knew otherwise. She sat at the head of the table, Ronald and I consorts on either side of her, wearing a plain blue-gray commonsense sort of dress; a dress that was good for the heat and ready to go to work in. The way she refused to cast a normal glance at me when she came in to the dining room, nod with a perfunctory smile or recognize my presence in any manner, didn't impress me as rude—that was the thing. It *was* rude but it didn't impress me as rude. What I decided to do with these people, at least for starters, was not to make a fool of myself by trying to be cheerful or convivial when they didn't want to be. I didn't want to be listening to the sounds of my own words and waiting for responses I wasn't going to get. It was certainly true to say that they weren't people who rejoiced in seeing their own kind. Isn't that the whole point of sitting down with strangers and swapping irrelevant stories about one's sleeplessness on a riverboat, the size of the mosquitoes and the heaviness of the heat? To get us to exercise our faculties of sympathy for one another? . . . If you talk about the terrible and unpredictable death rate around you and are made to look with the mind into the hollowed-out eyes of a child, isn't the message unmistakable? That we're feeding with words our love for our own kind? Unpacking our hearts?

That had been my only experience in that room with which I was so familiar. I had sat there often with another man, looking up toward the fourteen-foot ceiling that was always populated with small lizards that could make nothing of our conversation. The walls around us were all whitewashed, and the rough wooden table at which we sat was set squarely in the center of the room, large enough for ten persons. The chandelier overhead had six paraffin lamps in it and they were already burning even though the sun coming through the window in the far corner gave us sufficient light for the time being. It was the first time I had sat at the dining room table in the mission house with anyone other than McGowan, who had sat there nightly for twenty-eight years. And what he definitely had was the faculty for rejoicing in his own kind. He did it, of course, at the most basic level: he began with the body. He exchanged smiles with every man, woman and child in Ndami because he prodded the muscles below the skin and knew all the buried bones beneath the muscle we carried around. His love for his fellows was based on that kind of understanding, one that Nancy either had or could surely come by easily; that fundamental form of communication. But if she could or would, it was unavailable to her at the dinner table. She sat frozen-faced—and yet I felt nothing coming from within her to cause that coldness. Nothing seemed to cause her rigidity and severity. No force. Her silence had the resigned and melancholy quality that lurks among the markers in a cemetery. If sympathy and love make us speak up, even trivially, asking about the taste of the food that we're all sharing, then something must have laid its long gray finger on Nancy's lips. It wasn't hate. It was a recoil, a withdrawal from the world, so complete that I wonder how she could have withdrawn so far and yet stayed alive. I wonder if her plainness, her lack of all physical presence and grace, can really account for it? . . . Though it's true: everything about her—her posture, her averted eyes, the way she kept her elbow close into her body as she used a fork to reach for the food on her plate—seemed to say that she didn't want to inflict her presence on anyone.

When I decided to say something, and it was a conscious decision, I decided to talk about something that was already beginning to concern me:

"Are the two of you planning on staying after the epidemic is over?"

My question forced Nancy's head up from her plate. She hadn't expected it even though it was a natural one. A doctor was obviously needed in Ndami and I was sure they could have the mission house if they wanted it. I looked at Ronald after I waited for her to say something but looking at him didn't bring much about either. They were without plans? . . . I had never met any white people in Africa who were without plans, even if their plans were illusions. I took it as one more dangerous sign of their instability, their untrustworthiness to do what they had come to do.

"I hadn't thought about it," Nancy said uncertainly.

I was sure she would in time.

"When you do, you'd better think about what consolations you'll need. People who come to a place this remote usually have to be offered considerable compensation for being here."

"What's your compensation?"

I was surprised by the quickness with which Ronald asked that.

"I wasn't offered any—that's because I volunteered to come here. Most people don't. They're usually asked—'hand picked' is the phrase, I think. The two men who came with me had been told they were specially selected for the assignment—chosen. It makes them feel important to be chosen for the job, although they soon discover that they aren't important at all. It's the same with the priests, I'm afraid . . . although it's even sadder. God seems to have a habit of sending people to remote places with some kind of promise that He'll be along soon. But He never seems to arrive. I've seen a lot of chosen people in Africa waiting for a word that never comes, something that's supposed to tell them that they haven't been abandoned. After being certain of their special status in someone's eyes they become very lonely. Even bitter. So"—I looked at Nancy—"I was glad to learn that you had volunteered to take McGowan's place."

"I didn't," said Ronald.

I didn't know what to say. But I didn't feel any responsibility to say anything to him so I just continued with my thoughts to Nancy.

"McGowan was able to avoid the usual pitfalls that lie in wait for exiles because there was so much physical suffering to cope with. He hated disease."

"Another one?"

I couldn't ignore Ronald twice in succession. "What?" I said—pleasantly, I think.

"Did you know that's what people fear and hate the most?"

I knew he wasn't talking to me. He was bouncing something off me that was supposed to land in his wife's lap. I smiled at his game, although I didn't know what it was, and asked, "What's that?"

We were answered by drums instead of Ronald. The sudden sound of them made them both straighten up. They looked at me—startled, frightened, and for the first time I really wanted to smile, to smile genuinely, broadly, with deep satisfaction. For my feeling was that, thank God, something had finally got through to these self-centered, self-preoccupied Americans. I looked squarely at Ronald and jerked my thumb over my shoulder.

"That's what people fear here, right now. There isn't anything else worth fearing alongside of that. Death is running through these streets, unstoppable. It's created terror, and any way to deal with the terror is acceptable. Beginning at sundown every night you'll hear drums and just about anything else coming from various quarters of the city, depending on what group happens to live there. We counted over eighty dead yesterday, eighty. Since the people are Muslim here, fear isn't drowned in alcohol or palm wine, although a lot of them have taken to it again. But most of them rely on time-honored methods of dealing with what can't be dealt with. You may not get much sleep tonight, but after a few nights you'll get used to the sound. . . . I don't envy what you have to face," I said to Nancy. "We don't have much civil authority at the moment. People aren't only dying—there's robbing, burning, looting, all sorts of things have gotten out of hand. When word gets out that a merchant's dead his place is a wreck in a few hours. I guess you start to grasp at any kind of life when you're in the midst of death—wildly. We've got one stable figure in all this disorder—Embu. Colonel Sada. I'm not sure where he got the title but he's the head of the local police, which has become a small army, a kind of militia, in the past few weeks. Embu's probably getting ideas of taking over the local government when this is done with, and it might not be a bad idea. He went to England to study economics and wound up learning policemanship instead. He's all spit and polish, efficient, reliable . . . and he's going to be your greatest help. You'll have a car and driver to get about—in fact, you're being picked up here tomorrow morning at six thirty. I hope that isn't too early. The driver'll take you to Embu's headquarters and he'll let you know what sections of the city seemed to have been hit worse than others, and see to it that your instructions are carried out, when you start to give them. He and his men are the best resource we've got for disposing of the dead, too."

They both became even more alert.

"Oh, yes. We're using mass graves. No one will embalm the dead. Families sometimes flee their homes—just vacate. Several hundred have started out into the desert along the old caravan routes, and leave the bodies behind. We don't discover them for hours, sometimes for days, so you can imagine what the corpses are like. That's my job tomorrow, and for the next few days—I told Embu I'd head one of his burial details. So I may not see you for a while, although you can always catch me across the way at night. I've arranged for Embu to take you to Father Jovet. The old convent—did they tell you there were nuns here before they were replaced by priests?—is the only hospital we have. It was the only place McGowan could set up some kind of infirmary. I think you'll want to have most of your medical supplies sent there, and you'll find that the priests have become pretty good nurses. McGowan began training them. There are only four left—Father Marcel died yesterday—and they're ready to drop from overwork, although they won't admit it." ·

I smiled at Nancy.

"Even if you aren't a Catholic, Father Jovet's going to look on you as some kind of angel, I can tell you that."

Nancy's eyes lowered and I believe I saw a flush come to her cheeks.

"Father Jovet was a good friend of Pelissier's," I said. For I expected her to be able to make the connection between the two of them, and to know who Pelissier was. But she didn't seem to. "Didn't you know him?"

"No."

"How about Wheeler?"

She shook her head. That seemed curious because the expatriate community in The Port was a small and closely knit group.

"Nigel Heseltine then?"

I wasn't just going down a list of random names. Nigel had come to Ndami within the last eighteen months and had done a lot to improve our livestock. He was a veterinarian.

"No."

I found that very hard to believe. And I was teasing when I said, "Do you know Alan Angle?"

"Of course. But Ronald knows the Angles better. He plays bridge with Alan."

Ronald looked at her sharply. I didn't know why he should seem so astonished, unprepared to be reminded of it.

"Do you?" I asked.

His eyes went down. He seemed embarrassed. Why? . . . At being on personal terms with Alan?

"I have once or twice."

"Do you know his wife?" Nancy asked me.

I was glad to find that she was interested in something and I couldn't help but smile.

"Vivian?"

"Yes."

"For a good many years."

Ronald's head lifted.

"Do you like her?"

I was surprised that she asked, but my surprise was overridden by my inevitable, even irrepressible, response: all men liked Vivian. Most women did, too.

"One can't help it, can one?"

"Oh? Why? Why can't one help liking Vivian Angle?"

This was something new. Not only the way she came to unexpected life but the aggressive way in which she did. Had I been alert enough I might have detected something of the force of her will. But her challenge was too specific: it kept me smiling. How was I supposed to say that Vivian Angle was a splendid animal? . . . Vivian had, I thought, more personality in her body than most people do in their characters. Moreover, she was almost unconscious about it, as any instinctively graceful animal was.

"Well," I started searchingly, "you sort of get the same enjoyment watching Vivian as you do watching a cat leap into the air after a butterfly. She's energetic, attractive, she's a very good hostess, puts on wonderful dinner parties, makes you feel especially welcome when you sit at her dinner table, and, let's see, she's—"

"Loose?"

I think I was stunned. And I hadn't been stunned in a long time. My cheeks reddened. I kept on smiling, too: not from amusement but because I had to conceal my confusion and embarrassment.

"Well, yes, maybe, I—I suppose."

"You agree?"

I already had. My hand spun in the air.

"If you say superlatively, *superbly* loose."

A burst of laughter came from somewhere. I say somewhere because I couldn't believe that it came from Nancy. But it had. Her head was back, her open mouth aimed at the ceiling. I wouldn't have thought that such a sound could have come from her small body. That behind her severe eyes there was a vision of something humorous, even if it was maliciously humorous.

A chair crashed to the floor.

I wouldn't say it brought me to my senses but it made me realize I had paid no attention to Ronald. He had pushed back his chair—too suddenly, too far—and he was standing, looking down at me. At me, not her. The muscles, or a nerve, were jumping in his right cheek. He was staring at me miserably, struggling to say something. In his look of misery it was impossible not to glimpse the facts, if not the truth, about something. He cleared his throat. It made a small struggling sound of someone under great emotional strain.

"Loose?"

Nancy aimed her mouth at the ceiling again and laughed. I noticed her teeth for the first time. They were beautiful: white and absolutely straight. It was hard to believe that the hideous sound I heard came from behind them. Ronald's single word had come out hoarsely and it was put to rout by her laughter. He whirled to one side and stalked out of the room. Nancy stood up, surprised; too surprised. She put her hands on the table as if for support. But she sounded as if she needed no one's support when she spoke.

"Are there wells?"

"What?"

"Wells."

I concentrated on her narrowly set eyes.

"I'm sorry, I don't know what you're asking."

"Surely the city has got a number of wells, wells for water."

"Well, of course it has."

"You've sealed them off."

She said it matter of factly.

"No."

"What!"

"No one's been able to persuade the people not to use them, even though they've been told it's certain death to drink from them."

She picked up her fork from the table only to slam it down again.

"That'll change. I've no interest in seeing Father Jovet or his infirmary. That's a waste of time—those who are dying are dying, they'll just have to die. The thing to do is get at the living. I want the wells sealed off, by force if necessary. Is that possible?"

Now I stood up.

"I suppose Colonel Sada could put police around them."

"Then he must."

"Tell him so in the morning," I said skeptically.

"I will. And all water has to be boiled and portioned out . . . And access to the river must be blocked."

"But the river moves quickly."

"I don't care how it moves. I want control of the water of this city."

She had gone to the heart of the problem and I admit that she had taken me with her.

"If we can seal off the wells, can you treat them?"

"I won't know that until I've tested them, which will take a lot of time."

"And in those crates you've got something that can purify the water supply?"

"I think so," she said curtly, smugly.

But I didn't care how she said it.

"There are ten major wells, and about as many lesser ones—some in the outlying districts."

"Twenty wells for a hundred thousand people?"

"Half the population takes their water from the ditches."

"The flow will have to be stopped. Can it?"

I hadn't dreamt of it, but I said, "I suppose so."

"Then it will be. You said a car would be here at six thirty?"

I nodded.

"I suppose you can find your way out?"

That she was even pretending to be some kind of a hostess amazed me. And I nodded again. When I did, she turned and walked out. I didn't go to the door right away. I sat down in my chair and thought *My God*. . . .

12

WHAT DISTURBS ME IS THAT
I had no thoughts for four days.
From dawn to dusk I buried the dead
with three of Colonel Sada's men, and it did nothing but
tire my body. It quickened no thought. I might just as well
have been born without a mind. It seemed no more than an
activity, one of a hundred possible activities; hard, unpleasant. But an activity that didn't add a dimension to my life
that wasn't already there, or take away a dimension that
was. How was that possible? I refuse to understand why it
made no difference and still makes none. I suppose I was a
bit more aware of myself. Each morning when I got up and
stood at my screens, looking out at the beginning day, I felt
the wooden floorboards beneath my bare feet a little more.
One afternoon I burned my forehead up when my hat fell
into one of the graves and I wouldn't retrieve it. I lost
weight. I wanted to go home at night but I thought I should
stay close to the Keanes, be available to them, and so Funa
and I had agreed I would stay at the cottage that belonged
to the mining company. I drove by the mission house the
very first night I returned from working with the burial
detail but no one was there. I wasn't surprised that Nancy
hadn't returned yet, but I was surprised that Ronald wasn't
there. I wasn't disappointed. I was glad to go to my rooms
by myself, have a drink alone and fall onto the bed almost
without having eaten. And what I awakened to each morning I had awakened to for years: the mist and the smoke of
wood fires, which always hung over Ndami, gradually being pierced by dawn. Two or three minarets cut into the
white film. And a single dark line ran to the east before it

faltered, rose up again and then fell off, disappearing: it was all that remained of an old city wall. I have never lost the habit of turning the beginning of the day into the promise of dawn, and I suppose the promise at that time was that—with that day—the death rate might not rise. It took a while before that promise was kept.

On the afternoon of the fourth or fifth day after our dinner together, I drove over to the mission house and found Ronald in the middle of the courtyard, dressed in khaki shorts, without a shirt or hat, reading a book. A book was in his hand at least. Sitting in the sun instead of on the porch seemed to point to one more suspicious thing about the two of them. Apparently he didn't hear me drive up or walk to the gate.

"Are you trying out for sunstroke?"

He turned his head, looked for a moment and then stood up. He seemed dazed or lost. He hadn't shaved for some time but looked more rugged than unkempt.

"Oh, hello."

"Hello."

He gave a small smile.

"I'm drying out."

I didn't understand what he meant.

"Been through the wash?"

He laughed. Then I saw the puffiness below his eyes and realized that he meant he had been drinking. When I got close to him I could smell his sour breath, not at all fresh, from alcohol: stale.

"I hope you haven't felt that I've forgotten about you over here, or neglected you. I did stop by one late afternoon, but didn't find anyone in. Have you been getting around?"

He didn't answer and seemed embarrassed. He even lowered his head as he shook it. . . . Had he been drinking that much?

"I was just on my way into one of the markets. I thought maybe you'd like to come along."

From the way he looked at me I almost thought he was going to say *Why?*

"Oh. Sure, yes. I'll get my shirt."

He put the book in his hand down on the chair and I glanced at it. It was one of his wife's medical books. I looked at the table of contents to figure out what he was reading: there was a section in it on cholera. When he returned he was still pulling on his shirt.

"I don't think I've known anyone to take the African sun the way you seem to."

Again he seemed embarrassed and he didn't say anything in reply. But he did ask, just as I was getting behind the wheel of the car, "Have you been with, ah—Nancy?"

What else was he going to call her?

"No. I've been working with a burial detail for the last several days. I haven't seen her since the other night."

I thought he looked at me a little quickly.

"Oh, don't worry . . . there's no need. Embu—Colonel Sada—he's with her most of the time, or one of his men. I saw the two of them pass us yesterday."

"Do you know how she's doing?"

I was surprised that he asked.

"Don't you?"

He shook his head, looking at me frankly; openly enough to tell me that he was a stranger to her.

"No."

"Well, I've heard," I said. "Everyone seems to. She's closed off every well in the city to access except two, and got Embu to stand a twenty-four-hour guard at every one, three police in three shifts. I heard the men on the detail talking about the tables she sets up at each one. She takes samples from the well, works right there with test tubes—putting on quite a show, I take it . . . treats the well, goes on to the next, one after the other, then returns to sample and test what she's treated in continual rounds. Unendingly. Does she always work at that pace? . . . I understand that at the two open wells—wait, let's take a look. There's one just down this road."

I swerved into Chad Lane. In a few hundred yards steam began rising in the air. Fires were burning under huge pots, cauldrons.

"There . . . See? She's having the water boiled right at the well and doled out until some of the other wells are purified."

A dozen women were drawing water from the well, watched over by four of Embu's militia, replenishing each cauldron as it became empty. Another group of women were supplying those who stood in line with urns.

"It looks as if she won't trust anyone. That's wise. I know she's been in Lambatown with one of the priests, inoculating people. That's about the most infected section of the city. The death rate's still up. It was over a hundred the day before yesterday. But yesterday it rose only by two. That's a sign of something, I don't know what—but it seems hopeful."

His response was only a sullen look. Maybe there was a softening in his shoulders. His head sank a little into his body and he sat there docilely. At that precise moment—in a cholera epidemic in Ndami—he was a man without a function. A consort to a female doctor. A reluctant visitor that I was taking on a tour.

"What *is* cholera?"

"I noticed you had a medical book in the yard with you."

"It didn't say anything I could understand."

"Well, I know that the chief problem comes from the fact that the vibrio—that's the germ or bacillus, or whatever—has a very short incubation period, and that's why it's so explosive. Gets out of hand rapidly. When you first get it your stool has a kind of rice-water appearance and has flakes of mucus in it. There's the usual retching and hiccuping, cramps in leg muscles and feet, and gradual prostration. Dehydration is the enemy, I guess. It brings on the 'classic cholera face'—haven't you ever seen it? Sunken eyes, hollow cheeks, wrinkled skin, an apathetic voice. That's the second stage. I forget what the third and final stage is—McGowan told me. But I know that death comes from some kind of circulatory failure. They look for the victim to start urinating again. If they don't pass any water after a few days, they know they're going to die."

"You die because you can't urinate?"

I shrugged.

"The body's become a desert. No water."

He breathed heavily and I looked at him. His shoulders were still sagging, his neck was sinking into his body.

"You've been inoculated, haven't you?"

He nodded.

"You're all right then. You can still get it—"

He looked at me quickly.

"—but inoculation keeps you from dying from it. Or is supposed to."

I turned the car around, glancing back over my shoulder at the crowd around the well. The steam from the boiling water was a beautiful sight, and I said just that.

The loud and incessant drumming we soon heard didn't sound beautiful. Not to Ronald, anyway. His sunken neck came up from between his shoulder blades, and he looked around. It must have sounded the same as the slower, low-toned drumming that went on at night.

"How would you like to go to a funeral?"

He didn't expect to see me smiling when he looked at me.

"A funeral?"

"Sure. You're in Africa—you ought to see it while you're here."

I pulled off the road and turned off the motor.

"This isn't for a cholera victim."

I pointed to a large compound and got out of the car. The presence of drummers and the two open huts that had been built out of mats meant that the festivities marking the "final" funeral of a dead person were in progress. I started for an open gate while Ronald followed.

"Can we just go right in?"

"Everyone's welcome. They've been burying this man for weeks."

"Weeks?"

I liked his astonishment.

"Weeks. They're good embalmers—very, very good." I smiled as I said, "The only thing you can't do is steal the dead person's hair or nails." I waited for his surprised look, got it and then explained: "They always cut the hair and nails off the body right after death and the family carefully guards them so they won't be stolen. If they are, someone might make a powerful charm out of them." I pointed to a group of tables where men, women and children were seated, dressed in their best attire. "Let's sit over there." The tables were covered with white cloths and an array of drinks. The best way to describe how the funeral celebrants sipped from their glasses would be to say that it was with a quiet cheefulness. I decided to sit down with a group of younger people, and they greeted Ronald and me with smiles; and then, as was the custom, left us respectfully alone. A young girl, perhaps thirteen or fourteen, wearing a yellow dress, approached us carrying empty glasses. "Here's our waitress," I said to Ronald. "She'll speak either French or English to us."

It was English: "What do you wish to drink?"

I looked at her and suggested, "Maybe I should tell him what there is." She waited politely and I turned to Ronald. "You can have Dutch beer, French wine, English gin or Jamaican rum. Local fruit juice or lemonade"—I looked at the girl for confirmation, received it in her smile, and then added—"or American Coca-Cola."

It didn't seem that Ronald would be able to speak.

"All that?"

"Any of it," I corrected. "*All* would be impolite."

"Coke," he said.

"Two Cokes, then," I said to the girl. When she walked off I told Ronald it was a good choice. "It's safe for drinking under the present conditions. It isn't bottled here."

When the girl came back Ronald reached in his pocket for money.

"No, no," I said.

The girl smiled, saying, "All drinks are free. But"— she looked at me as if she sought my permission to suggest—"you may make a gift of money to the dead man, if you wish."

Ronald looked at me for guidance. He had a bill in his hand so I took it from him and gave it to the girl, saying: "This is for him then." When she walked off I pointed to one of the huts. "Those are the dead man's gifts. Cloths, robes, pipes, mats, soap, sponges"—I was naming them as I recognized them—"or money. See the man she's going to? He's the crier—she'll come back with him."

"What for?"

"His job is to cry out the names of all the donors."

Ronald sat up.

"What's going to happen?"

I laughed at his nervousness. "Don't worry. Nothing's going to happen." That wasn't strictly true. It just wasn't going to happen then, even though the crier handed Ronald a book.

"What do I do?"

The girl answered.

"Please sign."

I elaborated: "You put down your name, your address, and the amount that you gave. There's a column for each one."

I watched him write.

"My address in America?"

"No, your address here. Just write CMS—that's for Church Missionary Society, and means McGowan's old house."

He returned the book into the arthritic hands of the crier who bowed and thanked him in native.

"Now in a day or two the whole of the dead man's family, accompanied by drummers, will serenade outside the houses of all those who made gifts. Yours, too."

His surprise almost bordered on fright.

"Oh, I think you'll like it," I reassured. I thought I sensed that he wanted to hide. That to be looked at, seen or noticed, was in some way to be found out.

He swept a hand toward the mourning musicians: six men with funeral cloths tied around their necks, playing *seli* drums and shaking calabash rattles. One man struck bells with a stick.

"How can they do this in the middle of an epidemic?"

"How?"

"It looks like they're having fun."

"I don't know if they're having fun, but they're not in pain. There are pains like cholera and toothache, childbirth and typhoid fever—involuntary pains, always physical. But after those we're in pain because we need to be in pain."

A girl leaned toward me and whispered in my ear.

"You're about to get a song sung in your honor," I told Ronald. We looked down the table together and saw everyone smiling in our direction. Ronald moved in his chair uncomfortably. He smoothed the short sleeves of his shirt and stroked his cheek, as if he wished he were better dressed and clean shaven. "I think they're going to sing in praise of you for your gift."

I pointed out a musician who had stepped forward.

119

"I'll try to catch the words."

I could. It was a short song, sung twice. Ronald seemed alert, intent, almost as if he was trying to pretend that he understood what was being sung. But I think he only meant to appear appreciative.

"He's singing about a stranger who has come from a far land—that's you—to live in the great healer's house—that's McGowan—and has given twenty shillings to the dead man."

When the singer finished Ronald straightened up.

"Is there something I should do?"

"Well, if you want, you can walk over to the musicians and point to one of the sticks the bell player has. See the man with the orange scarf around his neck? He'll hand the stick to you. When he does, strike one of the bells."

He looked at the band, then at me.

"Should I?"

"Go ahead."

He did: to the delight of everyone and for his own pleasure, obviously. He came back to the table as any self-conscious adolescent might, with downcast eyes and flushed cheeks. But that's exactly how he should have reacted, in my opinion. Most of the tourists who happen to participate in a local ceremony in Africa, at least the ones I've ushered around, behave as if they're in a colorful kindergarten. They have no notion or appreciation that they're in a complex and antique culture. And Ronald's shy demeanor was absolutely correct even if it was accidental. I smiled as I stood up when he returned to the table, and pointed to a corner of the compound.

"See that woman? Watching those others count the cloths? She's called the *akovi*. Her job is to keep the death watch, and the shroud she's starting to wrap around herself means she's going to begin a song to that man's accompaniment." I pointed to the gravedigger. "And if she calls for gongs and rattles before we get out of here, we'll have to stay until midnight out of politeness."

"We have to go?"

"I think we'd better."

I started away from the table and everyone wished us polite farewells.

"What are they saying?"

"Oh, the usual. Thanking us for coming, telling us to *go well*, and so on. You seemed to like it."

He nodded. And it was obvious that he liked the market I pulled up to in a few minutes even more.

"You can just leave me here," he said.

"Well, I'm getting out, too."

"I mean when you're ready to go. You can just go on. I'll stay awhile and then walk back."

"You like African markets?"

We started into the first lane of stalls together and he nodded.

"A third of the stalls are closed because of the epidemic, but you'll still find quite a bit. If you go over in that corner"—I pointed off to the southeast corner of the market—"you'll find a dyer who makes an indigo fit for a Morris wallpaper.

He probably didn't understand my reference but there was no misunderstanding my boast. For he smiled.

"I'll go there."

Then a child ran into me, clasping me around the legs, almost knocking me over. I didn't think it was the moment to say that the child was mine. But I smiled, touched his head and gave him a message to deliver to his mother, who was my wife. He looked up at Ronald before he ran off.

"You seem to know people."

"I know a few."

I smiled because I had made a claim; modestly, I hope. But I had made it with pleasure.

"How do you do that?"

"What?"

"Get to know people. I'd like to get to know people. Does it just happen if you stay long enough?"

I looked at him to make sure he was serious.

"Do you really want to know?"

He gave me a look that wondered why I doubted him. So I pointed toward a corrugated tin roof at an intersection of the lanes. "When the epidemic's over, eat there." I knew I said it challengingly and explained: "You're making me touch on a subject that gets my blood going. . . . No, you just don't get to know people if you stay here long enough. You have to eat with them, that's how you get to know them. If you reject their food, you reject them. It's an old story—as old as Moses, telling his followers that those who eat forbidden food become unclean. To keep up religious distinctions, and social distinctions . . . any kind of distinctions. Back in England a pork-eating Gentile like yourself would never have got in on one of my family's communal feasts." I smiled to take the sense of exclusion out of the remark. "But you can't have communion, you can't get to know people when one person despises the other person's food, calls it uneatable, or says it's dirty. And that's just what the whites do in Africa: they say African food is unsafe, unclean. In an epidemic they're right, clinically speaking. But what's behind it is the same thing that's behind sending the servants into the kitchen to eat, or having one mess for the officers and one for the enlisted men, one table for the captain and a hundred tables for everyone else. It keeps up distinctions, gives the right social veneer to injustice and exploitation. The right to eat at the same table and the readiness to eat the same food—that symbolizes equality. Oh, it doesn't do any good to eat at the same table down in The Port. Vivian Angle always invites Africans up on The Hill, certain select ones—educated, European-trained—but she never returns the honor by sitting at an African's table, not unless it's spread with tinned food from Europe."

I shook my finger at the corrugated tin roof again.

"For all his sense of humanity, McGowan never ate there—and the priests never eat there either, for all their notions of divinity. They say it's the fear of infection. *Infection!* That's an excuse for avoiding intimate, personal relationships. Infected in what way, eh? It's a loaded word, it camouflages discrimination—the sense of superiority is disguised as a revulsion from microbes, not people. Clever, isn't it? I can't get over how clever it is, and convenient, too. So when the epidemic's over, eat there. And I'll show you how to eat *fufu*, too. . . . Speaking of the priests, Father Jovet wants me to bring you around to meet him, and see their infirmary. As soon as the wells get cleared up, that's where your wife will be spending the better part of her day. I'm sure she's spent quite a few hours there already, even though she had other priorities when she first got here."

I waited for a reply. I didn't think I was going to get it.

"Father Jovet and the other priests are the only other Europeans I can introduce you to here."

"Sure, fine."

"How about if I come by for you midmorning tomorrow?"

"All right."

I was going to go to Funa's stall but he made me hesitate. He lowered his head in the manner of someone searching for words and pushed something on the ground with the toe of his sandal.

"I'd like to talk with you about Vivian Angle sometime."

That reminded me that I had mentioned her. And it

made me remember my remark the other night and Nancy's burst of laughter. I think my cheeks warmed.

"All right," I said evenly, maybe a bit lightly, too. "Anytime you like."

13

WAS I DELAYED A DAY? Something at the mines? A call from Embu to work with a burial detail again? I forget. . . . But it seems possible because when I saw him two days later, as I think, I imagined that he thought I might have avoided him because I didn't want to talk about Vivian. Or listen to him talk about her. I was sure I wouldn't have anything to say. Ronald looked very good: clean shaven, no puffiness under the eyes, and neatly dressed. And apparently glad to see me. Nothing he said made me think that, just something in his manner that was outgoing, pleasant, possibly eager. But perhaps the section of Ndami that we had to drive through did away with some of his anticipation. For the litter of weeks was more noticeable; the smell was bad and the signs of a demoralized people were more visible. We passed by doors that had masks affixed to their jambs. And from behind at least one of them we heard the sound of wailing. Someone must have just died.

"I don't know what to tell you about the Catholic mission by way of preparation. If you're taken through certain rooms in the infirmary you might feel that the living are worse than any dead you've seen. Father Jovet's a little remarkable, which is something you might not be able to see right off. He's been here for eleven years and never left. The Catholics aren't like the Protestants or the colonial staff in The Port, going home, getting vacations, being 'rehabilitated' every few years. Since I've been here every priest that's come has come to stay. It's a choice they make, I guess—but not on the basis of the people, since they don't know them, or the place, which I really don't think they care for. I don't know what basis they make it on."

We followed the winding clay wall that bordered the road until it became more and more like an ochre-colored fence. The road finally narrowed, I slowed down and came to a halt at a doorway cut into the wall. A white cross had been painted in its middle.

"This is it. Don't expect much. Except that after the Holy Family and one or two saints, they may worship your wife next."

Ronald looked shocked.

"Oh, yes. They're all admiration, believe me. Admiration and gratitude. Well, they should be—everyone is."

We were standing in front of the door and I pulled a rope that sounded a bell in the corridor beyond the wall. A young boy opened the door. He recognized me and let me go first along the corridor. I found my way to what Father Jovet called his *salon*. It was a small room with one table covered by an oil cloth. Several straightback chairs were around the walls and on one of the walls there was a plaster-of-paris Virgin Mary, painted its inevitable blue. A short heavyset priest named Father Jean came in and looked very directly at Ronald.

"*C'est le monsieur du docteur?*"

He grinned out the question.

"*Oui. . . . Père Jean*," I said to Ronald, gesturing to the priest. They shook hands and when Father Jean's hand became free, he blessed Ronald, making the sign of the cross in front of Ronald's wide eyes. I was a little surprised myself. He and I then began carrying on our usually voluble and, for me, inaccurate conversation in French. For some reason I always got involved in a stream of facetious comments that seemed to convulse that good-humored priest. He kept shaking a finger at me, as if I had to be constantly scolded for one thing or another. I could tell from the way Ronald watched us that he didn't expect this kind of nonsense, lightheartedness, in a Roman Catholic mission. But it ended quickly when Father Jovet appeared, standing at the entrance to the room, pausing briefly—something he always did when he entered a room, as if to give you an opportunity to prepare yourself for his entrance. As usual he carried a grave smile on his lips. He was a gray-looking man, thin, angular. I once told him he looked like François Mauriac. It pleased him, not because Mauriac was a Nobel laureate but because he was such a good Catholic. He looked at Father Jean and myself, making sure we understood that his eyes had bestowed their recognition on us, then he came forward, holding out his hand to Ronald, speaking in his heavily accented English.

"Mr. Keane?"

His body gave a very slight suggestion of a bow as he shook Ronald's hand.

"We cannot tell you what a pleasure it is to make the acquaintance of the husband of our good, our very good and brave, untiring *docteur*."

It sounded eloquent, gracious and it was embarrassing to Ronald. But at least Ronald didn't have to suffer another blessing. Father Jovet wasn't spontaneous like Father Jean. He was a sincere enough man but he was a professional. A man who knew his craft. And his craft was religion. I've concealed a smile of sneaking admiration more than once for his indefatigable style. He had given up the world, as all Frenchmen consider they have done when they've given up France, whether they're priests or not; in addition, I

126

suspected that he knew the exact moment at which he had given it up. A lesser man would have periodically reminded God of the date. He was sometimes engaging and always incorrigible. For different reasons, in entirely different ways, he and I survived well as foreigners in Ndami. I think we respected each other's ability to do this. Had I been a rabbi—making us a little competitive—it probably would have become a matter of pride with us who lasted the longest, which of us would stand over the grave of the other, sadly, but smiling thinly. His gray-green eyes held Ronald in a long look of appraisal, for he was a man whose business was forming spiritual judgments. Judgments of others. Just at the moment when Ronald might have shifted from one foot to the other with uneasiness, he made an affable but dignified gesture for us all to sit down. Father Jean didn't take the gesture literally—he stood behind Father Jovet's chair with his hands clasped in front of him.

"I've ordered some tea, properly boiled. Mr. Cline-mark prefers cognac, I know."

He directed that quiet and misleading remark to Ronald and Ronald looked at me wonderingly.

"But I am afraid I cannot offer him that."

Then he smiled at me. I always detected a hint of malice in his eyes when he said things like that. He knew I disagreed with his proselytizing and he suspected that I considered him the father of all paternalism. He was right, I did.

"You speak, *mon pére*, as if I were a confirmed drunkard."

He didn't answer me. He confided to Ronald smilingly, "We make allowances for Mr. Clinemark because twice when we had no funds and did not know how we were going to feed the children who depend on us, he came to our rescue."

The boy who had opened the door came in with a tray bearing three cups, not four. Father Jean excused himself and went out with the young black convert. We talked of commonplace things: how long Ronald had been in Africa, what he thought of the climate, how he was managing in Ndami with his wife so busy and away most of the time. It was trivial, friendly, and marked by Father Jovet's cool courtesy; and it lasted until we drained our cups of flat, weak tea. Then the priest turned to me and spoke as if I were some sort of intercessor between him and Ronald.

"If Mr. Keane would like to see the buildings now, I would be glad to show them to him."

We stood up.

Father Jovet put his deprecating smile on and turned it toward Ronald.

"I regret that you should have to see our mission house when everything is in upheaval and disorder. There is too much work to do and too few of us to do it. Colonel Sada has insisted that we put our infirmary at the disposal of his sick soldiers as well as the critically ill, so our *refectoire* has also been turned into an infirmary. We are using all available space for the afflicted, though we continue to care for our children."

He let Ronald pass out of the room first. We walked along a corridor that valiantly strived to be white, going first into a room where young boys were making baskets. They all stood up as we entered and Father Jovet picked up specimens of their work, showing them to Ronald.

"We keep on with our little activities because it takes their minds off the danger around us. We like to think that our trust in God and the peace which comes from it is taken into the homes of the boys when they leave us each afternoon."

"It's a school?" Ronald inquired politely.

"Such as it is." The familiar sad smile came to Father Jovet's face. "But not much of a one these days."

"Still," I said, "give us the child until he is six and you may have him everafter."

Father Jovet and I exchanged thin smiles. We were accustomed to throwing harmless barbs at one another. He leaned toward Ronald to make a show of speaking confidentially to him.

"More than Mr. Clinemark's palate has been ruined by African cooking."

Ronald looked at me. He had caught the reference to food and I couldn't have been more pleased. I almost wanted to say *See?* as we went into another room where girls, younger than the boys, were sewing; being instructed and supervised by two Ndami women. These girls didn't rise or interrupt their work and we passed right through the room into a third where very young children were playing. None of them could have been over five years old. The room wasn't only crowded, it was overcrowded, and noisy, chaotic. One priest was there and two women. Not yet taught the restraint the others had acquired, the children flocked around Father Jovet, grabbing his trouser legs or reaching for his hands. Now the smile that lit up his face was warm, spontaneous, real. And he fondled them, stroking their heads as he spoke to them. It was impossible not to like him at such a moment. Yet I never understood why he drilled out the spontaneous affection he inspired in them within two years' time.

"You can see that we are caring for more than usual," he said, continuing to address himself to Ronald as if Ronald were a school inspector. "Not only those where the mother has died through childbirth or disease, but where they are healthy. They think their young ones will be safer here from the cholera. It's not true, but they beg and beg until I relent." He shrugged at his helplessness, knowing I would appreciate his next remark more than Ronald would: "I must learn some discipline." He used a gentle force to free himself of the clinging children and we went out through a corridor leading to the inner courtyard where the moans of the cholera victims reached our ears.

Just as they did Father Jovet said over his shoulder to Ronald, "It's in the nursery that the *docteur* relaxes when she is with us. I think your wife goes there even when she doesn't need to—she loves children so. Yesterday I had to tell her not to exhaust herself playing with them, for she could do it for hours and hours. When they cry she has only to pick them up and she makes them comfortable, instantly, instantly."

I think even I was surprised. At what? . . . Whatever it was, Ronald was, too. He looked at me as if he expected me to confirm what Father Jovet had said.

"The nursery?"

I shrugged.

We suddenly had to sidestep two oblong shapes lying side by side, wrapped in muslin.

"We are short of beds. The moment someone dies, we have to bundle them out here like this in order to make room for another." Father Jovet turned to me. "Can you bury them for us?"

"The trunk of my car is very small," I said. "But I'll go around to the district offices when we leave and get a lorry from Embu."

"Of course. A lorry is more convenient."

As we stepped into a shaded entrance a door opened and Father Paul came into the corridor, out of sorts. His head lifted high when he saw us. Something was clearly wrong from his point of view but Father Jovet didn't seem to notice it.

"Is *docteur* Keane in there?" he asked the priest.

Father Paul came forward hurriedly, drew him close to him and whispered something. Father Jovet pulled back and the other priest turned around and started for a door up the corridor. Whatever was going on we weren't about to learn for Father Jovet faced us with his hands gripped together in a priestly clasp.

"No, he says the *docteur* is not here. She is gone to

130

one of the wells and will be back later. Did you know that four of the wells are now clear? We have pure water from four wells for our unhappy city?" He smiled at Ronald serenely, expecting some response. Ronald had nothing to say about this accomplishment and Father Jovet pointed to the door from which Father Paul had emerged. "There is no need to go inside and look upon what suffering is there, or to our *refectoire* where even more bodies lie side by side, waiting for the mercy and the judgment of God. But"—he smiled with restraint and the facial muscles at the right side of his mouth quivered—"I will show you our chapel."

As he turned, Father Paul came out of the room he had just gone into. He passed us hurriedly, returning to the infirmary. I knew he was breaking the priests' custom of more peaceful days, which was to bow slightly, especially if Father Jovet was present, or speak some pleasantry. He certainly knew who Ronald was. Or if he didn't, he would have guessed and guessed correctly. Under ordinary circumstances he would have said hello or Father Jovet would have introduced the two, so he must have been trying to save a life. And Father Jovet was obviously trying to preserve appearances or his own sense of decorum by pointing to the door Father Paul had just come through.

"That is our dispensary."

We went through another courtyard filled with sunlight and the heat of the day and paused outside the chapel door.

"Unhappily, our chapel is not what it once was."

We stood inside the doorway of a long room, lower than the ones we had been in but with the same whitewashed walls. Rows of benches without backrests created aisles wherever there was a break in them. The center aisle led to an altar on which another plaster image of the Virgin stood, painted not blue but in bright colors. Above and behind it was a crucifix. The stations of the cross had been painted by one of the priests, crudely. Midway in the ceiling there was a gaping hole where the plaster had fallen. A rotted beam protruded from it.

Father Jovet put on his gravest air.

"We have been unable to make the necessary repairs to our ceiling, so only we use the chapel. Our converts are deprived of worship here. If it were safe I'm sure we would be using it for another infirmary. The benches could be strapped together for beds. There would be places for another sixty persons."

He shrugged.

"Don't you have the timber to replace the beams?" asked Ronald.

"Only in the mines. For the mines there are such things, not for chapels."

"Father Jovet knows I can get them for him," I said to Ronald since it was to Ronald he had spoke. "He has only to ask."

And he was a man who hated to ask.

"We shall do it after the epidemic is over," he replied calmly. "Already we cannot manage to do all that we must. It is more important now to assist the *docteur*." He smiled. "You do not know how good and helpful your wife has been to us. I asked Mr. Clinemark to bring you here so I could tell you, for all of us. She has been sent by Heaven. We are glad that you came with her for it must be a great comfort to her to have you here."

Ronald, who had looked steadily at him until that point, lowered his eyes.

Father Jovet admonished, "You must take care of her and not let her work too hard. When she returns home tonight, do something that will please her. You must look after her for all our sakes."

Even though Father Jovet smiled and Ronald nodded, it was obvious that Ronald wished a hole would open in the floor and swallow him up. His discomfort was total, complete.

I said, "We'll all look after her."

"Of course. Since we have ended our little tour of our mission here, I would like to remain behind and pray for her. She needs all our prayers. Will you make allowances for me if I ask you to find your way out?"

"I know the way," I said.

He extended his hand to Ronald.

"At a happier time we shall visit again, together with your wife, the *docteur*."

He gave a slight bow and we left him standing in the chapel.

As soon as we stepped into the sunlight of the court-yard Ronald asked me, "What are the mines?"

I was surprised he didn't know, probably because I was connected with them.

"The Continental, although the name's going to be changed. I'm the last white man to monitor what's left of the private interests. They're being nationalized. My house on the hill across from yours belongs to them."

"What do you mine?"

"Gold."

"Gold?"

He said the word the way everyone did: impressed by it.

"There's not much left. In fact, it won't be operating at all in a few years—it won't be worth it. But they didn't call the southern coast the 'Gold Coast' for nothing . . . although there was more gold in black skins than we ever had in the ground up here. I should go there to pick up some ledgers. Would you like to ride out? . . . As a matter of fact, there's something I'd like to show you."

"All right."

We walked across the road to my car.

"What did you think of Father Jovet?"

He seemed to think about what he thought but then all he said was, "He seems to be a nice man."

133

That isn't what I had in mind but I don't know how Ronald could have known what I had in mind when I asked him just that. I really was wondering how Father Jovet had made him feel when he said he should take care of Nancy, be a comfort to her and that she needed our prayers.

"What do you want to show me?"

"Not the mines—we can't go in them anyway. They're too hot. The view. The river bends not far from there and the land drops off, straight down. The desert starts to the north. You can look at it from up there.

We were silent. It was about five miles to the mines, and I thought I felt a slight tension rise up, an expectation, the kind that does when you imagine someone has something on his mind that he's afraid to reveal. I tried to do away with it by pointing to an old poster on the side of a general store. It showed Olympic winners holding up their medals.

"Look," I said, "that's Ndami gold they've got in their hands." I shook my head. "I used to think it was the fault of London and Zurich, our fault—the West's. The fault of capitalism and our colonialist policies—"

"What is?"

He almost interrupted. And I found myself looking at him in a surprised way. I had such fixed ideas about the gold industry that I had almost forgot everyone didn't have them.

"The madness there is whenever anyone agrees on the value of one thing. Like gold, the gold standard . . . even here, having it is the best thing that can happen to you. When London wasn't any more than a village, the court crier for the king of the Ashanti was wearing a gold cap. But if you can't wear a gold cap the next best thing is to be able to shape it. For centuries the most respected artisans in this part of Africa were the goldsmiths. And if you can't work with it, you work for it, you go down into the mines: that's next in the order of prestige. And I mean *prestige*. Any man in Ndami would rather work in the mines than anywhere else. They actually compete with one another to work in that sweat box—and not because the white man says *Get it for me*. The older men keep in condition like athletes just so they can stay on. There's a fellow named Oyebisi who's famous because he's been down in the mines for more than twenty-five years. He's a kind of folk hero. If you stayed around long enough and knew the language, you'd hear them singing ballads about him, the way he brings up the sacred and precious metal year after year. After twenty-five years you know how much he's getting? Twenty-one dollars a week—but he thinks it's a privilege. It is, by God. Since everyone agrees on the value of it, he never has to doubt the usefulness of what he's doing. He's a real snob, Oyebisi is—he walks around the markets like a pigeon in mating season, his chest way out. Have you known people who never doubt the usefulness of what they're doing? Or the usefulness of what they are? . . . You can't live with them. And it all comes when you agree on the value of any one thing. Who's ever heard of a *silver* opportunity? Or a 'heart of copper'? It's the heart of gold you've got to have, the golden opportunity, being worth your weight in it, or 'as good as gold.' Those aren't just words, damnit. The world's faith is in metal instead of wool or milk, where it should be. Do you know that every morning in London the leaders of five banks get together, match their buy and sell orders on gold, and announce the gold standard for the day? . . . It's like taking a pulse. How does the world feel about gold this morning? How the world feels about the daily terrorism in South Africa, or the daily malaria rate, isn't measured because the standard by which we judge everything—including the health of nations—isn't brutality or malaria, but gold. It's a kind of madness or insanity. I'll be glad when the whole operation shuts down."

Would I really? I was going to be out of a job.

I drove into the mining compound's scattered assortment of shacks and buildings, pulled close to the building where my office was, and pointed off.

"You can walk down to a ledge right by that rock. I'll meet you there."

It was one of my rituals to do what I was asking him, or telling him, to do: periodically turn aside from the outbuildings of the mine and walk toward the desert. Did I really expect him to take pleasure in one of my necessities? I believe I thought so. For the plateau that the mine was situated on was the highest point in the surrounding land, eight miles from the river and irrigation canals that make Ndami possible. The irregular carpet of green vegetation that runs over the earth comes to an end, an end so final and absolute that it forces you to think about it if you look at it long enough. In one slow turn of the head from south to north, the color of the land goes from green to ochre to yellow to an ashen white. At the very edge of the plateau you can find your way down among the rocks to several ledges until you're cut off from the view behind you. The rock forms a wall against your back. It's possible to sit there and have a still-hot wind sit down with you as you face the desert beyond. Desert insects move at your feet across the rocks. There are lizards with heads of brilliant blue. The segments of skin on their heads shine in the sun like gems. And on rare days a faint sound can sometimes reach your ear. For ten or fifteen miles north, too far for the eye to see in the quivering heat waves, is one of the oldest caravan routes in the world. When the camels are on it one can hear the striking of their bells. . . . This is where I joined Ronald in a few minutes. He was seated, clasping his knees, looking out. And he didn't turn his head even though I knew he could hear me climbing down to where he was. He was preparing himself to say what I was at that moment totally unprepared for.

"You asked if we were going to stay on here."

I sat down next to him and nodded without knowing whether he saw me nod.

"Do you think we should?"

I looked at him. Then I looked out at the hazy desert below and beyond, as if the question or the answer could be seen out there. I shrugged. I even laughed a bit. For I knew I wouldn't touch a question like that with a ten-foot pole, not for someone else.

"If you did, it would only be a question of for how long. We need a doctor, of course. We need several, even without an epidemic."

He looked at me and then he looked out again, this time with a difference. In my mind there wasn't a doubt that the stare in his eyes to the north came from realizing that he wasn't needed. Only Nancy was.

"I'd like to tell you why I came here."

I looked at him. He must have seen my head turn. Perhaps he waited for me to say *All right* or something like that. When I didn't he turned to see if it *was* all right and when he did I never saw anyone who wanted to tell anyone anything less than he did. Still, he did. And from the start I knew that he didn't say anything freely. He was expecting, wanting something in return. And I even think I knew what that was, too: information about Vivian. Knowledge that I didn't have, or, having it, would have never given, probably. Nevertheless we sat there for almost two leisurely hours as I listened to him start backwards, beginning with why he had come to Ndami, gradually moving into how. At first he left no room for any interpretation other than that he had been blackmailed, forced. He sounded as if he needed sympathy but I imagine he needed judgment even more. I mean, specifically—spelled right out. For isn't sympathy judgment? Judgment on your behalf? And if not

137

on your behalf then against you. Getting the matter settled, that's all that counts. Lining up the debts and the debtors. I would say that he very definitely went from being acted against to stumbling his way through his own actions, getting more hesitant as he stepped on each one again, wobbly stones in a stream he shouldn't have crossed. Or have gotten stranded in, bewildered by the current. His hesitation told me he was guilty, had some kind of conscience; for the guilty are always uncertain. The condemned are filled with security, strong in the knowledge that they're standing on the solid rock of their own damnation. But he was only guilty, looking around for judgment with the abject look of a beggar, hoping for a light sentence. How he reminded me of what we all are.

"Is this supposed to be able to help me answer whether you should stay on here?"

That was disingenuous. He didn't have to answer and he didn't. I knew that he wanted to know whether Vivian was real. Adequate. That the cause was equal to all the effects. But that was hard to answer, however much I felt that Vivian was real in whatever she was. Because she had the same effect on everyone that she had on Ronald, and I don't think he was ready to be told that: to hear that she wasn't just a person who existed for him, but that she was a type that existed for everyone, for Everyman. Isn't the strictly human aspect of love, isn't intimacy born when we see something in another that no one else sees? Or that others, seeing it, neglect? We're lucky, and answer our luck with love, if we can find one person who is able to show us to ourselves: honestly, truly. Or as truly as the human heart can. But Ronald—whatever his hopes were for the effect that he might have on Vivian—would have to be disappointed. For he couldn't show Vivian to herself in a unique way, in any personal way. All men reflected her equally, in the same way. And he didn't want to know that. And if I told him, he would believe something about her that I didn't think was true: that in her emotions she was false. Not sincere.

"You have to understand Vivian," I said. And I believe I regretted having said it. It implied that I did. "I've seen more beautiful women than Vivian—"

He looked at me quickly enough not to make me doubt myself but to make me pause. I suppose he thought I was going to run her down or at least a little sideways.

"Haven't you?"

He shrugged.

Well, I had. I almost wanted to shrug in return. I remembered coming right there, to that very place, and sitting for hours when I had received word that Ericka had taken her life. I watched the sun go down until its slant threw crystal streams across the desert. I wouldn't have minded if they had blinded me and I had never seen anything else again. I felt that a kind of permanent night had come because I would never see her beauty again.

I threw out a hand toward what was in front of us.

"That's beautiful, isn't it? Really beautiful? Doesn't it have the lure of this world? . . . I think it does. It has it for me, anyway. It's physical, it touches my eyes, it puts a kind of longing into me—it assaults my senses even though it doesn't move. No?" He didn't answer, he just looked at it. "I knew someone beautiful who was as silent and as motionless as that. Sometimes I would say, 'What?' to her after an hour of silence, just as if she had said something and I hadn't caught it . . . to, to . . . well, she existed like that"—I threw out my hand again—"but I wanted to end her silence because even though she was breathing, and I knew she was, I wanted to bring her to life. . . . That sounds ridiculous. She was alive so how could I bring her to life?" I don't know whether Ronald knew I was questioning my own words. Talking out loud to myself. "For some reason I got taken to the Folies-Bergère when I was about fifteen," I said, more directly to him. "It was something to see all that nudity, all that nakedness. Have you ever been there? All those faultlessly formed breasts, those perfectly proportioned lengthy legs—beautiful, beautiful women. I guess. But they just couldn't *look*, do you know what I mean? All that bodily beauty just couldn't stand there, it just couldn't look, it had to move. It had to run around and jump, it had to kind of dance. It was ridiculous." And I felt ridiculous trying to discover whatever it was I was trying to say. "That's what Vivian's all about." I almost faltered before his shocked look. "No, no, listen . . . it's not how her body looks, it's what it does. It's always going somewhere, it's always doing something, it never trips on a rug, it never struggles to get out of a chair. *Prowess*, that's what she's got, bodily prowess, not just bodily beauty. You know what I'm talking about. You should. You told me about the first time you went to Hamsun's Bay. To push yourself off a rock and go straight down a cliff into the water is what a seal does, not what a human body does . . . or a pelican does it, or some other thing. But when a human body does it, does something it isn't supposed to do, or what other bodies can't do, when it"—my hand went out again—"when it has something more than the beauty of that desert, when it overcomes what your body couldn't overcome, and with ease, *ease!* When it's got agility, prowess—"

I stopped.

"Forget it."

I said it abruptly, suddenly. He looked at me as if something he had done, some gesture or the way he might not have been paying attention, had turned me off.

"I can't put it together. In words. I'm sorry."

How could I tell him that even though I thought he and I were night and day, black and white, as different as any two men could be, Vivian had the same effect on me that she had on him? He wouldn't have stood for that. He would have denied it up and down even though I would have tried to explain that I just didn't do anything about the effect, that's all. It was possible to overestimate the importance of Vivian's bodily looks but you couldn't overestimate the importance of her bodily presence. She was undeniably, unavoidably there—*there*. She and her body presented themselves to other human beings the way a body on the stage presents itself to an audience when the curtain goes up. You didn't have to approach her on tiptoe to see if her beauty was alive. She was a body in action. You didn't have to whisper *What?* to see if she was drawing breath. What fascinated everyone was not how her body looked but what it did, even though it looked good. Ericka looked better to me, far better; I think she would to anyone. I imagine anyone who compared her with Vivian would say, "Now *that's* beauty." For beauty can be silent, motionless, as still as the desert, without action, seemingly without life. Beauty can have just a body. But Vivian had that agility which overcomes the difficulty we all feel in having a body. In our physical dis-ease we observed her ease with a kind of fascinated awe. Prowess is action, prowess is life, and what we need is life. Her legs not only came in a shape to be admired, they were filled with a movement which we envied.

"Vivian affects a lot of people the same way. She can't help it. It isn't her fault."

I smiled.

"It seems that it should be someone's fault because it creates a little chaos every now and then, but—"

I shrugged and stood up, to his surprise. Because I was stopped I thought we should stop, and I would have said so if something else hadn't surprised him more.

"What's that?"

"What?"

I actually hadn't heard anything.

"I hear something."

I would have thought my ear would have picked it up

first: that faint tinkle on the wind. It's always wonderful. I smiled and said, "Camel bells. They're out there on the caravan routes . . . somewhere." I pointed a finger into the nothingness to the north. We listened and I got pleasure from the look on his face. "It's hard to believe, isn't it? It's like being becalmed at sea and swearing you can hear the bells from some lost Atlantis."

We started up the rocks toward my car.

"Can you come for dinner tonight?"

He didn't ask me casually; he asked worriedly. I don't imagine he wanted me to get away, at least not yet.

"All right."

I accepted readily: I wanted to see Nancy again.

We could see the Dalaga River bending its way below, and the smoke and haze that always seemed to hover in the air above Ndami. It was just midday and a *muezzin* pierced the air from one of the minarets on the outskirts of the city.

Allah akbar! . . . Allah akbar!

14

I WANTED TO SEE NANCY AGAIN? I see her twice: that night and now when I remember her again. I went to dinner once and find that I don't want to walk into the dining room again. Or perhaps I would prefer to forget the first time and live with only what I can now visualize. For it's natural for me to put eyes into my head that weren't there then . . . to see anew, to see afresh. I don't see Nancy's plainness tonight, I don't see her bodily looks at all. What I see is the truth or the half-truth in what I said to Ronald. I see her immobility. Perhaps her own self-judgments had made her decide that she would give as little movement as possible to the body she was bound to. Somewhere there was an energy in her, a fierce energy; but it was hidden. She concealed it behind the rock of that exterior which turned everyone away. Was disease her absolute? Her gold standard? She had decided that disease was what people hated, feared and wanted most to avoid. . . . That was clever of her. She had chosen to fight what she knew best: her own *dis*-ease. I said that when I first saw her she reminded me of someone who had been confined indoors, who had been sick and was convalescing; unsteady on her legs, uncertain in the movement of her limbs. *Ill*-at-ease, exactly. She too was one of those whom you leaned toward and said *What?*, not to hear her speak so much as to know whether she was alive, where she was living—since her bodily presence didn't mean she was in the same room with you. That's it, *where*. I never knew another person whose physical presence was such an absence as Nancy Keane's. And it wasn't an accident of birth, it wasn't a misfortune. It was an achievement.

Could she live anywhere?

I had thought about Ronald's question: *Do you think we should stay on here?* And I thought about it again as I walked to one of the windows in the dining room and looked out. For Ngolo had come to the door and let me in. Ronald and Nancy must have both been upstairs and I decided not to wait in McGowan's old receiving room. I couldn't help but answer Ronald's question to myself, particularly after he had told me much, already, about his personal circumstances. I didn't think that he should stay. What for? . . . And I couldn't see why Nancy would want him to. But she should. *Yes*, I thought. She could have used a place like Ndami to bury herself: in the open air, in the house where I stood. A place sealed off but where she could still come to life. She didn't need to seal herself in a laboratory in The Port. And she spoke French, for God's sake! Father Jovet would make a pediatrician of her, making her care for all the children in his school and orphanage. She'd love it. And because she could associate with the priests on a professional basis, I wouldn't have that nagging sense of being responsible for her, as I did for anyone whom Alan sent to Ndami. Which is exactly how I would have felt about Ronald had he stayed on.

"Hi."

Ronald came in from the kitchen, surprising me. And I didn't have a chance to say hello before Nancy came in from the hallway, surprising both of us. There was a third surprise: when she saw me. But Ronald assured her that it was all right for me to be there.

"I told Mboye we would be three for dinner."

He obviously hadn't told her.

I don't suppose it would have made any difference if he had. For she was probably more indifferent to her surroundings than she had ever been—withdrawn, impassive. And with every reason to be, if she needed a reason. She was overworked. She was pale and her hair looked unwashed, unkempt; that may have been the most physically noticeable thing about her. It was matted into strands about her ears. Her skin was dry; her lower lip had several deep cracks in it. Small as she was, she looked even smaller. Her shoulders looked like they were trying to disappear beneath her thin dress. And she didn't have that look of intensity in her eyes even though she was surprised to find me there and was looking at me, adjusting to my presence. I tried to help her by saying something.

"We haven't seen each other but I've been in touch with Embu and Father Jovet, keeping track of you." I smiled. "I know what you've been doing—and accomplishing. It's remarkable."

She wasn't looking at me any longer. And that avoidance always had the same effect: you didn't know whether she wasn't listening; and if she wasn't listening, there you were—reaching out to her with words but not touching her. The result was that I tried harder and normal congratulations became praise.

"You're saving the city. No one could have done more, no one . . . or have done it any better."

She didn't say thank you. She cleared her throat softly and sat down. We followed her, unfolding our napkins, waiting stiffly, uncomfortably, for Mboye to come in with the first course. I suppose it was as plain as the plague that she didn't need compliments or encouragement or cheering up, nothing social or human; just sleep—hours of it, days of it. Physical rest. Ronald I didn't like, for the moment. He was self-conscious and doing his best to make me the same way. He kept looking at me in a manner that suggested he and I had formed some kind of partnership. Now that he had given me knowledge I was bound to offer him something in return. We were both looking at Nancy with the same set of facts, or from his experience. There was a two-against-one air about him. I had the feeling that he was watching me and saying to himself *So what do you think?* All that did was make me turn directly to Nancy and try to ignore him. What I said must have surprised him a little.

"There's a place for you here, you know, after the epidemic is over."

Since Mboye now came in with three bowls of rice soup, it might have been natural or seemed natural for Nancy to wait to reply. Or show some sign of response. But when our bowls were set in front of us and Mboye left she didn't look at me. She lifted her spoon instead of her eyes. So Ronald and I did, too.

"I'm sure you could have this house permanently, if you wanted it. And I've been thinking about your facility in French. You and Father Jovet could set up a health

145

program for the children. We could use a little preventive medicine around here."

Her impassiveness didn't anger me but it may have set one or two of my nerves vibrating just a little bit. I didn't expect conversation—assent, enthusiasm, even curiosity; but I at least expected her to look up from her plate. It was a kind of outrage that she didn't. Not necessarily against me personally but against something. It was threatening. Not accepting her own existence, she didn't accept yours. There was a connection there somewhere. Because she didn't believe in her own existence she didn't recognize yours?

"Maybe we could get funds from Alan or the new government to build a real clinic."

"Build one?" interjected Ronald.

I didn't see the necessity in repeating *Yes* so I continued to her: "The usual difficulty in getting started—I mean, getting the people to trust you, which can take a while—is taken care of already. You're famous for the shows you put on at the wells." I smiled but got no smile, no recognition, in return. "And honored," I flattered. "How many wells are purified now?"

That she would not or could not answer that simple question seemed unreal.

"How many?"

I think I repeated it because I was bordering on an attitude that wasn't going to let her get away with it. The only sound any of us made was with our spoons, when they clicked against the sides of our bowls. I looked at Ronald, then at her.

"All ten?"

I knew that wasn't true. I asked it the way you played with a child, deliberately guessing wrong so you'll be corrected. Nancy cleared her throat and I looked at her expectantly.

"Only eight."

"Only?"

She began to cough. She lowered her spoon toward the bowl but it didn't get there before she let it fall, using her freed hand to help the other one cover her mouth with a napkin.

"Careful," I said.

Ronald and I both watched her. She coughed until her pale cheeks began to get red and her eyes brimmed with tears. There seemed to be nothing to do but wait and watch. Which was absurd—but true. At any other table, in any other household, someone would have got up and gone behind her, to stand there futilely perhaps, make meaningless gestures and speak meaningless words, but do something nevertheless. She finally stopped and when she did she leaned back in her chair, wiping the tears away from the corners of her eyes. Then she extended a hand toward the table and held onto it as if for support, breathing deeply.

"Can't you get some rest for a day? Stay in bed for the morning? I'll drive to Embu's in the morning and tell him you're not coming in until the afternoon."

She didn't look at me or answer. Her doubled up fist was pressed against her lips and she cleared her throat.

"I've been thinking that maybe I could help inoculate," said Ronald. I looked at him, wondering what had made him think that, and then I looked at Nancy. But she didn't make any response other than look down at the soup bowl that Mboye was just picking up to take away. Ronald looked at me, directly. He was about to justify himself to me rather than her by saying, "The priests have learned to do it, haven't they?"

They had.

"McGowan taught them."

"Why can't I?"

I thought Nancy was going to say something. She seemed to move.

"The serum's only an alkalide salt solution," Ronald said with a hint of a put-down in the way he said *only*. He must have picked that up in that book he had been reading the day I found him sitting in the sun. Naturally Nancy didn't answer him.

Mboye came in with a salad bowl. He set it down next to Nancy and I looked at it a second time to make sure I wasn't making a mistake about what I saw in it. Salad. But you didn't eat greens in a cholera epidemic, ever. I spoke to Mboye in his own dialect, sharply. He gave me a look that was old and familiar, hateful, cutting: that blank look of an African when a white man or woman makes a baseless accusation. He answered me calmly but when he did I nevertheless thought he was lying. Then Nancy picked up the salad bowl and began to help herself. Mboye gave me a look of vindication and walked out. I felt humiliated at the same time that I was dumbfounded, watching Nancy dip into the salad bowl. I had to watch her do it twice before I could find enough wits to say anything.

"What are you doing?"

She didn't answer, as usual—but this time I needed an answer.

"What are you doing?"

She continued to take more and then she pushed the bowl toward Ronald. She didn't pick it up and hand it to him, she shoved it at him across the table, aggressively. And Ronald immediately reached for the salad spoon.

"You haven't been eating uncooked vegetables? You haven't been eating salad?"

My voice was high.

"He likes it."

Nancy spoke quietly, unassertively. I looked at Ronald. He seemed nervous; his fingers were jumpy, his head was lowered. He was heaping salad onto his plate. What in God's name were they doing?

"You can't be serious! You know better than that—

148

boiled water, no fruit, no uncooked greens . . . never. Never! It's absolute in a cholera epidemic, absolute!"

"He insists that we eat some every night."

I looked at Nancy quickly, sternly—I hope, even menacingly; but quickly because she had spoken with that same detached, almost superior, tone in which she had said *He likes it.* Because I had taken my eyes off of him, Ronald, apparently, was able to speak.

"We've been inoculated."

"Yes," said Nancy, echoing him in a kind of toneless mockery. "Haven't you?" Her question wasn't sincere, I knew it wasn't. Not for one minute did she mean that therefore everything was all right: inoculation took care of it. They were what they had been the first night I met them—two people who couldn't untangle their arms from some hateful struggle.

"McGowan was inoculated! That didn't prevent him from dying!"

"That's right," said Nancy. "It's only an alkalide salt solution."

Her voice was still flat, toneless, without inflection. It made a horrifying sarcasm possible. But there was resignation in it, too. And today I hear conspiracy: a willed, macabre defeatism. I hear it, I can't prove it. I don't think I could handle, get over, the way they were ignoring me, putting my attitude as well as my protests aside. And they were doing it out of a perverse impulse, as well: they were being accused, challenged in what they knew was wrong, absolutely *knew*—and they were trying to defeat me not by answering me but by routinely continuing what they were doing, almost with an air of outraged innocence. But I didn't think it was going to go as far as it did. Nancy pressed a fork into her salad and started to bring the fork to her mouth. I looked at Ronald fast enough to see that he was surprised even though he hadn't stopped helping himself to what was in the bowl in front of him. Me? I? I didn't even think. Or my thinking on the whole matter was so clear, so unequivocal, that I just leaned forward, reached out and slapped the fork right out of Nancy's hand.

"Oww! Oh!"

It was a small scream followed by an even smaller moan. But she pulled her head back, jerked it. I didn't think the fork would go into her. A red spot appeared just above her lip on the right, and almost as soon as it did a trickle of blood came from the spot. I sat like a parent who's just struck out at a maliciously disobedient child with a high sense of justification, righteously, and has unwittingly drawn blood; injured an eye, split a lip, cracked a tooth. Suddenly the consequences of anger were out of proportion to its causes. I sat possessed by that mixture of guilt and injustice which made me want to shout at her *Now see what you've made me do!* I was startled, ashamed—angry, unnerved. That's why I *did* shout at her.

"You close the wells—you ring them with Sada's men —you don't trust the people with water—you don't trust them to boil it so you boil it for them—and then you come back here, close your doors, and, and do—*this!* This! Anything green is every bit as polluted, every bit as foul, as unboiled water! You'll be dead before the week's out!"

She did shrink back a little.

But I didn't: I glowered at Ronald.

"We'll bury both of you."

Then Nancy dabbed her napkin to her mouth. When she looked at it she sat forward. It was as if the sight of the red color gave her a whole new opinion of me, a murderous one. Her eyes flashed, her shoulders came up, her chin lifted. Her whole body was filled with life, ready for action.

"Sada needs to put a ring of men around this place, not the wells," I said.

"It's—it's my fault," fumbled Ronald.

"I don't care whose fault it is!"

Maybe I did.

"I started it," Ronald confessed.

"Yes, he started it. Tell him how you started it," said Nancy. "I told him not to—Mboye brought it in the very first night, and I told him he didn't know what he was doing by serving us salad."

"I had been drinking," Ronald protested . . . but it was a feeble protest.

"All he said was '*So! . . . So?*' "

I looked at Ronald. He tried to look down.

"He just kept piling it on his plate."

Ronald looked at her and said, "I thought that was the idea."

"The idea? What idea?" asked Nancy. She looked as if she was amazed.

"How was I supposed to know what you had inoculated me with?" Ronald's cheeks reddened even before he had finished with his question and gone on to defend it. "For all I knew, you could have been shooting some kind of poison in me." His flush was the flush that came with the unwitting, unwilling confession of his paranoia, his stupidity. His shoulders sagged. His neck began sinking into his body as it had in the car the other day. "I thought you were deliberately—deliberately exposing me to, to danger —to disease. Isn't that what you were trying to do? Isn't that what you wanted in making me come here?"

Nancy sat motionlessly. The forward-leaning preparedness had gone of out of her body. The sternness left her narrow set eyes.

Ronald spoke again.

"I'd joined her, I had come along—that's what she wanted. I wanted her to join *me*."

I looked at him. When I did his eyes fell to his plate.

"Join you?" I said. "For God's sake, in what?"

"He began eating it," Nancy said tremulously. When I looked at her a kind of fright had taken hold her eyes.

"*He* began stuffing it into his mouth"—she paled—"he was going to eat *all* of it. He said if I didn't eat some of it, he was going to eat all of it."

I looked at him, as if in search of proof . . . Was it true? Was that it?

Pathetically, convictionlessly, he repeated: "We had been inoculated."

"I thought," said Nancy, on the verge of tears, "I thought that if I ate half of it, he'd have—we've each have less chance of contracting, of—"

She didn't finish.

She had shared it to save him from the effects of eating all of it? . . . As I was looking at him—to see if he was worth it?—I heard her fork strike her plate. Ronald almost stood up, for his eyes were on her. Nancy, on the verge of whimpering, was eating the salad again.

"So—so that's why we do it."

But she didn't want to be doing it this time. I didn't even decide one way or another if that was true, if I was believing what I saw or wasn't. She was just re-enacting their morbid ritual with martyred resignation, and when I reached for her hand my fingers didn't come within a foot of hers. But that was close enough to make the fork fall from her hand. It struck the side of her plate with a sharp ring and was like a summons that made her stand up. She turned quickly and started out of the room. But there was nothing decisive about it. It was only necessary. For she was going to cry.

I didn't expect Ronald to start after her but I looked at him as if I did.

"It's a suicide pact! That's what it is—you've forced her into a suicide pact."

"That's not the way it happened at all!"

"She's lying?"

He didn't answer.

"I didn't hear you protest."

The only sound that came from him was a small clicking one. It was the first time I noticed his habit of picking at the split nail on his thumb.

"No, she isn't lying but, but that's not how it was."

"Oh," I said sarcastically. "Those are the facts—somehow they just aren't the truth, eh?"

Click . . . *click* . . . was his only response. He didn't look up. He sat there with a genuine look of suffering about him: the suffering of not only the misunderstood but the misunderstood guilty.

"Well, I want to see this city breathe normally again, that's all. I can't give a damn what the two of you"—I seemed to need to prove that I didn't give a damn by pushing my plate away from me and standing up—"do to each other. I don't care who joined whom or who started what, you had your reasons for coming here, your motives. Dying people only have one motive—to stay alive. Usually. That's been our motive around here for some time, and as long as your wife cures this city I don't need any more facts about anything. When you both leave you'll take your reasons for coming here back with you. And I'll stay behind with mine."

I gave him a chance to say something. To change my posture if not my mind, I might have sat down again. Possibly. But he just stared in front of himself, miserably and I suppose self-pityingly, giving as his answer to everything that small sound . . . *click* . . . *click* . . . *click*.

15

I WENT STRAIGHT TO MAROC Nè-gre—"Black Morocco's," a high-life place, and joined a group of young men and women who seemed to be celebrating the decline in the death rate. What I did was lose myself in their language. Life doesn't have a different pulse in Africa. The human heart has the same beat; it thumps out the same music. What life's got is a different language. . . . Walking out of the old mission house didn't free me from what had happened there. My mind was left traveling along the lines that the English language laid out in front of me, which is a mental prison: pacing one-two-three down its narrow syntactical corridor of subject-verb-object. I've learned a lot of things in Africa and one of them is that you can only travel where a language lets you. You go where it takes you. When I went from the old mission house to Maroc Nègre I just didn't go from one noise system to another, I went to a place where I had to change my way of thinking, the way I looked at the world. Granted, that way was confining, too. So I may have just gone from one linguistic prison to another when I stepped out of English into an offshoot of Yoruba but it was freedom to me. However narrowly I had to travel along the lines a different language laid down in front of me, that path led me away from Ronald and Nancy Keane for four wonderful hours. And while it did Ronald traveled to the Catholic mission to see Father Jovet, which is something I heard about both in English and in French. Ronald's English version was a little different than Father Jovet's French version but not all that different, for the two languages have all those Latin words in common and we know how the Normans invaded not only England but English. Still, two versions rather than one. It is when I imagine Father Jovet exercising his cool and superb control that I get the most vivid image of their encounter.

Shortly after I left him Ronald walked out, aimlessly, into the city. The idea of seeing Father Jovet came gradually, he said. He saw a poster at a crossing at two of the roads, identical to one he had seen the day he had been with me, and he started to follow the lane that curved toward the Mwase district. Soon he was no longer aimless but striding with purpose. The white cross which marked the door to the Catholic mission made him a bit nervous, but he pulled the cord which rang the bell inside resolutely. Again the door was opened by an Ndami boy and Ronald had to simply say, "Father Jovet . . . Father Jovet" since he didn't speak French or Yoruba. And he was led to the same room where we had sat and had tea. He waited there patiently, uneasily. When Father Jovet appeared he didn't seem surprised at all to see Ronald. He seemed to act as if it was the most natural thing in the world for Ronald to return to the mission, and at that hour. There wasn't a look of concern on his face. His eyebrows weren't even raised in expectancy. He merely smiled, kindly.

"How good of you to come back to see me. I have just been thinking about you and your wife."

Ronald was unprepared to be treated as a husband.

"Thank you," he mumbled.

"I shall pray for the *docteur* continually, and with your permission, I shall pray for you."

Ronald was too embarrassed to respond.

"What I came to see you about, what I came to talk about, was whether I could repair your chapel for you."

Now Father Jovet couldn't respond. He was too surprised.

"Didn't you," asked Ronald, "didn't you say sixty more people could be cared for if the chapel could be used?"

"I did. Yes, that's true, but—"

"It can be fixed. I can do it easily. My father owns a small construction company where I was born, and I've worked with him since I was a kid. I know just what needs to be done to your chapel, I'm"—his self-advertisements were making him more excited that he had meant to become, and he lowered his voice, trying to finish more modestly—"a carpenter, a good carpenter."

I can imagine the sagacious look that the priest gave Ronald.

"Mr. Keane, you need not feel that you must do something because these are difficult times for us. Life"—Father Jovet's sad smile appeared—"life is difficult at any time."

Ronald lifted his hands. They were open, empty and ready.

"I have nothing else to do."

"You have your wife to look after, the *docteur*. She is very precious to all of us. Keep your strength, reserve it, until the time she must call upon it."

Must? . . . However strange the words were they didn't strike Ronald as being strange. They just seemed to be off the point. He couldn't conceive of a time when Nancy would have to "call upon his strength." He had no strength she needed. He had no strength anyone needed. He had, so far as he knew, no strength at all. What he was offering Father Jovet at that moment was an ability, one that would enable him to play a small role; not the role of husband which he was incapable of playing.

"I can see that some timbers are needed to replace the rotten ones, but not much else—only some mortar. If I could get right at it, it wouldn't take me any time at all to have it fixed up again."

He didn't mean to sound boastful, just practical.

156

Whatever he sounded like to Father Jovet drew a charitable smile.

"The surroundings here are not what you may think, Mr. Keane, not even after your little visit. There is much unpleasantness and death—"

"But the chapel is way off from the rest of the rooms."

"Even now," said the priest steadily, "Father Jude has fallen very ill. I'm sure that you are very anxious to help us, and you are very good and brave to be willing to be surrounded by such sickness. But it is not fearlessness that conquers these things, only faith."

Naturally Ronald wanted to talk about the ceiling, not faith. It needed a workman to repair it, not a believer. But Father Jovet—often perceptive, always inflexible—was a hard one to deal with. A person's spirit meant nothing to him, even though it would mean a lot to a previously spiritless individual. Only the Spirit of God working through that person interested Father Jovet. He'd be suspicious of anyone who suddenly appeared with an offer of help, even if the offer held out the promise of tangible good. There was an atmosphere inside that mission—Catholic, French, Christian—that he regarded as more vital than anything. Not that he wasn't interested in saving the lives of others or attending to their death. But he would prefer that they died at the hand of a patient saint rather than be saved at the hand of a sudden and questionable volunteer. To Ronald, of course, there was nothing questionable about fixing a ceiling that was falling in. And he put the question in the form of a puzzled look on his face, to which Father Jovet attempted to reply.

"I am touched by your offer, Mr. Keane, moved, and I will pray about it. But it is not enough for us to want what we want, to be able to want it, in the modern fashion. What concerns God's Kingdom must be asked for by Him, not ourselves. May I tell you that when I was a boy I wanted to be a great violinist? I worked very hard to become one, and I was very capable, I think. But the violin did not want what I wanted! I assaulted the poor instrument with my whole heart, as well as with bow and fingers. I kept summoning it, calling upon it to sing at my touch, but however much I called, it wouldn't. I now know that it was God's wisdom teaching me the difference between what I, a glory-seeking boy, wanted for my life, and what was needed in my life. . . . I also want the chapel ceiling repaired, Mr. Keane, but I must seek guidance whether that it is what is needed at the moment. Please understand that I am not rejecting your offer. I only need a little time to learn if God has sent you to work among us, as He has sent your wife to heal the sick among us. We are called to our work, especially here, within these walls. These walls have chosen us, we did not choose them."

Father Jovet gestured to the walls of the room in which they sat. The smile of deprecation assumed control of his face and Ronald felt not only embarrassed; he felt humiliated for his presumption. I wonder if he was forgetful or mindful that he had been chosen not by walls but by a pair of moving hands, by beauty, and that he had rapidly expected to be chosen by other forces in life not very long ago? In any case he should have understood the position of a man like Father Jovet, and gone off wondering about his touching story of the boy violinist.

What he did immediately was to stand up and stammer.

"I—I only wanted to be helpful."

"Of course, of course, naturally . . . and who knows? Perhaps you will be," said Father Jovet cheerfully. "But since we need Mr. Clinemark's assistance with procuring the necessary timbers, we must wait and consult him in any case."

Ronald's face lit up. He took, or mistook, this for a favorable sign.

"Shall I talk to him then? Is it all right if I ask about getting timbers from the mine?"

Father Jovet was not accustomed to this kind of insistence, even though it came in a questioning form. His restraint was in his smile and his smile was at the impetuousness of a child. He played with Ronald.

"Well, if you wish. You may talk to him if you wish."

Ronald didn't know that he was supposed to abandon his wish and he came straight to my place after he and Father Jovet had parted formally yet amiably. My headlights shone squarely on him when I came home from Black Morocco's. He was sitting on the single stone step of the Commonwealth Mines' house. I didn't know how long he had been waiting and since I didn't know what he had done, I thought he might have been there the entire time. He looked haggard enough to have been sitting there four hours and that made me think he must either have been desperate about something or that he was going to be uncontrollable about something else. Maybe both. I wasn't glad to see him in any case. When the headlights of my car struck him full, he stood up; and when I got out of the car, he came straight toward me, purposively.

"I went to see Father Jovet."

I knew the next line was mine.

"Oh? What about?"

I said it flatly enough. And he answered energetically enough as we stood outside. I didn't feel like inviting him in. I don't think he thought I was being rude. But then I don't think he read people very well or even tried to. I leaned against the fender of my car and listened with increasing interest as he went on, especially when I thought I heard Father Jovet trying to get rid of him, trying to keep him out of his thin gray hair, by talking about the proper motivation—the wishes of men and the wills of the gods.

"So," said Ronald, finishing, "what do you think?"

"Me? Think?"

"Yes."

"I think the idea that you have to consult the universe before you can put a solid roof between it and your head is fascinating. And silly. That's what I think."

"So my idea is a good idea? You think it should be done?"

"Of course it's a good idea and I think it should be done. I think any use of that room at the moment is better that the use to which it's being put, but" . . . I shrugged. "It's not what you or I think that counts here. I'm not convinced that Father Jovet is really all that interested in providing sixty more beds for cholera victims. He's God's man before he's a good man, so he likes that chapel for what it is—a reminder that Africa isn't home, that even France isn't home. Heaven is home. Well, maybe that doesn't matter—what matters is that if it's your generosity that repairs the chapel ceiling, he's got to be grateful to you unless a little praying can convince him that God sent you to repair the chapel ceiling, the way he sent your wife to heal the sick and cure the city. Because then, you see, all you are is a pawn in the hands of the head man for whom he works. He needs that assurance to stay comfortable, and to be able to order you around, if necessary. But then no amount of praying can change the spots on the leopard: that's me. The timber has to come from me, or through me. That makes them very difficult to accept because he knows that they belong to the Commonwealth Mines and the mine won't donate them. I have to steal them—which he knows I'll do at the drop of a pin. I'm unscrupulous when it comes to property, a regular Marxist. I'll rob the mining company of anything in a matter like this, change the figures in the inventory or say the timber was devoured by termites. For sixty more beds, why not? Who wouldn't?" I laughed, realizing. "Father Jovet wouldn't. Just imagine: stolen timbers donated by a Jew and concealed in a Roman Catholic ceiling! How could anyone's prayers get past a barricade like that?"

"Can you get them then?"

"Of course I can get them. You can go out and get them yourself."

Ronald's face was even brighter than it was when I first agreed he had a good idea.

"Have you got six by sixes?"

"I think so. That's about the smallest we would have, though. How long do they have to be?"

"It looked like about twelve feet to the center of the ceiling from the walls."

"They're fourteen-footers. You'll have to cut them."

"Well? What shall I do? He told me I could ask you."

I shrugged.

"So you've asked me. I said yes."

I was mischievously leaving it up to him.

"Maybe if I got the timbers and brought them to the chapel, he'd see that it could be done."

"Well, in that case, what you need to do is go to Colonel Sada's office in the morning. Just say you're Ronald Keane—Nancy's got him wrapped up in that little black bag of hers—and he'll give you all the help you need, whatever you want. He's there at six sharp every morning."

"What do I want?"

"A lorry, for one, to go to the gold mines. He'll provide it and give you a driver to go with it. And when you get to the mine, just find Angoli—ask anyone for him. He speaks good English. In fact, you'd better keep him with you when you go back to the mission. Tell him I said that it's all right. He can be your interpreter."

"Won't you be at the mine?"

"Not in the morning."

"Don't I need something from you in writing?"

I shook my head.

"Just tell Angoli I said you could have some timbers. He'll believe you—especially if you tell him who you are."

It wasn't the wrong or the right thing to say, it was just a fact. But it was a problematical fact to Ronald, for his face clouded a bit and he seemed to fidget. Who was he? Not Ronald Keane, or if he was that was irrelevant. He was Nancy's, *docteur* Keane's, husband. That's who he was. In Ndami he got whatever importance he had from her.

"Has she really done that much? That well?"

His eyes were lowered so there was no point in nodding. I had to say:

"Yes. She has."

His face came up.

"Do you know Alan Angle?"

My God! What was the connection between that and anything else? That he would have preferred to be Vivian's temporary choice than Nancy's husband? Or was he just suddenly fishing for whatever he could catch? For he must have known I knew Alan, judging from the way I had talked about Vivian the other day.

"Of course I know him. I had a letter from him yesterday."

"I mean, personally? Do you know him personally?"

"No one knows him personally. Not even Vivian."

That took him back. I'm glad it did.

"What do you mean?"

Not what he thought, I'm sure, or what he hoped: that Alan and Vivian had no relationship.

"Alan Angle is more interested in the dying British Empire than he is in any living woman. And maybe for very good reasons, who knows? A dozen men have been ready to lay down their lives or careers for a woman like Vivian, but not many men are ready to give their lives for a political ideal that's already dead. And only because it'll give them satisfaction to see to it that it gets a decent burial.

Alan's one of those human particles of dust floating in a ray of sunlight on a very late afternoon. He hasn't any existence apart from that ray, none at all, and he's grateful to have passed through it even if it's dying. Even if the sun is going out. Have you ever been in his office on The Hill?"

Ronald shook his head.

"He's got a letter from Churchill framed on the wall. It hangs there like a passage from the Koran or the book of Isaiah, promising him eternal life. British immortality."

It was my turn to shake my head. And while I did I looked at Ronald, thinking: *Vivian, on the other hand, stands for everything mortal. Thank God. . . .*

"Does that answer your question?"

There was a kind of glaze on the surface of his brown eyes, noticeable even though it was dark.

"You . . . you said a dozen men?"

"What?"

"A dozen men have been ready to lay down—"

"Oh," I interrupted, "that was just a . . . a number out of a hat. I was trying to make a comparison. I didn't mean anything by it."

Didn't I? He must have wondered himself for I began to hear that clicking sound he made with his thumb nail.

"Well," I said, "I need some sleep. You don't need a ride, do you?"

It wasn't much of a walk down the hill and across the bridge that spanned the gully between our places. Yet I knew I wasn't being very generous in asking him that way. He shook his head, as I expected and hoped he would, and I walked into the house, hearing that *click . . . click . . .* behind me.

16

I SAW FATHER JOVET SOONER THAN I had expected to see him the next day. I was planning on going to the Catholic mission sometime in the afternoon but about ten o'clock in the morning I saw him walking along Nkosa Road, leading a small funeral cortege. I pulled to the side of the road, surprised, maybe even startled. Not that someone had died but that a funeral ceremony was actually taking place. Between three boys and one of the priests a shrouded body was being carried in a mesh of ropes. Two other priests were walking behind them, reading from their prayer books, just as Father Jovet was doing at the head of the small procession. It could only mean one thing: the fifth priest, the one priest absent from the procession, was actually present—in the mesh of ropes. Only a strong and sad need could have made these men walk three miles in the intense heat. The loose white muslin gowns they usually wore had been replaced by the heavy black robes they had brought from France. The reverence they were showing for one of their own dead meant that dozens of dying yet living people had been temporarily abandoned back at their mission, or that Nancy had been left alone to care for two infirmary rooms filled with sick and prostrate bodies, not to mention the children. I was sorry at the sight but I was not completely sympathetic with their need to maintain the primacy of their own rituals, to draw close together in dwindling fraternity, separate and distinct from the community around them. I got out of my car, sought the shade of an acacia tree and watched them perform their graveside rites. I waited because I thought I could drive some of them back to the mission, sparing them an hour's walk. When they began ritually sprinkling dirt into the grave I walked to the cemetery wall so I could be seen. Father Paul noticed me first. He must have said something for Father Jovet turned his head and looked in my direction. He came toward me in a minute or two, without—for once—his professional, deprecating smile.

"Father Jude died last night."

"I'm very sorry."

I hope he knew that I meant it. I didn't like to see their group get smaller. He shrugged, and I thought it was unlike him to make such a gesture of hopelessness. I pointed toward my car.

"I thought you might like a ride back."

He looked back at the grave site. It was obvious that he didn't know whether he should desert the others.

"I *have* been wanting to talk to you," he stressed in a way that was meant to tell me that that would be his justification for accepting my offer, if he did.

"We could take two of the others," I suggested. "There's room for four."

Without answering he went back to the grave, said something to Father Stephen and returned.

"I will go with you alone."

We started across the road together.

"I didn't even know Father Jude was sick."

"I did not know it myself until it was too late. But it is always too late. He was brave in not telling us. He is with God now."

As soon as we got into the car he turned to me, looking very tired and burdened.

"I must tell you that she is sick."

"Who?"

"*Docteur* Keane."

I gave an inward start. Outward, too: my body moved toward the wheel.

"How do you know?"

"She was in the *refectoire* when you were visiting with Mr. Keane. It happened just then, as we were passing, when Father Paul came out."

How well I remembered! I looked at him, feeling cheated if not betrayed.

"You could have said something to me then."

"I thought it best not to, because, because her husband does not seem to be very"—he hesitated again, he found the word he wanted—"very secure."

"How sick? What happened? What do you mean?"

"She fainted."

I wanted to groan. Perhaps I did.

"But she says it is not cholera."

"Not cholera?"

"No."

"How does she know that?"

He shrugged. He pursed his lips and made a smacking sound with them.

"She is a *docteur*, isn't she? Who can argue with her? I wanted to put her to bed but she would not hear of it. Perhaps you can speak with her. She is not a Catholic so she will not obey me."

I looked at him to see if he was being facetious. But he had made that last remark in all seriousness.

"Where is she now?"

"With the children. She was there when we went to bury Father Jude."

We drove the rest of the way in silence. I didn't tell him what I had seen and learned last night. And what was I going to say to her? I admit that I thought she could have had no more than a dizzy spell for a number of reasons, especially overwork. How could she function with the strain in her marriage? Maybe that's where the strain showed itself. Speculation was pointless. The only thing to do was to confront her stubborn will with the fact that she had fainted and make her do something sensible about it. But how? I really didn't think she would.

"Maybe she's not a Catholic but she's not a Jew, either. Why should she listen to me?"

"Try."

I shrugged.

"Anything."

He opened the mission door with his own key and we went down the corridor, stopping in front of the nursery. Father Jovet whispered conspiratorially, "I will leave you alone and go on to the chapel for a moment by myself."

I nodded and opened the nursery door. The room was filled with children and I could see right away that Nancy wasn't among them. I was going to go right on to one of the other infirmary rooms when I recognized one of the Ndami women, Orana, a miner's wife, and asked her where Dr. Keane was.

"Sudi."

"Sudi?"

That wasn't surprising in itself: Sudi was the most infected area of the city, not strictly in Ndami but about six miles east, across the Dalaga. But if Nancy was there it meant that with the priests gone she had left all the patients in the mission unattended. It seemed like total desertion to me: irresponsible. I could only get a vague idea from Orana about how long ago she had left. Then I went on to the chapel to tell Father Jovet that she was gone. I thought that I would probably drive out to Sudi and find out what was the matter. I assumed that Father Jovet had gone on to the chapel to pray and set a candle burning for Father Jude. But as I stepped into the courtyard one had to cross to get to it, he came out of the chapel, his eyes down, his face dark with rage, his whole body jerking to a halt when he saw me. I had never known him to look hateful.

"*Mon Dieu!*"

He threw an arm of outrage into the air before it fell toward the chapel door.

"*Mon Dieu!*"

He pulled me toward the chapel with a snap of his head and turned. When I stepped inside the door what I saw was remarkable: Ronald lying on a bench in midair, a leg dangling over the side and a hand beneath his head, contemplating the ceiling like a Renaissance artist who had been commissioned to turn it into a fresco for the glory of God. He had got in that position by upending all the benches in the chapel and stacking them against each other, thirty or so from one wall, the same number from the other, moving toward the center like leaning dominoes. It was possible to get through to the altar but to do it you had to pass under a bridge. And Ronald was on the bridge: he had hoisted another bench and suspended it across the last two upended ones that came from either side of the chapel. He had made a ruin of the ceiling. Gaping holes were in it. Mortar was all over the floor. Angoli stood below, supporting one of the last upended benches, his black hair and skin powdered with the ochre-colored dust which had fallen from the loosened ceiling.

Father Jovet demanded, "What is this? What is this!"

Ronald sat up.

Without waiting for a reply, Father Jovet rushed forward and passed under the bridge that Ronald was on. Ronald lifted a leg. Angoli jumped back, frightened. Ronald, startled to see us, managed to look innocent as well as bewildered. Father Jovet pulled the crucifix from its hook on the wall; he seized the candelabra and the statue of the Virgin from the altar, like treasures about to be defiled, and came back toward us. Only then did Ronald start to answer.

"I—I just wanted to see how loose that beam was.

How much damage there was—to tell you. And it just all fell out, it—"

"You have misunderstood!" Father Jovet interrupted acidly. "The matter was settled. It was clear, *clear* that nothing was to be done! The ceiling was not to be done!"

"But you said it was all right to ask Aaron about the timber."

The priest looked at me menacingly.

"Ask, ask! Is this your doing?"

"Of course it isn't. I offered to give him timbers—I did that much. I'm sure you knew I would."

Father Jovet clutched the things from the altar as if they were his protection against both of us.

"He is *your* responsibility! Yours! This is your matter —I leave it to you." He drew himself up, stifling his anger. "I must look after the sick and the dying," he said importantly, and started off.

"I'm glad someone will," I retorted, "because your *docteur* isn't here, either. You both went off—the doctor and the priests—to leave everyone alone."

He stopped.

"She isn't here?"

"No. She's gone."

"Gone?"

"Yes."

"Where?"

"To Sudi."

His eyes widened.

"Sudi?"

"Yes. While the four of you went to bury Father Jude, to perform your ceremonies. I'm sure Sudi is a better place to go than a cemetery, under the present circumstances. She's probably dealing with the living. I thought the dead were supposed to bury their dead. Isn't that right?"

The muscles in one of his cheeks twitched before he turned and went out, quickly. A bit guiltily too, I think.

"Is he really mad?"

I looked up at where that naive question came from.

"You don't think he was trying to be *helpful* in clearing off the altar, do you?"

"I didn't expect it to fall apart like this—"

"Obviously not. What a mess!"

"It could have fallen on someone's head at any minute!"

"Well, that's a point in your favor—if you can get anyone to believe it. But didn't you *talk* to him this morning?"

"I was going to, I wanted to! But when we got here, he wasn't here—and I just wanted to—"

His hand went toward the ceiling.

"I know, I know," I said. "You just wanted to see how rotted the beam was. Now we know. There's no point in talking about how we got where we are—we're here. How fast can you get it cleaned up?"

Cleaned up meant fixed up to him.

His head pulled back and he looked at the ceiling with a professional air, saying: "There's too much weight up there, that's all. It's unnecessary." He swung a leg from one side of his scaffold-bench to the other and sat there, swinging his feet as if he was on a bridge. "Who built this place anyway?" he asked critically.

"Let's not talk about the builders—there are no architects to sue or anything like that. Just tell me what you're going to do about the damn thing. What do you need to take care of all this?"

"Bolts," he said breezily. "It has to be bolted. I'm going to bolt it."

"You are?"

"Yeah."

"How? With what? I can't get you any hardware."

"Don't they have a supply room? Some kind of maintenance routine?"

170

At another time, on another day, I might have laughed.

"Where do you think you are?"

He looked at me blankly.

"Look," I cautioned, "my advice to you is not to look around here for supply rooms or anything else. Don't bother the priests and stay away from the infirmary area and the rooms where the children are. Did you happen to use the back entrance?"

Angoli did the nodding and smiled.

"Okay," said Ronald solemnly, "I won't bother anyone, and I'll hurry. I know they want this done right away."

"Right away?"

I looked around almost stupidly. Not only was the ceiling a mess and plaster all over the floor, the dust from it had floated everywhere and coated everything.

"How do you expect to do this *right away?* It would normally take two men a week to make this much of a mess to begin with, and then a month to get it back in order. At least in this part of the world it does. Do you expect to do this 'right away' by yourself?"

He pointed to Angoli.

"Can't I use him?"

Angoli smiled. They both waited. But I knew Angoli didn't have a carpentry skill anywhere in his black limbs. I shrugged.

"Of course you can use him. Anything to get it done. Tell me what you'll need besides bolts."

I *was* talking as if he were my responsibility. Maybe he was, I don't know. But Ronald let me know that I was talking impatiently, peevishly.

"I thought you wanted this done?"

"Cleaned up, naturally!"

"No, *done*—for more beds."

"I do, I do. That's why I want to get down to basics. Tell me what you need," I repeated.

"The usual things."

"What are they?"

"A couple of ladders, a little better scaffolding than this, some cement—mortar, a mixer, trowels, nails. That kind of thing."

I shook my head at his naivete.

"You think you're going to find a cement mixer? And you'll have to buy some of this stuff yourself."

He was very agreeable.

"All right, no problem."

"Providing you can find it. Angoli can take you to the Ede—that's the best market for these things. Start in the furniture maker's quarter. You'll have to hunt for what you need but you'll find it, and"—I turned to Angoli—"tell everyone it's for more beds at Father Jovet's mission."

Angoli smiled.

"Will do!"

He never did learn the use of pronouns.

"Maybe you can borrow some ladders and tools that way—anything that's returnable, anyway."

"Is there a welding shop?"

"No. Will a blacksmith do?"

"A blacksmith? Great!"

I imagine it sounded romantic to him.

"We have several. Who's best, Angoli?"

"Samson."

"There, you see? A convert. You'll have yourself a Christian. You should be able to get him to do whatever you want for the chapel."

Ronald pushed himself off the suspended bench and dropped to the floor.

I asked, "How long is all this going to take?"

"We'll work straight through the night."

"I don't think you will. There's no electricity."

He looked around the chapel without a sign of disturbance in his face.

"I'll figure something out."

"Figure something out? Like what?"

"I don't know," he said casually.

There was a shrug inside of me. It was out of my hands. I didn't really care.

"I have to go to Sudi to see your wife."

"Oh," he said brightly, almost pleased. "How's she doing?"

He sounded as if I were going to pay a social call on her. He was in his own world, whatever that was made of. Mostly himself, I guess.

"How's she doing?" I echoed as if I were considering an answer. But there was no point in taking him out of his own world or making room in it for something else, especially when I didn't really know what it was. "I don't know," I said, starting out. "I'll let you know."

17

I THOUGHT I WOULD FIND NANCY if I located her driver and car. But I found her by seeing a crowd of women at the west end of the Sudi market where the well was located. Nancy had to be working there, attracting an audience. The way in front of me was blocked because olive oil was being pressed under large wooden wheels, running off into bins in the road; so I had to park several hundred yards away. Smoke from a couple of braziers filled with sandalwood hung in the massively hot midday air and, a bit strangely, extended up the road toward the well like a pale finger that was pointing the way I had to go. When I think of it, I think *Oh, was it hot.* But typical. I wasn't a stranger to it. It was that time of the day when the sun, crossing the sky, is like a pole vaulter: straight over the bar, poised, hanging. Light and heat beat straight down. Everything stops moving at that time of day. The birds desert the sky, the cattle—standing in the shade of a tree—don't move. If a fly buzzes in the stillness you figure that it's dying out of sheer protest. It was at this time of day that I approached a circle of more than one hundred women, standing two and three deep. And I approached them with a regard and love that's grown up in me for the way human life here doesn't desert the sky at this time of day, doesn't always seek the shade. In the most motionless human figure you can feel the presence of human will. Of strength, of quiet endurance. The women in the circle around the well didn't yield one drop of perspiration to the unyielding glare of the sun that struck their foreheads. I wish I could have said the same for myself. In their ringed closeness their elbows sometimes touched. All their bodies were without shape, looking the same, anonymous, because they all wore the same loose muslin gowns. A few women kept their baskets on their heads. All their expressionless faces were turned on Nancy, on a woman—one of their own kind. Yet not like them at all. They were a human ring of silence and patience and she was a center of concealed energy and restlessness. They looked at her, with her tubes and chemicals and microscopes —Nancy the alchemist—as all the powerless ones look on magic: mutely, fascinated.

They were like a medieval crowd watching Merlin.

I had to maneuver my head around from behind the women to get a glimpse of her, and my first one was through a brass ring that was hanging from the earlobe of a woman two rows in front of me. Nancy was seated. Three boards supported by crates at one end and the edge of the well at the other made up her table, her laboratory bench. She was using a crate for a chair. Two microscopes were in front of her. On her right was a flat wooden case, on her left was her squat black satchel. Jars, vials, chemicals, calipered tubes and miscellaneous glass were scattered around. She was looking through one of the microscopes, her hand on the focus knob. Then her head lifted: she squinted in front of her and blinked, pressing her lids together slowly and tightly, like someone who's trying to relieve eyestrain. She looked back into the microscope again but she couldn't have seen anything for she lifted her head too quickly, too impatiently. She pulled the slide from the clips on the microscope stage and inserted it in the other scope. She barely focused that one before she pulled her eye away, then reached for a slide, or a rectangle of glass. She picked it up and dropped it. It made a faint tinkle when it struck the boards. That was followed quickly by another sound, delicate, too, like the striking of Japanese glass. She began rummaging among the thin cylinders of tubing, found the one she wanted, inserted it in one of the jars, capped the end of it with her finger and drew out some liquid. She let a few drops fall onto the slide she was preparing. But instead of setting the glass tube down she just let go of it. It broke when it fell over—but that didn't seem to surprise her. She put another piece of glass on top of the drops of water and fastened the slide under the clips. Instead of looking at it, she took a corked vial from the flat wooden case on her right and held it up to the sun. I almost started toward her but I was fascinated, too—like the women. I enjoyed spying on her, especially since she was someone who concealed everything. How she could keep her eyes open from the glare made by all the glass around her, I don't know . . . unless she was already half blinded by the sun. She lowered the vial finally, set it down carelessly, and rubbed her eyes before putting one of them to the microscope. She didn't look into it long. She stood up and went for something in her black satchel, striking the top of the microscope on her left. It toppled over. The accident stopped her from getting whatever she had wanted in her bag, and she sat down, so suddenly that the crate beneath her wobbled. I thought she was going to go over backwards but she leaned forward, put her elbows on the table and dropped her head into her hands.

That's when I began pushing through the circle of women.

I no sooner did than Nancy lifted her head, turned, saw me and looked forward again. She had looked like an animal detecting a scent. I saw her hand go to her mouth as I approached her and I heard a rapid clicking: it came from tapping her front teeth with the nails of her fingers. It was the first time I ever knew her to speak without being spoken to first.

"I—I can't clean this well!"

She exclaimed it, that much was clear. But I didn't know whether she did it angrily or whimperingly.

"I can't! The water in this well won't purify."

A close look at her scared me. Her eyes were filmy. Behind the film her pupils wandered, vacantly.

"Get out of the sun. Whatever you're working on or whatever won't purify, leave it. You've been working too hard at it."

I think I expected her to stand right up, as a sensible person would have.

"No, I haven't."

"If you don't stop, you'll *be* stopped."

She looked at me quickly, defiantly. She must have thought that I meant I would stop her. So I explained that I didn't mean by force of arms.

"What's above our heads will stop you. You've got to get out of this sun."

"I need the light."

"You need the light? It won't do you any good—you won't be able to see it after you keel over."

Ignoring me, proving that she needed it and God knows what else, she picked up the vial she had held in her hand a minute before and lifted it to the sun. It was effective in showing me how ineffective anyone could be with her. At least for an instant. Then her arm started to drop, her fingers loosened and the vial fell. The vial itself didn't break but it dropped on one of the thin glass cylinders and shattered that. Nancy's shoulders jerked at the sound. She was unsteady; the crate beneath her wobbled. I caught her by the elbow to steady her and was surprised that she stood up.

"I can't put any more into it—"

There was no question about the tone in her voice this time: she sounded as if she might cry. I didn't know what she was talking about but I didn't care; that didn't matter. I kept a grip on her elbow and started to lead her away.

"You don't have to," I said.

"Where are we going? Where are you taking me?"

"To Father Jovet. You're sick."

At the moment I said that a single observation made me panic: my hairline was damp with perspiration, the shirt under my arms was ringing wet, where my hand gripped her arm my palm was moist, and in one or two places my pants clung to my legs. But nowhere was she the least bit damp from perspiration. I thought: *dehydration . . . dehydration.*

"But my things . . ." she started to say, without really seeming to be concerned about them. She just uttered the three words, half wonderingly.

"I'll get them, I'll get them."

What I did was lift my hand in the air and wave to her driver, Mbopi. He started toward me and I spoke to him in his dialect. That made Nancy pull her elbow from my hand.

"What did you say to him?"

Her voice was filled with suspicion.

"I told him to get your things."

"No," she said emphatically, and turned around, starting back to the well for them.

"Nancy, you're sick!"

"Oh?"

It was hard to believe how she said that. My own eyes widened. I was just about to grab her elbow again but her single, airy, almost mocking *Oh?* made me stop.

"Yes you are. Don't conceal it, there's no point in trying—you fainted in one of the infirmary rooms the other day."

That fact made no impression on her; had no authority.

"I should know whether I'm sick or not."

"Father Jovet *told* me that you did!"

"Well, he should mind his own business and give out the last rites. I know he likes playing doctor but he isn't one."

We were back at the well. Mbopi was standing on the other side of her makeshift table waiting to be told what to do. She reached for her black bag, rummaged in it and brought out a small plastic container. Pills rattled in it. She twisted off the lid and dumped a pill into her hand. But she didn't bring her hand to her mouth. She brought her mouth down to her hand, bending her body low to pick it up with her tongue. It was odd, odd—and I stared at her.

"What was that?"

"Nothing," she said flatly.

Why was she so fascinating? Because she was uncontrollable? Not uncontrollable as a spoiled child is, or a merely willful person, that wasn't it. There was too strong a sense of purpose in everything she did; you respected something in her. She made me back off, pull away. Or at least I started to until I realized that if I did, it might be the same as if I had helped myself to salad: cooperating in stupidity. So, even though I didn't retort with anything, I started gathering up the calipered tubes that belonged in the flat wooden case. And I ordered Mbopi to take one of the microscopes. That made Nancy reach quickly for the other one and put it in her satchel. After she snapped it shut, she picked it up and walked off, heading for her car. I was still picking up calipers and I told Mbopi to go after her and drive her to the mission. I told him not to take her anywhere else, anywhere—even if she told him to. And I told him I would follow. He was nodding at me when I heard a grinding sound, the sound of tearing at the throat for breath. As if suffocating. I whirled and there Nancy stood, thirty feet away, bent at the waist, doubled over: retching.

I ran to her and grabbed for the satchel she was still clutching. Her fingers loosened and she let me take it. She straightened, started to totter backwards. I put my arm around her. But then she pulled away from me.

"Let me get you to the car!"

But that wasn't it. She wasn't being willful or stubborn. She bent forward again and the unwanted—the fearful thing—happened: she vomited. She didn't just retch, she vomited. And the certainty that had been in me, the kind that wants to scream *I knew it!* in perverse triumph even at the sight of misfortune, came out in another pathetic exclamation to heaven.

"Oh, God. . . ."

As if to silence me, Nancy straightened up after one upsurge of her stomach.

"I'm sorry."

That apology left me gaping at her. Sorry? I was speechless. At least I didn't know what to say but I automatically knew what to do: I put my arm around her shoulder, as I would have with any invalid and started toward the car with her. Once more.

"All I need is a little nap," she said.

"You can do that at the mission."

She shook her head.

"No."

"You must. Then someone will be able to look after you—around the clock."

"I want to go home."

I insisted, "You can't be alone!"

"There's nothing wrong with me."

Now she *was* being stupidly willful and I raised my voice: "Quit ignoring the obvious! You just vomited!"

"That's natural."

That was still another response that boggled my mind.

"Natural?"

"I'm pregnant."

My shock wasn't pure shock. I did more than almost stand stock-still. I was confused and bewildered. I felt silly, embarrassed about my false assumptions. And I was defeated. Her announcement was totally effective in making me withdraw. It was as if she had said *I'm in a condition that men don't know anything about so why don't you and Father Jovet just stop telling me what's wrong with my body or what I should do with my body?* She knew she had won the minute I let go of her elbow.

"Are you satisfied?"

She knew I wasn't satisfied at all. There was a trace of smugness in the way she asked. Smartly triumphant, that's what she was.

I opened the car door for her before I answered.

"I guess I'll have to be."

"You seem surprised."

"Well yes, I am. A little."

"Why?"

The minute I said I was surprised I knew I shouldn't have, for now she had trapped me. Trapped me in what was perfectly obvious, somehow: that my surprise wasn't about her physical condition, but that her marriage, her relationship with Ronald, was one that allowed this. That she *could be* in this condition, not that she was.

"I just assumed, maybe because the priests—wasn't it Father Paul who was in the infirmary with you when you fainted? . . . Everyone just assumed—I mean, with the epidemic—that you had succumbed."

I was clumsy. I never sounded more false to myself. She knew my surprise came from someplace else.

"It happens, you know."

I looked at her and felt I wasn't the only one who sounded false.

"But you can still have cholera even if you're pregnant, can't you?"

"You can, but I haven't."

She slouched down in the seat of the car and rested her head against the back of it, closing her eyes. And just as hers closed, mine widened. Her right arm above the elbow was riddled with purplish-red marks. Like pockmarks, marks made by a needle—to excess.

"You've got a lot of marks on your arm."

She touched them without opening her eyes, gripping her arm as if she wanted to cover them up.

"I had some of them before I came here."

I couldn't imagine why.

"Are you diabetic?"

She laughed. And she actually managed to do it with enjoyment. I mean, her laughter wasn't totally at my expense.

"No. I'm sorry I had to tell you that I was pregnant," she continued, "because I haven't told Ronald yet. I want to tell him myself." Her eyes were still closed while she said this but then she opened them, turned her head to the right and looked up at me through the open window. "You agree that that's my right, don't you?"

Her *right*. She wanted that made perfectly clear, and the tone in her voice, suddenly severe, made me straighten up. I had been leaning down toward the window.

"Yes, of course. I won't say anything to anyone."

"Thank you. Drive me home, Mbopi."

Mbopi looked at me. I imagine he expected me to shake my head or repeat the order I had given him—to take her to the mission no matter what she said. But I nodded and told him to do as she said, and Nancy didn't question me about it this time. I watched them drive away, not idly, but as if I might discover something if I looked carefully enough. When they disappeared I turned around and discovered that all the women had turned their attention on me. That discovery led me nowhere. I felt lost. Disoriented? I walked back to the well and covered it with the boards that Nancy had used for her workbench. They could easily be removed, of course, if anyone wanted them to be. And there weren't any of Sada's men around to prevent it. But I think word had spread—not admonishing words about staying away from unpurified wells, but word about Nancy. Heads turned when her car passed in the road. Everyone knew who she was and what she was fighting and that her enemy was their enemy. So the populace had stopped drinking from the wells—to help her almost as much as they did to protect themselves. The circle opened at two places for me and I walked out of it, past unsmiling faces. No matter how bright the sun under which Nancy had worked, everyone knew there were powers of darkness in the well. And that the powers were defeating her.

Powers were defeating me, too.

The power of human wilfullness, so it seemed: the way Father Jovet and the priests had left the mission to indulge themselves in private ritual; the way Nancy had deserted the sick who had been left behind, to nurse her own compulsions to come to Sudi; the way Ronald had found a way almost to enjoy himself. It seemed that it

182

needed a hurricane to stop people from pursuing what they wanted. Or what they must pursue. I, on the other hand, walked slowly back down the road to my car, past the smoking sandalwood and wheels grinding out olive oil. I started for the mine, thinking about Nancy. I ran through that part again—and looked on us as playing "parts," even then—where she had noted, in a pleased high sounding voice, that I had seemed surprised that she should be pregnant. I began to feel or sense that she needed or wanted to portray herself as someone to whom pregnancy happened. Or could happen. And that she had taken the opportunity to sketch that little picture of herself for me. I know how I traveled from where I had parked to Dalbiri Road but I don't know how I got to thinking that Nancy had not only taken the opportunity to do that, but that she had made it up on the spot. That saying she was pregnant was on-the-spot cleverness. It wasn't just because she had made me agree I wouldn't tell Ronald, who of course would know the truth of it. Or the possibility of it.

My car slowed down. For a moment I thought it was doing it by itself but I had obviously taken my foot off the accelerator. I steered to the side of the road, let the motor idle in the heat and let both hands rest on the steering wheel as I stared out of the front window. *What if she lied?* I thought, asking the question because a crazy kind of certainty was growing within me that she had. I imagined myself driving to McGowan's old place and confronting her, bluntly saying *You're lying.* And that only made me imagine her laughter, which would have precisely the same effect as her announcement had: make me withdraw once more, retreat, even apologize for my "craziness." That is, if she laughed and didn't remind me of her *rights* again. When my imagination took another route, telling Ronald and Father Jovet what had happened at the well and what she had said, it dead-ended in a picture of three of us huddled together, discussing Nancy in a way that seemed absurd to me: three grown men, all rather large, conniving to control one extremely small, shy woman. And it's possible that even at that moment I thought her "rights" included her right to lie, if that's what she was doing. In any case, I continued on to the mine and spent the afternoon with the foreman, Masaka, preparing to send off the last small yet valuable shipment of gold to The Port. It was scheduled to take place in three or four days. The transfer of the gold from the mine into Ndami, then to the river, onto the docks, into the steamer and finally onto the train always involved setting up elaborate security measures. It was something of a ritual, too. A ceremony. Passing boxes from one pair of hands to another, from one checkpoint to the next under the watchful eyes of constantly changing supervisors. What heightened the ritualistic importance of the shipment this time was that it would be the first transfer of gold from Ndami to The Port unaccompanied by white overseers or white militia on the steamer and the train. It freed me from thinking of Nancy—Nancy fainting, Nancy retching, Nancy vomiting, Nancy with needle marks in her arms—for several hours. But when I stepped out of the mining offices near sundown, there she was again, right in the front of my mind. I walked to the edge of the plateau where Ronald and I had climbed down, and sat among the rocks, looking out and down to the desert to the north. I climbed down again, which was a ritual of my own, I guess; one that had a calming effect.

I thought about my daughter instead of Nancy.

Not long before cholera broke out in Ndami, my youngest child told her first lie to me. Or it was the first I recognized. I had already recognized that she played certain games or turned to one special activity when she wanted to put a barrier between herself and the demands of our household—mainly the demands of her mother and myself, but also of her brother and sometimes other playmates as well. A certain "style" started to show in whatever game she was playing. But only to me. It was undetected by her brother and playmates. I could see her learning to keep secrets from others. On occasion I could see that she was afraid of being caught, found out. And she was right to be afraid, for everyone around her—especially her mother, brother and myself—the whole outer world, just assumed that it had a right to barge in on her five-year-old self anytime it wanted. It was at a moment when I had assumed that right unthinkingly that she stopped me from barging in by turning her head and uttering a lie. It stopped me cold, naturally. And I had to stop myself from instantly challenging her with the truth and shaming her, from exercising my adult power. Something both sad and wonderful in her child's eyes made me stop. Wonderful because I saw her staking her little claim to a self that could be free from the prying eyes of the world. My approach toward her that afternoon had been like a sudden pounding or even ruder opening of the door to her own small self, and her equally small lie was no more than a *No, stop, I don't want you to come in right now.* It was wonderful because I saw her standing on the threshold of becoming human, of arriving at that moment of freedom and liberation that comes when we discover we can lie and not be found out. That we can cultivate a self that others cannot probe. But it was also sad, not only because I felt turned away, but because I could see the sadness of the coming price in her eyes: the price paid after years of turning people away, of protecting that small inner self by withdrawing from humans in order to become more human. I hoped, of course, that she would never become so separated from others, from me, her mother, brother and playmates, that all she could furnish her inner world with would be her fantasies and dreams. And so I did the only thing I could do: touch the outside of her when she didn't want me to reach inside of her. I touched the brown lobe of her ear and put my own pink lips on her dark forehead. And when I had done that, I smiled and walked away.

And in my mind I walked away from Nancy.

I stopped trying to probe her inner world. I stopped my sleuthing, eying her lack of perspiration and then saying it was dehydration. Eying her puncture marks and believing she was excessively injecting herself with serum. She had told me what to think. She had said *Stop knocking. I don't want you to come in any further*. She may have fabricated an untruth in order to say it. I may have believed that telling me she was pregnant was artifice. But if it was artifice she was only, like all of us, imprisoned by her own art.

18

THE DAY HAD BEGUN WHEN I saw a funeral cortege in Nkosa Road and it ended when I saw an old war canoe in Feli Lane. I recognized it, lying atilt in the road near the rear entrance to the Catholic mission, because it was still used on the river for ceremonial purposes. Twenty or thirty men, women and children were gathered around it, looking on, laughing, talking. Urns and wooden buckets were everywhere. There were bales of straw in the road, making it impassable. And Ronald was standing in the midst of it all, eating a banana. Heads turned at the sound of my car. So did his. He waved and ran toward me, shouting:

"These people are marvelous! I can't get over it! I can't!"

His words weren't enough for him. He had to shake his head back and forth to show that he couldn't get over it.

"Everyone's helped, everyone! You should have seen us!"

"I should've?"

He nodded, laughing.

"I had twenty or thirty of them trailing me back from the market, carrying stuff. I looked like a white hunter on safari!"

I didn't appreciate the picture that put in my mind, and I looked at the canoe, which weighed several hundred pounds. A dozen men must have been needed to carry it. And he saw me staring at it.

"That's my cement bin."

"Your cement bin?"

He smiled.

"My cement crew is going to get started any minute, as soon as the straw gets here."

His cement crew!

"You'll ruin that canoe if you mix mortar in it."

He shook his head.

"No, I won't. I'll clean it up like new. *Better* than new," he boasted. "Come on in, I'll show you what's been done." Before I got out of the car he started across the road with vigor, too much vigor. He was being obnoxiously Yankee. He had stopped being any kind of an individual and had become a type. Filled with confidence, ready to boss everyone around. As soon as we entered the chapel he waved his hand toward the ceiling, making sure I looked up at his handiwork immediately. His handiwork in this instance meant the lighting. "Since I'll be working until midnight I had to tackle the no-light situation. It's already too dark in here for what I have to do. What do you think?" Hurricane lamps of different shapes and sizes were hanging from each side of the chapel ceiling in two rows of five, ten lamps in all. "I was just going to hang them for temporary lighting, but I thought, why not for good? Then they can use this place for evening services when this is all over. The only problem's the heat on the ceiling—but it's not a problem," he added quickly, "if you know what to do about it. When Nancy and I get back to The Port I'll send up some asbestos and show Father Jovet what to do with it before we go. Don't worry about those holes around the spikes." He was pointing somewhere again.

I didn't even see any holes. I certainly wasn't going to worry about what I couldn't see.

"I'm going to patch them."

He bent over and picked up a large hook from the floor, holding it out so I could see.

"Railroad spikes—from downriver, I'll bet. I had the blacksmith shape them like this. That's what I anchored in the timbers. Look at this."

My eyes seemed to be going from one thing to the next.

"You see that hole?"

He took me by the elbow and pulled me forward. Then he pointed to a small round hole that had been burrowed through the end of one of the timbers from the mine.

"I had to whittle that myself with a knife and a couple of other things. I couldn't find a drill anywhere."

He paused so I could appreciate that fact to its fullest extent.

I admitted, "It must have been quite a job."

The chapel door opened and Angoli entered. When he saw us a white gash appeared in his black face; he smiled ridiculously. Ronald beamed at him and put his hand on his shoulder in what seemed to be genuine affection.

"Angoli's okay."

"I'm glad you think so."

I said it a bit flatly; dryly. Genuine affection or not, it smacked of the typical expatriate attitude: that an African was okay if he performed in the way a white man wanted him to perform.

"Have either of you seen Father Jovet?"

Ronald looked at Angoli, which meant he hadn't. And Angoli shook his head.

"So he doesn't know whether he wants hurricane lamps permanently installed in his ceiling?"

Ronald's eyes filled with hurt surprise.

"You mean he won't want them there?"

"If they make midnight mass possible, he might," I said, "but you had better volunteer to take them down before you just announce that they're permanent, or that you've installed them for his own good."

"Right, right," he said, contritely, but even his momentary penitence was pragmatically inspired. "I'll ask him. And if you see him before I do, tell him I'll be finished by eleven or twelve o'clock. We've got the cement crew lined up to come in and clean everything off the floor and the benches as soon as I've got the mortar replaced. Right, Angoli?"

Angoli nodded.

Ronald's confidence in his American know-how was oozing out of every pore of his perspiring arms.

"Cement crew? What do you mean, *cement crew?*"

"Sure! Angoli, start soaking the straw. Ten minutes," he said, with a finger held up in warning.

"Ten minutes," parroted Angoli.

Ronald pulled the watch off his wrist and handed it to Angoli, who smiled and walked out.

"I've got rope for the benches so we can put them together for beds," Ronald said to me. "You can tell Father Jovet that, too." He went toward coils of ropes that stood in a pile against the wall and took one of them in his hand to show me. "We'll have to lash them together at the feet. I hope we can get them tight enough—there might be a half-inch space, or even more, between them at the top. What do you think? Will it do? If we use a girth hitch at one end, looping it here—underneath, see?—and then a half hitch at this end."

So he had been a boy scout, too. I cautioned, "The priests might not be able to handle another infirmary room right now. Not since Father Jude died."

"But I thought that's what they wanted."

"Father Jovet *wished* for it," I countered, "in a moment when we happened to be with him. But he may be able to do it," I also encouraged. "So I'll tell him."

"If they can't handle it, Nancy can," he boasted.

The mere mention of her was menacing to me. I glanced at him in such a way that made me feel I was really going to say something.

"I saw her earlier today."

"That's right—at Sudi," he remembered.

I nodded at his casual recollection.

"She has gone home to take a nap."

"Oh, good! That's good—she needs a rest."

"How do you know?"

I asked that quickly, searching for information. But he didn't have any information. He was just making conversation and shrugged.

"Well, she's been working day and night since we got here."

"I think it's more than exhaustion. Aren't you planning on going home for supper?"

His expression told me he wasn't. He looked at me as if I had made him feel guilty. And he justified himself.

"I have to get this mortar in."

I nodded, agreeing with the necessity of doing just that. But I also made a suggestion.

"But I think you'd better have a conversation with her."

He didn't seem curious, he just looked amused.

"With Nancy? You don't know Nancy."

I wasn't about to debate that.

"Nevertheless, I think you'd better look in on her and see how she is."

He was agreeable. Too easily agreeable?

"Okay, I will," he said, grinning. And then his eyes surveyed the task in front of him. "I'm going to put this mortar on in two batches. I need to let the first one set for about an hour before I put the second one on. I'll take a run home then." He turned around and looked up, explaining, "They didn't need to make this ceiling as thick as they did, so I've lowered it where it's been fixed, inside. Oh, don't worry—you won't notice it. I did it"—he turned his head back toward me, smiling—"with chicken wire."

"Did you? Good. Well, if you're going home I won't look in on Nancy then. But if you need me for anything, remember: I'll be right across the road. At home."

His misunderstanding was complete when he said, "I've got everything under control here."

"I meant where Nancy was concerned."

"Oh, right. All right, I'll do that."

"I'll see Father Jovet now," I decided aloud, "and tell him about the lamps. And the benches."

"Why don't you tell him to stop in and have a look?"

I nodded as I walked off. I wasn't going to mind telling Father Jovet that his ceiling would be done by midnight, since he had implied that Ronald was my lowly responsibility while the sick and the dying were his lofty one. He ought to be pleased; even a little apologetic, I thought. For it was obvious that Ronald hadn't bungled a thing after he had first brought the plaster down on himself. He knew exactly what to do and how to do it, cleverly improvising, which was something neither Father Jovet nor I myself would have believed, or was ready to. I walked along the corridors, satisfied and relieved. But I didn't find Father Jovet in either of the infirmary rooms, the refectory or his little receiving room. So I found the door to his own quarters and knocked on it. I guessed, first from the silence, then from the quiet movements I heard behind the door, that he had been lying down. I assumed a slightly more official air than I normally would have because I had disturbed him. When the door opened he looked at me blankly, then gravely expectant.

"I know I'm disturbing you, but your chapel will be done tonight. Finished. You'll be able to celebrate mass in it tomorrow morning if you want, or to expand the infirmary facilities. Ronald's got the necessary rope to bind the benches into beds, and he's ready to go ahead with it if you wish. I think I can get Embu to requisition mattresses and bedding."

Alert, if not alarmed, he stepped out of his room and closed the door behind him.

"Beds?"

"It's hard to believe that it's possible, but it is. And you won't have any trouble at night. You have lighting now. There are ten chandeliers hanging from the ceiling."

The expression on his face went from disbelief to fear.

I reassured, "Oh, only if you want them. Ronald says they can be easily taken down, so there's no cause for alarm. He only put them up so he could continue working tonight, but you might want to look at them before he takes them down. He's still there."

He turned his head and looked down the corridor anxiously. I thought he was going to start running to the chapel. The muscles in his neck had started to work.

"But we cannot handle any more patients without *docteur* Keane's advice and help, especially since Father Jude is gone. Has she been so long in Sudi? Her presence is necessary! Two of the children have fallen seriously ill and have been calling for her."

"She seems to be a bit ill herself."

His gray eyebrows lifted.

"I saw her working at the well and she vomited."

"*Mon Dieu!*"

He crossed himself.

"But she says she's all right. She insists on it."

His mouth opened, exposing the silver work along the edge of one of his front teeth. And I delivered the message that she was pregnant, in French:

"*Elle dit qu' elle est enceinte.*"

He stared at me, doubly struck.

"*Elle attend un enfant?*"

"*Oui,*" I said but I shrugged. "That's what she says . . . and therefore the vomiting is natural." I shrugged again.

He stared off and shook his head grimly, as if he were preparing to come to a profound conclusion.

"Then she must take care of herself for the sake of her little one."

"That's why she went home—to rest, to take a nap."

"Ahhh. . . ."

"Ronald's going home after he applies a batch of mortar to your ceiling to see how she is."

His look of concern for Nancy was replaced by his anxiousness for his chapel. The two struggled for possession of him and he looked along the corridor again.

"I will go see him."

I said quickly, "She hasn't told him yet that she's expecting a child."

He nodded without appearing that he knew what he was agreeing to: not mentioning it. I imagined that he would forget all about Nancy the minute he stepped into the chapel anyway. He started off down the corridor, quickening his pace as he moved away from me. And when I stepped out into Feli Lane and went toward my car, the sounds in the air—shouts, laughter, voices calling to one another—came together in a chaotic celebration. Thirty to forty people had gathered to watch Ronald's "cement crew": ten boys tramping in the war canoe, having the time of their lives, mixing the ochre soil with finely cut straw and what was probably cholera-infected water. I went up to the canoe and warned them about getting water onto their hands and then near their mouths. But they only shouted joyfully and excitedly about how finely they had cut the straw at Ronald's orders. And they cried even louder about their coming reward. I asked them what that was and found out that Ronald had been passing out coins by the handful. The ceiling was going to be not only a triumph of American engineering but American finance. So it seemed.

19

THE SUN RISES WITH AN EARLY morning heaviness in Ndami. The ground starts steaming after the first rays strike it, so the light's sluggish. I looked out one of my windows and watched the insects drift up from the ground where they'd spent the night. They seemed to be rising from a bed of dreams just as much as I had. I could see Ronald and Nancy's place from where I looked out. I had often walked across the small gully at this hour of the morning to drink coffee with McGowan, taking a dish of goat's milk and rice with me, made a bit tastier by raisins and ginger. And I had an impulse to do just that on this morning. So I walked down the hill and crossed the small wooden bridge where children were already playing two hours before school, with a readiness—though lacking in eagerness—to see Nancy again. Ronald, too. I was ready to face the possibility of moving more of the seriously ill from their homes and hovels to the newly repaired chapel, *if* Father Jovet was going to approve of that. I thought they would see me walking across the bridge and up the hill because their dining room windows faced that way, so I only knocked lightly when I reached the door. I had to knock again when no one answered and finally opened the door myself, poking my head in. The rooms of the house were too big for me to attempt to call through them. My voice wouldn't have carried beyond the wide outer hallway unless I shouted, but I said, "Ronald? . . . Nancy?" for my own benefit as I let myself in and walked through to the vestibule that went left and right in front of the stairway. I echoed their names again, got no response and walked into the dining room with my bowl of rice as an offering against any rudeness. The room was empty. Only the sun filled it. The table was set for two, waiting. I pushed open the swinging door that led to the kitchen and found Ilema at the table slicing guava. I set my bowl of rice in front of her so she could dish it up, and learned that Ronald and Nancy weren't up yet. At least she hadn't heard them moving. And Nancy hadn't come down for dinner the night before.

Fear, not curiosity, made me ask about Ronald.

And the answer was fearful: he hadn't come home last night. I looked up at the ceiling as if I could see through it to the upstairs room. I told Ilema to go to Nancy's room, following her out of the kitchen, telling her to knock but not go in. I thought politeness was still in order, I suppose. I stood at the bottom of the stairs, waiting; but Ilema's knocking was too gentle and when I heard the soft thumping of her knuckles on the wood a second time, I started up the stairs. No door opened, no voice inside answered to the knocking, and I took the last steps two at a time, swearing at Ronald in my mind.

"Nancy? It's Clinemark."

I knew what the inside of the room in which she was sleeping looked like. For it had been McGowan's bedroom, and less than a month ago I had removed the books that had been in the one case he kept there, and other personal effects for shipment to his sister who was still living in Scotland. The only other furniture in the room besides the bookcase was a dresser and a chair along with the large bed. It was huge, empty and cheerless. I opened the door and the light was dim because the windows were on the west side of the house.

"Nancy . . . ?"

No answer, no answer. I don't remember if I was terrified. I took three or four steps into the room before what I saw and what I smelled paralyzed me. Nancy was lying on the bed on her side, bent at the waist; the bulge in the pale green bedcover was made by her knees. The blood seemed to crawl in and out of my heart as thick as oil. What kept me from standing motionless, afraid for myself instead of her, were the flies. To the end of my life I think I will see them, eight in all—exactly eight, not seven or six, but eight, in two groups of five and three. Three were near her upper lip and five were gathered around the lower one, and one of them was burrowing into the corner of her mouth, a mouth that was stale and flaked with vomit that had dried. I cried out:

"Ilema!"

And then everything became a series of rushes. For an hour, a half hour? I rushed to the bed and pulled back the green cover. She was still wearing the dress I had seen her in at the well. The terrible smell from the emptying of her bowels rose up and I didn't want to touch her. But I did.

"Ilema!"

I suppose I wanted some help in carrying her or avoiding her but I didn't wait for it. I shoved my hands underneath her and picked her up. It was much easier than I thought. I don't think she weighed much over a hundred pounds, maybe even less. When I twisted myself through the door with her I saw Ilema leaning against the stairway, and when she saw Nancy she put both hands to her cheeks.

"Get *water!* Boil it!"

Ilema came behind me and I took Nancy to McGowan's old receiving room for patients and laid her on the high examining table. It jolted me to see one of her eyes opening. I should have shouted for joy but I was just jolted.

"Nancy?"

Naturally she couldn't talk. The lid just slid back over the green eye again.

I ran to the kitchen. Ilema was at the stove, putting a pan on the fire. I wanted her to clean Nancy, wash her, change her clothes. I knew she would hate to do it, would be afraid. They all were. Why not?

"I'm going for help. Can you take off her clothes?"

She gave me a helpless look. I laid my hand on her arm in pity.

"Do what you can, do what you can. Just wash her, get it away from her mouth—"

I began running as soon as I was out of the house. And just when I got through the courtyard and beyond the gate, I saw Mbopi coming up the hill to collect Nancy for the day's work. I waved and began yelling at him. When he stopped, pulling to a halt with his head forward behind the steering wheel, amazed, he jumped out of the car quickly. I told him Nancy had collapsed, to rush back to Embu and have him send a van for her and take her to the

Catholic mission. I told him I'd go directly to Father Jovet so we could get a bed ready for her and that I'd be there, waiting. I didn't say hurry. I just said:

"Cholera, cholera!"

And when I started running toward my place I heard Mbopi spin the wheels of his car in the dirt and for once was glad that all Africans were born racetrack drivers. The children playing in the gully near the wooden bridge heard my feet strike the boards and they scampered up the slope and stared at me. To see a frightened white man running is a sight worth seeing. I was going to jump right in my car and maybe I should have. That judgment, that I *should*, came from my feeling that I was taking care of myself before taking care of Nancy. But one of my shirt sleeves and a spot on my left trouser leg was dirty—with Nancy's dirt. So I took them off outside my front door and threw them aside. I went into the house, washed my hands and arms with barely enough boiled water to do the job properly, pulled on some clothes while my hands and arms were still wet, and ran to my car. I started driving to the mission, hitting potholes in the road at high speed, blaring the horn at pedestrians—which I seldom did—and sending goats running for safety. Because I didn't want to stand at the cross-marked door at the Catholic mission and wait for someone to open after I pulled the rope to ring the bell, I went around to the rear entrance. I walked into the inner courtyard at almost the same moment that Ronald and Angoli were coming out of the chapel. Both of them had bundles of straw under their arms. I had caught them, especially Ronald, smiling and talking. Both of them hung on to their smiles when they saw me coming quickly at them. I think Ronald's robust boyishness made me flare up in anger.

"You *told* me you were going *home* last night!"

He gaped.

"Then why didn't you?!"

"The mortar didn't set—"

"*Set!*"

"—the, the way I thought it would, so I couldn't get away." He looked at Angoli for some kind of support, either against me or for the truth of what he was saying. The sight of Angoli must have reminded him of his accomplishment for he smiled at him and then said proudly, satisfied with himself: "But we did it. We worked until two o'clock and decided to sleep right here—on the floor." He hugged both bundles of straw under his arms to show me how they had done it in comfort.

"Well, your wife's damn near dead!"

That took care of the stupid smile on his face and it gave me a little satisfaction to get rid of it.

"That's right! I went by there this morning to have breakfast with you, and Ilema told me you hadn't even come home! And she hadn't come down for dinner last night! If you had done what you *told* me you were going to do—!" I broke off because of the stupidity of it all, including the stupidity of my own bungling: not telling him she had vomited at the well, not telling him she had told me she was pregnant, whatever her "rights" about telling him herself were. "She's got cholera, cholera! I found her on her bed, collapsed, still dressed since yesterday—"

He dropped the two bundles of straw.

"Get out in the road," I ordered. "I met Mbopi and he went to Colonel Sada's for a van. They're picking her up and bringing her straight here, any minute. I'm going to tell Father Jovet so he can get a place ready for her."

I could hear him running across the courtyard as I went to the door that led through the corridor to the refectory. There were no priests in the refectory, only two women looking after the patients, but when I opened the first infirmary door the heads of both Father Paul and Father Jovet swung around at the way I burst in. Father Jovet was on his knees next to a man stretched out on the floor. He held a needle in his hand, ready to inject him. Father Paul was seated on a stool next to one of the cots, cleaning a man's face. Both stared at me expectantly.

"*Embu apporte le docteur Keane! Elle a le choléra.*"

"*Le Choléra!*" exclaimed Father Paul.

"*Oui!*"

Father Jovet deserted the man on the floor without injecting him. He stood up, saw the needle in his hand and looked down at the prostrate man at his feet; his face was a turmoil of guilt and confusion. He put out his arm toward Father Paul, holding the needle in the air, and Father Paul stepped forward to take it. It had seemed like an order and a brotherly appeal at the same time. But then Father Jovet just stood there and stared at me.

"I went there just a while ago," I said, "and found her in bed. Mbopi's gone for a van—he and Embu should be here any minute with her. Where shall we put her?"

He walked by me out into the corridor, turning his head left and right.

"I've already told Ronald—he's waiting in the road for them. Tell me where they should bring her and I'll go out there, too."

He shook his head, saying, "We will find a place, we will find a place alone, not with the others. For herself." He stopped, looking about distractedly, and lifted his long nose into the air. "In the chapel. Have them bring her to the chapel."

He went off one way, I the other, out the front entrance into the road. I saw Ronald half a block down to my right at the crossroad and waved. He came running. I could see from the helpless and fear-ridden look on his face— guilt-ridden, too, I imagine—that he wanted more than another order from me. He wanted some assurance, for me to say *Never mind. It wouldn't have made any difference if you'd gone home or not.* I suspected that it wouldn't but I didn't know. The only difference it would have made is that we all would have felt better, no matter what she felt like.

"How is she?"

"I said damn near dead."

My mood hadn't changed.

"Go help Father Jovet—he's putting Nancy in your chapel. *I'll* stay out here and show them where to bring her."

I had closed the door behind me and realized it when he started for it.

"You'll have to wait if you ring the bell there. Go around the other way."

He went up the road, running. And I went after him, walking. When I reached the crossway I already heard a horn in the distance. It was Embu himself. No other van made a sound like that. And when I was able to see him I could see that he was driving at breakneck speed. Our emotions or attitudes, the way we were behaving, suggested that we had an operating room, that surgeons and anesthetists were waiting, that scalpels and blood were ready. It was all, all unnecessary, absurd. . . . Embu swerved into the mission courtyard through the already opened gates, his bullfrog face half concealed by the huge sunglasses he hardly ever took off. He jumped out of the van and ran to the back as if he didn't weigh two hundred and forty pounds. Mbopi had been riding in back with Nancy and before I got a hand on one of the back doors of the van to hold it steady, they were already pulling Nancy out on a stretcher.

None of us said anything.

Ilema had taken off her clothes after all and Nancy was wrapped in a sheet. There were dark spots on it from water, places on her body where she hadn't yet been dried before Mbopi and Embu had come for her. Her hairline was wet around her forehead. And most astonishing of all, her eyes were open—both of them. The ride must have jolted them open. She wouldn't have had the energy or the will to open them herself. For they had no life in them, only the "classic cholera look"—vacancy. When the sun struck her face, her head barely turned to the side, and the lids didn't lower. I let go of the door, pulled off my hat and held it over her face.

"Take her to the chapel."

Ronald and Father Jovet had brought in a cot which looked like one of the priests'. Ronald started to rush toward us but then backed away immediately, probably because of the way Embu—always forceful looking—was moving forward. With authority. They transferred Nancy to the cot in the middle of the chapel where Father Jovet stood with a vial and syringe resting on a cloth in his hand. He was the only one of us who could find refuge in some role, and it was a double one since he had a robe on, always ready for death. But he had a problem with Nancy's sheet. Her arms were wrapped in it and she was undressed underneath. I went to the cot and helped him. She stared right straight at me and through me. I don't think she actually saw me, I can't imagine it—and yet to protect myself from her stare I spoke to her, softly. As if it would help if we were all quiet.

"This will help."

I tried—for whose sake? Father Jovet's?—to keep the sheet close about her while exposing her arm but I couldn't. I uncovered her chest. She had no breasts and even her nipples had all but disappeared. They had been sucked into her dehydrated body, collapsing inward the way the skin around her cheekbones was beginning to. Father Jovet bent over her with the needle, ready to stick it in her arm, when he saw what I had seen at Sudi: the purplish pockmarks made by previous injections. He stood straight up. He drew in on his breath, pulling in his cheeks; his gray eyes widened as he looked at me. I just nodded, meaning that I knew they were there. His pursed lips popped open and I heard the soft whistle or air escaping from them. Then he injected her, put the sheet back over her himself and made the sign of the cross over her body. He looked around—for Ronald, primarily, I think. For he had something to say.

"It's what she would have done."

Ronald was seated on one of the benches near the wall. He was wearing sandals, khaki shorts and a short-sleeved green shirt. He was dirty. His hair was still filled with the dust that had fallen with the ceiling. The lines in his neck were creased with it. His elbows were pressed into his legs just above his knees and he was holding his head in his hands, covering his ears, looking down. God knows what he was thinking. But it's easy enough to imagine what he was feeling. The rest of us seemed to have taken up positions like official members of a delegation. A motley delegation at that: a French priest, an Anglo-Jew, a coal-black man with ceremonial scars on his cheeks who outdid his British educators in style and decorum, and Mbopi, whose nose showed that he had an Arab lurking in his background.

"Why didn't she tell me?"

Heads turned to Ronald who hadn't moved. Only Father Jovet went toward him because only he would have some kind of official response, whether it answered Ronald's question or not. I wanted to say *She might have if you had gone home*. I was troubled but I remained detached.

"Those who ease suffering," said Father Jovet, standing near Ronald, "know how to suffer without seeking what they give to others so freely."

I turned around and walked out. I wished I had answers at my fingertips like that. I still had my hat in my hand when I stepped into the courtyard and the sun struck my forehead. All it made me think was that the sun didn't give a red hot damn what it burned up next. Almost by the time I put my hat on, Father Jovet was standing next to me. When I looked at him he seemed to have changed. He had certainly changed from the time I had burst in on him, when he was on his knees before the man he forgot to inoculate. His face was grave but a certain confidence emanated from him for he had official reserves of gravity to draw upon; he had no confidence where Nancy's life was concerned, but he had a personal confidence where death was present. He knew where it belonged in the scheme of things.

"How long will she live?" I asked.

"She will be dead in six hours."

I was shocked. For no reason. There was no reason to be shocked, yet I was.

"Do you think you would like to select a grave site for her?"

I looked at him.

"Me?"

He shrugged. He was assuming my partnership, I suppose; relying on me.

"Where did Angoli go?" I asked without waiting for an answer. "Maybe he could find a coffin somewhere." He didn't expect me to say that for coffins were a luxury. We had been bypassing them for shrouds and lime after the first week of the epidemic.

He said, "I would like to say mass for her."

"I don't think she's a Catholic."

"I will ask Mr. Keane first. If he allows it, will you attend?"

"*Jamais de la vie*," I muttered and walked off. Maybe "Not on your life" was unnecessarily harsh but at least I muttered it softly. I found Angoli and asked him who could build us a coffin in six hours. He looked a little bewildered but I nodded *That's right* and said it was for Dr. Keane. He thought Koli, a furniture maker in the Ede market, would be able to make one, and we drove there. Then we went on to Colonel Sada's offices, got some shovels and drove to the cemeteries in Nkosa Road. The

Christian and Muslim ones are easy to tell apart because the tombstones rise so much higher in the Christian cemetery. They're like outstretched hands appealing to heaven for help. Because the epidemic had caused so many bodies to be put into the ground in a short period of time a lot of graves were still without markers. But they would spring up as if the dead had been planted like seeds, flowering from every head. Angoli and I walked to the place where McGowan had been buried. A marker hadn't been erected for him yet either, saying, as it would, how he had healed the sick. There was room to put Nancy next to him—two doctors, both white, both dead from the same epidemic—so I suppose that's where she belonged. No, not *belonged*. She didn't belong to this sienna-red soil the way McGowan did. What's a cemetery anyway? A humanized plot of ground? . . . Well, I had no sense that we were humanizing some dirt six hundred miles north of the Bight of Benin by putting Nancy Applegate in it. But my sense of things wasn't important. I told Angoli we would dig a place next to McGowan and we perspired from every pore as we did. When I had worked with the burial detail I had helped fill holes that had already been made, so I had never dug a grave before. I'm not sure I've ever really dug into the ground for anything, since I've never gardened. And I went at it mechanically. I seemed to have little sense of what I was doing except that I knew I had to do it. Although I fantasized Ronald doing it with me rather than Angoli. That might have made things different.

When we were done I decided not to return to the chapel, at least not then. Four hours were still left of the six. I told Angoli he could go home and didn't have to come to work at the mine the next day. He was so tired that he didn't even smile his appreciation but he nodded, eyes down. Most everyone in Ndami was going to have some response to Nancy's death even though they had never set eyes on her. The women who watched Nancy in

Sudi were going to say that she was defeated by the powers of darkness in the well. In any case, they would know there was greater magic than hers. I drove Angoli toward his home, let him off when he spotted some friends in the road, and then went on to Nancy and Ronald's house. I thought I should see if Ilema had taken the covers off Nancy's bed and burned or boiled them. I found her in the back of the house, outside, doing just that: boiling the bed-clothes in an old oil drum whose top had been cut off. McGowan had kept most of his dressing clothes sterile in that way. And then I went up to her room; to see, I suppose I thought, if there was anything that needed doing. I'm not sure I gave myself a reason. I think I just wanted to see where she had lived rather than return to the chapel where she was dying.

She had not filled that large room with much of anything. The closet had only five pieces of clothing hanging from its rack. The tabletop and dresser top were bare, nothing was draped over the back of the one chair, although there was a pair of shoes beneath it. There were no cosmetics anywhere, only a single hairbrush, and that was on top of the bookcase. It seemed as if the person who lived there was poor. In need. There were eight dresser drawers and I opened all of them. Only two of them had anything in them; they were so sparsely filled that in places I could see the bottom of the drawer itself. There was a trunk in one corner of the room and I lifted the top of it. It was half filled with miscellaneous bits of clothing, most of them without labels; scraps of this and that. There wasn't anything that unmistakably looked as if it belonged to any one individual in particular. I realized her purse wasn't around anywhere, if she had one—and she must have somewhere, someplace. I was sure Ilema hadn't removed it. I didn't think it would have much money in it but it probably had her passport and things like that in it, unless they had been left at her home in The Port, which was possible.

Behind the glass doors on the bookcase were a dozen or fifteen books and two larger notebooks bound in heavy black covers. I opened the doors of the case and began pulling out the books. They were all medical texts. The first one was entitled *Tropical Toxicology*. As I held the third or fourth in my hand, I noticed something—or felt something—like an absence. I had opened the covers of the books and each of the inside covers was blank. There was no imprint of any library where they might have come from, and no name, nothing to declare ownership or possession. I pulled out all of them and discovered that they were blank. I looked about and realized that if I had not known who had lived in this room, if I had not known that these things belonged to Nancy Applegate Keane, I could not have discovered it. There was nothing in the room that would enable anyone to establish the identity of the person who lived there.

Then I took out the two black notebooks and opened one of them.

The first page leaped up at me. It burst from the book like fireworks, a riot of color. And the explosions of color came from intricate designs. I was so taken back—and curious—that I had to sit down. I took both books to the chair and began turning the pages. It became clear to me what they were: drawings of the inside of the body—cells, organs, tissues. My first thought was of the work that had gone into them, the amount of work—for it had to have been staggering. Tens of hours for each page. For they were minutely, precisely done. There were no large areas of hastily smeared on color. Any large area had been filled in to contour with dozens, hundreds, of fine lines, all done with colored ink or pencils. I turned one page after the other until I finally gripped all of them and flipped them with my thumb. The book was filled in from front to back. I set it on my legs and opened the other one. At first I thought the opening drawing was like the others, for it was large, fanning out against a background of pastel blue and consisting of hundreds of fine strokes. But it was a flower instead of some cell or bodily organ. The petals were veined like the underside of some leaf and then I was startled to find words, words that crawled around the page on the edge of the flower, as if they were resting on its petals:

A FLOWER IS A DIFFERENTIATED ROOT

I didn't know what it meant. I still don't know. I mean, I understand its cleverness, and possibly its correctness, but I can't guess why she wanted to make the root so all-important. Why she wanted to make me think, as the statement did, of the straggling roots in their darkness and not of the petals in the sunlight. For there were no roots in the drawing—only the flower. And the words seemed to cancel the flower out completely. While looking at the petals against the light blue, one was forced to think *Here is a differentiated root*. I turned the page, ready for more. But it was another cell, or maybe something she had seen under the microscope. And the next several pages were the same. What she had drawn looked like bacilli or seaweed: long, thin, wavering forms of life, beautifully segmented into a rainbow of colors. But then a page of horizontal black lines hit my eyes—heavy, bold, straight across the page. They were black bars locking me out. Two more pages just like it followed and then I saw that she had written something on these pages and had blacked it out. For every now and then I could see a fragment of color, a fraction of a loop or line, rising above or dropping below the heavy black line that went across the page. And then the next page was chaos—"doodles," nonsensical, with no recognizable shape or form. Lines just seemed to follow one another, chase each other, twisting into forms that represented nothing. I couldn't say one looked like a cup or another looked like the letter "U" or anything. They were just shapes. And sometimes there were changes of color in midline.

I turned the page.

And there was nothing but language, words—no design. And every letter of each word had been done in a different color ink. Or if it was the same color it was a different shade of it. The lines were encompassed by quotation marks:

"*I do not want you.*"

"*I do not want you. You are not worth wanting.*"

"*I do not want you. You are not worth having.*"

"*I want you. You are worth knowing.*"

I looked up and stared out the window. I blinked. Going through those notebooks had made me lose my sense of where I was and what I had just recently done—dug a grave. And that people were waiting for me. That the woman whose room I was in was dying where they were waiting. But when I stopped looking out the window and lowered my head to the book in my lap again, that's all that seemed to exist for me: what was in that book.

The next page had been crossed out.

And the next. And the next. The black lines were thick; carefully penned but heavily, forcefully. When I kept turning the pages and kept encountering the same thing I felt a maddening frustration, almost as if I had found a hidden chest and couldn't get the lock off. On page after page she had written out, poured out thoughts that she had buried again. Colored fragments were visible everywhere, straggling from above and below the thick, horizontal black lines like the antennae of crushed insects. Small frail creatures given a death blow by a huge iron bar. I brought my eyes to within inches of the page, then held the page up to the light coming from the window, but nothing showed through. Not one word.

The next ten pages were drawings of cells again.

And then the next was titled. The words THE HEART were printed at the top left of the page. Each letter was a maze of design; not like a medieval illuminated manuscript but geometrical, diamond shaped, segmented like a lizard's skin. And in the middle of the page, just slightly off center, floating in a red-black pool, was a shape I would not have known was the human heart unless it had said so on the top of the page. Colored stems ran from it, arteries and veins. Little lines meandered across it like rivers on a mapped bit of land. She had drawn it a second and third time on the next two pages. But the arteries and veins were bigger: bulging, overgorged with blood. I found that I began counting the number of lines she had made on the crossbar of the "T" at the top of the page, for not only could I not understand why she would have titled the pages again, I couldn't get over the amount of work she had done. I counted forty-seven lines in the crossbar alone before they blurred against all my efforts to keep them separate. I began to feel that she must have spent not just hundreds of hours drawing and printing, dipping her pen, wiping it clean, but thousands . . . *thousands*. It seemed staggering to me. So staggering that when I turned the page I was unprepared to see it filled with Valentine hearts of all shapes and sizes: upright, tilted to the right or left, one lying on its side, two hanging upside down. And just above the lower right-hand corner of the page she had embellished one of the hearts with two dots: two black firm dots. They were nipples. For the first time in my life I saw that the two swelling parts of a Valentine heart looked like two ballooning breasts, and the bold emphatic way that she had drawn the nipples made them fan out obscenely. I felt a jolt in my chest, lowered the book in my lap and stared blankly in front of myself. I glanced down again and had the same sense of shock. I almost didn't want to turn the page.

But I did. And there again was:

"*I do not want you.*"

"I do not want you. You are not worth wanting."
"I do not want you. You are not worth having."
"I want you. You are worth knowing."

This time I felt I had read something terrible and turned the page quickly. It was a large letter "V" that filled the page. Inside each slanting arm of the letter were hearts: Valentine hearts on the left, human hearts on the right. Six on each side. Right away I thought the letter stood for *Vivian*, and I still think so. Black horizontal bars ran across the next four or five pages, very evenly. Whatever she had written had been precisely spaced. I held each page up to the light, always hoping something might show through but only one word did: the word *although*. I made another word out as *skin* but it could have been *slim*. Only the *s* and the *i* were unmistakable. But when I turned the page a whole phrase was unmistakable: *just because it's easier to die than it is to work*. It made no sense to me when I read it but it didn't need to. It sprang up at me every bit as much as if she would have directly addressed me, saying, *Aaron, I've been wanting to say something to you for a long time.* She had just started to black out the page and she was doing it in sections, it seemed. Something, maybe cholera, I don't know, had kept her from getting to all of it, and I read it as if it might disappear before I got through it. My eyes went back and forth, reading:

just because it's easier to die than it is to work. He wants life to claim him. Anyone should be determined to live another day if they've gotten through the night — *wedded pollution. It's easier. I said* — — — — — — — — — — — — *and I told him, "A silent life is different than a silenced one,"* *and then he didn't say anything himself. He was silenced. When I talk to anyone, really talk, they're silenced and then I'm the*

*one who's left alone. They walk away from me but still
think that being silent is worse than being silenced. He
never stopped talking about his father the whole way
to Rabat in the car. What he said was painful and it
made me as angry as it did him, then when I said, "I
think everyone should smash their cradle and use it for
firewood, don't you?" he didn't answer me. He
wouldn't even ask me what I meant, if he didn't
understand. I could have silenced Vivian. Anyone who
doesn't think they're living unless they're loving or
being loved, like her, is —— — —— —— —— —— —— ——
—— —— —— —— —— —— —— —— —— —— —— —— ——
—— —— —— —— —— —— —— — Once in the body,
twice in the soul. —— — —— —— —— —— —— —— ——
—— —— —— —— —— —— —— —— —— —— —— —— ——
—— —— —— —— —— —— — what's it like? I tried to
tell him, I tried saying —— —— —— —— —— —— ——
—— —— —— —— —— —— — a stone, a stone at the
bottom of a stream. It's not the stream, it just troubles
the stream. It shows the life in the stream but it isn't the
stream because everything you feel once in your body
you feel twice in your soul, sometimes more —— — ——
—— —— —— —— —— —— —— —— —— —— —— —— ——
—— —— —— —— —— —— —— —— —— —— —— —— ——
—— —— —— —— —— — stupefying himself, squeezing his
eyes shut, sucking her breasts and having his genitals
stroked. If he saw her everyday of the month he
couldn't stupefy himself for more than a hundred
minutes solid, but he thinks that if you do that with
someone something in the end will be all right. I — ——
—— —— —— —— —— —— —— —— —— —— —— —— ——*

That was the end of the page.

The next five or six had been torn out. Three letters,
clo, were visible near the seam of one page. But that's all.
The rest of the notebook was blank. From there to the end

the pages were unused. I felt lost. My head swung toward the bookcase. I supposed I hoped to find another notebook there, which was ridiculous. I knew I hadn't missed seeing one. I gripped the pages of the book in my hand and flipped them along my thumb, trying to see if I had missed something, anything—a drawing, a word, or even a message half hidden in one of the designs. I knew that was ridiculous, too, but I did it anyway. When I gave up I was staring at the page which ended with someone saying: "You are worth knowing."

I stood up as suddenly and quickly as if someone had called out my name. With the two notebooks in my hand I hurried out of the room. I went down the stairs noisily and when I got outside I ran across the courtyard to my car just outside the gate. I threw the notebooks onto the seat and the top one slid off the other onto the floor. I scrambled after it fearfully, as if I were retrieving something breakable rather than indelible and enduring. And when I got it safely back onto the seat I threw myself down next to it, more in a hurry than I had been because I had lost a few seconds. I pulled the door shut and opened my eyes at the same time that I did my mouth, to let out a bellow of animal anguish: I had caught my ankle between the door and the car. I let go of the door and swung my left leg out so I could reach down more easily to clutch my right ankle with both hands. My moans were half self-pity and anger, half pain. I couldn't believe I had done that to myself, especially at that moment when it seemed so important to race back to the chapel. I spent less than a minute groaning through my clenched teeth as I hung on, waiting for the initial pain to subside, but it seemed like half an hour. When it did I pulled my left leg back into the car and rested my head back against the seat. I had been stopped . . . stopped. A spell of temporary insanity had been broken. For I had lived a swift dream—from the time I had started out of Nancy's room to the time I had slammed the door against my anklebone. I was going to race down the road to the Catholic mission as I had earlier in the morning. I was going to burst into the chapel with her notebooks, rush right to where she was lying, without paying attention to anyone else and she was going to struggle back from wherever she was at the mere sight of me bending over her, magically. And if my presence and eagerness weren't magic enough, I was going to, to—

What, . . . what?

What did I think I could do?

Give her some insane comfort? Open one of her books and hold it up in front of her? Encourage her to live and tell her she was worth knowing? . . . Perhaps my fantasy wasn't foolish. Or the need that gave birth to it was not. But the way I was running around in my head and down the stairs and across the courtyard to satisfy that need was foolish. I don't know why something can be worth imagining or worth dreaming and not be worth living, but apparently it can be. At least that's the way I felt. The slam of a car door had rebuked me. I felt punished and reached down once more to rub my anklebone before I slowly started off for the mission. When I got there I parked in Feli Lane and walked, or rather limped, around to the back. Embu's van was gone and I wondered what that meant. But I stopped wondering when I opened the chapel door and saw all of Ronald's chandeliers burning. The altar had been reassembled; the statue of the Virgin was in its place and the crucifix was above it on the wall. Father Paul was at the altar rail, praying. Nancy was on the cot in the center of the chapel. Ronald was still on a bench, in almost the same position I had last seen him in, except that he was on the opposite side from where he had been before. Father Jovet was standing near him.

"Jesus . . . Jesus."

It was hard to know where that low call was coming

from at first. But when I heard it again I could tell that it came from Ronald. And then it wasn't easy to know how it had come from him. I've heard that name constantly even though I've never been in a church other than Father Jovet's chapel. But it didn't sound like a plea. It sounded more like it did when I heard it on a street: a complaint.

"Jesus. . . ."

I walked straight toward Nancy even though my swift dream was past. Her eyes were closed. I could have held no book up to them. She was still breathing for I saw the sheet move slightly below her flattened and collapsed chest. I remembered the Valentine hearts I had seen and I reached down and touched her shoulder.

"Nancy . . .?"

I didn't expect her to respond. But I felt better for having touched her. I even pressed my fingers against her shoulder a little more firmly. The last and the only time I had reached toward her I had slapped a fork out of her hand. I suppose I tried to feel that I had undone something.

While I did this Father Jovet had approached me.

"It will not be very long."

I looked at him.

"I think," he added.

"Pointless, isn't it? Stupid."

He shrugged.

"Jesus . . ." moaned Ronald.

I looked over at him.

"He has been saying that for an hour. I cannot get him to stop."

"Is he praying?"

Another shrug was the only answer I got to that. Then Father Jovet suggested, "Perhaps you should take him away. He has been sitting there too long."

It was true. He hadn't been home yesterday morning. He had begun to look like someone who had slept on a bale of straw all night. There was a stubble of beard on his face and he seemed to be breathing through his mouth rather than his nose.

"Where's Embu?"

"Colonel Sada has gone with Mbopi. He will be back with others."

"I see."

What I saw was preparation. Minimal preparation, but nevertheless preparation for a death.

"All right, I'll take Ronald home."

Father Jovet almost sighed with relief.

"Tell Embu that Koli will have a coffin. What shall I do? Wait there with him, or come back?"

The priest shrugged.

"Well, let's wait and see," I said.

"Jesus. . . ."

I went over to Ronald and he looked up. His eyes were bloodshot from crying and the rims were red. From the way he was breathing his nose was obviously stuffed up. He was just a suffering human being without resources. I don't think he even knew why he was suffering. He looked bewildered that he was.

"You've been here a long time," I said. "Why don't we drive back to your place? You can clean up and we'll have something to eat. A cup of tea."

He didn't say anything. But when I touched him on the arm he stood up, willing enough. He looked toward Nancy.

Father Jovet said reassuringly, "We will look after her."

He was so obviously lost that I took him by the arm and said, "Let's go."

We did. We walked to my car in silence. I wondered what to tell him and when: that she had been sick, that she said she was pregnant . . . that I had just been to her room and found some things of hers he might want to see. That I had brought them in the car with me. But I waited until we got there. I had to pick up the notebooks so he could sit down, and after he had I held them out to him.

"Here."

And then I drove off. I must have thought I had been clear about what I was doing just by the way I said *Here*, that I had intoned it in such a way that I meant I was handing him something that belonged to him. But he seemed to take them as if I had given him an order to hold them. Which is exactly what he did: set them across his bare legs listlessly, obliviously, without curiosity. He stared out of the window for a mile before he said anything.

"Why didn't she tell me?"

I didn't want to be too direct in my response.

"I'm not sure whether she would have said anything last night or not."

He looked at me and I shrugged the possibility off.

"Remember when we first visited the priests and Father Paul came running out of that room? I guess she had fainted then—but they didn't want to alarm us, and I guess she insisted she wasn't sick."

I was doing a lot of "guessing" and I waited until he looked back out of the window again before I said anything else.

"She wasn't feeling very well when I saw her at Sudi yesterday. She vomited."

"Vomited?"

"But she said it wasn't cholera. She said it was natural —because she was pregnant."

The impact of that seemed to register in his chest, in a jerk of his shoulders upwards. His mouth opened but nothing came out of it. He stared through the windshield, dumbfounded. Then his mouth closed and as I looked at him his cheeks reddened.

217

"She's lying."

He said it so emphatically that I shrugged again, this time more from self-defense than casualness.

"That's what she told me—and also told me she wanted to tell you herself, which is why I asked if you were going home last night. It was only accidental that I happened to be there at the time that she threw up. I should have said something to you. I'm sorry. That much is my fault."

He said flatly, "It isn't so."

I didn't shrug again. I gave it up internally and refused to be mystified. It wasn't as if I or anyone had to settle something between them. We were silent and when I reached their gate in five minutes I sounded as if we were done with it.

"Well, now let's see if Ilema can make us a cup of tea. Here, let me carry those."

I took the notebooks from his lap, carried them in, set them on the dining room table and got ready to call out for Ilema when I remembered that she was probably still outside.

"I'll see if Mboye's here."

I went into the kitchen. He wasn't there. But some of the water that Ilema had boiled to wash Nancy with was still warm and I lit a flame under one of the pans. When I walked back into the dining room Ronald's chin was in the air. So was his right elbow. He was draining a glass that had had brandy in it—how much I didn't know, but there was a bottle on the table in front of him.

I asked, "Have you eaten anything?" . . . which was a very indirect way of saying *Now let's not be foolish*. And his only answer was to take hold of the bottle and refill the glass. Or almost fill it—a squat one that held maybe four ounces. It was enough for a whole evening's consumption. I was afraid that if he drank even half of it he wouldn't be able to go to the cemetery, or anywhere else

218

for that matter, in another hour. But when he sat down he picked up the glass and took a drink from it right away. A normal one, I suppose: the level of the brandy in the glass only went down a quarter inch. Still I cautioned, "If you haven't eaten anything, you'd better go easy on that."

He looked at me. He was incapable of looking at me challengingly or even inquiringly. He only looked pathetic, just as he had when I had first looked at him in the chapel.

"Why would she say a thing like that?"

He was troubled about it but I don't exactly know why he was. Now I imagine it was because, not having touched her since he played tennis that day with Vivian or since he had first gone to Hamsun's Bay, he had turned Nancy into one of the Untouchables. And maybe he was reminded of it too strongly.

I echoed, "Why *would* she say a thing like that?"

For I couldn't answer him. Not to his satisfaction, anyway. I had answered myself: that she said it not only to make me stop meddling in her affairs, her fate, but because her fate tempted her to make me think of her in that way. I imagine she had understood soon enough that Ronald wasn't going to realize that she was worth knowing. And once she had given up her desire to be known, a desire she shared with everyone, she would wish and even settle for merely being wanted, or . . . had. Terrible word, that: *had*. Even when we say *worth having*. But I could see her playing with me at the well at Sudi, in effect challenging me: "See? I'm wanted—occasionally. I'm worth having." To me she displayed in an unfortunate, even humiliating, way what Vivian could display proudly. Because I'm not sure Vivian was worth knowing but she seemed to be worth wanting and having. But Ronald was married to the one worth knowing.

"Oh," I said, "I don't know why she would say something like that—if it wasn't true. She was probably distracted, overworked . . . the sun, the heat. I suppose she wanted to put me off, make me leave her alone. Get rid of me. . . . It worked."

"Jesus."

This time the name sounded like a plea, a lament. Ronald leaned forward and reached out with both hands for the notebooks. He did it so suddenly that something inside of me sort of leaned toward him and I started to say:

"Those are—"

But I stopped because he just pulled them, slid them across the top of the table until they were in front of him; then he crossed his arms over them and put his head down. And I didn't think it was necessary or possible to say what they were as long as they were being used as a pillow. I turned and went back into the kitchen. I cut some bread and found some cheese. There was a little honey in a wooden jar and some lemon marmalade in another. I put them on a cutting board and brought them out. The glass was at his lips again and I felt that I had caught him. Unfortunately he didn't feel caught. He took a long slow drink, set the glass down and then stared at some spot on the table.

"If you go out into this sun after drinking all that, you're going to keel over."

"I'm not going out in the sun."

What did that mean? Surely he knew we would be burying Nancy soon. Or didn't he? Where was he living?

"Have something to eat with it, anyway," I said, putting the things in front of him. He reached for the bread as I sat down. I started to cut some cheese for him but he barely lifted the bread off the board before it dropped it again.

"I killed her."

"I don't think it mattered that you didn't come home last night. You shouldn't feel that way."

I immediately minimized his responsibility because he

220

was exaggerating it. Dramatically. At first he answered me by taking a drink. The way he threw it into his mouth seemed to emphasize his feelings and his right to them; his hopelessness.

"I forced her to eat that salad."

"I don't think she died from that," I said, although I didn't know whether she did. And didn't realize I was assuming that she already had. "She had the same inoculations that you had."

He didn't look at me to consider the truth of that. He just stared at some spot on the table. Then he shifted his eyes to his glass of brandy again.

"Eat something."

That stopped him from reaching for the glass but it didn't start him eating. It started him crying. He put his head down on his folded arms again and I didn't know how to respond to his tears except with a sense of helplessness. Grief was grief, if that's what it was. Maybe it was remorse, guilt, self-pity . . . I didn't know which. In one spot he was getting the cover of Nancy's notebook wet and I wanted to pull both of them away from him.

"What am I going to do?"

I didn't pause too long before responding to that.

"Why don't you go upstairs and lie down?"

I looked at the top of his head of thick brown hair—since he didn't look up—and wondered what I was going to do *with him* when this was over. From all indications it appeared that he was going to need taking care of, or looking after; especially if he was going to consume brandy. The steamer was leaving at noon or before tomorrow and it would be almost two weeks before it left again. When I thought of that I was reminded of things I had to do, whether the time to do them was appropriate or not.

"I should wire Alan Angle about what's happening here."

Ronald stirred and lifted his head. God knows what

was going through his mind but his brown eyes looked across at me like a couple of rodents squatting in rounded cages. I had raised a specter and he didn't want to look at it. I didn't either. I regretted doing it and tried to get him to look in another direction.

"Maybe I should drop in at the chapel again, too."

He stood up as if he were going to do it. Abruptly. But what he did was take hold of the bottle of brandy by the neck and start to walk away. Was he taking advice and on his way to lie down . . . Or carouse alone?

"I didn't mean for you to take the brandy with you."

He didn't answer and he didn't look at me. He just hit the corner of the table with his hip as he went around the end of it and was thrown off balance. I got up and followed him when he started out of the room into the hallway.

"I won't be gone long," I said, as if that would prevent him from doing something. But it didn't prevent him from continuing right on up the stairs. "I wish you'd leave that bottle down here." Obviously my wishes didn't have much to do with his and he just kept on climbing. It seemed to be a contest—whether I could stop him or he would keep moving. "We'll bury her next to McGowan. Angoli and I dug a grave next to his in the cemetery on Nkosa Road. Not far from the river."

He won.

Despite the fact that I uttered each sentence like a separate threat, he wasn't threatened. He disappeared at the head of the stairs.

I went straight out of the house to my car and directly to the post office on Jaffa Road. I began to write out a wire to Alan that said Nancy was dying but then I crossed out *dying* and said *dead*. After I had done that I crossed out *dead* and put *dying* back in again and added *DEATH EX-PECTED TODAY*. I stood at the crowded high table, touching elbows with those on either side of me, and stared at the streaked wall in front of me for a minute. Then I wrote *RONALD KEANE MAY DEPART ON STEAMER TOMORROW. WILL CONFIRM.* I didn't know whether Ronald would be willing to do that but I thought I'd suggest it to him.

When I pulled up at the back entrance to the mission I saw Father Paul's back as he crossed the inner courtyard toward the chapel door. In his arms he carried a ream of white cloth. I sat inside the car for a minute with both hands on the top of the steering wheel. The pain in my anklebone seemed to flare up and I reached down and rubbed it. Then I got out and went inside. Father Paul and Father Jovet stood opposite each other, unravelling the white muslin. Seeing them do it, as I often had before, made me realize again what good caretakers they had been of afflicted and helpless people: unskilled but tireless. They didn't see me and I looked at Nancy lying on the cot. But I didn't see her as she was there. I suppose I didn't want to. I remembered her fruitless and desperate search to find something in her microscopes at Sudi. It remained incomprehensible, or perhaps awesome, that the tiny creatures she was looking for held the power over life and death.

"*Morte?*"

I startled both priests with my question. They turned their heads, their arms outstretched, holding the drooping muslin between them.

Father Paul answered, "*Oui.*"

I shook my head as if I couldn't understand it, although I could. It prompted Father Jovet to say something for my benefit.

"She did not die of the *choléra.*"

"No?" I said skeptically.

He shook his head.

"She died of being a human being."

I forced myself to look at her sunken face.

"I didn't know that was an affliction."

"Only a frailty."

I looked at him. He regarded me both gravely and sadly, and I nodded.

"Do you need help wrapping her?"

"No."

I was glad.

"Monsieur Keane isn't with you?"

"No."

"We could perhaps wait a bit—until this evening? If that would be better for him?"

I looked at her again, against my will, for that was a reckless suggestion. Even if she was wrapped we both knew the carcass that had contained her silent spirit would be crawling with maggots. And I was sure it would be worse to wait where Ronald was concerned. It was going to be bad enough as it was.

"No. I'll go back and wait there until you come by."

"All right. Father Jean has gone to find some flowers."

I nodded and started to leave. Father Jovet spoke to my back after I had taken a few steps.

"Colonel Sada says that the death rate dropped to fifty-seven yesterday."

His remark momentarily stopped me, and I couldn't start up again until I had said, "Good for her."

Ronald was upstairs, stomach down, on his bed. The bottle of brandy on the floor next to him appeared to be at the same level that it had been, but I couldn't be certain. He wasn't asleep and he wasn't awake. His head was turned to one side and he lifted an eyelid when I came in and let it drop again. He was clearly in his own world—whatever it consisted of, wherever it was.

"Can you get up?"

He didn't move.

"Do you want to?"

He still didn't move. Not even an eyelid. . . . I didn't care. I didn't think it was important whether he came to

224

the cemetery or not. He was going to have to make whatever he could of it one way or the other. I looked around the room at his suitcases and trunk. He had brought more with him than Nancy had, it appeared. I looked down at him and thought that he was going to be sleeping soon even if he wasn't now, and that he was going to wake up with a very bad headache. And stomach. I went downstairs into the dining room, saw three bottles of liquor setting on the table between the two high windows, took them to the kitchen and emptied them down the drain. I was going to take the notebooks from the dining room table but I didn't know of a better place to remove them to, unless it would have been back in Nancy's room. So I left them there, looking at them for a moment. I don't mean I opened them. I saw the edges of a few circles where Ronald had gotten one cover wet and I rubbed them out with my thumb. Then I went to the back of the house and asked Ilema if she thought she could pack all of Nancy's things and get them ready to go on the steamer tomorrow. After that there was nothing to do but walk to my car, which I had parked in the shade of a cottonwood tree, and wait. It wasn't very long before I saw Embu's van and Nancy's car, driven by Mbopi, come up the hill. Father Jovet and Father Paul were with Mbopi. Father Jean was seated in the front of the van with Embu and I could see a couple of heads in the back. I walked up to Embu first and told him that Ronald wouldn't be coming, that he was on his bed, drunk. Embu sent a swift, dark look at the house, conveying his judgment. But then his black face softened when he looked at me again. And I nodded to encourage him to think that Ronald's sorrow was so great that he had drowned it in drink.

I went up to Father Jovet and said, "*Il a trop bu.*"

He looked at the house also, distressed. But when I shrugged he seemed to show that he too thought Ronald had succumbed not to wilfullness and brandy, but to grief.

"I'll drive my own car," I said.

225

Four black men carried Nancy's wooden coffin to the open grave—Mbopi, Embu and the two militiamen that Embu had brought along. It didn't seem strange that Ronald wasn't there. No one really associated Nancy with him. I think I was the only person who had ever seen them together. Certainly I was the only one who had been with them together. And my own feeling was that Ronald had become attached to her so haphazardly that he could hardly have much of an idea of whom or what he had been severed from, if he felt severed at all. We all stood back and observed Father Jovet as he read in Latin from his small black book at the foot of the grave. I don't know what he considered appropriate for a non-Catholic but he mumbled musically enough. It filled the heavy air with a kind of softness. I didn't have any philosophy for the occasion so I accepted easily enough whatever it was that he had, especially since I couldn't understand it. I did look at the piece of ground next to her, under which McGowan was stretched out, and thought about bodies "being at rest." I thought that McGowan's was because I felt he died somewhat complete or, more accurately, that he had passed a number of mile markers that he had intended to pass. I couldn't imagine that Nancy had completed anything. At least not an emotion: all of those were still wandering inside her, homeless, when she died. I accepted the way the priests and I stood watching the two militiamen of Embu's shovel the dirt into Nancy's grave, with Embu and Mbopi looking on with us. We were all in some way members of the funeral party, and the other two men were only attendants, attending us. But then I couldn't accept it. It was irrational of me to see the scene from the standpoint of Nancy's body, as if it were sentient and was aware of the two strangers standing over it. Yet that's how I did see it and felt it. And I didn't like it. The land was too strange, the soil was too strange and she was estranged from too much herself. I found myself going forward, causing the heads of the priests to turn to look at me, and I took a shovel from one of the men. The other stopped digging for an instant when I began shoveling the dirt in, but then he started again until Embu came forward and took his shovel from him. We filled in the grave without looking at each other. We all seemed to feel awkward when we were done.

"What shall we do about the well at Sudi?" I asked. "It's the only one she couldn't purify."

Embu laid his big hand out flat and sent it through the air.

"I will seal it off from normal use."

"And then what?"

"Have it boiled."

"All right," I said, "until something can be done. The Port will have to do something about it. I'll tell Alan Angle that a chemist is needed. He should be able to find someone."

We walked back to our cars, nodding, agreed on something. No one said anything about Ronald, although Father Jovet seemed to be searching in my direction for something. So I told him I would be in touch with him. And then I drove back to McGowan's old house. I believe I thought it was for the purpose of satisfying myself that Ronald was in fact out cold on his bed. Which he was. But when I came back downstairs I went into the dining room and didn't hesitate to move toward the black notebooks. Only when I reached for them did I pause an instant. When I picked them up I said out loud, "Nancy Keane, these are mine"—as if I were justifying myself to someone. I still have them and I never did tell Ronald what they were.

20

PITY FLOWED FROM EVERYONE to Ronald when word that Nancy was dead circulated through Ndami. For it also became known through Sada's men and Mbopi, I imagine, that Ronald had been struck down by misfortune. Was bedridden. By midafternoon people started coming to the house with gifts, people whose families had been touched in some way by Nancy's ministrations. The entrance to the house was filled with gourds and kola nuts. I had to tell Mboye to pack them in the crates that had held medicine on the trip upriver. For they were going to have to go back with Ronald: it would be an insult to leave them behind. Four of the boys who had danced for Ronald in the canoe, mixing mud and straw, and whom he had rewarded with coins, came by with a basket of figs while I was there. I had to rub my hand on all their heads with appreciation on his behalf. For the crime of it all, if it was a crime, was that he didn't know what was happening. He was in a deep sleep. I tried to rouse him from it by shaking his shoulders and by telling him, close to his face, "I'm having Ilema and Mboye pack your things." But it had no effect on him. Not even when I tried to warn him: "I think you should go back to The Port on the boat in the morning." He just rolled out of my grasp. I don't think it was particularly willful. He was probably genuinely sick with self-pity, which is why I withheld *my* pity. His stupor struck me as a sign of total cooperation on his part to make himself ill with whatever human poisons were necessary to him: guilt, self-hate . . . the usual things. All toxic.

I had a good many things to do other than worry about

him and so I did them. I must have made half a dozen trips from the mine to the river and I also sent a three thousand-word telegram to Alan Angle, which cost Continental Mines about twenty pounds. I told him Ronald would be on the same train that arrived with the gold shipment and gave him a full report of the progress that had been made against the epidemic. I was sure Nancy's death was going to jolt him and I took the opportunity to ask for special funds and assistance to improve the general sanitation facilities in Ndami. I also told him I would be coming down to The Port in a week with all the company records. A final bookkeeping report was going to be made prior to nationalization, and then. . . .

And then?

As Vivian had asked *What are we going to do without you?* Fortunately I only had to think about the immediate future. And that was how to get Ronald on his feet and give him a chance to protest that I was literally shipping him out in the morning. I had told Ilema to try to get him up at six and give him some tea or soup but she had failed. When I stopped by at about six thirty to see if she had succeeded, she just shook her head. I told her to go home and not come back until morning. Then I drove home and told Funa I would be bringing Ronald back for dinner about nine o'clock.

It was just after eight when I climbed the stairs to his room, carrying a paraffin lamp. I lit a half-dozen lamps throughout the upstairs, and the two in his own room, before I set about getting him up. And I started with every intention of succeeding.

"Ronald!"

I gave him a whack on the arm.

"Ronald!"

He bolted right up and looked about, dazed.

"It's Clinemark. Get up. I'm taking you back to my house for dinner."

No longer dazed or startled, his head started to lower and so did his shoulders, probably with his realization of where he was.

"No, no," I said, grabbing his arm. "Get up. Go in and wash."

I waited as he sat there, staring straight ahead.

"You'll feel better in the morning if you get up for a few hours and then go back to sleep. . . . Because you're going downriver with the steamer. Back to The Port."

That had no effect on him. He gave no indication that he understood what I was saying. His silence wasn't stubbornness, recalcitrance or anything that I would have termed hostile. It seemed to be sheer willessness, passivity.

"You don't have to change clothes, just go in and wash up."

I pulled at his arm and he moved his legs and got up.

"That's right. Just a little water."

I walked behind him to make certain he went into the bathroom and stood outside the door, watching. He went through all the proper motions, slowly, mechanically, and didn't look at me when he came out.

"It's not far to my place. I told you I was going to show you how to eat *fufu* before you left."

He followed me down the stairs. I looked back once to make certain that he was and saw that he was holding onto the banister, looking at his hand as it slid along. I didn't try to carry on any further conversation for the moment. I knew what would wake him up—or I thought I did. All I wanted from him was some look of recognition that he knew he was leaving in the morning and that that was all right. I looked over at him once or twice as we drove, especially whenever we hit a pothole in the road and got jostled. I thought the bump might jolt him awake a bit more. It only seemed to make him belch at one point: his cheeks were a bit puffed out and his lips pursed as if he were trying to hold something in. He seemed to take no

230

interest in the dull lamps or dark figures that were moving in the night. And no interest in my house when we pulled to a stop and got out. He didn't look up when I held out a hand and said, "This is it." Funa, wearing her best white *agbada*, was standing at the door when we walked in, and the children were just behind her. I gestured again.

"This is my family."

I looked for his reaction in vain for he seemed to have none. But when Funa bowed and held out her hand, Western fashion, he responded. He reached for her hand and shook it. Both of the children followed her example.

"That's Laoye—he ran up to me that day in the market—and this is Ewumi. He's four and she's seven."

He had no smile or words. No questions, no comments. So I gestured once more.

"I see the table's ready. We'll sit on this side together and have them sit opposite us."

Anyone else would have asked why the plates were face down, even if they guessed it was customary, but he didn't. When we sat down Ewumi turned them over and Funa and Laoye went into the kitchen, returning together. Funa carried two steaming bowls and Laoye had one filled with water. He went around to Ronald and held it out to him. Ronald looked at him without asking me what he wanted.

"You're supposed to wash your hands," I explained. "I know you just have but it would be bad etiquette not to."

Ronald put his hands in the bowl.

"When he gets older and taller, he'll kneel before guests."

That didn't seem to interest him.

Laoye put down the bowl and dried Ronald's hands with a towel. Then he held the bowl for me, his mother and sister.

"And now," I said, "I'll show you how to eat *fufu*."

I took a ladle from one bowl and scooped meat, vegetables, and broth onto my plate. And then I pointed to the bowl of solid mash toward which my fingers were moving, kept going, put my hand in and brought out a small lump.

"See? Not much. You make a kind of oval shape out of it, press your thumb in right here . . . like this, see? And make a little hollow. There. Like a spoon."

I dipped it into my plate and turned it in the sauce.

"Try to make circular tosses with it when you do it. There are pulpy fibers in the vegetable that make it stick to the dough."

I told Funa and the children to begin so Ronald could watch them as well as me and then I brought the *fufu* to my mouth, giving him a satisfied look after I had. Then I scooped some meat and vegetables onto his plate and pointed to the *fufu* bowl.

"Go ahead, try it. Dig in."

He did. He tried. The lump wasn't very well shaped and when he pressed it with his thumb, it broke. Part of it splashed onto his plate and I sympathized with him by laughing. What he had left in his hand he rolled in the sauce, picking up whatever he could with it, and then bringing it quickly to his mouth. Long yellow threads hung down to his plate and the lump in his hand almost broke before he got it to his lips. And I saw his fingers stay there. Their tips were on his tongue as if stuck, motionless. I thought *Ah ha, now I'll get him to wake up*. His eyes widened a bit.

"Funa made it especially mild just for your sake," I said.

Yet I knew it was scalding him. He didn't want to lick his fingers but he tried it. Then he fished into his pocket for a handkerchief and blew his nose—which meant the insides of his nostrils were burning. For the first time he looked directly at me. It might have been an attempt to give me an angry look, but it was a look of recognition as far as I was concerned. Or it might have been. For he could hardly see me because of the tears in his eyes. He wiped them and then made the mistake of taking a deep breath to cool the inside of his mouth. That made matters worse. He emitted a small gasp and Funa, being very polite, tried not to smile. And I wanted to laugh but I didn't: I wanted *him* to laugh. What he did was put both hands on the table, one on each side of his plate, and look down at the plate—severely. He hadn't been that alert since he had walked out of the chapel with Angoli, carrying bundles of straw under his arms. But he didn't say anything. He wouldn't talk.

So I kept at it.

"The meat's red because it's cooked in palm oil and chili pepper sauce. I assume that's what you're looking at. Maybe you'd like to cut it with a knife. The chunks of meat are a little large—they usually are—and when you don't know how to bite portions of it off, or it burns too much to do it, it's permissible to cut it. I mean, it's still good manners—as long as you hold the meat with your right hand and cut it with your left."

I told Ewumi to go into the kitchen for a knife.

"I'll show you."

When she brought the knife to me I cut a piece of meat on my own plate.

"It's a little awkward, but you get used to it. Food's only touched with the right hand here. Want to try it? The meat'll go down easier."

I offered him the knife which he took without looking at me or saying anything Then he cut the meat, all of it— very small, small enough to gulp down his throat without chewing it. Which was clever if that's what he had in mind. It would make his mouth less of a furnace. He went for more *fufu*, tried to mold it, swiped it on his plate and tossed it in his mouth, swallowing fast.

"Better?"

His eyes widened but he nodded.

A response, I thought, and said, "Good! It gets better if you eat more."

He seemed to believe me and reached for more *fufu*, wiping it around in the sauce on his plate. After he ate that portion he blew air out of his mouth and both of the children laughed. Funa got up and returned with two glasses of *akara* and another plate on a tray.

"Want to try something to drink?"

There was perspiration along his hairline. He reached for one of the glasses and poured half of it down his throat. He didn't expect it to go down like fire and he lurched forward, coughing and sputtering. He tried to look at me as he coughed, his face getting fire-engine red.

"It burns worst only when you take your first drink. Take another."

He did and swallowed nervously but discovered that what I had said was so.

"There. . . . And why don't you take one of those things that Funa just brought in? They're a kind of dough-nut—made out of bean flour, and they're mild, very mild. It'll be like eating a plain piece of bread after choking on a fish bone, soothing . . . go ahead."

He reached for one and held it in his hand, looking at it.

"Those little green things you see *are* pepper pods, but they're absolutely harmless, totally bland. You won't even notice them."

He ate one, swallowed it down and reached for an-other.

"See? I'll send some along with you tomorrow so you can have them on the journey downriver."

I hadn't mentioned that he was leaving since I had tried getting him up, and I thought he might say some-thing. He blinked in a way that made me think he would. What he did was to look at Funa—sharply; almost rudely.

She turned her eyes on me for an explanation which I couldn't give her.

"She isn't very attractive, is she?" I said.

His eyes fell to the table and he coughed. I wanted to challenge him with *But she's not as plain as Nancy, is she?*

"She's as common as the African earth she walks upon, but she's an *abiku*."

At the sound of that word Funa said something to me. I laughed and the children did, too.

"She heard me say that word and she doesn't want me to talk about her. An *abiku* is a spirit child, a child that the parents think is going to leave this world as soon as it can, to join its spirit companions—which the parents don't want it to do, naturally. But if it does, the mother prays for the child to be restored to her."

This didn't impress Ronald.

"Funa's mother gave birth to her four times."

He looked at her again, his lips slightly parted. I waited for something to come from between them but, no, nothing did. Not even an incredulous *Four times?!*

"That's right. They can always recognize when a spirit child's reborn because there's a mark that's been made somewhere on the dead child's face or body. And if the scar appears on the newborn baby in the same place, they know it's an *abiku*, back again."

I said something to Funa. She argued with me—but not seriously. Then she turned her head and dipped her chin. There was a small gash on the side of her neck that was lighter than the rest of her skin and I pointed to it.

"See?"

Ronald looked at it disbelievingly. Then he looked at me. I waited for him to speak what was on his mind but he looked down at his plate instead.

"I'm glad you didn't ask me whether I believe it," I said a little sourly. "I almost thought you were going to. You can imagine with what care Funa's mother treated her after giving birth to her four times. She satisfied every want and whim and put up with every mood, which—believe me—covers quite a range, because if a spirit child doesn't get what it wants, it threatens to die. You can imagine what a hit that makes with mother and father. I think what it boils down to is that an *abiku* is a problem child—"

I was looking at Funa as I said this, smilingly, even though she couldn't understand English; and it was through her eyes that I saw something was wrong. As I turned to look at Ronald he started to get up, his cheeks puffed, his right hand pressing into his stomach.

"What's the matter? Are you going to be sick?"

I got up.

"Here—"

But before I gave him directions he turned around and went for the front door, running down the stairs to the car. He put both hands on the front fender and leaned over it. If he had vomited he would have done it on the hood of the car but he only retched. I went after him, following him out. Funa and the children stood on the porch above.

"It isn't the food," I said, "it's the brandy."

Funa called something down and I asked her if we had any mineral water. She said no. Not that it was needed. . . . Ronald pushed himself away from the car and started to walk around to the passenger side.

"I want to go home."

I turned around and looked at Funa. I told her what he said and then, just as he was closing the car door after him, I told her he had said thank you and was sorry he wasn't feeling well. I got in the car, looked at him and nodded. I don't know what I was agreeing with but I remember nodding.

"Home? . . . To *America?*"

He looked at me. I knew that isn't what he had meant.

"All right, home," I said . . . "to bed. But first we'll stop someplace where we can get you a glass of mineral water. At least I think we can. I've never tried. It's a place called *Maroc Nègre*—Black Morocco's. It'll give you a chance to see a group of Africans who don't like living here—who can't live anywhere, really. Africans who have lived in the West, abroad, and have come back."

He looked as if he was about to protest.

"The mineral water'll help your stomach," I assured. "You'll sleep better."

He looked out the window while we drove for about a mile and then he said something.

"Do you like living here?"

I was surprised to be asked.

"Yes, I like living here. But you don't have to like living at all to be able to share certain things with other people, common concerns—with people who happen to be living at the same time that you do. Do you? No one around here has the secret to life, but I like the way they don't think it's a mystery. Why? Are you thinking of staying on?"

To that I got no answer. Not even a shrug.

I turned into Corra Road, pulled to a stop and got out of the car. Ronald followed me. The noise of the band could be heard half way down the street. Black Morocco was considered one of the best high-life bandleaders north of The Port. His place was no bigger than a medium-sized room, filled with rickety chairs and crooked tables. Its six-man band thumped its percussion instruments and one of them sang into a microphone. They didn't need loud-speakers in that small room but they had them and you couldn't understand what the person next to you bawled into your ear. But then no one came to Black Morocco's to make conversation—not in the evening, anyway. They came for the sake of the music which they didn't only want to hear but feel, feel it physically. Everyone's bones finally vibrated with it. The dance floor was no more than a patch of cleared space, giving room for three or four couples.

Naturally there wasn't an empty table but I pushed my way forward. The heads on the bodies I touched didn't even turn to see who was shoving them this way and that. I saw a girl who called herself Mickey seated with a huge Nigerian, a favorite dance partner of hers, at a table right next to the dance floor, and I went up to her and shouted two inches from her sweaty and perfumed ear. I said I had Ronald Keane with me—*the doctor's husband*. I had to say it twice, and when I did they both stood up. I asked for their table while they danced for us. They nodded their heads, smiling, and the Nigerian shook Ronald's hand. I had to shout into the waiter's ear for mineral water—and cognac for myself—and he brought it almost as soon as we sat down. Black Morocco saw me, waved, guessed who Ronald was, left the band, and came over to shake Ronald's hand and tell me there was no charge for the drinks. Ronald let his hand be pumped again, passively, but his eyes were definitely open. He looked around as if he were frightened. I pointed to his glass and shouted in his ear.

"Drink!"

I even tried a whole sentence:

"You've got to get the poison out of you!"

But I don't think he understood because I had to say *poison* two or three times and I'm not sure he had understood the words which came before and after it.

Mickey and her Nigerian friend, already shiny with sweat, took the dance floor. I poked Ronald in the arm and pointed to Mickey for I knew she was magnificent. Her movements precise but relaxed, she danced with her partner for ten minutes, waggling her hips in her tight skirt, crooking her knees, putting one leg forward and stretching the other backwards. Her massive partner, foot to foot with her and knee to knee, swayed the upper part of his body in rhythm with hers; their hands twitched, occasionally interlocking, although their bodies never touched. Once Ronald looked away towards the frantic musicians, who, with beads of sweat on their brows, were furiously belaboring drums, wooden boxes and electric guitars. Black Morocco was bawling into the microphone until the music from the loudspeaker turned into a blare so loud that your aching eardrums could no longer stand it. Your very skin seemed to vibrate and twitch with it, and Ronald was pulling his head away. The trunk of his body was leaning backwards, as if he wanted to get six inches further away from the band. Suddenly the singing stopped, and when it did the clapping that was going on could be heard. The instruments also stopped but the drumming went on. Ronald looked around. He must have seen the gleaming eyes and flashing teeth of everyone whose faces were pressing toward the dance floor toward Mickey. When the drummers changed their rhythm he turned around and looked. She was moving toward him, her head at knee level bent towards the floor, her arms twitching to the ground as if they were going to pick something up. With her swinging, twisting pelvis sharply defined in the taut skirt, impelled by the drumming and now by the music that broke out after a shout from Black Morocco, she swayed along in front of her partner who followed, leaning backwards as far as he could, his trunk twitching. Then Mickey threw her body backwards as she came close to Ronald. Her skirt was hiked up high onto her thighs and while the band played itself into a frenzied climax, the enthusiastic crowd began putting coins on her almost-level forehead. Her head was no more than two feet away from Ronald's legs and she looked up at him, sweat pouring off her face, her white teeth shining brightly as she smiled. I hit Ronald on the arm at the same time that I held out a coin for him to take and put on her forehead. He didn't seem to want to do it and I had to nod and shout, "Go ahead!" He placed it partially on top of another coin and it slid off her forehead onto her face. Mickey grabbed it, lifting herself up, laughing—and the crowd cheered. Ronald had stood up and Mickey's huge partner clapped his arm around him, wiping all the perspiration from his arm onto the back of Ronald's shirt in the process. I handed Mickey a handkerchief and she wiped her face, handed it back to me and then kissed Ronald on the cheek. I picked up his glass of mineral water and held it out to him. He took it and drank it down like a child who had been ordered to drain a glass of milk. I took him by the arm and started to lead him out, waving goodbye to the band, which broke into a departing fanfare for us.

I'm sure he was relieved to be out on the road.

"Now don't you feel better?"

He shook his head, not in denial but bewilderment.

"There are half a dozen places like that in The Port," I said. "Have you been to any of them? The Paradise Bar, Low Life, Dark Donna's? They're better than the Hamarttan or the National Hotel when you need a drink."

He apparently hadn't been to any of them. And he apparently wasn't going to establish any kind of contact with me. Not even to question his departure, which I gave him another chance to do.

"Do you know how long you'll stay in The Port?"

Again all I got was a shake of his head.

"Well, I'm sure you can stay on at your house for as long as you wish, and we may see each other again. I'll be driving down to Samasi in a week and taking the train in. I have to be up at the mine at six o'clock tomorrow and I'll stop by at about eight to make sure you're awake, unless you hear the steamer. Odutola—that's the captain, you'll like him—starts blasting the whistle ninety minutes before sailing, then every fifteen or twenty minutes after that."

He slumped down in the seat and put his head back— just as I was going to ask if he wanted to stop at Nancy's grave in the morning before he left. I thought I could ask him next morning if it seemed I should, and I didn't say anything else until I pulled up outside their gate.

"Can you find your way?"

He looked at me and nodded.

"Wait," I said after a sudden thought. "I'll pull the car around so the headlights shine to the door." I did, to my satisfaction. "There. . . ."

He cleared his throat.

"How are Nancy's mother and father going to be told about her death?" he asked.

I hadn't thought of that.

"I don't know whether Alan will have considered it his place to have sent them a cable. Probably not, you're her husband. I suppose it'll be up to you to write to them?"

Click, click. . . . There it was again: the sound he made by picking at his thumbnail: *click, click.* He nodded and drew in his breath. Then he opened the door, closed it and started for the house without saying anything else. He was still wearing the same khaki shorts and shirt that he had put on almost two days agao. I thought I'd probably find him in them in the morning, still stretched out on the bed with the remainder of the brandy gone.

But I didn't find him there at all. I couldn't believe it. I asked Ilema a dozen quick questions: Where he was? When he had left? How he was dressed? Where were his bags? How did he look? What had he eaten? And then I jumped in the car and drove down to the dock. For that's where he was, sitting on one of the dock pilings. A hundred people were milling about, paying no attention to him because his back was turned toward shore. He was looking downriver, thinking God knows what. When I got out of my car and started for the dock I saw Embu's van coming down the river road.

"Ronald!"

He turned around and I waved to him as I made my way through the crowd. He got off the piling and stood on the dock. He had shaved and was cleanly dressed but didn't look as if he had slept much.

"You surprised me. I went to the house and you weren't there."

"I . . . I wanted to go to the cemetery."

He looked down at his feet. He seemed embarrassed. And I was even more surprised.

"Did you find it?"

I'm not sure whether I meant the cemetery or the grave. For even though I had said we were burying Nancy next to McGowan and assuming that Ronald had remembered, no marker had been put on McGowan's grave yet.

"I think so."

I didn't want to question him any further. His intentions were enough. There was no point in finding out whether he had stood over the right plot of ground.

"Look, here come Embu and Mbopi."

Odutola blew the ship's whistle as if to announce it.

They both were carrying something. Embu handed me the bag in his hand and spoke to me in his own dialect. I laughed and handed Ronald the paper sack.

"I forgot, but Funa didn't. She brought some *lepi* to Embu's headquarters this morning—those 'doughnuts' you had last night, remember?"

"Oh. . . ."

What Mbopi handed him he didn't want to take. It was Nancy's black satchel of medical instruments which must have been in the car Mbopi had chauffeured her around in. Ronald looked down at it, up at Mbopi, continued to hesitate and then reached for it. With something in both of his hands it appeared that none of us was going to be able to shake hands with him. And we didn't. But Embu, who had become a little politically ambitious in the wake of his good record in handling the epidemic, wasn't prevented from speaking a few grand words.

"We will build a momument to her someday in Ndami."

Ronald swallowed. That didn't fortify him. If he

242

didn't walk away he was going to start crying, so he turned and moved toward the gangplank. I followed him for a few steps.

"I'll probably see you in a week or so. If you're still around."

And if he wasn't? I ignored the possibility.

"If you are, we'll have *fufu* together someplace."

He just nodded the back of his head at me as he walked onto the steamer. I dropped back and joined Embu and Mbopi. We took a place further away from the bank and waited, without saying anything to each other. Ronald stood at the railing a bit sideways, facing upriver, not looking at us. For a while he held the bag and the *lepi* but then he set the black bag on the deck at his feet. Someone above ordered the gangplank taken away and in a minute a white jet of steam shot of the whistle's mouth and it blasted for the last time. The ropes were thrown off and the bow of the boat began to draw away. Odutola let the current take the steamer to midstream before he ordered the engines to churn. Ronald looked like a boy on a raft, sliding off. I didn't think he was going to turn to look at us but he finally did. By then I didn't expect to hear a goodbye or a call of thanks to any of us come across the water. And no such call came. I waved once more and when I did Embu and Mbopi joined me. At the last moment, it seemed, one of Ronald's arms lifted. I sometimes think he should have known that the steamer's destination—the new docks at Samasi—had been named for Alan. It was called Angle's Landing.

21

I COULDN'T BELIEVE IT," RONALD told me in less than a week, "*I couldn't believe it*." And before he did believe it, he would have liked nothing better than to have been able to stand at the railing of that riverboat until it had carried him back home, home to America. He wished he could keep on drifting. Even the fantasies about Vivian, which alternated between guilt-filled longings and satisfying scenes of revenge, scenes of triumphant accusation and punishment, only drifted through his mind. They had no power to seize it. He dozed fitfully all night on the train and arrived in The Port sleep-drugged, passive, unprepared. I knew, of course, that he would be met. It was common courtesy in the circumstances of Nancy's death. It was also standard procedure, etiquette, good expatriate manners. But I suppose Vivian had arranged, at least a little bit, for it be more than just good manners. For she had to, didn't she? Had to have felt some twinge of guilt or, if guilt is too strong, then a pang of uneasiness? Nervousness?

The station's diesel fumes don't completely suffocate the smell of ocean air in The Port's train terminal. And I imagine they mingled in Ronald's nostrils. A half a dozen porters always start wrangling among themselves for your bags, and they crowded around Ronald, appealing to him as "Master," using the word cleverly, hoping it would get him to intervene on their behalf. He was tongue-tied by their cries, not knowing how to arbitrate. But he was saved from having to try.

"Mr. Keane! . . . Ronald!"

He turned and saw a face he didn't immediately recog-

244

nize. Seeing it wasn't within the range of possibility. But when it was clear that it was not only possible but true, his heart took a sudden turn. Blood went to his head. It was Alan Angle, coming toward him through the crowds, half a head taller than anyone else, dressed in white—white shoes, white slacks and a short-sleeved white shirt open at the neck. He looked like a figure in a dream, pulling a small group of subordinates behind him as if invisible strings were attached to him. Still, Ronald didn't grasp the reality of it until Alan reached out with both of his large hands and found one of Ronald's, smothering it between his two warm palms.

"We can't tell you, Ronald . . . we can't tell you what we've been feeling since we heard. We're dreadfully sorry, dreadfully."

Ronald tried to look at him as his hand was being gripped, squeezed and gently wagged up and down. All of him was jostled. When he replied he could only mumble.

"Thank you."

Alan made a single gesture and one of the men behind him stepped forward to deal with the porters who had already become attentive and respectful when they saw Alan Angle take Ronald's hand, then his arm, turning him toward the station entrance. Together they began moving through the crowd.

"Your train's early," said Alan. "We very nearly didn't get here in time."

That Alan knew he was on the train was too much like magic of the wrong kind, witchcraft.

"How did you know I was coming?"

"Aaron sent me a wire giving me a report of the whole terrible business. We need to recognize the part he played in this, too. I want"—Alan increased the pressure of his already firm grip on Ronald's elbow—"you to do us a very great favor."

Ronald looked at him nervously. He felt he was being

asked to agree to do something before he knew what it was. It took all of his effort to say nothing, just to wait.

"Vivian and I want you to come and stay with us while you're here."

Ronald pulled his elbow from Alan's hand.

"I couldn't. No, I couldn't—thanks."

"Of course you can. Vivian said you would protest but that I mustn't let you, and so I won't. You can't go back and live in that house of yours by yourself, not now, not after what's happened. It'd be too miserable for you, too lonely, so we're especially prepared to make you comfortable. One of our guest rooms has a sitting room with it, so you can even take your meals alone when you don't care to join us and share our table, although, of course, you're always welcome to do that . . . always, and we hope you will."

That Vivian would say *anything* and that Alan would say what it was made Ronald's cheeks go red. And he already felt feverish. He hadn't intended to go back to Nancy's house. He had forgotten that they had one, very nearly. For it had never occurred to him that it might be his in some way.

"I was going to stay at the hotel until I could get a plane reservation."

Alan drew his head back.

"You're not staying on a while? We thought you might . . . and let us pay our proper respects, too. The National's full up at the moment. So's everything else. Trade delegations from East Africa have taken over everything. I doubt that you could get an accommodation—even with my help," he added modestly. "So please say that you'll come with us. I give you our promise that Vivian and I won't bother you, for we understand what you must be feeling." He retook Ronald's elbow in his hand, paternally. "We need to make amends to you, show our proper appreciation. When I learned that you'd gone into that death trap with your wife without a moment's hesitation, and when I read Clinemark's report on your expansion of the infirmary facilities in Ndami . . . well! We all realized we hadn't taken your measure. You've both made the rest of us look second rate, you and your wife. After all, it's our affair, isn't it? It's not as if you had had to go, being Americans. I've already sent in a report to the Colonial Office. I shouldn't be surprised if some recognition will be coming to you. God knows there ought to be something . . . something more than the little we can do to express our thanks and admiration. Of course, we know nothing can make up for your terrible loss, but we want you to know how deeply we feel for you. So, won't you please allow us to do a little something for you? It will be a privilege."

Ronald was dazed.

"*I couldn't believe it*" was the phrase he kept repeating to me over and over again after each thing he told me.

Alan's black Jaguar and driver were waiting just outside the station, and another man was standing beside the car, someone Ronald remembered seeing at the Hamarttan Club several times.

"You know Eliot, our chief secretary, don't you?"

Eliot shot a hand out toward Ronald.

"I say, Keane! What a job you've done!"

Ronald was becoming will-less, shrinking into nothingness. Recoiling from praise he didn't deserve. Eliot opened the door to the car and Ronald crawled into the back seat, pressing himself into the corner. His ability to think had deserted him. His throat was stuck. He couldn't take charge of himself. There was no hotel to go to and he didn't know how to order Alan's driver to take him to Nancy's house, even though he hadn't wanted to go there. He was unable to imagine how Vivian could possibly face him when he walked into the Angle residence on The Hill. Yet he tried. He tried to visualize where she would be standing, how she would position herself, what she would say, how she would behave in Alan's presence. How could she play this part? This role? He didn't think it was possible. He felt a sickening panic at his unpreparedness for what was happening, for such an occasion, for the scene that swam before his mind's eye. He looked at Alan, hoping to see something in the narrow, angular face. And Alan, seeing the movement of his head, mistook it for sociability and spoke.

"Aaron reported that the death rate dropped to twenty-nine the day you departed."

Eliot, seated next to the driver, turned around and responded when Ronald didn't.

"I shouldn't be surprised if it's *zero* in a day or two. What a smashing thing!"

The gold work in Eliot's mouth glittered when he smiled. And Ronald tried to acknowledge the smile with a nod but a memory of his last meeting with Vivian was taking possession of him. He remembered her refusal to see Nancy, to alter her way of life for him. His face became grim and he tried to make a mold of it, intending to keep it that way until they arrived on The Hill. But when they did he didn't need his grim look. Vivian wasn't there to receive them when they walked into the sitting room.

"Tell Mrs. Angle that Mr. Keane has arrived," Alan said to a servant adding to Ronald with a smile, "Vivian's probably ducked into the kitchen to see to some final touch for our luncheon."

Ronald thought no such thing. He was sure Vivian was upstairs in her room, hiding; trying to get control of her wobbly knees, redoing the makeup she had smeared during an unexpected, final fit of weeping. For he imagined only two possibilities: either that she was arranging a reunion between them behind this facade of officialdom, using Alan as a means to bring them together; or that the invitation to stay on The Hill had originated with Alan, and that she, dismayed and nervous, had concealed her own feelings. He imagined that Vivian was frightened that he was returning in this manner, not only alive but free of a wife, filled with the knowledge of how she had treated him, of what she was. This last possibility was the one that made most sense to Ronald for Alan seemed perfectly at ease, in control of everything. The initiator. Incapable of being used by Vivian. He was, in fact, calmly telling Ronald about the visit some Soviet warships were paying them when Vivian appeared, barefoot, carrying a pair of white sandals in her hand. Her hair wasn't in place. She was wearing a thin, patterned, pale blue dress and didn't appear prepared to receive anyone. It was at Alan at whom she looked when she came in, Alan alone, ignoring Ronald completely, yet talking as if there were a large crowd in the room listening to her speak to him.

"Am I late? Oh, I hope I haven't kept you waiting! I had our table put out on the terrace, and Selso called me, and—wouldn't you know? Look what I've gone and done!"

She held up her sandals.

"Broken a strap!"

Alan seemed embarrassed at the sight of her bare feet. He looked at Ronald smilingly, his veined cheeks a shade pinker than his usual color.

"Well, I hope we're among friends, dear."

"Oh, I'm *sure* we are."

Only then did she turn to Ronald. She dropped her sandals to the floor so she could clasp Ronald's hand in both of hers.

"I'm so very glad you've come to stay with us. I know Alan has told you that we want you to stay as long as you can, as long as you wish . . . and that we want, so *very* much, for you to look upon our house as your home while you're here. If there's anything I can do for you, I shall only to be too happy to do so."

Her fingertips seemed to be pressing into and kneading Ronald's palm. He lost his sense of balance, if he had it.

For she was talking just like Alan, sounding like him except for her intonation. Ronald tried to look into her eyes. He thought they were filled with sincerity but he didn't know. He couldn't keep up with anything, especially when her tone saddened.

"Oh, dear! I'm not very good at moments like this, am I, darling?"

Darling was Alan at whom she cast a glance before looking directly into Ronald's eyes.

"I know the perfectly proper thing to say at a dinner party and some silly diplomatic function, but at a moment like this I'm awkward, so awkward. But I *do* want you to know how much I sympathize with you in your wife's unhappy death. We"—she seemed to falter—"we're all proud of her, and grateful. She was a wonderful person, a marvelous doctor. She'll be missed here more than we can say."

A wonderful person? . . . A marvelous doctor?

To whom was she speaking? About whom? Perhaps Ronald withdrew his hand, perhaps Vivian released it. He didn't know. He was too shocked to know, too shocked by her words. He couldn't believe them. Alan must have seen him struggling with something, for he took a step forward.

"Don't, Vivian. He should be spared remembering."

Then a servant entered, carrying a tray.

"Here are our drinks."

Alan looked at the tray.

"What's this?"

"Nothing for you," said Vivian quickly. "I remembered Ronald's fondness for alexanders, so I had one made especially for him, even though it is only lunchtime."

Ronald shook his head.

"No, no. I don't care for anything to drink."

"Oh, but you must!"

Vivian lifted the glass off the tray and held it out to him. Her thin native bracelets clicked softly against one another. "It'll do you good after your long train ride, and I know you haven't had one since you left. Am I right? And nothing cold, either. I'm sure there was no ice to be found anywhere in Ndami. Am I wrong?"

She kept asking, needling him, for a response. And he felt Alan standing close by, observing, waiting for it.

"No."

"You see?"

She pushed the glass an inch or two closer to his body and he took it. She smiled beautifully.

"Let's all sit down then, shall we? and have Ronald tell us everything. We just don't know"—she turned her eyes on Alan—"what it is to be away from our luxuries and comfort, do we? After what Ronald's been through and what he's done, coming back here must be like coming to stand on the sidelines. Please, please tell us everything."

Did he try? He said he tried. But what was everything? Everything seemed to be the way Vivian crossed one leg over the other as he began to answer some question of Alan's. Her legs were stockingless. One foot and its slender ankle hung in the air. Her toes pointed toward him, each one tanned by the sun, each small nail daubed with a milky polish. Ronald struggled against being dominated by memories of having touched them. Once he thought she deliberately dipped her toes and then lifted them, as if she were using them to wave at him. His alexander was cool, liberally sprinkled with nutmeg; its fragrance was welcome to his nostrils and he drank it as if it were a milkshake. Vivian filled his glass again from a decanter on the tray, a silver urnlike thing whose surface was streaked with cool drops of condensation. When she bent close he mistook the scent of the wisteria in a nearby vase for perfume coming from her. He could see quite clearly that the rims of her eyes were not red, that she hadn't had an uncontrollable fit of weeping just before he arrived. Her knees weren't wobbly; they were lovely. The thin material of her dress arranged itself around her first this way, then that, collapsing against a breast, then into her lap, rippling up at her waist and falling against her again, depending on how she moved.

At some point Alan interrupted apologetically.

"Vivian, I'm afraid we do have a schedule, damnably inconvenient though it is."

"The Russians, of course. How tiresome! We'll go to the terrace and Ronald can continue. Ring for Selso, will you, dear?"

Alan did as he was asked. And Vivian seemed to explain why she couldn't do it, which she usually did.

"If I don't bring my sandals I'll never remember where I dropped them."

They had all stood up. And as Alan went to a table to pick up a brass bell, Vivian stooped adroitly for her sandals. When she did Ronald felt something brush against his leg, below the knee. His eyes dropped: Vivian was reaching for her sandals with her left hand and her right was quickly leaving his shin where she had given him a secret stroke. The brush became a blow. She jumped right up as the bell rang and walked directly toward Alan, her sandals dangling in her hand. Ronald lifted his swimming head. When he looked at the back of Alan's, his vision was blurred. He saw Vivian linking her arm through her husband's.

He couldn't believe it. . . .

Vivian was saying, "You won't forget to tell him about A. J. will you, dear?"

"No, no, certainly not."

Alan looked back at Ronald who stumbled behind them as they made their way toward an umbrella that was shielding a table from the sun that was set for lunch.

"But," said Alan, "I'd like to hear about your expansion of the infirmary facilities, Keane."

Ronald returned Alan's backward glance with a confused nod, for his leg, where Vivian had stroked it, was burning. The skin beneath his slacks had leaped to life. He stared at Vivian's bare feet and legs. Her ability to deceive, her daring . . . he couldn't put it together. The sun struck him heavily.

Vivian threw her hand out.

"Look at the fleet! What a clear day!"

Eight gray ships sat in the bay like eels that came up to bask in the sun. Ronald looked where he had been directed to look. And then his head went back and forth, from Vivian to Alan, whenever each of them spoke.

"Yes," said Alan, "and I have to be on board one of them in an hour. I can't be much of a host, I'm afraid. Tell us about the infirmary, Keane."

Chairs were pulled out by black hands and they sat down.

"You mean the chapel?"

Alan looked at him.

"Aaron didn't say anything about a chapel."

"I fixed a hole in the chapel ceiling, that's all."

Alan looked at Vivian, his lower lip thrust out doubt-fully.

"Listen to him! Another fifty or sixty beds and he says it was only a hole in the ceiling. That's something measured by the standards we have to settle for here, I can tell you. And without proper equipment, too. Improvising —that's what we need in this country, and a lot of it."

"Alan, *do* tell him about A. J."

"All right, all right. We've had another unfortunate death in our colony. One of our best men died of fever in Mlane, about two hundred miles along the coast from here. It's nothing certain, of course—there are channels to go through and I can't make promises. Still, if you like, I could try to suggest that you be his replacement. That is, if you think you can handle the sort of thing they're doing, and I gather from Aaron's report of what you did with the in-firmary facilities that you can. It would mean looking at the site and talking with Sickles, our head man. What's going on, in general terms, is a fight against pollution in the center of the city: water supply, surface drainage, that kind of thing. The whole system needs reconstruction, with a good deal of ingenuity, in beginning with what's there and making work what can work. I don't know if that's in your line, but I thought . . . well, Vivian suggested that after the jolt you've received you might not be quite ready to return to the States, and having something to put your hand to might be just the thing. It would be to our advantage, too; it's not just a favor by any means. It takes time to bring a man out from back home, and there's nothing like finding one on the spot.

Vivian suggested. . . .

Ronald looked at her. A line in one of her cheeks betrayed pleasure: she was holding back a satisfied smile. Her lips were parted; she appeared to be breathing through her mouth.

"We naturally can't expect him to make up his mind right this minute," she said softly to Alan. "He needs to rest and have time to think about it."

Now she allowed herself to break into a frank smile as she looked at Ronald solicitously.

"Certainly," agreed Alan, "all the time you want, Keane. You'll find our overseas pay scale doesn't rank with American scales, but I think you'll find it adequate."

He lifted his head and looked toward the house. A servant was approaching them, one without something for the table.

"Now what is it I must do?"

Alan sounded officially tired, not genuinely disturbed. But Vivian turned her head and stood up quickly anyway.

"I'll see to it, darling."

She plucked a strawberry from her fruit plate.

"Obligations! One is never free of them in this kind of life, never free."

She popped the strawberry into her mouth and started toward the servant, leaving Ronald's jaw tightening at the recollections that the word *free* brought back to him.

Alan said, "I hope it's nothing from the Admiral's flagship."

Vivian stopped.

"Maybe Ronald would like to go on board with you? Surely they wouldn't object to your bringing whomever you please."

She didn't wait for a response to her suggestion.

"I hadn't thought of inviting you," said Alan, "Would you like to tour a battleship?"

"No, I don't think so."

"I don't blame you. It'll be a bore."

From thirty feet away Vivian called, "It's for me, Alan." Which sounded like an announcement that she was leaving, until she started back for the table. "It's Mrs. Albert, so I can't say no. It's about our dinner with the Russians tonight, I'm sure." She bent over and picked up her sandals. "I'll just be a second." She looked directly at Ronald when she said, "We're sorry that we have obligations this evening. Please understand and forgive us, will you?"

He had no choice but to nod even though he didn't understand a thing. She could prepare an alexander for him, stroke his leg—and yet talk as if she had met him only an hour ago, constantly saying *we*, talking for herself and her husband, whom she kept calling *dear* and *darling*. It was making him wake up. He was being forced to become more alert. He even realized that he and Alan weren't sharing Vivian's fruit plate. They were eating creamed fish. When Vivian walked away they each seemed to take mouthfuls of it in silence. And then Alan cleared his throat and coughed softly into his napkin. A polite embarrassment hung in the air between them. Alan spoke without looking up from his plate.

"Vivian's had some sort of shock."

To hear it shocked Ronald.

Alan was severing the toast underneath his creamed fish with the side of his fork.

"She was terribly upset at the news of your wife's death."

Ronald was all eyes but Alan didn't look up. He was all ears, too, and he waited, resting the side of his hand on the table, holding his fork above his plate.

"Vivian's very delicate, really, for all her vigor."

Nothing could have seemed farther from the truth. It was like saying that Iceland was on the equator.

"She puts most of us to shame, what she can do in this climate—"

Alan stopped talking because what she did at that particular moment in that climate was come clacking out onto the terrace in shoes. Alan dropped his fork onto his plate, brought his napkin to his lips and pushed back his chair.

"I'm afraid I have to join our Comrades below."

He dropped his napkin right onto the food that was left on his plate, lifted his eyes quickly to Ronald and turned the corners of his mouth up just as quickly, in a nervous, apologetic smile.

"See you this evening, I hope. Before our dinner. A drink together, perhaps?"

Ronald stared as he started off for Vivian, meeting her in the middle of the terrace. They stood together talking for a minute, then Alan's head dipped toward hers, she tilted her cheek upwards smilingly and he kissed her. When she started toward the table Ronald kept staring. What was this? . . . Was something happening? When Vivian went toward the table Ronald couldn't turn his head aside, couldn't conceal his captivity at the way she moved across the surface of anything—a terrace, a tennis court, a beach —as if it liked to feel the weight of her. The heels on her white shoes elevated her, lifting her skirt to knee level, making the calves of her legs firmer.

"You can see I found a proper pair of shoes."

Yes, she could see him seeing. That was like her: cleverly, happily reminding him that he was looking. He turned his head and when she sat down he didn't look at her, not even when her voice sounded out caressingly.

"Oh, Ronald. . . ."

She put her hand on top of his. He withdrew it, moving it closer to his plate. He had felt almost frightened by her touch.

"Everything that has happened to us has been so terrible! So horrible! But it happened, we can't help that, and we're here again. You're here again, we're together again. I didn't think we ever would be! But now, now you can stay on—I *know* Sickles will have you."

There was joy in her voice, real joy. And it was odd the way she said things had happened to them, *us* . . . saying *we* couldn't help it. She put her hand on his and he withdrew it again.

"You're right. We shouldn't talk about it now," she said.

In not looking at her, by not letting her touch him, he was starting to get some distance from her. He was using his "condition" to hide behind, deliberately. It was like standing behind a screen and he began to enjoy it: listening, waiting to hear or see out of the corner of his eye what she would do next—which was to eat a wedge of pineapple, then a small ball of melon. She couldn't keep silent even though she had said they shouldn't talk about it.

"Ronald?"

He didn't move or answer.

"I've been afraid that you would misunderstand what I knew I had to do for us, so afraid! Seeing Alan here with you, seeing those"—her voice seemed to be faltering, and she distracted him from it by holding a hand out toward the bay, passing it through the air, over the ships below—"your being back, knowing how everything in the colony depends so much on us now, I hope you understand. Surely you can see. . . . Ronald, we've both suffered, both of us! Please believe that."

He looked at her whether he was ready to believe it or not. He didn't know that she had suffered; he couldn't imagine that she had. He couldn't because she was leaning forward, trying to urge the truth of what she was saying upon him. The tension put upon her dress by her shoulder slackened. The top of her dress fell away from her, forward, revealing part of her bra and the line where the sun had stopped tanning her skin. And he started undergoing something again: even though he was not in Ndami but was seated at a luxuriously arranged table on a spacious terrace, facing an ocean and a sloping canopy of rich vegetation, he was undergoing something again—but undertaking nothing. He had not under*taken* anything except the repair of the chapel ceiling since he had come to Africa. He had under*gone* everything. . . . Was there no end to undergoing?

"You're back, darling, that's all that matters. I knew there wouldn't be any risk if you took the proper precautions."

He undertook the effort to speak, to emerge from where he was hiding. To assert the sense of guilt he knew they both should have.

"Nancy took the proper precautions."

Vivian's head lowered and her eyes dropped. She reached out for his hand but he pulled it away and her hand struck the handle of a spoon. He had to make her pay, he *had* to; somehow, some way.

She said, "There isn't anything I wouldn't do to have Nancy back again."

"We killed her."

There was a moment's silence. It was long enough for him to feel the effect of his own words on himself. He began to sink down in his chair. But as he sank her voice raised itself, not in loudness but in pitch.

"Really! Don't you think that's a bit thick? Don't you think so? After all, it wasn't *our* suggestion that she go there."

Her Australian accent had become more pronounced. He wasn't prepared to be crossed by her. His efforts to undertake anything were at an end, routed. Her gaze was demanding, even more demanding than her question and she shook her head. She moved her hand back and forth in the air over a short area of space, quickly, as if she were rejecting an offer of food or drink.

"No more, no more—not now. We shouldn't talk about it now. Were you able to sleep on the train last night?"

He only shook his head.

"I didn't think so," she said as if that explained why he was being nothing but unreasonable. She reached for the bell on the table and rang it. "You need some rest, you look exhausted."

He nodded his head without even thinking about it. He felt exhausted. His agreement with her judgment mingled with self-pity, though I doubt he knew what part of himself he pitied, what part of his life or recent experience he pitied himself for.

Vivian stood up.

"Selso, see if Paddy's brought Mr. Keane's things to the guest room, will you?"

Paddy was just coming from the car port with them when Vivian asked and the three of them, she, Ronald and Paddy, walked down the long corridor, past the sun room and up the stairs to the second floor guest room with its balcony that looked down on the garden that was so well cared for at the rear of the house. Vivian herself opened the door.

"Just set the bags inside, Paddy. I'll show Mr. Keane how to do the shutters."

She walked directly to the low wide windows.

"There's a trick to them. The catches need redoing. You have to pinch them in the middle. Do you see, Ronald? . . . Can you get the other one?"

He couldn't get the other one. For as she was reaching, making a mock-sound of mock-effort as she stretched, he threw himself on the bed. He turned his back on her and the still unshuttered windows. He closed his eyes and even with the dimness that he brought on himself by doing so, the dimness increased after he heard one of the shutters close. It closed off a portion of his mind, it seemed: part of the room. He hadn't put his body down on a bed so comfortable in weeks, maybe even months. Vivian was right: he needed rest, that was where he belonged, withdrawing from everything right there and then, especially her. He was only in her house because it was worse to go to Nancy's and because there were no hotel rooms in town. He was only going to accept the Angles' hospitality for the day, maybe even only the afternoon . . . he would sleep, get hold of himself and leave.

I imagine Vivian stood looking at him for a few moments when she turned around and saw him on the bed, motionless, with his back turned on her. But I cannot imagine what she thought. Whatever it was, it gave Ronald time to drift toward sleep, gently down an incline . . . even the bed began sinking beneath him. At first he didn't realize that it was from the weight of someone sitting on the edge of it. But then he felt a hand touch his shoulder, bringing him into wakefulness with care, calling his name softly, whispering it into his ear. He felt breath on his cheek. He rolled over, his eyes open, looking up. Vivian's hair had fallen forward with the tilt of her body, and the sudden quickness, the force with which the side of her head thudded down on his chest, jolting him, the fierceness with which her arms gripped him, was the closest she came to confessing guilt, admitting shame, declaring a need to be reconciled to something if not him. Ronald's hands leaped to her arms, gripping them. He lifted himself up, pushing her up, her head glued to his chest until he swung his legs off the bed and slid around her, leaving her seated on the bed's edge. He walked away—somewhere into the room, anywhere—his heart pounding. He was about to speak, or he thought he was about to speak, until he heard her voice behind him.

"You can't think I was wrong, or that I treated you badly, just because I loved you so."

He turned. She was getting up from the edge of the bed, and all he could do was stare at her in the shuttered darkness of the room, speechless. His silence must have given her her chance, for she started toward him, moving as directly as her words had been aimed. She walked straight into him. Her arms came around him and the fulness and softness of her breasts were such that his eyes closed at the sensation as her cheek slid along his. For all her desirableness his emotions didn't rapaciously surge through him. The tenseness went out of his arms, the tightness out of his chest. His throat loosened up. He was able to swallow. The dimness of the room, even though the shutters cut off the breeze at the same time that it kept out the glare of the sun, seemed like a mercy. The tip of Vivian's nose struck the corner of his mouth and opened his lips as it bumped across his teeth. He might have spoken if he could but it took a few minutes. And after the minutes had passed he was moaning in the same tone of voice that he had moaned for Jesus in the chapel.

"Vivian . . . !"

22

I RECEIVED THE FOLLOWING WIRE:

PLEASE COME IMMEDIATELY. DON'T DELAY.
CAN YOU? ALAN SAYS SO TOO. WIRE BACK.
VIVIAN.

Vivian? . . . Right away? . . . Right away meant two and a half days. That's how long it took me to get there: to pull myself and things together. I put both myself and my things into one of the company cars along with Angoli and together we drove over the almost impassable roads from Ndami to Samasi. I boarded the train, told Angoli to wait for me until the end of the week—he had two half-brothers there—but then to drive back alone if I didn't return. I'd get the steamer whenever I did return. I took a bedroll along with me on the train and slept in the baggage van, tolerably well. So I arrived in The Port not overly tired from traveling.

And, unlike Ronald, I was expecting some kind of reception committee. The moment the train pulled into the station I looked about for someone and was surprised to see no one. I didn't expect Alan to be there but I expected someone from his staff to be. I started out of the station a little wonderingly if not confused until, two steps or so through the main entrance, I saw Vivian standing only where Vivian would stand: in the sun, next to a blue Peugeot. She threw a braceleted arm into the air when she saw me, forcing my lips apart. I couldn't help but smile because she always waved that way, tossing her fingers straight up as if she were pointing to something in the sky.

"Aaron! Over here!"

Both my hands were held down by my bags so I lifted my chin into the air and smiled some more. I imagine all my teeth showed. Vivian started toward me, quickly as always, making a brown-black blur of herself between her neck and her knees: the dress she was wearing seemed to be patterned like a native mask. One of her arms came around my neck, pulling it forward; one of her breasts squashed against me and I got a kiss on my unshaven cheek. Her hand dropped onto the top of one of mine and she pulled my smallest bag away from me.

"Oh, Aaron! Still refusing to let a black man carry your bags."

"I didn't refuse," I protested, "there weren't any around."

"Oh, you liar. Just because you live native, speak native, and half think like one doesn't mean you have to lie like one!"

"I'm glad to see you, so let's not start an argument. Besides, you look a little native yourself."

She poked her knee out from under her dress, causing the skirt to lift a little.

"Do you like it?"

"It?"

"Why, yes, *it*."

"I like the way it looks on you."

"I'm not fishing for compliments. It's one of Tufola's best patterns. So don't be inappreciative of local art."

She handed me back my bag as if to punish me.

"You can lift it into the back seat."

I did.

"Why are you my reception committee?"

She was already opening her door and getting in when I asked, but she didn't answer. Instead she turned over the motor.

"How do you like my car?"

"It must be new."

"Isn't it wonderful?"

"If you like machines."

"Don't be so superior."

I looked at her and smiled: "Why not?"

She blared the horn on principle, not because someone was actually standing in our way. It was just a general announcement to everyone in the street everywhere, even halfway down the road behind us, that we were leaving. It seemed to be a custom among people who owned machinery in this part of the world.

"So where are you taking me if you're not going to explain why you're my reception committee?"

"To your hotel."

"What's my hotel? I was going to stay with Msago."

"On the floor?"

"No, they have a bed."

"If they push someone else out of it they do."

"Vivian, you have the damndest ideas about how people live in this country."

"I know exactly how people live in this country, so don't lecture me," she said lightly—lightly enough to let me know that she didn't feel I was. "We're not having you up because I have a house full of French women."

"French women?"

"*Wives!* Alan has run off for two days with three Frenchmen from Abidjan—petroleum, of course—and left me with their wives. Have you ever tried to fill the empty hours of idle wives?"

"No, but I believe other men have."

She surprised me with a disgusted look.

"That isn't what I meant. They're like their food—all

sauce. I can't stand them! They're incorrigible snobs, and two of them can't even speak English. Where do they get their nerve?"

I laughed. And then something occurred to me.

"If Alan's gone for two days why did he want me to hurry down?"

"He thought you might enjoy a few days relaxing here."

"Vivian," I said suspiciously and coaxingly, as if I were trying to pull the truth out of a child.

She looked at me.

"What?"

"I know you better than that."

"Oh?"

She turned her eyes back on the road before saying more.

"No one else does. Why should you?"

She looked at me again, a little challengingly; and I was surprised again. And, answered by a question, I couldn't and didn't answer. It was she who broke the brief silence.

"All right. . . ."

The stiffness went out of her shoulders.

"Alan doesn't know you're here. I put in the wire that he said to come too because I was afraid you might not otherwise . . . if it were only I who asked you."

I looked at her and she made certain that I didn't look into her eyes. She kept her profile to me, steadfastly.

"You fox," I said with a mock sigh, because, to be honest, I really didn't care. "You crafty woman. Do you know what it's like driving from Ndami to Samasi? Do you have any idea of the condition that road is in?"

"Don't, please. I'm sorry, but you've got to help me find Ronald."

"Find him?"

"He's up and gone, disappeared!"

"How do you know?"

"Because he was staying with us."

I must have looked surprised.

"It was Alan's idea, not mine. He insisted upon it, he felt that under the circumstances it was unthinkable not to do so. Alan met him at the train, he came up for lunch, we had a perfectly normal visit on the terrace, then Alan went off to tour a Russian battleship, and Ronald went to sleep— he was exhausted. We were having a dinner party that night that we couldn't cancel, and we couldn't invite Ronald, but Alan thought we could all have a drink together before our guests arrived. But when Alan went to his room he was still dead asleep so he didn't ask him, and then—in the morning he was gone! No warning, no word, no *reason!* He was going to look at a position that Alan had found for him in Mlane—"

"He must have had a reason."

"I can't imagine what it was."

"And someone must have seen him go. He had to get a taxi, didn't he? Didn't one of—?"

Vivian shook her head and interrupted me.

"No one saw him. Nothing, no one. If they did he must have bribed them to lie plenty. He probably walked out in the middle of the night."

"You've got watchmen at your place. They would have seen him."

"They all go to sleep on us, you know that."

"Maybe he's at home."

Vivian shook her head.

"At a hotel?"

"No."

"How about the Afrique?"

"Not even there. I've tried them all."

"Has he gone back?"

"To the States?"

I nodded.

"He hasn't gone through immigration. Alan's checked. He can't have just disappeared into the bush! What are we going to do? We feel responsible, after all."

I gave her a questioning and significant look which she probably didn't observe.

"Why should you feel responsible?"

But she observed the more than casual way that my question came out for she looked at me.

"Well, someone's got to feel responsible for him. He's come back filled with the effects of your epidemic."

"It wasn't *my* epidemic."

She didn't reply.

"His wife *did* die, you know."

"That has nothing to do with it," she said sharply.

"Nothing to do with it? Then what does?"

"If you got to know him at all, you know that he didn't give a damn about her."

I was a little surprised how authoritatively she said that. And it made me realize that I had been a little too solemn when I had referred to Nancy's death. I looked out the windscreen and admitted the truth of what she said.

"No, I don't suppose he did. But her death made him a little guilty. Remorse, you know? Maybe he's gone on a drunk."

"Oh, dear, no!"

"It's possible. Some place like the Up All Night?"

She shook her head distastefully.

"I told Paddy to check around a few places. He says he did."

"How about Solly's?"

Her head swung around at me. She gave me a frank open stare, a brilliantly clear scrutiny. I must have withstood the intensity of it because she swung her head forward again and looked out the windscreen.

"Solly's?"

"Solly's," I repeated. "Solly Dodide's."

She released her foot from the accelerator and let the car drift to the side of the road, braking it. Even after we stopped she kept her foot on the brake pedal so that her knee was high in the air. Tofula's patterned dress slid up to the middle of her tanned thigh. She had both hands on the steering wheel, kept them there, looked at the dashboard and then at me by tilting her head sideways. She looked as if she were listening to some sound in the engine.

"What's the matter?" I said.

"You know what's the matter."

I suppose I did but I didn't say anything.

"What do you know about Solly's?" she asked.

I shrugged without looking at her.

"A few things."

She didn't ask what, I didn't say what. At last I looked at her and we exchanged a glance of recognition.

"Don't tell me he came apart?"

"I guess you could say that."

She reached for the ignition keys and turned the switch. The motor died. She supported her right elbow on the bottom of the steering wheel and rubbed the fingers of her right haand along the bridge of her nose, her eyes closed.

"What must you think of me?"

I wasn't supposed to answer that question. Or it was clear that I didn't need to. But we were silent just long enough for me to feel that I should.

"Well, I don't know. I might think that Ronald's lucky, you never can tell."

"Oh, Aaron—"

She reached for my hand, squeezed it quickly and withdrew her own.

"Don't be kind."

"Why not?"

"Because I need to feel down on myself, that's why.

Oh, why, *why* didn't I think of Solly's? Why didn't I think of that! It would be just like him to moon about in that room, wouldn't it?"

"Am I supposed to answer that?"

She took hold of the steering wheel with both hands at the very top of it. She might have been trying to control the car at full speed.

"Will you do something for me?"

"If I can."

"You can. Will you?"

She looked at me.

"Don't I get to know what it is first?"

"Say that you will."

"All right, I will."

"Drive out to Solly's and see if he's there?"

"And if he is?"

"Get him out of there—take him to his house."

"And if he isn't there?"

"Then I don't know. I'll just have to wait."

She didn't want to wait a minute longer then. She reached for her purse on the seat between us, opened the car door and started to get out.

"Take my car."

"Wait a minute! What about my hotel?"

"You can go there later."

She slammed the door and I scrambled into the driver's seat, not because I was eager to get started. I was just going after her. I put my head out the window.

"Don't you want me to take you up The Hill?"

"No."

"Or somewhere—"

She sent her braceleted hand back and forth through the air, trying to stop me from talking, telling me no.

"Do you know how to get there?"

I thought I did.

"Ah—"

"Take the first road on your left after Hamsun's Bay. And then come to the Palm Wine Terrace."

"Where? Look," I protested, because I wanted to get her back in the car. I wasn't ready to drive to Solly's. . . . "Look, let me take you wherever you're going. You're in the middle of nowhere."

"I know exactly where I am, and a walk will do me good."

"Well, where's the Palm Wine Cafe?"

She looked at her watch.

"Oh, you know the Palm Wine Terrace—in Cecil Street, just down from the Soho Market. I'll meet you in the room on the second floor."

"The second floor—"

"Yes. In two hours. Is two hours enough time?"

I looked at my watch.

"If he's not there, it's too much time."

"Well then, your room is at the National."

"Vivian, I'm not going to pay those prices—"

She silenced my objection with a wave of her hand.

"Alan will pay."

"Alan doesn't even know I'm here," I reminded her.

"Aaron, quit acting like an ingenue. Why are you so distracted? You haven't just arrived from the provinces. Alan will be informed, Alan will pay. Now go!"

It was she who went, turning around quickly, starting across the road toward the wavering lines of people who were walking along. She was wearing a pair of high sandals that had no ankle strap, and each time she lifted a foot the back of the sandal came up and softly struck her naked heel. I sighed, turned on the motor and then looked up the road once more to where she was walking before I started to pull away. When I had been looking at her out the side window, her waist was at my eye level. The thin inter-twined lengths of leather that went around her as a belt were made, I'm sure, from water-buffalo hide. And she had something on beneath Tofula's natively-patterned dress, a beige slip; but she wasn't wearing a brassiere. It didn't seem possible that a woman her age could look the way she did.

Had I been distracted?

23

SOLLY'S . . . THE RIGHT PLACE *where all the wrong roads of life had led.* I wasn't sure that the only thing Ronald was doing there was "mooning," as Vivian had said. I imagine that was part of it but I thought there was another part, too: when all things seem wrong sometimes there's an impulse to return to a place where something was right, a place where something had "worked." It doesn't need to be much. Whatever the reasons, if he had to escape, Solly's was as good and probably better a place to go than anywhere else. I didn't particularly want to see him. I don't think I wanted to see him at all and when I was driving past Hamsun's Bay I wished that Vivian hadn't asked me. But she had, and I had said yes. Why? Because there was no reason not to? Because I was involved and I also felt responsible? Or because I was like every typical male: when Vivian, with a decisive and energetic movement, said *Take my car*, you took her car? I didn't like to think of it that way even though I thought of it smilingly. And I wondered why I laughed with Vivian and not at her when she had made her remarks about her guests. Wasn't she also an idle wife—unproductive, narcisstic? As Alan's wife didn't she lead a life of camouflage and idiotic ritual? Didn't she go about with her apron off and her scent on? When I thought about a little detail like that, it confused me: I don't believe I ever smelled perfume on Vivian. She never seemed to enhance herself by cosmetics and other forms of sexual display. I can imagine her being annoyed at the competitiveness among the three French women because she seemed to be so free from sexual competition. Why? Was she so sure of herself? She seemed such a type and yet she was so untypical. She was never gaudy, never seemed to employ the arts of sexual bargaining with men or women. Even though she may have distracted me, I would be hard pressed to point to anything about her which suggested that what she wore or what she did was intended to distract me.

It was curious.

When I turned off the motor of Vivian's Peugeot I heard the crows squawking. The man inside who was poking around in bins of maize I assumed to be Solly. I saw a closed door, pointed to it and said, "Mr. Keane?" He didn't nod. He only looked surprised and walked past me and opened the door. From the position I found Ronald in—sprawled across the bed, not asleep, not awake—he must not have heard me ascend the stairs. Or he had assumed that it was Solly. For there were dirty dishes on a tray on the floor—he must have been having meals up there —and there was a bottle of Scotch next to it. He was some-place, all right, or had been somewhere, for when he squinted and raised himself up on his elbows he looked at me as if I might have been Nancy: I mean, for someone to come from Ndami was like coming back from the dead.

"Aaron."

I nodded.

"Tell me what's happened," I asked.

He didn't or couldn't. So I told him why I was there asking him that question: that I had gotten a wire from

Vivian, that she had just met me at the station, that she had told me he had disappeared, that I had her car outside and that she wanted me to bring him back to Nancy's house, presumably so she would know where he was. He got off the bed and went to a small table where there was a pitcher and basin. He poured water into the basin and washed his face with his hands. All he had on was a pair of square undershorts.

"So how long have you been here? What happened?"

He turned toward me while he was drying his face with a blue hand towel.

"Alan met me at the train."

"I know that."

"*I couldn't believe it. . . .*"

That was the first time I heard him express his incredulity as he told me what happened and shook his head over his confused feelings. He didn't tell me what happened in the guest room so much as he confessed it, guardedly. And he only did that, I think, because it led to the next event. When Alan came to the guest room to invite him to have an evening drink, he hadn't been dead asleep. Alan hadn't left him undisturbed.

"But Vivian said so," I objected.

"Said what?"

"That Alan had found you asleep and didn't wake you."

Ronald wasn't surprised. He said flatly, "He lied."

"About what?"

"About what?" he echoed.

"Yes."

This is about what: When Ronald woke up Vivian was gone. He didn't know when she had left; he didn't know what time of the afternoon or evening it was until he opened one of the shuttered doors to the room's balcony. And then he could see from the softer light of the sun that it was early evening. Waking and remembering were almost as bewildering to him as living and experiencing had been. He pulled on a pair of pants. Shirtless and shoeless, he walked out onto the balcony which faced the top of the hill that rose behind the Angle's residence. Some servant was still working in the garden below. Dressed for dinner in a white coat and tie, Alan stepped into the garden from the house moving slowly along one of its stone paths. Ronald straightened up and drew back—he didn't say *from guilt*, but I imagined as much. He continued to look down at the back of Alan's graying head without being detected. Alan reached the center of the garden and stopped; but instead of looking around randomly like a man who was waiting for his wife to finish dressing for a dinner party, he turned and looked up at the balcony to the guest room. Ronald pulled back too late. Alan had seen him and his voice floated up from below.

"Taking the air?"

Ronald had to nod before he could find his voice. He stepped forward again, making an attempt to appear relaxed by putting a hand on the railing.

"Yes, I am."

"I'll come up and join you."

He couldn't believe it, Ronald said. Alan didn't wait for an answer. He turned and started toward the house and Ronald backed into the room in a panic. He pulled on a shirt and scrambled into a pair of socks as if clothing would protect him from something. He saw the unmade bed: both pillows had head imprints on them. He put one pillow on top the other, threw back the sheet and was straightening it, palming down the wrinkles, when Alan knocked. He tried to put a smile around his mouth as he reached for the door handle.

Alan immediately commented on his appearance.

"You're looking fit."

Ronald tried to keep smiling. It wasn't easy for Alan looked distinguished, well put together, fortified. Ready for

274

the Russians. His white dinner jacket seemed to do away with his normally bluish gray, heronlike complexion, even though he was smiling, . . . Alan looked around the room as he stepped in. Ronald, understandably paranoid, was sure he gave special attention to the disarray of the bed.

"How are you getting on?"

"As you can see, I slept hard."

"Good. A night sitting up on the train entitles you to a bit of a rest," Alan said calmly. "I'm glad that you got some."

Ronald flushed. He grew warm even though there was nothing in Alan's voice to suggest that he was saying anything other than what he was.

Alan walked past him onto the balcony.

"I haven't seen the view from up here in a long while. I used to enjoy watching the way those creepers climbed and twisted their way up the hill on top of those trees."

He paused. The pause seemed to be intentional: to give Ronald a moment to observe just how the creepers twisted. So Ronald looked toward the summit of the hill and tried to appear appreciative, interested. But he didn't know how to convey his appreciation or interest except by nodding. And his nod brought forth a further fact for his appreciation.

"It's filled with bird life up there," said Alan.

Ronald kept looking, thinking nothing, only feeling trapped on the balcony with Alan.

"Have you been thinking about Mlane?"

Ronald looked at Alan but Alan didn't return the look.

"Well, I haven't thought about it much yet."

"No, of course not," Alan agreed, "you've just awakened. But I hope you'll take the offer seriously." He put his hand to his mouth and coughed. "Have . . . have you enjoyed Vivian?"

Even the cough and the hesitation didn't prevent the

remark from seeming sudden, abrupt. And Ronald's head swung toward Alan. It was an animal reaction: thoughtless. He wished he hadn't done it. *Enjoyed?* The question sounded like it could mean anything, no more than *Have you enjoyed Africa?* Alan had turned his own head toward Ronald so that their eyes had met and Ronald had to force some answer from himself.

"She's been . . . very nice."

He grew warm. He had to do better than that, had to say that he meant she was considerate to visitors, nice to guests, a good hostess. But he couldn't. Nothing else would come out of his mouth and he looked away.

"She," began Alan thoughtfully, deliberately, as if he were analyzing a stranger, "she puts most of us to shame, I suppose, by what she can do in this climate. But . . ." Alan coughed softly. He smiled thinly, glancing at Ronald, who was looking at the hill beyond. "You should have known her twenty years ago the way I did." Alan seemed to remember something for he laughed a bit, privately; and the laughter relaxed Ronald enough so that he looked at him. Alan took immediate advantage of it, turned his head and caught Ronald's eye again. "I understand you played tennis together."

Ronald's head swung toward the hill again. Alan's understanding seemed to encompass something fatal. Ronald felt caught by the most insignificant of facts: playing tennis. Nevertheless he felt caught and his Adam's apple pulled in and popped out again as he swallowed.

"Yes, I did."

"Vivian mentioned it. Did she take you to Hamsun's Bay, too?"

It wasn't clear that Vivian had mentioned that also, and Ronald didn't know whether Alan was fishing, whether he was seeking information. He didn't want to answer yes, yet he didn't want to be caught in a lie. His tongue sat thickly in his mouth and he nodded.

"She was on the Australian team, you know."

Alan was looking at him . . . waiting for Ronald to admit that he knew?

"Didn't she tell you?"

Ronald nodded.

"Yes, she did."

"Watching her go off that cliff! The native boys enjoy it, I can tell you. It made Vivian a winner overnight. Can you imagine? The wife of a colonial official doing that? Every visiting dignitary and blackguard enjoys her, too. I don't think the admiral would be coming to dinner tonight if he hadn't seen Vivian. Enjoyment is what Vivian's all about—it's her great talent, giving enjoyment to others. And we've had the way of life, at least until recently, until now, that's allowed her to do what she can do best. When I started to talk about her today at lunch"—Alan put his hand to his mouth and cleared his throat—"I had been thinking that I've been wrong to put her through the round of obligations we've had thrust upon us these past months." He showed Ronald a wan smile, one to accompany the tone of self-reproach in his voice. "She needs a change, a bit of rest. And I expect you do, too. I was thinking. . . ." Alan coughed softly, lifting his hand again to his mouth. "I was thinking that she might be just the one to take you to see Sickles. I assume you want to look the job over, and give it some thought. The country between here and Mlane is well worth seeing—if you haven't, you should see it. Vivian's familiar with it, of course. Knows it well . . . she could show it to you, give you, ah . . . well, point out a lot of things you couldn't find on your own. You might think of taking a week or ten days before seeing Sickles. So you can be at your best. I know it's an important decision for you."

Ronald, fearfully hypnotized, was staring at Alan's profile. Then Alan turned his face full on him.

"I don't have to tell you," he said, "that it's also important for us. I mean, it'll settle the matter of A.J.'s replacement."

That Alan was arranging for Ronald to be alone with Vivian was clear, so clear that Ronald blurred it by responding to Alan's final words. And at their surface value. "No, no, of course not. I know it's important."

Alan waited for him to say more: for ten strained seconds. Then he put both hands on the balcony railing and ran the fingers of one along the top of it, back and forth as if he were gauging its smoothness.

"Actually, I expect to be going to London in the next ten days myself. I can't say for how long. They're starting some fairly high-level deliberations. I haven't told Vivian yet." He glanced at Ronald to be sure it was understood that this was between them. And then he lifted his chin into the air and looked at the summit of the hill. "It's possible that I won't assume the high commissioner's post here after all. Oh, I have a promotion with the Colonial Office, a future, a very good one I might say, but—what they want here is a fresh start, a totally new beginning, totally. I can't say I disagree. In fact, I'll help find the right man. But it's Vivian I'm worried about, not myself. Her lifestyle—I mean, our way of life out here, well . . . it isn't meant for London, for England. We've been away too long. Here in Africa. Clinemark can tell you what that means. I'll probably try to arrange something else other than London after about six months, of course. It's at times like these that I wish Vivian had some, some . . . ability of her own, some vocation, some interest here in Africa to, well . . . to occupy her, to satisfy her. I mean, until the future is more certain, until I could give her another way of life outside of England."

Alan stopped, sure of getting a response from Ronald; but all he got was silent amazement, hypnotized comprehension.

"Alan . . . ?"

278

Vivian's voice sounded out from the garden below and Ronald was struck swiftly and decisively in the crook of his arm, as swiftly as Vivian's voice had struck Alan. Alan knocked him back from the balcony railing, hissing between his teeth, "Don't let her see you!" After they had backed into the room Alan glowered at him. "For God's sake, Keane, don't look at me that way! Don't tell me—" Alan stopped moving and talking. His face reddened with frustration and anger. He was standing near the bed and reached for an edge of the sheet that Ronald has hastily smoothed back. He tore it away from the pillow and it flapped in the air like the wing of a bird, floating down to the bed again. "Don't tell me you haven't enjoyed my wife! You've got a hell of a lot of cheek, pretending not to know what I'm talking about, forcing me to stumble around in my own home! You run around the world making a mess of it with your impulses, you damned Americans, and then when others try to take some kind of reasonable account of your bloody impulses, you—why, look at you! standing there and gaping at me as if *I* had been cuckolding you with *your* wife! Don't flatter yourself by thinking that's what you've done, Keane. It's your damned simplemindedness that puts me off. I've had my pound of flesh—in more than one market, too, and other things weigh more with me. You'll never be in a position to know what that means, but I've enjoyed running this country . . . that's the kind of thing *I* enjoy, and I intend to continue to enjoy running things in whatever way I can. You owe me something, you owe us all something—you can mark my words on that, for coming here and getting in over your head! Well, I want you to paddle your way out. They won't enjoy Vivian's native costumes and bracelets in London so I've arranged for Sickles to take you on. I'm telling you to take that job in Mlane and have Vivian go with you until it suits me to have her someplace else. I'm not *asking* you, is that clear? I'm supposed to be inviting you to join us for a drink before our guests arrive. I'll just assume that you don't want to, and I'll tell Vivian that you were still sleeping!"

Alan walked out.

He didn't even bother to shut the door after him.

"*I couldn't believe it,*" Ronald said to me as he sank down onto the edge of the bed at Solly's. I believed it but was filled with questions.

"And Vivian doesn't know this?"

Ronald shook his head.

"Huh! That's just what she said, isn't it?"

I got a blank look from Ronald.

"What?" he asked.

"Vivian. . . . About Nancy and Alan having their activities, their self-importance. Their egos—not interrupting their fun. That's what you said she said."

Ronald looked at me as if he hadn't said it, or having heard it from me didn't see the point of it. I admit I was having a half dozen reactions and was voicing only one of them, maybe not the most pertinent.

"Well," I said, "you can't stay here. Get your bags. Let me take you to your house."

He was willing. I don't think he had the same doubts or misgivings about going to Nancy's that he had when he first arrived. Life and the Angles had intervened.

"Where are you staying?" he asked.

"Nowhere yet."

"Why don't you stay with me?"

I picked up one of his bags while he closed the other.

"Well, we'll see. I have to get Vivian's car back to her first. Do you owe Solly any money?"

"A little."

We started down the stairs. He handed Solly a bill and we walked to the car in silence and went as far as the coast road before either of us said anything. I remember that I doubted that Alan felt as authoritative as he sounded. *Not going to be high commissioner!* kept going through my mind. His personal world must have been shaken, even tottering, although I would have agreed that his professional life was secure. But his personal world was the one where Vivian had had her part. I myself couldn't imagine it gone, being taken from her. Not only would her skin go pale in England, her life would pale. I'm sure Ronald didn't know how easily Alan could maintain a hold on both his professional and personal existence if Vivian stayed behind in Africa, if she went to Mlane. For there was probably more than one government residence there, not only the vacant house left by A. J.'s death. Appearances could be maintained. Vivian could have her own house. Alan would be flying back to The Port frequently and they would be meeting in Rome or Paris for a week, somewhere en route to and from London; or spending long weekends in Dakar or Mombasa after some conference Alan was attending.

Ronald broke our silence.

"What do you think?"

"About what?"

"Going to Mlane."

"Do you want to go?"

He didn't hesitate to say, "I'd like to go. There isn't anything back in the States. I don't have a job."

I nodded, thinking that Vivian wasn't back there either. But I said something else.

"That's a wonderful coast."

"You've been there?"

"Oh, sure. The Dutch slavers used to come into Mlane. It's got quite a history. If they didn't speak another dialect down there—it's wrong to call it another dialect," I corrected, "it's really another language—I might have gone there myself. The sea air's even better than it is here. I think it's got something to do with a current a few miles offshore that never gets this far east. Sickles is a Welshman . . . at least his mother was Welsh. He's a little different than the usual expatriate. He reads Dylan Thomas. And he likes his work, likes the people, is into the food a bit, and isn't totally given over to the automatic gin or Scotch at five o'clock every afternoon. . . . Sorry," I apologized, and looked at him quickly.

"That's okay."

But it wasn't okay. For he slumped down and put his head on the back of the car seat.

"I don't want to be totally given over to it, either."

I was surprised to hear him say so. At another time I might even have been glad. I looked at him, expecting more; but his eyes were closed as if he were considering his wish to be other than what he was or had been, and neither of us said anything until I turned off the coast road and started north along the last six mile stretch.

"I think a lot about Nancy," he said from his slouched position.

"Oh?"

I waited for more and when it didn't come, I prompted him.

"What do you think?"

I had to wait some more.

"I just think about her."

Somehow that made sense: a thought process without a thought product.

"And what about Vivian?"

His eyes opened. He straightened up.

"Do you want her to go with you?" I asked. I think I meant *Do you think she should?* but that isn't what I said. And I imagine that he wasn't going to confess that he did, outright; not so soon after he said he often thought about Nancy.

"Do you think she'll want to?"

"I don't know what she wants," I said shortly. "All I know is that she wanted me to find you, get you home, and call her." I was careful not to say that I was going to meet her. "And that's what I'm doing."

He sat up and put a hand on the dashboard.

"Don't tell her that Alan came to my room, will you?"

"And that you've got an arrangement? A gentlemen's agreement?"

"We don't have an arrangement!"

I tried to look at him no more than questioningly but I suppose I did it challengingly, too.

"Oh?"

"No."

"If Vivian drives you to Mlane and she doesn't know that Alan has told you that—that giving enjoyment to others is her great talent, and, ah, he's going to let her do that in Mlane because no one will enjoy her ways in England, and—"

"It's not an arrangement!"

His face was a litle red. He had turned it full on me but when I looked at him his eyes went off someplace at the same time that he continued his denials.

"I didn't say anything to him! Not a word, I didn't agree to anything."

"That's true."

"And I left the house that night."

"Well, don't worry. I won't say anything to Vivian because that would be interfering with Alan's life a bit too much. I'm sure he'll tell her something when the time comes. I don't know what goes on between them. I don't see how I can make it my business."

I was glad to reach Tintolo Road.

"Here's your street."

Ronald anxiously looked out the front window.

"I assume you've got a key."

He nodded.

"Are you going to come in?"

I shook my head as we pulled up to the small front gate.

"I don't think so."

"Why don't I take your bags?"

"Not right now. That can wait. I'd better get back to Vivian—I mean, leave her car where she told me to. One of us will call you."

He got out of the car reluctantly. When he closed the door he bent down and looked in through the open window, seeking some kind of reassurance.

"I'll call you," I said.

He turned and passed through the front gate just as I pulled away. I don't think the weight of his bags was pulling his shoulders down: he just didn't want to face his ghosts alone. And I didn't want him to use me to avoid facing them. I had forty minutes before Vivian expected me and I drove to The National Hotel and checked into the room that she had reserved for me. I wanted my own room—to myself, by myself. At that moment I believe I felt that Alan, Vivian and Ronald deserved each other And that I deserved a rest from all of them.

24

THE SECOND FLOOR OF THE Palm Wine Terrace in Cecil Street had a narrow balcony which hung out over the walk below. Four tables—all small, for couples only and covered with eggshell-blue tableclothes—were thrust against a wrought-iron railing. And Vivian was seated at one of them.

"Aaron! Up here!"

I saw her hand in the air from across the road. I waved back and cut cater-corner through the traffic, mostly pedestrian. I had left her car in Stubi Lane nearby and was going along at my usual pace, maybe a bit more slowly; but she shifted the weight in my body, pulling it up from my legs and sending it into my chest and slightly straightening shoulders. My legs moved more quickly.

"Did you hear from him? Was he there?"

The heads of the people at the other three tables turned and looked down trying to find me, or whomever she was calling to.

"Yes."

"Oh, *good!* Hurry!"

All the inside tables upstairs were filled, too—with Africans and a few Arabs, Lebanese or Egyptian. I don't remember seeing any woman. Vivian's face was not only the only female one, it was the only white one, though not much paler than some. Everyone observed me as I came in and passed among the narrowly separated tables, not because I was interesting but because they were interested in seeing who was going to join Vivian. Maybe some of them knew she was Alan's wife. I felt the heads turned on my back, following me and going right on where the eyes in them wanted to go: to Vivian—her face, a bare arm, the foot that was thrust out from under the table, some part of her covered body. I had thought, not long before, that it must have been hard for Nancy to have been Nancy, but I also wonder what it was like to have been Vivian Angle. She apparently didn't notice the others in the cafe. She didn't seem to see anything or anyone but me. Her expectant eyes were turned solely on me and she didn't seem to be interested in anything but how I was twisting myself toward her through the crowded room.

"Can you squeeze in?"

I got a smile from the heavyset man in the chair back of me and I momentarily surprised him by speaking about our predicament in his dialect. It not only pleased him—I could see that it pleased Vivian, too. The way she smiled at me indicated that she didn't have the vaguest idea that her world was falling apart. That might have been a little responsible for my opening lighthearted remark.

"I don't think I've ever been this close to you even in private."

She laughed, briefly, anxious to hear other things.

"Tell me, tell me."

"Well, there's nothing to tell you."

Which is exactly what she wanted to be told, exactly what she wanted to hear: for it meant that there was nothing wrong. Everything, especially Ronald, was under control. I could see that she was already completed satisfied, ready to sigh, and I shrugged.

"He was there, that's all . . . drinking a little bit, but not too badly. Mulling things over, thinking, I suppose."

"What did he say?"

"Oh, how Alan met the train" . . . and on I went, telling her what she knew, and perhaps suggesting a little bit more: that he was understandably nervous to be met by Alan, that he was unprepared to sit down with both of them—probably even her—so soon, so suddenly.

"But why did he just run off in the middle of the night?"

I think I looked away at the same time that I shrugged.

"You'll have to ask him that—"

"You mean he didn't say?" I must have hesitated for she half pleaded, half questioned: "We didn't do anything wrong!"

I knew she meant that she and Alan hadn't done anything wrong, hadn't made a social error, said the wrong thing. But then—each of them, separately, one after the other . . . what had that been? Possibly not wrong but if not wrong, what was it? I looked at her and she glanced at her bracelets and adjusted one of them.

"He probably thought he shouldn't have been enjoying all that luxury," I said.

She made an impatient sound and flicked her hand.

"Why ever not? That's as bad as not wanting to stay at the National Hotel! You deserve a little luxury after what you've both been through. Do you want one of these?" she asked immediately, as if I deserved a little luxury right then. She was pointing to the glass in front of her. "It's spiced tea."

"All right."

She waved a waiter to her and was going to speak but stopped herself.

"You do it," she said smilingly. "You do it with such style."

"I don't do anything with style," I replied self-deprecatingly, probably because I didn't like the role I was playing or the way I was playing it. The concealment troubled me.

"You do, too."

I ordered a spiced tea and the waiter walked off. Vivian smiled.

"I never hear you speak the local language."

The minute I thought she was being deliberately carefree she asked to be informed.

"Tell me what it was like, Aaron."

"What *what* was like?"

"The epidemic, being there—McGowan's death, and Nancy's, too. Everything."

"Well . . . all right." I did or I tried to. And I think I was glad to, glad to get my mind away from the present. And as I more or less succeeded in telling her everything, two things happened. She became rapt. A perfect listener.

Her eyes never left my face, not even when she sipped her tea; they stared at me over the top of the glass. She grimaced when I would have grimaced, said *Oh, no!* at the same time that I felt something akin to that, mirrored my astonishment and even horrified disgust when I told her of the dinner I had with Ronald and Nancy, smiled thinly at my description of Ronald on his scaffolding—as if the memory of him offering Nancy the salad bowl was still in her mind—and smiled at me and my attempts to bring him from his alcoholic stupor after Nancy's death. And as I drew pictures of myself for her I reencountered myself: carrying Nancy's body down the stairs, observing how the flies had been grouped around her lips, digging her grave with Angoli, going through her notebooks, standing in the hot noon at the well in Sudi. The end result of it was that I felt finished with Ronald, the Ronald I had just retrieved from Solly's. In drawing back to Nancy I had drawn away from him.

Vivian's hair was short, auburn, curling forward around her ears. She looked down into the road when I stopped, touching a strand of hair near her right ear. She looked contemplative, not aware of the people, cyclists and carts below, and let out a long breath. Her breasts lowered as all the air went out of her diaphragm.

"Oh, Aaron! . . . take me there."

She had spoken that into the road below, and only after she had did she look at me, tilting her head, still playing with the strand of hair above her ear. I didn't understand.

"Where?"

"Ndami. Take *me* to a funeral celebration, take *me* to Maroc Nègre, show *me* where you sit and look into the desert, have Funa cook a dinner for *me!*"

It was not only said charmingly, it was said longingly. And I found myself smiling with pleasure at her and at the thought.

"All right. Anytime you like—just tell me. I'll meet the steamer."

"It upset you, didn't it?"

I couldn't follow her.

"What did?"

"Telling me. Remembering."

"Oh, maybe it did. A little."

"What should I do? Can I help him?"

"Who?"

"Ronald."

"How? By going to Mlane with him?"

"Going to Mlane with him? Why should I go to Mlane with him?"

She was so surprised to hear me suggest it that I was a little shocked to realize I knew Alan had stood on the balcony with Ronald arranging it.

"Oh, I don't know," I said quickly, my eyes drawing away from hers, "I just thought maybe someone would take him down and introduce him to Sickles."

"Does he want to go?"

"I think so."

"Good! That'll be a relief to Alan."

I looked at her, searching her face for some concealed meaning that might have been behind the words.

"Why will that be a relief to Alan?"

"Well, he needs an immediate replacement and he would like to do something. For Ronald . . . he was very upset about Nancy. That's like Alan."

I nodded.

"How is he?"

"Harassed—and I can't forget for too long that I am, either. Where did you park my car?"

"You don't have to go?"

"Not this minute. But we can have a long visit when Alan gets back, just the three of us, have you to dinner, spend the whole evening together."

"When is he coming back?"

"Tomorrow night."

"Has there been anything in the air? Any developments—in the air? Any developments—in the government, I mean?

"Corruption already, lots of bribery. Let me tell you what happened not ten feet from Alan's nose. . . ." I let her tell me and I barely listened, though I pretended to. She was only doing it because we couldn't talk of other things; not really, not easily. And I didn't really want to talk about Ronald even though he was the reason for our being together. Could I say *Well, if you're not going to Mlane with him what are you going to do with him?* And however rapt she was about all I told her of Ndami, it led nowhere. It put her somewhere—that was clear, made plain by the way she had said *Oh, Aaron, take me there.* It had put me somewhere, too. It just hadn't led us anywhere together. That happens, I guess. I was sorry it had and I wished otherwise for I didn't want us to be so unreal as to be talking about someone else's avarice. As I pretended to listen to her I was watching her, a woman so apparently in control, oblivious to how she was being controlled, or might be, until she suddenly reached a hand across the table and laid it on top of mine.

"Aaron, you're not listening."

I was a little surprised to have been caught but I smiled at her rightness; laughed it away as cleverness, flushing a bit as my eyes lowered. She kept her hand on top of mine for an instant longer than she needed and rubbed my knuckle bone. I was looking at the top of her extended forearm and when I responded I seemed to be confessing to that part of her.

"You're right, I wasn't."

"Is it something you want to talk about?"

I withdrew my hand at the same time that I smiled to let her know her touch wasn't what was unpleasant.

"Maybe it's something we'll talk about after Alan comes back."

She didn't ask what that was or why I thought we might. She said nothing. No doubt because she thought it was a need of mine. And I no doubt suggested such a possibility, not because I assumed I was, ever had been or would become, her confidant, but because I wanted to be ready to help her by talking in the future, in the event that any silence of mine was injuring her now. Even though I wouldn't talk about it now, she still seemed to want to satisfy some need of mine.

"Please say you'll stay at the room I've reserved for you at the National."

"I've already checked into it."

"Oh," she said blankly.

"So you see you've persuaded me."

She smiled.

"Well, I should leave and do what I have to do. Go back to my guests, call Ronald. . . . If I need to ring you after I talk with him, may I?"

"Of course."

"I hope I won't have to bother you. More than I already have," she added. But I don't really think she felt she had bothered me. "And I'm sorry for making you drive to Sumasi. Wouldn't you have driven anyway?"

I nodded to say I would have.

"Vivian, if you call me again—after you talk with Ronald—what *is* my business? Tell me my business. What can I . . . ?" I trailed off momentarily for I didn't know what to ask or how to put it: how to find out how much or what part of her life was *my* business. I fumbled. "I mean you were right: when I said something about knowing you better than that, and you asked why should I, for no one else did? Well, I realize I don't, and I also realize that it's only by accident that I ran into Ronald and so here I am."

None of that led us anywhere.

"Aaron, what are you talking about?"

"Vivian, the reason I thought you might take Ronald to Mlane is because Alan suggested it to him."

She looked at me for what seemed a long time. And her body lifted just a little, not very much. She didn't cry out against his having done so. She didn't throw a hand to her forehead and wonder how he could possibly do such a thing. She said only one word and she said it very quietly.

"When?"

"Apparently Alan walked into the garden just before dinner, or after he had gotten dressed, and he saw Ronald standing out on the balcony of your guest room. He went upstairs and talked with him."

"Then he *lied* to me? Ronald wasn't asleep?"

"No."

Her eyes lost their usual brightness; alertness.

"I don't believe it," she whispered without looking at me. But after no more time than it took for one breath to be expelled, she corrected herself: "No . . . I can believe anything."

I didn't know why she could.

"Tell me more."

I did: but not all. As well and as carefully as I could remember I told her how Ronald had said that Alan felt she had been overworked, that a rest would be good for her, that seeing the country would be good for Ronald; and that Alan suggested they might want to take a week or ten days so Ronald could be in the best frame of mind when he met Sickles. What I observed in Vivian's face as I said this much was something that I had only seen once before in my life: the horror of a woman learning that one man has been talking about her to another, secretly. The level of the talk and its purposes can extend the range of the horror. It was the look on her face that kept me from saying how Alan wished she had some skill to occupy her, and that he was going to England and would probably never be high commissioner.

"And is that why Ronald wants to go? Because he thinks I'll be going—because Alan is sending me off with him?"

I shrugged.

"I see. . . ."

She looked down into the road, seeing it and God knows what else. I sat there for as long as I could, waiting for her to come out of her long, long stare. When she wouldn't, I spoke.

"What do you see?"

She looked at me, seemed to think about what she might say, and shook her head, slowly.

"Oh, Aaron. . . ."

What I said next I seemed to say on Alan's behalf, as an excuse for his suggestion: "Ronald said that Alan mentioned he might have to, *was* going, to London soon—for talks in the Foreign Office . . . that might take a long time." Each bit I said made saying the next bit a little easier; possible. "He seemed to think they might last for some time."

"London?" she echoed softly.

I nodded.

"Apparently he had just found out about it and hadn't had a chance to tell you yet."

"He's had plenty of opportunity since then."

Vivian's lower lip trembled. She bit it quickly in one corner to stop it.

I tried to detract her from her own emotions by asking, "Do you think it means anything?"

She answered me by reaching across the table and laying her hand on top of mine again, but not lightly; this time she gripped it, rubbing her fingers into me. I saw the heads of the two men at the table to my left turn toward us.

293

They had probably seen Vivian do the same thing a minute before. Vivian saw me turn my head toward them and she looked at them with me. Both men looked away but not before one of them showed his frank smile.

"Maybe one of them," I suggested, "knows Alan, and is enjoying himself by imagining the worst."

"Do men do anything with women except enjoy themselves and imagine the worst?"

She said it so quickly, withdrawing her hand from mine at the same instant, that I almost couldn't respond. And she looked at me firmly.

"I'm not enjoying myself," I said.

She smiled . . . but quickly, too quickly. It wasn't sincere. She reached down for her purse which was at her feet, leaning against the balcony railing. Her head was down when she spoke.

"Well, I'm going to leave."

I was so unprepared for that that I couldn't respond again. Certainly not with words. I started to get up.

"No," she ordered.

She must have seen from the bewildered expression on my face that I was confused, or even a little hurt, for all the energy went out of her body, her stiff preparedness to move. Her shoulders sagged and her head went to one side a little, limply.

"Do you mind?"

There was a kind of half plea in her voice.

"I need to leave by myself."

I knew I minded but I couldn't object. What trouble there was was her trouble, so how could I not do as she asked?

"Naturally I can't mind, I just wish you wouldn't."

"I'll call you, I'll see you. Will you be at the hotel?"

Her question seemed to decide that for me because I found myself saying, "I suppose so," and giving as my

294

reasons, "I need to shave and clean up." But I must have wanted to be where she could reach me.

"I'm going to go see Ronald," she said as she stood up. "I want to hear him tell me what Alan said to him."

"I told him I wouldn't say anything about it to you," I objected.

"Alan could have told me, for all he knows. I'll find a way so that he doesn't suspect you."

I was going to say something else, something explanatory, apologetic, but she put her hand on my shoulder and stopped me.

"Aaron . . . ?"

She waited until I looked up.

"Thank you. You make me feel as if I have a friend. I don't think"—she smiled with a trace of lightheartedness and intoned with a trace of sarcasm—"I've ever had a man for a friend. Not a friend. . . ."

She turned and left and I didn't watch her go out. Not because I knew enough men were watching her go already but because I had let her know that I had agreed to cooperate with Ronald, to keep silent about the conversation he and Alan had had on the guest room balcony. And I was troubled even more by the fact that by going directly to Ronald she was going to discover that I had concealed things from her: she was going to learn that I knew Alan wasn't going to become the next high commissioner, that I hadn't told her their whole way of life was going to come to an end. That's what I had felt apologetic about, even a little guilty. I thought I had told her enough, enough to prepare her. Breaking it slowly seemed the right thing to do, and anything more than that, other than slowly, brutal. I hadn't really thought I was being deceptive or cowardly; that what Alan was withholding should come from him. But now she might think otherwise, hearing it from Ronald. I saw her emerge from the cafe below and start immediately across the road. I had expected her to turn around, look back and wave to me. So I had been watching. But she didn't. . . . I suppose I had hoped she would more than I had expected it. She obviously wasn't in a back-glancing mood. I only might have guessed that her easy energetic stride meant she was ready to walk into a hurricane. For there was nothing burdened about the way she moved, or unnecessarily forceful. It was just Vivian walking, moving her body in that self-possessed, graceful and effortless way that troubled men. And in troubling men gave trouble to herself. To her life.

25

I DID AS I SAID I WOULD. I WENT TO my hotel, showered and shaved, laid down on the bed and then surprised myself. Not by going to sleep, which happened too fast for me to realize that the baggage van had not been as restful as I had imagined, but by waking as late as three o'clock in the afternoon. Vivian had certainly left Ronald long before then and I thought she might call at any time, so I ordered tea to be sent to my room. When I had left Ndami, hurriedly, I had filled one of suitcases with records from Continental Mines—chaotically, so I sorted them all out. I should have gotten a number of summaries together, so I started to write one up but tired of it after thirty minutes. That made me call Eliot's office. He wasn't in but I asked one of his assistants if I could get a dictaphone to use in my hotel room. As I expected, he said he'd have one sent over. I decided to go for a short walk while I waited for it. On my way out I told the desk clerk I was expecting a delivery and a phone call. It was easy to be distracted by the changes that had taken place in the city since I had last been there. I walked through several of the markets and I listened to a discussion about the future of the plantain crop fifty miles to the northeast where a disease was attacking the fruit. I helped settle a dispute over an accident between some German tourists in a rental car and a taxi driver. The Germans clung to me as their deliverer even after I got them to accept that they were completely at fault, so I went to the car agency with them after we had settled with the police, and when I got back to the hotel both my dictaphone and Paddy were there, waiting.

"Mr. Clinemark!"

I knew Paddy and he smiled when he saw me, handing me a note.

"From Mrs. Angle. She says no reply is necessary."

"Oh?" I said, disappointed, for then I couldn't open it right away. There was no need to, and Paddy expected me to regard him as more than a messenger and to stop speaking English. So I did until he himself said he had to go. He used the expression *I must fly*, and we both laughed, for that was what Vivian always said when she wanted someone to hurry: "Go, Paddy—*fly!*" After he was gone I turned aside and opened her note.

Aaron,

I have decided to leave with Ronald at seven tonight. You didn't tell me why Alan was going to London, or didn't you know? When you see him please don't talk about me, don't even say you saw me. I'm leaving him a note, which will explain and ease his mind. It's funny that in looking after myself I'm forced to look after him. I know you didn't enjoy yourself

this morning and don't, don't imagine the worst about
me, don't imagine anything at all. Forgive me for
bringing you down here. You will be in Ndami forever,
won't you? So I know where I can find you?

Vivian

I felt for a moment that I didn't know what to make
of it. But I knew perfectly well what to make of it: just
exactly what was in it. And maybe that Vivian had decided
to make her own hurricane rather than walk into one of
someone else's making. I didn't know what to do with myself, that was it. I felt cut off from something, so fast that I
couldn't connect—not with the hotel lobby, the room I
had on the third floor or the dictaphone machine that was
sitting on a table in front of me right next to an elephant
plant. I guess I decided to connect with the dictaphone
machine, for I picked it up. But instead of going to the lift I
continued down the corridor to the bar, deciding, apparently, to disconnect myself from everyone and everything.
But there was a flaw in my decision, if that's what it was:
the moment I stepped into the bar, the air rang with my
name. Half a dozen voices cried it out. Not that the voices
belonged to people who were especially glad to see me;
they were just glad to see someone else, anyone else they
didn't see every late afternoon of the month. I was taken
possession of and served two Scotch and sodas. I was
regaled with expatriate news and regaled others in turn
with news a bit more newsworthy—of Ndami and its epidemic. I didn't leave the bar for two hours. When I did the
grandfather clock in the lobby of The National Hotel let
me know it was twenty minutes to seven. I went to the lift,
brought the dictaphone to my room, set it down, and
looked around. I felt like exactly what I was: an almost-
stranger in a hotel room. And then I thought of the time.
The fact that I had fifteen minutes or so before Vivian and

Ronald were leaving seemed to say to me that I still had fifteen minutes to catch them. To make it to Nancy's. I didn't know what I wanted to say; it just seemed that because I still had a chance to see them once more, I should seize it. It seized me, anyway, and I went out of my hotel room door and ran down the stairs because the lift was engaged. It didn't occur to me to call Nancy's house to say I was on my way. I wouldn't have been able to say for what, if I had. And I felt I was sure to be late, sure to have missed them. Nevertheless I found myself walking, half running, walking again, then running faster, perspiring to what I thought was no end. For when I turned the corner into the lane where Nancy's house was located, it was already ten minutes after seven. But when her house came into view so did Vivian's Peugeot, slanted toward the ditch at the side of the road. I felt triumphant, particularly since the front door was halfway open, ready to emit people about to go on a trip, carrying bags. I hurried up the walk, ready to help with the bags that Ronald had taken in only hours before, and poked my head through the door.

"Ronald? . . . Vivian?"

I walked in, saw the French doors that had seemed so important a few months before, heard voices and walked in their direction, intending to call out again.

"—no abilities?" I overheard Vivian say from upstairs.

"I shouldn't have said anything else."

"I asked you to—and Alan will tell me anyway if you don't."

"Then why don't you let him?" pleaded Ronald.

There was a pause and I had a chance to call up to them to let them know I was there. And when I didn't my faster heartbeat let me know what I was doing.

"Because," said Vivian, "I want to hear it from both of you."

"There's nothing to hear."

"There had to be *something* to make you walk out in the middle of the night! and—and create all that suspicion, and worry me half to death."

"I'm sorry."

"Why did Alan boast about his future?"

"He didn't *boast*."

"You said he did."

"I said he just talked about the future of the country, and that his future was a good one, that's all."

"And that mine wasn't."

"He just—"

"Because I don't have any abilities."

"He just said that your way of life wasn't meant for England!" Ronald said with exasperation. "You'd been out here so long, in Africa, both of you—that's all he meant. That's reasonable, isn't it?"

"No. His way of life is meant for England but mine isn't. I don't understand. What's my way of life? What's the matter with me?"

"All he said was that you had been doing too much lately," Ronald said in a tone of complaint, the tone of someone who found another person's exaggerations trying. "Why are you twisting everything that I say?"

There was a pause.

Ronald pleaded softly, "Why can't we just go?"

"We can as soon as you tell me about your conversation."

Making it plain that he was tired of it, Ronald threw at her: "Because of all the diplomatic obligations, the Russians or whatever it was, he said you needed a change, a rest. That's all." He said it as if he expected it to be all.

"What a lie!"

It was silent.

"A lie," Vivian repeated, and then said a little shrilly: "And what's all this *just* business? He *just* said this, and he *just* thought?" Why are you trying to make so light of it?"

"Because it *was* light!"

"So that's why you ran away in the middle of the night?"

There was a pause.

"I was thinking of Nancy," Ronald said quietly.

There was another pause. One of them moved.

"Think of her all you want, Ronald," Vivian said as quietly as Ronald had, "but don't ever get tragic with me about her. I know how you felt about her," she said with sarcasm, "so don't use her, don't blackmail me with her."

"I wasn't trying to," he protested.

She didn't answer.

"Vivian, I didn't say two words to Alan. I couldn't, I was afraid to—"

"Afraid of Alan?" she said surprised.

"I thought he would notice something in the room. I had just awakened, walked out on the balcony, and I didn't know why he wanted to come up."

"What could he notice?"

"I don't know, I didn't know. 'I understood you played tennis together,' he said, as if he had some special understanding about it—and then right away he asked if you had taken me to Hamsun's Bay, too, like he was trying to find something out."

"Well, didn't you say yes? I swim all the time. It's perfectly normal for people to swim with other people."

Ronald must have nodded.

For Vivian said: "Then what?"

"He said that you had been on the Australian team and began praising you—"

"Praising me?"

She seemed more interested.

"The way you went off the cliff, how the native boys

301

enjoyed it, how none of the other men's wives could do something like that—how everyone enjoyed you, the visitors and officials from other places. That's what he said about you—that giving enjoyment to others was one of your talents. A gift."

It was clear that Ronald meant it to be complimentary. Something to appease her. He must have thought it would for he was silent. But if he was waiting for a response, none came.

"It is, you know," he said softly.

Again I heard one of them move.

"Don't," she said quietly. Then added: "Don't interrupt what you were saying. I still don't know why I have to be lied to and shipped off to Mlane."

The switch in tone was abrupt. There was a pause. They must have been looking at one another.

Vivian said suspiciously, "Did you and Alan hear me call him from the garden?"

While it was silent I lifted my hand and put it on the post at the bottom of the stairway, waiting for the answer. I was sure it was going to be *No*.

"Yes."

"Yes? Then why didn't he answer?"

"He knocked me back into the room."

Ronald must have waited to observe the effect that would have or was having on Vivian.

"He hit me in the arm and dragged me off the balcony."

"I don't believe you."

"It's the truth."

"You're exaggerating."

"No, I'm not."

"Alan never hit anyone in his life."

"He tore the sheet off the bed," Ronald said, as if he had said it before, challenging her to remember when she had been wrong another time. His tone was unmistakably the tone of someone who was feeling the triumph of informing a person of something they didn't know about another, when that person thought she knew everything.

"Vivian, he knows we're having an affair," he said smugly.

God knows what Vivian did but I closed my eyes. I winced, forgetting for an instant that I was worried about what I was doing: eavesdropping. And worrying about being caught. What did he think he was doing? I had heard men enjoying themselves like that before, forcing a woman to acknowledge—to see herself—as the man's sex object. And in the eyes of another man, too; even if that man wasn't present. Ronald was proud that Alan knew; his pride came from another man's knowing. It was silent for so long that they must have been staring at each other, Ronald doing it overbearingly; or if not overbearingly, from one of the few points where he held a temporary advantage over Vivian.

"What—"

The word came from her, breaking off. In a quiet but courageous way, the way some people speak after their speech has been momentarily taken away and they have swallowed, she continued.

"What did he say?"

"That he knew I had been *enjoying* you."

There was a pause.

"That doesn't say very much."

"Enjoying *my wife* was the way he put it."

There was another pause.

"Well, I thought that was my talent—giving enjoyment to others. That could mean anything. Tenniis or swimming," she suggested, but not very convincingly.

"He didn't mean that," Ronald said decisively. "I was standing there like an idiot and he told me to stop looking at him as if he had cuckolded me with *my* wife."

"Cuckold?"

Vivian echoed it faintly.

"Alan said *cuckold?*"

"Oh, don't worry," Ronald said breezily, "he doesn't give a damn. He's had his pound of flesh."

"Who?"

"Alan! 'I've had my pound of flesh,' he said." Ronald was swept along by his own sense of maleness, announcing with a mocking bravado, "What *he* enjoys is running this country!" Vivian must have been considering the truth of it, or the possibility of it, and Ronald must have been looking at her, for he seemed to be answering a look of scepticism when he repeated: "That's what he said."

"*This* pound?"

There was a pause.

"Is *this* a pound?"

It was impossible to know what she meant.

"Maybe it's more," she said. "Or is *this* a pound?"

"Vivian," Ronald said pleadingly.

"Let's go," she said darkly, her voice filled with misery and anger.

"Vivian, for God's sake!" said Ronald, equally pained and irritable. But there was no anger in his voice. She had done something that had totally transformed him and whatever was taking place between them. "God!" he whined pathetically.

"Let's get out of here," she commanded sadly.

I turned and ran, prancing toward the door ridiculously, taking long, hopefully soft steps. I pulled the door after me, almost closing it. When I was going down the steps I felt the panic in my stomach, its chaos at the fear of getting caught. And it got worse when I realized I couldn't do what I was doing. They might see me through the French doors, scurrying down the walk or dodging through the gate away from the house. So I turned around and went back up the steps, grabbed the still-ajar door with one hand and pounded on it with the other as if I were just arriving.

"Ronald! Vivian!"

I called out more loudly than I would have normally, pounded once more and called out again, poking my head through the doorway, leaning in, off balance, one foot in the air behind me. I saw Vivian coming down the stairs. Ronald was right behind her, carrying his bags.

"Oh, there you are!" I exclaimed. "I just ran over to say goodbye."

They were startled to see me, unprepared, possibly upset that I was there. I noticed several things at once. That Ronald's face was filled with pale fear; he looked nauseated, like someone about to be sick, or who already has been. That Vivian was no longer wearing the patterned dress I had seen her in earlier but was wearing a blouse and skirt, and that the two top buttons on her blouse were undone. That kind of exposure wasn't her style. I saw more of one of her breasts than I have ever seen and my face grew warmer than it already was because I realized what she had done when she asked *Is this a pound?* And that Vivian was shaking even as she moved. Either her mouth was already open, or it opened at the sight of me. Her lower lip was trembling.

"Oh, Aaron!" she said, her voice high and a little false as it strained to feign a natural excitement. "I've just had an idea! Do you think the new road's finished to Timbwe?"

"I don't know."

How could I? I wasn't up on things in the south of the country.

"Well, whether it is or it isn't, that's how far we're going tonight. You know the Pelissiers, don't you?"

"Of course."

She had walked right past me and I glanced at Ronald, giving him some look of recognition before I began following her out the door and down the steps.

"We'll stay with them tonight. I know it won't matter that they don't know we're coming, and then"—she stopped and turned to see that Ronald was coming. And to make certain that he was hearing. He had set a bag down on the porch to close the door and I went up after it quickly.

"Here," I said, smiling, picking it up.

"We might even stay with Marta and Bill two nights. Don't you think that'd be nice?"

"Very."

I did but I was agreeing because I had to, because I was supposed to.

"And what I can do when we get there is call ahead— to Sasso. Go on to the Muirheads', and after that the Hungerfords', and then the Beutners'. I'll call the Clarks! You remember Darlene, don't you?"

Of course I did. I think I nodded. What she was doing —eagerly and animatedly going down the list of all the expatriates—was almost lost on me.

"Do you think that's what Alan had in mind? That I should introduce Ronald to people?"

Ronald and I avoided looking at each other with a fierce determination. But Vivian had gotten through to me: she was stressing that she intended to socialize her way to Mlane, that she would be staying in homes with Ronald where I knew, and she knew that I knew, she would be treated as Alan's wife. And that Ronald would be introduced, known and regarded as the widower of the doctor who had given her life in battling an epidemic. Vivian had walked around to the driver's side of the car and looked at me over the top of it.

"We might even spend a night with Doc Bray and his family."

She was inviting me to join her, to respond in a way that acknowledged I understood what she intended me to.

"You'll like him," I said to Ronald. "The first thing

you'll hear about is a three-hundred-pound catfish he swears he saw in some tank when he was a boy. His will to believe in that fish is one of the strongest forces in this part of Africa."

Vivian laughed and got in the car.

I helped Ronald in with his bags.

"I thought Ronald should see the country near Khosa," she said from inside, and I looked down through the window as soon as Ronald—confused, bewildered but listening—got in and shut the door. "The Bowmans and Greers are both close by."

"The men work at the dam," I said to Ronald.

"And then our last stop before Mlane could be in Ghoba with the Harts. Al and Jo are leaving soon, you know."

I bent low and looked past Ronald to Vivian.

"No, I didn't."

"Going home for good. That's what I should do, at least for a visit."

"Jo Hart's voice alone is worth hearing," I rhapsodized to Ronald. "It sounds like a cello."

Vivian laughed appreciatively. She should have. For with every name that she named she was saying *Not one night will I be with Ronald alone. I'll have my own room, be in my own bed. And so will he.*

"Well, you're lucky," I said to Ronald. "You're going to have an interesting trip. Expatriates like to be visited. They make wonderful hosts and hostesses, and you'll be treated royally"—I paused to look down and across at Vivian, smiling at her—"because you're with the First Lady." Then I straightened up and touched Ronald's arm as a reminder. "Don't forget to write to me. I'd like to know what you're doing in Mlane and how you like it there."

He nodded and managed to say, "Thanks for everything."

307

"Yes, Aaron, thanks for running down after us."

"I was afraid I wouldn't catch you. I just wanted to see you off and say goodbye."

"You're a dear."

I looked down at her once more.

"Have a safe journey."

"We will."

Several goodbyes echoed back and forth and then they pulled away. I watched the car go up the road and even walked into the middle of the road myself so I could see it better after a hundred yards. The taillights flickered once, quickly, but the small blue car kept going. Then the red lights came on again and stayed on. The car came to a stop and the driver's door opened. My first thought was that some detail had been overlooked or some minor thing forgotten, and I started toward the car. But Vivian leaped out and began running toward me as if it were something urgent. She didn't stop running until she thudded against me. Her arms went around me, her head slid past mine and my neck got wet. I didn't know why: from an accidental brush of her mouth or an intentional kiss. My arms lifted instinctively—to hold her, support her; and she squeezed me tightly.

"Oh, God!"

She was crying. My neck had gotten wet from tears.

"Think of me, Aaron!"

She pulled back, gripped my shoulders and gave them a little shake as if I needed to pay attention.

"Think of me!"

She turned and ran back to the car, leaving me startled. So that I almost responded too late. The car door was already closing when I started after her.

"Vivian!"

The Peugeot pulled away.

"I will!" I shouted, both hands cupped around my mouth. Her hand came out of the window and she shook it in a wave. The last thing I remember seeing was the way her native bracelets fell against each other.

26

AND I HAVE THOUGHT OF HER. And all of them, right away, returning to Ndami on the train. I didn't wait for Alan to come back with his French visitors to discover that Vivian had already gone off with Ronald. He would only have faked his way with me and I would have lied about why I had come down so soon, concealing what I knew. For I had no more interest in exposing his masks than I had in assuming one. So I spent a long night summarizing the activities of Continental Mines for the past twenty-nine months and got sleepily onto the train the following midmorning. I was glad Angoli would still be in Sumasi with the car. I didn't want to ride the steamer upriver.

But if I thought of Vivian on the ride back, I confess that I didn't think much. I stared out of the train window at the moving landscape, lulled by the heavy, monotonous turning of the wheels. I could imagine her and Ronald going the rounds of their social itinerary but I couldn't imagine anything of significance. Nothing insightful. Most of their hours would pass frictionlessly by, lived on a smooth and pleasant surface; so smooth Ronald would often be distracted from the fact that anything was seriously wrong. Beyond that I couldn't picture their circumstances because I had never been in the homes they were going to, except the Clarks'. I knew everyone, of course, and even had sharp recollections of this one's habit and that one's gesture. But the images that were thrown at me from beyond the train window made more impression on me. I found relief in an almost anemic lassitude. For I hadn't really experienced anything except my own concern about everything since our epidemic showed its first signs, and even though I was returning to Ndami, I felt that the train was taking me away from something. It was refreshing to see the world again: walkers carrying long sticks, healthy or half-starved animals staring dumbly at the train as it passed, the bent bodies of men and women in the sparse fields. Every village threw up signs of the limited and meager life which it encompassed, and I submitted to these signs, as one learns to, with contentment, even though it was solemn contentment. For an epidemic, in speeding up the processes of death, had accelerated the responses of life unnaturally. And the emotional fevers I had witnessed seemed part of the same chaotic framework. To return to Ndami was to return to days, if I have not already said so, whose pace was measured by the steps of a water buffalo, an animal whose movements reflect the slow and inexorable changes silently taking place in the trees around one, to the blades of sharp grass beneath one's feet and even to the cold blood of a harmless snake coiled in the sun for warmth outside one's door. Returning to that pace and joining its rhythm makes it hard to believe in the primacy or even importance of certain endocrine secretions.

A month went by before news reached me. Not news from someone but news from somewhere: *The Saturday Expatriate*, a six-page weekly that contained harmless gossip about who in the colony was recovering from snake-bite or mourning the loss of an aunt in Devon. In a column entitled "The Travelogue" there was an item which said that after traveling with her husband to Lomé, Vivian— *Mrs. Alan Angle*—was flying on to Australia for a visit with her family in Cairns. It didn't say how long she would be gone but it did wish her a "very happy reunion." I suppose there was a *Well, well . . .* inside of me. It wasn't a head-shaking one, a superior *I knew it,* because I didn't really know what I knew—how many of those four or five weeks had been with Ronald, how many of them had been in The Port, or whether it still left Ronald in Mlane, brown and alive. I do remember a half thought passing through my head, a kind of judgment: *Brown and alive with Nancy dead and Vivian in Australia* but it wasn't a thought worth examining. I was a little unhappy perhaps that I had learned about Vivian's trip home from somewhere instead of someone. I suppose it was petty of me to feel neglected but I confess that I did. If keeping in touch with people wasn't in Ronald's nature, I thought it might be in the arrangement of things, a gesture in return for certain gestures of mine; but we obviously lived by different kinds of human reckoning. And since it was in Vivian's nature to dash off notes, I could only assume that how she was living didn't allow her nature to express itself as it had in the past. People who drift away like rafts that silently work loose of their moorings in the night do so for good reasons. Or necessary reasons. I accept the necessity which lurks at the bottom of all sad and guilty silence, but in this case I hoped the silence would break; break under the sensible pressure which tells us that as long as we're on Earth there's no point in being as silent as Heaven. But I heard nothing. The end result was that I spent far too much time guessing at the size of other people's souls.

When an opportunity came along for me to hear or learn more I almost didn't take it. Out of the same anemic lassitude that had overtaken me on the train perhaps. There was going to be a reception on The Hill, about four months after Vivian's departure for Australia, for Victor Franklin, our first high commissioner, the day he presented himself to the new government. I received an invitation that wasn't marked *R.S.V.P.* so I waited until the last minute before I decided to accept. I believe the weather decided it for me. It was that time of year when a silver mist hung along the river banks until almost noon and I loved riding the steamer downriver whenever it did. I also loved the view from The Hill.

It's hard to imagine anything more deceptively festive than one of those Third World occasions that are made an excuse for a display of international good fun. The reception began at four o'clock and the terrace on The Hill, the gardens, the house and the lawn overflowed with people who might be mistaken for peacocks. The robes on black men vied for high-fashion awards with the gowns on white women. I wasn't competitive myself. I didn't have a white coat or any ribbons to wear above my breast pocket, but my beige pants and cream-colored jacket crumpled around my body well enough. I looked like a casual expert of some kind, a tropical entomologist. Vivian would have loved it. And if the occasion called for it there was always the language, or one of them: whenever I spoke a few words of native tongues, everyone within earshot knew I belonged. I heard English, French, German, and Spanish and recognized half a dozen varieties of Yoruba, Kikuyu and several offshoots of Swahili. The disharmony filled the air, joyously. People loved this unmixable flow of chatter because the confusion of tongues was the confusion of the world—the heart, the mind—and you could see them rejoicing in the disheartening fact that *This Was Life.* The unresolved conflicts between peoples and countries was more real than the resolutions we all made in our own little nests, our private cells of private hope and hopeless compromise. And it was all done with such grace, such style. The Roman Catholic bishop from the Ivory Coast, the same one who had been directed by Vivian's finger to eat more fish the very night Nancy and Ronald had come to dinner on The Hill, smiled and nodded at a noted Tanzanian radical, though both hated what the other stood for and were bitter verbal enemies. A sight like that can almost make you believe that life doesn't require substance at all, just this unmatchable style. And would you believe it? Because one stone—Vivian, the center stone—was missing from this emerald hilltop setting, I found the luster of it all noticeably dimmed. To my surprise I found myself looking around for a commanding gesture, a comparable spark or shape. The closest I came to it was in an Nigerian woman as black as ebony wearing a dress so yellow she looked like a tropical fish. The stones on her ring-laden fingers flashed like beads of water in the sun. If I had heard her speaking a language I knew I might have approached her. I had no alternative but to encounter the sadness I felt when I saw Alan standing without Vivian, in the company of Franklin and his family and Zimbwala, the country's first president, and his entourage. And I admit I may have only felt that sadness because of an unwarranted self-centeredness: had Vivian been among that important group of people, I imagined that a braceleted hand would have leaped into the air like a cat at the sight of me, even if the occasion demanded that she keep her hand demurely at her side. I don't know . . . In any case I waited patiently in the long receiving line so I could pass Alan. He looked as he always did—distinguished, always taller than everyone else; a man meant to preside. He saw me when I was a dozen places away. I thought I detected a glance of recognition in his eyes, but nothing else: no expectation, no eagerness, no warmth. Nothing personal. And the direct look that he gave me as I was about to shake his hand was the look he had given everyone, proper for the occasion.

"Good to see you, Aaron."

He was actually going to turn to Victor Franklin's wife on his right and introduced me to her immediately, which may have also been proper. But it wasn't what I wanted. Or expected.

I stopped him by saying: "Thanks. Is Vivian still in Australia?"

His head, already moving to the right, came back toward me but his eyes seemed to stay where his head had carried them. They lagged behind.

"Yes. I'm going down to see her next week."

Now his eyes landed on me.

"I'll remember you to her."

That was quick of him; expert, seizing the initiative.

"Will you do that, please?"

"Of course."

"Tell her I'd like to hear from her."

He smiled graciously, as if he had been complimented, and said: "This is Amelia Franklin."

Victor Franklin's wife named her two sons, both standing next to her. When they extended their hands to me I was drawn towards them, away from Alan, who was already smiling at a Latin-looking man who was speaking a heavily accented French to him. That was the way of it at these gatherings: whenever you spoke to someone you spoke to others. Personal questions were a violation of decorum and if you asked them you got general answers. I went after them anyway, trying to find anyone on the list of possible stops en route to Mlane that Vivian had suggested. I saw Jack Muirhead first, standing with a half dozen men, then Pam, John Clark, Basil Bowman, Linda Hungerford, the Brays—not one of them were with less than four other people or had had less than two glasses of champagne. I worked my way into each group and when the socially appropriate oppportunity came my way, I said: "I understand you met Ronald Keane" or "Did Vivian Angle pay you a visit a few months ago?" And I got a meaningless remark or two before someone made a remark about the next thing, whatever it was. "Oh, yes—Keane, the American" . . . "He was with you in Ndami, was he? Too bad about his wife. Surprising, both doctors going like that. You'd think they'd know how to look after them-selves better than that" . . . "He seemed a good sort. Is he staying on?" . . . "I believe they were with us one after-noon, before going on to Khosa. He was a *fine* young man, but he didn't say very much. He had been carsick all morn-ing, hadn't he, Harold?" . . . "How special of Alan to arrange for him to work with Sickles—and to have Vivian drive him there and bring him by to meet us! We shall miss the likes of Alan Angle, I can tell you that, no matter what qualifications Franklin brings with him from Senegal" . . . "She is just indefatigible, isn't she? Where *does* she get it? If I had half that energy!" . . . "Wonderful, wonderful!" said Darlene, who came the closest to suggesting anything, "but I don't think she was her usual self. She was content to listen to John talk about soil deficiencies for hours. She had him bringing out his little jars and sat on the floor with them, completely absorbed! Well, naturally, John was un-stoppable with that kind of attention—and from Vivian, too, so I had to try and carry on a conversation with that bashful American boy. He was in such a state of shock over the death of his poor wife, of course."

What was to be inferred from these remarks?

Days without happiness, awakenings without glad-ness? Or that Vivian was being highly successful at keeping Ronald at a distance, separating herself from him? I went in search of Sickles and the search lasted longer than I ex-pected, probably because he was passing from the garden to the house as I was coming into the garden from the east lawn, or leaving the terrace when I was starting toward it. But it was on the terrace where I finally found him, after sitting in one corner of the library for twenty minutes, thinking if I stayed in one place long enough, looking at pictures of birds of the Indian Ocean, he might pass through. I had forgotten that Sickles had the lidless eyes of a fish. The lids were somewhere in the top of his head for he blinked often enough; still, he had an open look about him that made you feel he was incapable of concealing anything, and therefore a man to be trusted. And he couldn't conceal that he had too many glasses of champagne. True to character, he didn't try.

"God! the only way to stay sane at these affairs is to get stinking. Look at me."

He belched.

"You mean listen, I think."

"I do."

"Where's Lydia?"

"Off somewhere being disgusted with me."

"Good. While she's gone, tell me about Ronald and Vivian."

He swung his head around at me.

"Tell you what?"

"Where is he?"

"Keane?"

I nodded.

"God knows, who cares? I put him on a mammy wagon six weeks ago. It was supposed to be going to Abidjan."

"Abidjan?"

"What's the matter with Abidjan?"

"You *are* stinking."

"Leave that to the Americans—they can't handle this Third World stuff. *He* was stinking, all right."

"Ronald?"

"Has your hearing gone on you up there?"

"Come on," I protested. "Didn't he work out? Wasn't he any good?"

"Ah, you were the one who told Angle he was such a boy wonder, fixing your infirmary or chapel or whatever the hell it was, that I had to try him!"

"I didn't tell Alan he was any *wonder*."

"Well, he told me he was! Oh," Sickles growled, "he was all right in that way, I'm not talking about that—"

"You're not talking about anything yet."

"Well, I'll tell you, and then you tell me. They came pulling in as breezy as you please one Saturday morning. We knew they were coming because"—Sickles made a half turn and jabbed at the air with his finger in the general direction of the receiving line—"him . . . that one's wife, Vivian, had called Lydia the day before, and before we sat down and had a chance to cross our legs she's talking about how I must want to take Keane out to the site. 'The *site*,' she kept calling it. You know we don't get any work out of our men on Saturdays, she knows it, too, but she insists how anxious Keane, who's not saying a word, is to see the site and get an idea of what he's going to put his hand to. What do I know? I mean, this is Angle's wife. How do I know what's required of me? I can't very well say, 'Let's not be silly now,' can I? So off I go with Keane while Vivian stays behind with Lydia and tells her the whole story of your epidemic and his wife's death. His wife was that weird one, wasn't she?"

Sickles looked at me for confirmation. But I didn't have a ready response to the word *weird*.

"Tiny thing?" he asked. "Shy and withdrawn?"

I nodded and he shook his head about something.

"So off we went and that was all right, but then when we came back we all had to get in her car and go over to A.J.'s to see the house, which is where Keane, she says, is going to be staying. *She*, Vivian. I didn't know that. Angle didn't say so. I though Keane was going to be staying with us, what with his personal circumstances and all, but it turns out that *she's* going to be staying with us. So over we went, came back, Lydia had prepared supper and then—out come the needles! Lydia's into crochet work, ever since Billy went back home to school. Every stitch, every sample . . . Vivian couldn't get enough of it. The two of them chattered the evening away in Lydia's sewing room—Vivian never seemed the type for crochet work—while

317

I, of course, was stuck with him on the porch, and he didn't do anything except finish the only bottle of Scotch I had. Oh, nothing excessive—not by expatriate standards, just keeping his misery good and damp, I supposed, and I had to tell him the history of the country, half of Africa and two thirds of the Middle East. I thought I was going to have to start on Wales. Do you know that it was three or four days before I caught on?"

"To what?" I said, maybe too quickly, for Sickles held up his hand while he took a swallow of champagne. He seemed to be signaling for me to *Wait*.

"On Sunday we all drove down the coast to Barufi. Ever been there? That was fine because I hadn't been there in five or six years and Lydia never had, and we ate at the old hotel—native run now—in Klusa on the way back. Then all day Monday and Tuesday Vivian ran Lydia around the countryside, every bloody hamlet—'looking for trinkets,' says Vivian. Bric-a-brac stuff. Lydia didn't even have supper ready. One night I got back before they did. We had to eat at the Bongo Drum two nights running. And, of course, by now I'm learning that *he* doesn't know the difference between a terminal and a sink-line."

"You mean he was no good?"

"Oh, he was all right, I don't mean *no good*. He just wasn't the Yankee wonder you made him out to be for fixing your infirmary or chapel or whatever it was."

"I didn't say he was any *wonder*."

"Well, Angle did. He was ready to have me think so. But Keane took it on the arm the third day out—there's a mark of a workman for you. How fast he gets injured. It wasn't bad, mind you, and not all his fault. A cable snapped, gave him quite a scare, and a chance for me to write another complaint to Angle. This damned Indian equipment they've been sending us from someplace around Bombay just won't hold up, but no matter how many reports I send in nothing gets done about it. Except to remind me of Commonwealth trade agreements and all that. Anyway, I drove him back to A.J.'s and went home early myself, before four o'clock, and when I got back Vivian was preparing our dinner. For making us all eat out two nights, she was cooking native for us—had spent half the morning going around to all the native markets, Lydia said. She dropped everything when I said Ronald had taken a hit on the arm from a cable, and off she went in her car. Do you know how long she was gone?"

Sickles looked at me for an answer. An estimate. When I didn't give him one he seemed to prompt me.

"And with us waiting supper? *Her* supper?"

I was afraid to guess. I expected him to say midnight.

"Two hours. Two hours to look at his arm. Well, I'll tell you." But instead of telling me, Sickles shook his head. Whatever it was he got over it and his mind went on to the next thing, for now he started nodding. "He came back with her. You should have seen him—all smiles, hummin' to himself on the porch while she walked straight to the kitchen. Straight," he repeated, looking at me significantly, "and hardly lifted her eyes for an hour. Downcast the whole time. It was pathetic. She never looked at him, not once all during supper, and she went all quiet like. We couldn't get over the change in her. Why, she's got more spirit than that, she could have made some effort to conceal it, but no, it was as if she didn't give a damn. And *him!* . . . just as cheerful as you please for a turn, talking about California, every inch a—a damn Yank who's had his way. There wasn't a mark on her but he'd had his way, all right. B'gees, it was pathetic! The way she went into the kitchen after supper—why, we've got Menna, one of the local girls, for cleaning up, but no, in she goes with Lydia after her, and straight off to her room so I had to sit it out with Keane on the porch while he serves us brandy from his own bottle. And that's not the end of it, no. Before we're up, we hear her car at six in the morning. Up jumps

Lydia and in a minute she's back with a note in her hand, one Vivian's left on the breakfast table—'Gone swimming,' it says. 'Let her,' I said—'she's some kind of champion.' The less fuss the better, I figured, and a swim might do her some good. Keane didn't need anything. He was in top form the next morning, if *top* means not letting the men work at their own pace. Not content to show anyone, are they? Americans? No instincts for training anyone, just getting the job done, even if that means taking over the controls from another man. I don't know where he learned to handle a tractor, but once he got the gears right, he was moving dirt like six men. And then about eleven o'clock Lydia shows up, waving to me from the bunker. That puts a smile on all the men's faces, if they'll show them to me— I've told her not to do that sort of thing. But Vivian didn't get back yet, and she's worried, so worried that off we go—not telling Keane. I thought we'd be right back anyway. But it took us an hour before we could find her car— first we drove west, to the beaches, then back along the shore to Benin. Finally I spotted her Peugeot down a copra track leading to the shore, off to the side. But no Vivian— nothing, nowhere. And there's no place to swim there. The water's not fit for a fish. We made fools of ourselves shouting for her, and then some native girls ran up to us and pointed to Huseman's Island. Huseman's Island! Do you know how far that is? Six miles, if it's a yard! With the shipping lane about three miles out, just past Mlane Shoals. Why, it'd take a quarter of an hour to get out of the way of any ship, thrashing for your life! Lydia was beside herself—not that I wasn't uneasy myself. Well, she had to be gone after, and that meant a harbor launch, which meant going to the harbor master, who—of course—enjoyed himself turning me down. 'Impossible, impossible!' One of that breed who would have murdered us all in our beds if he'd had his say. I had to tell him it was Alan Angle's wife, which made him popeyed all right, and meant there was sure to be something in the papers about it—including his heroic part.

"So off we went, the harbor master, two other blacks, and myself, and sure enough, about four miles out, on her way back, there she was—her head riding the swells like a beach ball, and her arms coming out like they're turning cartwheels. I was standing forward, waving to her—and she actually started to turn out of our way until I began to call to her. She stopped swimming, looked surprised, but not for long, I'll tell you—and then said, 'I can make it.' Huh! That wasn't the point at *that* moment, was it? 'You'd better get in,' I called, and she didn't object to it. So Mwoge—that's the harbor master—threw the rope ladder over, and there we all were, watching her . . . if you know what I mean. *They* were watching her, I can tell you that, pulling herself up while the ropes swayed her back and forth, with Mwoge, the cheeky bastard, reaching down for her arm before I did, getting ahold of her. She never set an eye on me. 'Am I being rescued?' she asks, and I could hardly get my tongue for the way she asked it: dry as dust, sarcastic—well, not quite, but damn close to being sarcastic, as if we had our cheek. And she never said a word of thanks to anyone. She did say, eyes down, as if she knew she was being a bit much, 'I guess I *am* a little tired,' walking straight off to the bow, stretching herself out—right on the deck, closing her eyes. Shutting me out, you know? Leaving me to the men and the human relations bit, standing with Mwoge at the wheel, watching them stare at her—and not a thing to cover her. I didn't think of bringing a wrap, and Lydia hadn't come after me with one."

Sickles stopped and stared as if he were coming to terms with their forgetfulness again. His head shook.

"She's a beautiful woman."

I nodded and let a little pent-up breath escape.

"Yes, she is."

"And she must be all of forty-five."

"Forty-two."

"Forty-two, then."

"Maybe forty-three. I don't know her birthday."

"How *does* she do it?"

"I don't know."

"No white woman'd do that, either—lay on a hot deck, face to the sun at two in the afternoon. And me, rattling to the blacks about one thing and another, trying all my local lingo, every word of it, to—to divert them, you know? But what for? Once she lifted herself—a bit, at the waist, pushing down on her heels, so she could pull down on her swim suit on her legs, tucking her fingers under it near the crotch. Pshew! I heard one of the men whisper to himself, and bloody whispering it was, too. I shot him a glance and all he did was look at me and grin. Show me his teeth! It makes you wonder when the mucking world is going to end, it does. When we got to the dock she walked off it quick enough, straight at Lydia, as if she were ashamed—and left me to bow and scrape to Mwoge. The thing was, she never said a word about it while we were driving back to her car, just—right off, too—'I think I'll be on my way this afternoon,' saying how nice it was of us to put her up, that she appreciated it, that she hoped Keane'd work out all right and that she was sure Alan would be writing to me, expressing himself personally. And all of it in this quiet way, this—this soft tone, like someone had died and no one could enjoy themself, or at least she wasn't going to remember that she had. All very correct, all very formal, not Vivian Angle at all. And when she got out at her car she closed the door right behind her, quick. Hell, Lydia could have driven back to the house with her, but no—and there was no saying, 'Would you mind?' and so on, so I could get back to the *site*—oh, no. She gets her way, you know—except for the night before when Keane got his. As if there was nothing between them, as if he was just one of the hundred visitors who pass through The Port each month, she says, 'Say goodbye to Ronald for me, and tell him I said good luck, will you?' She might have had a little inflexion in her voice when she said *Good luck*, as if she really meant it, but I wouldn't swear to it. Well, I told him, all right—but not until I drove him home, and not until I had pulled up at A.J.'s. Ever seen a man struck by lightning? . . . Neither have I, but he must have looked like however you look when you get hit. I could have told him that she headed out to Huseman's Island, and that he must have had rocks in his head for eyes not to have seen what she was like at supper the day before, but I left it up to him. I mean, it wasn't anyone's affair anymore—not mine. I told him what she said just the way Vivian said it, as polite as a stranger. He didn't say a word. He just sat there, breathing. When he got out of the car, like a man who weighed fifteen stone, I said, 'Like to take a bite with us?'—knowing the answer. He just shook his head, and I never saw him for three days. That is, he didn't show for work for three days. I figured I should look in on him at noon when he didn't, and I found him clean out—gone, stinking, drunker than six lords. Lydia finally got some proper food in him and when he showed for work again, he said, 'It won't happen again.' And it didn't. At least, not so he missed a day for it. He spent most of his nights at one of the high-life places, and got sick once eating native, but he was a workhorse for four months before he decided to go home. Now you tell me—look, there's Lydia—"

He pointed off to the south lawn.

I couldn't see Lydia among the hundreds there.

"Now you tell me," Sickles repeated, "what's behind all that, what was going on, what"—he made a movement with his head in the direction of the dwindling receiving line—"what himself's doing here without Vivian. *Now* where's she going?" he asked about Lydia, lifting a hand in the air and waving it toward the crowded lawn. "But don't tell me until I get Lydia. She'll want to hear this, too—and she likes to see the sun go down from up here as well. Take care of this a minute, will you?"

He handed me his champagne glass.

I liked to watch the sun go down from the terrace on The Hill, too. Burn itself down like an orange candle on an invisible wick that snuffs itself out when it reaches the heaving green-black sea. But Sickles spoiled it for me. *Tell him?* Tell him and Lydia about Ronald and Vivian, and explain why Alan was standing on his long legs like a solitary marsh bird, alone? No. When I would have said, "Well, when I first saw Nancy in McGowan's courtyard," they would have said *Who?* No. I set Sickles's champagne glass on the terrace railing and walked into the house, passing through the library and on out to the garden before crossing the east lawn toward the road. I looked back to where Alan was standing more than once, and would have waved to him if he had seen me. Once when I turned I had an impulse to go to him and say, "Have Vivian write to me, will you?" Naturally, it was an impulse I didn't act upon. At the moment I seemed content to pause at every turn of the winding road and watch the sky go purple and see the lights flicker on in The Port below.

And as time went by, darkening those who were once so visible, I had to be content with a guessing game: guessing at the size of Ronald's soul in America, guessing at the size of Vivian's soul in Australia. But the game ended, as games do, leaving Nancy clearest in memory and closest to me. I suppose it couldn't be otherwise since what's left of her body is just off Dalaga Road. And I've helped to keep her more alive, too. A few years ago I paged through one of her notebooks again and was taken enough by one of the drawings to remove it with a razor blade. I made a kind of matting and frame for it, and have it hanging on a wall. When people ask me what it is, all I can do is shrug. It's just some cell, some form of life; it might be a cholera vibrio or the origin of all impulse, for all that I know. And she's stayed close because I received a letter a few months ago that had been addressed to the American embassy in The Port and had then been forwarded to me with a note. The letter was from Nancy's mother, Clara Applegate Carr. She was planning a trip to Africa in the spring and asked if the embassy could assist her in finding her daughter's grave. The American cultural attache has asked if I will see to her visit in Ndami when she arrives this coming April. Naturally, I've said I will. Is there a more appropriate person to show a mother her daughter's grave than her daughter's gravedigger?